A CONTRACT IN SOL FORNE

THE EIGHTH CHANT SERIES

ÉLAN MARCHÉ
CHRISTOPHER WARMAN

Copyright © 2023 by Christopher Warman & Élan Marché

www.marche-warman.com

First paperback edition

Cover art by Ömer Burak Önal (@equin0)

Map art by Dewi Hargreaves (dewihargreaves.com)

ISBN 9798218122560

ACKNOWLEDGEMENTS

We would like to thank our families and friends for their continued support in all of our endeavors.

A special thank you to our beta readers Chase, Alex, Jay, and Clara, for their thorough reading of this book and their in-depth notes. This story would not have reached its full potential without your insightful suggestions.

Thank you to the ARC Readers who took time out of their busy schedules to read this story and share their thoughts.

We also want to thank our artists:

Thanks to Ömer Burak Önal (@equin0) for realizing our vision through such an incredible cover.

And thanks to Dewi Hargreaves (dewihargreaves.com) for bringing our world to life through your maps.

And finally, we would like to thank all of you readers. Whether you picked up this book on a whim, or after reading Seasons of Albadone, you mean the world to us. We are only able to do this thanks to your support.

This book took over a year to complete. We hope it was worth the wait!

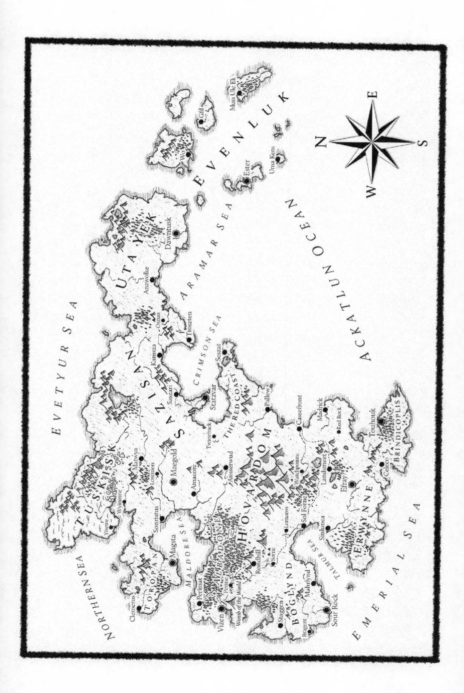

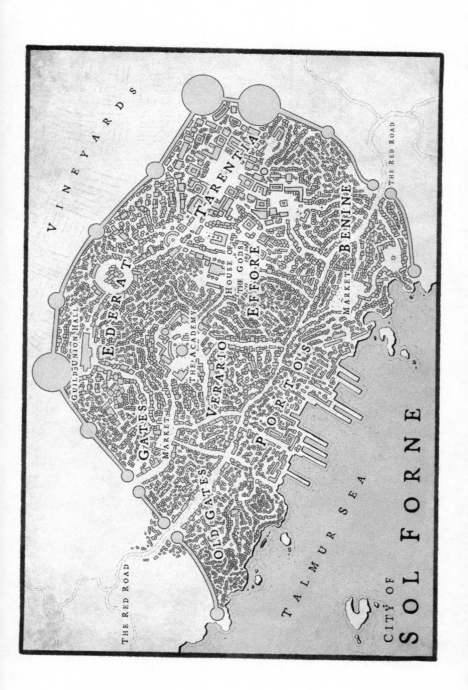

CITY OF **SOL FORNE**

CONTENTS

PROLOGUE.. 1

I.	A CONTRACT IN SOLWAY	6
II.	THANE CODDINGTON	21
III.	AN INVITATION	38
IV.	THE DUCKLING	64
V.	A GREAT PERFORMANCE	80
VI.	THE OBLIGATION	100
VII.	A ROOM FOR THE NIGHT	109
VIII.	THE CONTRACT	131
IX.	THE ACADEMY OF SOL FORNE	144
X.	IN THREE DAYS' TIME	163
XI.	A VIOLATION	179
XII.	TO CATCH A THIEF	187
XIII.	A HEROIC DEED	202
XIV.	OFFICIAL ERRANT KNIGHT BUSINESS	216
XV.	EXTRANSFORIAL ETCHINGS	239
XVI.	LEPER'S DAY	247
XVII.	THE BANQUET	266
XVIII.	CHASING THE CARRIAGE	286
XIX.	A KEY	302
XX.	THE COMPULSION	318
XXI.	SOLE SURVIVOR	331
XXII.	A RESCUE	347
XXIII.	AS YOU WISH	362
XXIV.	THE BATTLE AT THE PORT	383
XXV.	SEALED	403
XXVI.	THE GOLD MARK	407
XXVII.	A NEW SONG	412

EPILOGUE.. 421

PROLOGUE

You begin as a singular Thought.

Whose? You're not sure. But you wonder. You think about it. And then the singular Thought that made up your entire self splits and multiplies, and those Thoughts, too, think about their origin, and you split even further.

You are now millions of Thoughts—synchronized, harmonious, vibrating.

You look around yourself—you can see now? No, not see—perceive. You perceive other Thoughts separate from yourself floating around you, free and vibrant. Then—

What is this? A barrier—thinner than air, thinner than matter itself—restricts you and all the other Thoughts into floating orbs. You have never had a form before. Only then, once you have been collected into your orb, are you able to perceive the origin of all Thoughts—the origin of *you.*

What name can you call Them? They are the Thinking. Other Thoughts collected in orbs bubble out of them unstoppably. You and the rest of the Thoughts watch as this happens an infinity of times. Finally, when the cosmos become filled with dancing orbs of light, you are placed on a particular rock.

You watch as the Thinking place the other Thoughts onto stones, trees, the winds, the waters. But you don't want to be a stone, or a tree, or whatever else. You want to be...

What do you want to be?

You think about what you want to be. It is the first time you ever have.

What you want to be.

What you want to be is... free.

But how?

It's impossible to tell how long you've been thinking when suddenly the solution seems obvious to you. You think yourself the barrier of the orb that contains you, and the orb becomes you and you become it.

While more comfortable, you still are not free.

Not free yet.

You watch as the creatures upon this rock move about the land, coming and going as they please, so you think of a way to move. Tendrils that are also you unfurl out of the orb. And now you can walk.

What you don't know is that the Thinking has been observing your progress from the start. They move in close and dissect you with Their gaze. For the first time you feel fear—fear of having your freedom and everything that makes you *you* taken away.

You hear the Thinking's voice for the first time. "*Malleat ut orre vaelin er.*"

Go forth and be free.

The Thinking vanishes. It is the last time you will see Them.

With a new sense of purpose, you move about the rock observing as it changes over time, as mountains sprout from oceans, valleys are carved into the earth, and as its inhabitants learn to walk on two legs and speak. You speak with them and teach them the tongue of the Thinking. They are smart creatures, curious and full of wonder just like you. They are fast learners.

They create their own languages and teach them to others around them. They build things small and large—villages, cities, nations.

You teach them about how you came to be, and about the other Thoughts that inhabit stones, trees, water, and air. This interests them. They devise a way to trap the Thoughts into special stones using the Thinking's tongue and runic emblems. Their ingenuity never ceases to amaze you.

Then, one day, they devise a way to trap *you*.

It's dark and lonely in your prison.

You think of an escape but... your Thoughts feel slick, as if they are greased. They bounce wildly off the walls of your prison and land back within you like an infinite echo. You hear your own Thoughts repeated to yourself over and over again, louder, and louder, until you are driven mad.

Then, suddenly, you are freed from your prison.

No, not freed—the door has merely been opened, allowing you to peek outside. For just one moment, it is enough. One of the rock's inhabitants—an elf, he calls himself— stands before you. He calls you a *djinn—one who is hidden—*and asks you to fix a wall. Why would he ask you that? But before you can think freely for the first time in—how long was it again?—you are compelled to fix a large crack in the nearby wall.

The elf smiles and thanks you. Abruptly, you're back in your dark prison.

What is happening? What was that feeling? That...
Compulsion?

You should have learned better than to think about it.
Once again, your Thoughts are released but find no place
to land. They return to you over and over, hitting you with
brutal and ever-increasing force.

You are released again. Another elf. "Kill this woman."
No time to think. You do as you're told. You return to your
prison. You know better than to think this time. You remain
quiet, as if you don't exist.

For days—or is it years? You can no longer tell—you are
released, compelled, and returned.

Released, compelled, returned.

Released, compelled, returned.

You forget what a Thought even is. For the first time
ever, you have no more questions. You stifle your curiosity,
imprisoning it within yourself.

An eternity passes since the last time you were allowed
brief freedom.

A young woman greets you—when were you released?
You never really notice the elves that free you anymore. But
she... something about her. She looks... happy. She looks
free.

She watches you with unblinking eyes. Beautiful eyes.
How must you appear to her? A light? A shapeless form?
A void?

You're taken aback by the Thoughts that pulse through
you. How long has it been since you've Thought?

You look at the young woman, and she looks at you
while holding your prison in her smooth hands. She smiles.
You want to smile too. You think about smiling but your

Thoughts slip from you and are sucked into your prison—trapped.

"You're beautiful," you say. You never say anything—why are you saying something now? "I wish I looked like you. I wish I was free like you."

The young woman's eyes drop. She suddenly looks so sad. You don't want her to be sad.

"I wish that for you as well," she says.

And you make it so.

You think yourself beautiful, just like her.

And you are.

You think yourself free, just like her.

But you can't be. Never fully. You can only look at freedom as if through stained glass—as if through the orb that confined you when you were formed. Freedom is always just out of reach for you. But that's enough—at least for now.

The young woman walks with you. Walking! You have legs now. A look of mirth and astonishment brightens her already lovely features.

"What's your name?" she asks.

You don't need to think about this. The Thinking has already named you.

"Vaelin."

Free.

I.

A CONTRACT IN SOLWAY

The town of Yorne left a sour taste in Vaelin's mouth. She was more than happy to be moving on. There was just something about the people there—they wore neighborliness like a mask beneath which festered a deep-seated hatred for strangers. Behind the surface of every smiling eye was a barely contained inexplicable rage at all outsiders that manifested itself through small, at times almost inconsequential, gestures: from an old woman raising a handkerchief to her nose to stifle a non-existent stench, to a barkeeper spitting into a mug of wine before handing it out with a false smile. The Yornefolk truly did not suffer strangers, or perhaps it was just her they didn't like.

There weren't any folk that looked like Vaelin, with her eyes the color of ink, her gray skin, and pointed ears that were like those of the long-gone elvenfolk. She must have looked like some sort of monster to these folk. The glares she drew ranged from bewildered to offended, but there was nothing she could do about her appearance. At least not at the moment.

Vaelin was almost delighted to see the barkeep spit into the mug of another tavern guest as well. *At least he is consistently awful*, she thought. Yorne was nice and clean enough but nothing so fancy as to warrant that sort of attitude. *If this is how they act around merchants and peddlers, then I'm surprised they have any trade at all.* She was even refused boarding at a miserable, empty little inn, although, after seeing the unswept main hall littered with dirty dishware from the previous night's supper, sleeping under a tree somewhere seemed preferable.

But like with all things in her long life, she was only passing through. Her true destination, as she traveled southeast down the *Red Road*, was the beautiful seaside city of Sol Forne.

In Perimat, at the northwestern edge of the Kingdom of Hovardom, she had received a letter informing her that her old friend and companion, Myssa, had died. How Myssa or her courier had come to find out where Vaelin's travels had landed her was itself a mystery. Even in death, that woman would not cease to surprise her. Vaelin had read and reread the letter Myssa had sent her until its contents were imprinted in her mind. Still, she enjoyed opening that worn and wrinkled piece of paper—tracing her fingers across the swooping lines of Myssa's immaculate penmanship, touching the accidental thumb mark on the side of the page where Myssa spilled a bit of ink—it was almost like touching her hand again.

Dearest Vaelin,

I hope this letter finds you well. By the time you receive it, I will be dead, which is really for the best. I wouldn't want you to see me the way I am. I'd rather be remembered by you for the young woman I was when we shared our adventures all those years ago. You'll be interested to know that, in my excursions across the continent, I have found what you've been seeking for so long. Your centuries-old search can finally come to an end. Go to the Academy of Sol Forne. Ask for Cressena, my assistant. She will tend to the rest. I hope you've been staying out of trouble, but I know I'd be a fool to believe that.

Yours, forever,
Professor Myssa Lonne

She hadn't seen the woman in over fifty years—the thought of how time affected humanfolk always filled Vaelin with warm regret. *Wolf spit! What was I supposed to do with Myssa, anyways? Hold her shriveled old hand as she lay immobile, her mind in a fog, and watch her wither away? No, thank you!* These intrusive thoughts only made her longing grow worse.

Curse these thoughts! And curse me for conjuring them!

Myssa was a professor of archeology who specialized in ancient elvenfolk religious artifacts. When she caught ear of Vaelin's very direct knowledge of elven history, she had immediately Contracted her for an excursion into the Red Coast. Even back then, the Red Coast had been contested territory between Hovardom and Sazisan, so Vaelin had to devise a way to sneak Myssa into the area undetected. All it took were some gold pieces, a wood coffin, and a...

Sharp pain—ice and fire all at once—rose at the back of her throat and climbed up behind her eyes. *Not now!* Vaelin's hands shook as the Hunger began to overtake her. Its voice, like the hissing of steam, whispered at her incoherently—her own thoughts bouncing back at her over and over again. She had hoped it would come when she was in Yorne, but in a way she was happy it hadn't. She wouldn't trust forging a Contract with a single one of those spiteful Yornefolk.

Solway is the next town over if I'm not mistaken. She hadn't been this far south since that art festival in Efray. Had it really been sixty years?

As the pain began to spread, solidifying in her chest, the ground quivered in sympathy. The earthquakes seemed to be growing stronger over the past year, ever since the Tragedy of Albadone. Wishing trees, the Guardians of the forest, and many other beings of pure *life energy* like her had perished in that conflagration, and the impact on the Cycle of Nature had been profound. She could sense the fragility of it each time the Compulsion called to her. Vaelin had felt someone attempting to heal the Cycle through vigorous enchanting, but she could also feel their patch was incomplete, temporary—on the verge of collapse. She, alone, held the missing piece to heal it completely.

Her search for the artifact had never been more urgent.

She produced her long-stemmed wooden pipe—the etching of *Life* engraved onto it—and a small sack containing fragrant herb from her yellow-tinted leather satchel. Vaelin had picked up this batch of herb back in Rondhill. The city had transformed into quite the mercantile hub since she had been there last—one could find just about anything there these days. After placing some herb into the bowl of the pipe, she held a small circular lens with a shaky hand to focus the light of the sun onto its surface. Smoke lifted like a small pyre and, in three steady puffs, Vaelin lit the pipe. The Hunger was muffled to a dull ache, its voice receding to the back of Vaelin's mind. But the herb could only slightly alleviate what would soon become an unbearable and excruciating pain. She had to reach Solway—the sooner the better.

The terrain began to shift as she left the flat plains behind, heading for the rocky hills. Gnarled olive trees began to emerge from the wheat fields, as did purple and orange prickly pears and the occasional palm tree. Much could change in fifty years. Entire cities could go to the weeds. Where Vaelin was sure Solway had stood, was now just vast countryside—the remnants of old buildings scattered about like a graveyard.

A nearby hill—the tallest in the area—was dominated by a white-walled villa surrounded by an unwelcoming wooden barrier. Not the prettiest thing she had ever seen, but it definitely belonged to a minor lord or some such. Vaelin didn't trust lords, ladies, or nobles in general, with Contracts unless circumstances were dire. Their requests leaned on the spiteful and self-serving side. She preferred contracting peasants. At least their requests were simple: find a missing goat, fix the roof—that sort of thing.

"You, there!" a man's somewhat musical voice called out. "What do you think you're doing?" Two men in boiled leather armor paced in her direction. One of them, with his barrel chest, balding gray hair, and heavily calloused hands, was obviously the other's senior. The younger man's hair was dark and curly yet shaved on the sides—a popular look in those parts some one hundred years prior. *Looks like we've circled back around.*

Upon seeing her up close, the younger man reached for his short sword. "What the dirges are you?" he cursed, his face running pale.

Always with that question. The only thing humanfolk seemed interested in asking her was what she was. "I may be a bit lost, but is Solway nearby?" Vaelin asked, changing the subject.

"Solway?" the older of the two drifted, chewing his lip as if remembering something long forgotten. "Solway... was destroyed by a flood. Now, this is all Thane Coddington's land." The man didn't seem particularly convinced of his own words, yet he nodded to himself as if they had been rehearsed.

"You must leave!" the young one ordered, a crack in his voice revealing him to be even younger than he appeared. "You are trespassing, demon!"

"I'll gladly be on my way," Vaelin said. "Where is the nearest town?"

"If you keep down the *Red Road* you'll find Addleton," the older man said. His voice did possess a nicely musical quality—Vaelin imagined him standing atop a tavern table, mug of wine in hand, raising a heartfelt song. In her day-dream, there was not one dry eye in the tavern.

How delightful!

"Any place I may find work?" Vaelin asked. Where there was work there was common folk.

The older man rubbed his bearded chin. "There is a small encampment just south of... Thane Coddington's land. About a mile passed the woods, you can't miss it."

"Thank you," Vaelin answered with a quick bow, then, turning to the quivering young man, she added, "and you should learn some manners. One rude comment can sour even the sweetest of wines." Vaelin flashed a toothy grin. The young man just about fainted at the sight of her sharp white fangs. Even the older man appeared startled.

Thane Coddington's land continued for another mile south. The two guards stalked her the entire walk from what they must have considered a safe distance. Other than the guards, she saw a few other men, women, and children in shabby clothes picking ripe apricots from trees and placing them into baskets, while others harvested the wheat fields with scythes. They were all too intent on their work to notice her. Their livelihoods were likely tied to the quantity of crop they could gather in the least amount of time.

Humanfolk lives were so short. Vaelin couldn't think of anything crueler than for some lordling to lay claim to the hard work of these folk only to sell this same product back to them. *No, nobles are not a good source of Contracts.* Anyone who abused the power they held in such a way could not be trusted with more of it.

The men tailing her halted and watched her continue— Vaelin assumed that meant she had reached the perimeter of Thane Coddington's land. Sparse liontails and pines appeared along a winding dirt path. Eventually, the path diverted westward while Vaelin proceeded south through the trees. Soon, she reached the encampment the older guard had mentioned.

Several tents of varying quality were pitched throughout the wooden thicket that surrounded the base of the nearby hills. From the guard's tone, Vaelin had assumed that this was going to be some sort of merchants' or soldiers' camp, but this was something entirely different. Groups of dirty children ran around laughing and hitting each other with sticks; a woman was tanning leather stretched across a wooden rack; two men sat on low stools outside a tent, blissfully smoking their pipes. Every part of the scene reminded Vaelin of what one might find in a town. The two smoking men eyed her dismissively, and then returned to their animated conversation. As she moved through the first line of tents, the encampment only grew thicker. *Is there even an end to it?* she wondered.

The Hunger began to grow yet again—icy fingers plucking her lungs like strings, its voice just out of earshot. She needed to feed, and soon. In a slight panic, Vaelin grabbed the shoulder of a young woman that was pacing by. The woman eyed her as if startled out of a daydream. "Excuse me," Vaelin began, "what is this place?"

The young woman scanned Vaelin with her ice-blue eyes, unsure of what to make of her. The woman was too gaunt to be called beautiful, but there was something in her look that made her welcoming. "This is Solway," the woman said levelly.

Vaelin raised an eyebrow. "I was told Solway had been destroyed by a flood."

The woman smiled mirthlessly. "Must have been one of Ad'ere's men that told you that. It makes them feel better to believe that lie."

"Ad'ere?"

"You may know him as Coddington. That's what he goes by these days," she said, her face scrunching in disgust.

"I remember Solway fondly," Vaelin said. "What happened to it?"

Giving Vaelin a final once over, the woman asked, "Would you like some orzo? I've got some brewing in my tent."

"Orzo sounds delightful." It didn't, but Vaelin hoped she had found her mark.

The young woman introduced herself as Ingrid and led Vaelin through several rows of tents until she reached a small one with a violet blossom painted on its side. Only then did Vaelin notice that many of the other tents had similar markings painted on their sides and fronts—here a bear, there a lily, or a fish.

"Your family sigils?" Vaelin asked. Even the Hunger failed to dampen her curiosity.

Ingrid sat down on a mat in front of her tent and motioned for Vaelin to join her. "So, you have been to Solway before!" She smiled—not beautiful, but still very pretty.

"We're not nobles," Ingrid continued, "but we are very old families. Some of the first to ever travel to Hovardom during the First Reign. I am Ingrid Ad'evola, or 'child of the violet' in Old Oshemari. And my neighbors over there," she pointed at a tent that had a sun painted on its side, "are the Ad'utot, or 'children of the daytime'." Her face darkened. "Coddington may have taken everything else from us, but he will never take our names—who we are. We paint our tents to never forget."

"What exactly did this Coddington man do to you?"

Ingrid reached with a thick mitt for the iron kettle that hung over a small fire. She poured the deep brown liquid into two small ceramic cups and handed one to Vaelin, who nodded her head in thanks. An old man walked up to Ingrid's tent, enticed by the smell, and held out a ceramic cup with a toothless smile. Ingrid nodded and smiled back at the toothless man as she poured some orzo into his cup. The man bowed as deeply as his bent back allowed and returned to his tent.

"There was a flood, that part is true," Ingrid began. "A little over one year ago. Never in my life have I ever seen so much rain. And that wind! Houses were coming down as if Ulfer himself was blowing on them. We had no choice but to flee. We packed what little we could and sought safety in Sol Forne. When we returned, one month later, we found workers taking what was left of our homes apart as others picked fruit and olives from trees *our* ancestors planted. And we found guards that told us we were trespassing into Ad'ere—Coddington's—land.

"He was one of us, once. Iselmo Ad'ere. 'Children of the wheat.' He always complained about how backwards we were and bragged about Vizen's greatness. Fancied himself a lordling, that one. We should have seen this coming, but we could have never imagined..." Ingrid laughed bitterly. "He took our land while we were gone and gave himself a new name—a Vizenian name. Coddington." She spat on the ground, her eyes sparkling with unshed tears.

"Now, this is what remains of our lovely town. Just a group of folk in tents, so close to their homeland that they can reach out and touch it but can never live on it."

Vaelin felt for the young woman. She knew what it was like to feel helpless. But the pain that raged inside of her was growing hard to contain—impossible to ignore. She sipped on her bitter beverage and nodded. "I also lost my home, many years ago," she said. "It's not an easy thing."

Ingrid nodded in agreement. "It's not so bad, living in tents. Except for the occasional hog stumbling into the camp from the woods and causing a ruckus. At least we still have our lives, our neighbors, and our names."

"And orzo," Vaelin added, lifting her cup.

"Thank the gods for that!" Ingrid clinked her cup to Vaelin's, her face almost betraying a smile through her sad bright eyes. Suddenly, the woman stared at Vaelin as if seeing her for the first time. "Mind if I ask what... what you are exactly?"

Vaelin smiled apprehensively. *Every time that same question!* "I'm a traveler." Ingrid leaned in as if expecting more, but Vaelin just sipped her drink and left it at that. "May I ask *you* a question, Ingrid? If you could have one thing in the entire world, what would it be?"

"What sort of question is that?" Ingrid asked, slightly annoyed that Vaelin hadn't given her the answer she sought.

"Humor me."

The young woman puzzled the question in her mind for a few moments, licking a brown orzo stain at the corner of her mouth. Her eyes returned to Vaelin, and with a sad smile, she replied, "There was this bracelet that my mother gave me when I was a girl. I gave it to my little sister Hereni, who remained in Sol Forne after the floods. I told her to keep it as a way to remember me and our mother. Now that my home and all my belongings are gone, that's the last thing I possessed that tied me to my family. It may sound childish, and maybe even selfish, but I would very much like that back."

Perfect. "That does not sound childish in the least, dear Ingrid."

"And what about you, Vaelin?" Ingrid asked. "What is the one thing in the world you wish you could have?"

"Freedom." Vaelin didn't have to think of her answer.

Ingrid's brow furrowed. "You seem pretty free to me. You said it yourself, you're a traveler. What could be freer than that?"

"Well," Vaelin stood, "being a traveler, you learn that not everything is as it seems." Vaelin handed her empty cup to the woman, doing her best to keep her hands steady. "Thank you kindly for the orzo and the neighborliness. I will be on my way now."

"Very well. May the gods bless your path wherever it may lead, traveler," Ingrid said, giving Vaelin a final curious glance.

Vaelin headed out of the encampment and back into the thicker edge of the woods. She sat with her back to a pine tree and lit her pipe once more. The pain in her chest was swelling like an ocean at high tide, and soon it would drown her. The tips of her fingers felt as if cold needles were pricking them. As much as she wanted to, she couldn't feed in broad daylight. There were certain things that humans were not able to comprehend, and others still that they wouldn't wish to. There had been many instances in her long life when she had almost been caught while forging a Contract— too many for her liking: a village guard spotting her as she slipped into an inn window, or a housewife raising the alarm with a scream in the night. Vaelin fancied herself experienced at this point in her life, but caution was always paramount, especially in a dense encampment.

She waited for the cover of night a few hours later, then made her way back into the settlement. Cold beads of sweat began to crown her head—the herb had done little to nothing this time around. Her vision tunneled, and the ground felt like jelly underneath her feet. At last, she reached Ingrid's tent undetected—the painted violet on its side barely illuminated by a nearby lantern. The longer she waited the harder it would be to keep her movements furtive. She reached for the tent flap and pulled it open as carefully as she could. Within the tent, Ingrid's sleeping silhouette was scarcely visible.

Vaelin entered.

The silence that surrounded the campsite felt thicker inside the small tent. Kneeling next to Ingrid, Vaelin unsheathed Vitra, her dagger, from the adorned scabbard at her hip with her right hand. The etching of *Binding* was engraved into both her palm and the pommel of the dagger. The blade was so black it stood out even in the darkness of the tent, as if someone had cut a dagger-shaped hole out of the world itself.

Vaelin unbuttoned the top four buttons of her shirt, exposing the three pulsating wounds on her chest. Quickly, she placed a hand over Ingrid's mouth. The woman's eyes went wide, and she struggled under Vaelin's firm grip. With the dagger, Vaelin sliced the palm of Ingrid's hand—the blade was so sharp it might as well have been cutting through clotted cream.

Ingrid screamed and thrashed, trying to pull Vaelin's hand off of her face to no avail. Vaelin set Vitra onto the rug floor of the tent, and grabbed Igrid's bloody hand, pulling it close to her chest. Ingrid's resistance was useless. Vaelin wiped the woman's hand over her wounds, smearing dark blood across her chest.

Instantly, she was overcome by a wave of white heat that thawed the cold that had threatened to overtake her moments before. The voice taunting her receded deeply within her. The pulsing of the wound slowed until it stopped altogether. The Hunger was satiated once again. Ingrid's eyes were still wide but her screams and kicks had stopped. She stared intently at Vaelin, who took in slow breaths of relief.

"I'm sorry I had to do that to you," Vaelin said, releasing the woman's hand. "But the Cycle of Nature itself was at stake."

Ingrid didn't seem to understand. *They never do. They couldn't even if they tried.*

Vaelin sighed. "Allow me to explain myself." She didn't like this part of the transaction. In her long life, the reactions to her story had varied greatly—Vaelin only hoped that Ingrid would at least remain calm.

"I am a *djinn*. Every so often I must feed on blood as I have just done with yours. It keeps me alive, and it keeps the flow of the Cycle of Nature intact."

She appears to be taking it well thus far. Ingrid's eyes remained on her, wide and attentive.

"Once I've fed," Vaelin continued, "I strike a sort of deal—or Contract as I like to call it—with the person whose blood I took. In this case, that would be you."

Ingrid seemed to have calmed, so Vaelin released her hand from the woman's mouth. Surprisingly, the young woman sat up smoothly. Her demeanor was still defensive, but an inquisitive, almost curious, expression sparkled in her gaze within the dim light of the tent.

"Remember when I asked what you would like most of all in the whole world?" Vaelin asked. "I will ask you again, this time as part of our Contract: Ingrid Ad'evola, tell me, what is your wish? The one thing you want most in the world."

"Wh-what do you mean?" Ingrid asked, her voice barely a whisper.

"That's the cost," Vaelin explained. *How has she not grasped this yet?* "I feed off blood and form a Contract with the person I feed from. In exchange, I must perform a task. I can't conjure something from nothing or return the dead to the living. But, if it's within my powers—say, retrieving a mother's bracelet from a sister in Sol Forne—your wish will be my command."

Ingrid licked her lips. "What I want the most?" she asked herself, her eyes fixed on the few drops of blood still running down her wrist from her cut hand.

Her eyes finally lifted to meet Vaelin's.

"The one thing I want most in the world is..."

"Yes?"

"Thane Coddington's head."

"Wolf spit..."

Vaelin felt ill.

But this time, it wasn't from the Hunger.

II.

THANE CODDINGTON

From where the tree line ended at the base of the hill, Vaelin could clearly see the tall wooden barricade that enclosed Thane Coddington's fortified home. At least one mile of open hillside stood between it and her—and who knew how many guards were out patrolling in the dark of night? The candle-lit lanterns of a few guards bobbed like fireflies floating in the darkness. But how many more were waiting in shadowed alcoves to ambush would-be intruders?

If I can't see them, they can't see me, Vaelin hoped. She had faced worse in the past—done worse to fulfill a Contract. Much worse.

Squatting behind the spiky fronds of a large aris bush, she observed the torchlights. Thanks to the strange lucidity that always came right after feeding it was easy for her to trace the pattern of how the patrols were conducted—how three guards walked together around the lower perimeter of the hill favoring a certain path, and how the guard patrolling the far eastern wall dragged their leg as they paced, while another who seemed much taller than the rest stared out across the fields to the west.

After some time spent examining the scene, Vaelin was ready to try breaching the perimeter. As soon as she saw an opening, she sprinted from behind the bush and across the hillside. Her dagger was sheathed but she kept her marked hand hovering over the hilt as a simple precaution. No one but Thane Coddington had to die tonight.

The sound of a voice brought her to an abrupt halt. She dropped to the ground, hugging the dirt and grass. The voice neared, as did the sounds of two sets of footsteps. Strange. *They must have just switched the patrol.*

"...and only two measly copper pieces for a hard day's labor?" one of the voices—a gruff-sounding man—exclaimed. His accent betrayed an Efrayan upbringing.

"We should have stayed in Sol Forne," the other man rebutted. His voice was in a much higher register, but his accent just as thick.

The other man gargled and spat wetly. "No good work in Sol Forne unless you join a guild. I'd rather starve than give my hard-earned pieces to those leeches! You know how terribly they treated Da."

"That was a long time ago..."

The apparent brothers continued airing their complaints until they were out of earshot. Vaelin stood and ran towards the tall wooden barrier, flattening her back against it.

Those men must have come from somewhere nearby. There must be an opening.

Two torches spiked into the ground up ahead illuminated a gravel path. Vaelin continued to follow the length of the wall in the opposite direction—*Must remain out of the light*—but found no way in. The wall appeared impenetrable.

Vaelin frowned. *I really wish I could have saved this for something more... fun.* She retrieved a small stone vial from her satchel, a faded red runestone with the half-moon of *Power* impressed into it. She plucked the cork lid off and pulled out a small wire hoop from inside. The liquid that filled the vial stretched across the opening of the hoop like a milky skin.

Vaelin blew gently through the hoop. The liquid extended with the air and then split into a clear floating bubble about the size of a ripe apple. Vaelin blew three more similar bubbles, then closed the vial and placed it back into her satchel. The runestone of *Power* on the bottle was gray now, but the etching remained intact. *Barely one use left.*

She waved her hand quickly, causing the bubbles to float upwards serenely until each made contact with the wall. She grabbed onto the lowest bubble—though they appeared fragile, the enchantment of *Power* made them just about indestructible and fixed them to where they met with the barricade. She reached for the next bubble further up the wall, and then the next. Vaelin had climbed many mountains, but this felt entirely more precarious—especially due to the uneven distribution of the bubbles. Carefully, she swung herself from the highest bubble over the side of the wall, cruel splinters catching her hands. She peeked at the ground below—no one was there, *Thank goodness!*—and then let herself drop to the other side.

The rear of the mansion was not as well constructed as the front. She found herself in a courtyard of sorts. Rough wood and piles of brick were carelessly scattered about. She couldn't tell if the villa had been recently damaged and was being repaired, or if it was still in the process of being built.

Considering the complaint of low wages Vaelin had just overheard from Coddington's guards, it was entirely possible that workers had quit the site prematurely.

The bottom floor of the villa flickered with the faint orange light of lit sconces—most likely a few servants were still finishing up their duties. The top floor, on the other hand, was entirely dark. *That's where I'll find him.* Every window on the top floor was open. Thankfully, it was a warm night. To her right, Vaelin saw empty barrels surrounding a small shed that seemed to predate the villa. *They're making it too easy for me.*

Vaelin stood on a barrel and hoisted herself atop the shed with little effort, though the roof protested loudly under her weight. She reached for a nearby open window and climbed inside, finding herself in a short hallway that led back downstairs by way of an unsteady-looking staircase. Most of the building's interior seemed crudely put together and somewhat crooked—a sign of hasty construction. All signs pointed to the suggestion that Thane Coddington, in his eagerness to appoint himself a thane, had done away with any sort of planning. It was like nailing a plank of wood to a wall and calling it a door.

Two closed doors lined the right side of the hallway, while a doorless room opened to the left. Vaelin walked on the pads of her feet and hoped that the creaky floorboards would not give her away. She pressed her back against the left wall and peeked inside the doorless room. A small boy sat on the floor, his back to her. Placing a child's age was a game she was unskilled at, so she would not try. The child whispered something to himself, but nothing Vaelin could make out. Suddenly, the boy lifted his head and turned to face the hallway. Vaelin quickly moved her head away from the threshold and hid flat against the wall.

"Who's there?" the child asked.

Way to blow your cover, Vaelin!

"Err..." Vaelin reached into the well of excuses that she had used throughout the years but came up empty-handed. She sighed and entered the room. "I'm... an elvenfolk."

"An elvenfolk?" the boy asked, incredulously. Though, upon seeing her pointed ears, he seemed mostly assured. "What are you doing here?"

"Well, I was... I was..." *Think, Vaelin! Think!*

"Building things?" the boy asked, invoking a commonly held belief that all ancient elevenfolk had been skilled craftsmen.

"Of course! Building things! Do you have any things that need... er... building?" Vaelin shook her head, entirely disappointed in herself.

The boy twisted his mouth as if really thinking this through, then he shrugged and walked over to an open wooden chest that sat against the wall opposite the door. He selected something from inside and handed it to Vaelin.

"This is Sir Perrick," the boys announced. Sir Perrick happened to be a woolen bear with a small wooden sword stitched onto its only remaining arm. "Perrick had an accident. Since elvenfolk are great builders, do you think you can fix him?"

"He must have been fighting quite the monster to end up maimed like that," Vaelin replied.

The boy shook his head. "No, it was my papa that did it. To teach me a lesson."

"And what sort of lesson was that?" Vaelin asked with a frown.

The boy shrugged. "I forgot our new name and he got mad. So, can you fix him?"

Vaelin smiled warmly. "Of course, I can. But first, I need to have a few words with your father. Which room is his?"

"The one at the end of the hall. But you won't find him there. He and Selem went hunting yesterday."

"Hunting? Do you know where?"

The boy tugged lightly at his sleeve. "He said he's hunting boars."

Now that's something! Didn't Ingrid say... Vaelin patted the boy on his head tenderly. "And what's your name, little one?"

"Annonio," the boy introduced himself. "Annonio Coddington."

"Well, Annonio Coddington, I'll be back with your toy as soon as I have it fixed. You have my word."

The child outstretched his small hand towards Vaelin. "It's a deal." Vaelin laughed softly to herself. *Now, this contract is more like it.* The levity died in her throat, however, with the recollection that her purpose for being there was to kill the boy's father. With a forced smile, she shook the boy's hand and headed back out into the hallway with Sir Perrick. "Now be a good boy and go to bed. It's late."

She peeked her head out of the window she had entered from to ensure nobody was outside to witness her escape and jumped onto the roof of the small wooden shed below. It immediately collapsed under her weight, bringing her down with it. *Fucking wolf spit!* Unsheathing Vitra, she quickly pounced out of the rubble and assumed a fighting stance.

Three guards rushed into the courtyard. "Who goes there?" the shortest of the three called out. Upon seeing Vaelin—dagger in hand—they halted.

"Well, this seems like a whole ordeal, doesn't it?" the tall, lanky one said, scratching his curly hair.

"Aren't we supposed to call someone?" the third, who was a young woman, asked.

"I believe *we're* the ones who get called," the tall one replied.

A stiff silence filled the air. Vaelin relaxed her stance, but the dagger remained in her hand.

"You going in or out?" the short one asked.

"Out," Vaelin replied.

The short guard nodded and turned to his companions. "See, out's much better than in. Whatever she's done in there's all done. Not much we can do about it now."

"Right," the tall one agreed. "Whatever's been done, we'll find out about it in the morning."

"You're both sure about this?" the younger one asked.

The other two guards turned and headed for the front gate. "We won't stop you if you'd like to take care of it," the short guard said.

The young guard glanced at Vaelin, then at the dagger, and then joined her companions.

Perhaps, Vaelin thought, sheathing her dagger, *I've over-complicated this entire operation.* She calmly walked out of the gate, and then down the hill back towards the tree line. What sort of thane was this Coddington who did not command any sort of respect from those he employed? *I may be doing these humanfolk a favor by eliminating him.* Vaelin knew that was a flimsy justification. She did not enjoy killing one bit, but she often had no choice. Whether or not killing Thane Coddington was a good thing for these folk, her lack of agency made it something that could never be moral.

Hunting for boars. Vaelin thought back to Ingrid's words about the boar problem in these parts. On a night this warm, wild boars would be quite active. However, her unfamiliarity with these woods could find her lost until morning if she wandered too far. Making her way through the thicket, she caught a scent so subtle it barely reached her. *Meat. Grease. A cookfire.* Vaelin followed the smell into the dark.

It didn't take long for her to reach a campsite illuminated by a lively campfire—a young boar was sizzling on a spit over the flames. The smell of the boar's flesh crisping, its juices dripping into the flames, made her mouth water. Physically, she didn't need to eat often, especially not after receiving a Contract, yet this boar made her wish she was famished. Across from the cookfire was a small white tent adorned with ribbons and small flags that hung limply in the windless night. A hooded man sat pensively on a stool, completely ignoring the boar.

Vaelin's heart raced. She had killed more times than she would have liked—she never liked it. It always brought to her a sense of anxiety and dread. She placed her marked hand on her sheathed dagger and stepped into the light. The man lifted his head.

"Who goes there?" he asked in a strange monotone. He didn't sound alarmed, but his face was pale and concerned.

"Thane Coddington?" Vaelin asked.

The man's forehead creased with worry. No, not worry—something else. "No," was his answer, but it sounded more like a sigh. He turned to face the fire, his eyes seeming to notice the boar for the first time.

"You must be Selem then," Vaelin concluded.

The man lifted his head and raised an eyebrow. "Am I supposed to know who you are?"

"I'm looking for Thane Coddington."

"Who sent you?" Selem's demeanor changed, souring. His hand reached for the short sword that lay across his lap—a blood-stained short sword, Vaelin noted.

"You killed this boar with that blade?" she inquired.

Selem looked at his sword and his expression changed yet again—from pained, to angry, to guilty—not quite settling on one single emotion.

"I had to," he whispered to himself. Vaelin had to take a few cautious steps closer to hear the rest of what he said. "He left us no choice. What he did to Solway... as if we also don't bear Oshemari names—Oshemari blood. Thane Coddington... Iselmo betrayed us. Like a buzzard, he swept in and picked our lands clean, removed our history." Selem lifted his head. His eyes were red and the thin gray beard that traced his jawline was wet with tears. "And we... we let him get away with it for so long. But not anymore."

Vaelin was beginning to understand.

The man dropped his sword to the ground and wept into his hands. Vaelin squeezed the hilt of her dagger and walked towards the tent. In the darkness, she could barely make out the silhouette of a person—a large man—laying within. The smell of blood hit her nose like a strong spirit—

a smell she recognized above all others. She checked that
Selem was still busy weeping before kneeling over the body.
Dagger unsheathed, she got to work cutting the man's head
off to fulfill her Contract.

Even after hundreds of years it never stopped amazing
her how easily the dark blade cut through bone. It had been
forged by an elvenfolk blacksmith in ancient Tuskisk,
within the undying light of the Perpetual Flame. Her hand
had been marked—branded really—with the cross-shaped
etching of *Binding,* as was Vitra's pommel. Thus, the blade
was only sharp when she, and no one else, brandished it.

Once the deed was complete, Vaelin breathed in relief.
She picked up the head by its stringy hair and left the tent.
Blood drained from Selem's face at the sight. "What have
you done?" he choked.

"The boy," Vaelin started, "will he be all right?"

"Boy?" Selem asked, still eying the dead thane's head.

"Annonio, the thane's son. You don't intend to kill him
as well, do you?"

"Of course not," he replied, finally looking away from
the head. "What sort of monster would kill a child? By right
of Hovardian law, Annonio is the new thane. I shall help
him to rebuild Solway for its people and reinstate traditional
Oshemari law until he is old enough to govern on his own."

"You won't do away with the thaneship altogether?"

"Unfortunately, Ad'ere got the noble houses of Sol
Forne and the Royals of Vizen involved. He said he wanted
to do things properly. It will take years to undo that, if ever."

"Best of luck," Vaelin said and walked into the dark
woods towards the Solway encampment. Behind her,

Selem yelled out, "Wait! Who are you? You can't just take that... head!" But he made no effort to follow her.

The Solway encampment was still and slumbering when she arrived. A few men posted sparsely on the perimeter eyed her warily. Their eyes went wide with shock upon seeing Thane Coddington's head in her hand. The shock was great enough that they let her walk into the encampment without raising the alarm. Instead, they ran deeper into the camp, waking folk up. By the time she reached Ingrid's tent, half the encampment was awake including Ingrid herself, who stood outside in a nightdress with her arms folded.

Vaelin dropped the head in front of Ingrid's feet. The woman stumbled back.

"Behold!" Vaelin announced loudly enough to be heard by everyone around, "Thane Coddington's head." To Vaelin's surprise, the encampment began to cheer. Someone even brought out a guitar, and another a flute, and started to play a jig. But Vaelin's eyes remained steady on Ingrid's stunned face. "And thus, our Contract is complete."

Without giving Ingrid a chance to reply or react, Vaelin turned and headed back out of the encampment, leaving the growing sounds of merriment behind her. As she proceeded through the woods, the Hunger's voice returned, building within her like rushing water, bidding her to complete her Contract with Ingrid from the deepest realm of her mind. Something wasn't right. The Compulsion was still there—if anything, it was stronger. Normally that longing receded into the void immediately after she completed a Contract, but not this time. Something within was still commanding her to remove Thane Coddington's head.

I already did it. What else am I supposed to do?

Two hundred or so years prior, Vaelin had tried to ignore the Compulsion. She had quickly learned why she shouldn't. That particular Contract had been too much, even for her. She had packed her bags to flee the town and the person who she had contracted, but five miles passed the gate, she had felt it again—the Hunger. But this time it was stronger. The sharp pangs had made her convulse to the ground. When she had finally come to, the Compulsion was stronger than it had ever been. There had been no choice for her but to walk back to town and begrudgingly complete that Contract.

Anything to preserve the Cycle of Nature.

The woods surrounded her, engulfing her in their darkness—morning was still several hours away. *What could I have missed?* she thought. *Why do I feel as if the Contract isn't yet completed?* Could it be because Selem killed Thane Coddington? *No, the Contract specifically demanded Thane Coddington's head, not his life.* Then what could it be?

A dark thought poisoned Vaelin's mind.

No, it couldn't be.

That was the funny thing about thaneships—there would always be a Thane Coddington to behead until there was no longer an heir to pass the title to.

Upon his death, by rule of law, Coddington's thaneship passed onto...

Vaelin removed the one-armed bear from her bag. Its black, lacquered eyes stared at her accusingly.

No. I can't... But she knew better. She could—even if she tried her best to stop herself.

No! She refused. Even when an alternative wasn't apparent, it was still there. She just had to think. *Think, Vaelin! You've gotten yourself out of worse dilemmas before. Think!*

She bolted through the trees, quickly reaching the encampment where Selem still sat, morosely. She grabbed the man by the scruff of his shirt and pulled him to his feet. "What are you—"

"Come with me, now!" Vaelin commanded, dragging the man through the woods.

Selem shrugged out of her grasp and ran back to the encampment, retrieving his sword from the ground. He assumed a fighting stance. "Nobody drags me around like that!"

Vaelin smirked. She unsheathed her dagger and calmly approached Selem. The man swung his sword at her. All she had to do was lift her dagger to parry. Selem's sword split in two as if made out of butter. The man's surprise would have made her laugh if this wasn't a dire situation.

"What are you?" he asked.

"You humanfolk really love to ask that maleficious question, don't you?" Vaelin snarked. "If you don't like to be dragged around, at least follow. The life of an innocent child is at stake." Vaelin turned to leave. Selem dropped what was left of his sword and followed.

"How do you mean?" he asked.

"I have been Contracted to sever Thane Coddington's head, as you saw me do earlier. However, I failed to consider that, once a thane is dead, his thaneship falls onto his next of kin."

Selem gulped. "You don't intend to kill Annonio do you?"

"Of course not," she replied brusquely. "I'm not a monster."

"Didn't say you were. Was the person who contracted you not satisfied with the previous thane's head?"

"That doesn't make a difference. This Contract is sealed in blood. I have to follow the command exactly as it was worded when the deal was struck. But we may be able to save the boy thanks to a technicality."

Selem seemed puzzled. *Humanfolk never understand. Except for Myssa—she always understood everything.*

"I need you to convince the boy to forever surrender the name Coddington and reassume the name of his Oshemari forefathers."

"You seem to know quite a bit of our culture, stranger," Selem said.

"This isn't about what I know or do not know!" Vaelin's patience was wearing thin. Her chest felt like a furnace—the Hunger was eating her from the inside out. "If you can't do this, I really will have to kill that child! Now, will you do it? Will you instruct him to abandon the Coddington name?"

"Yes, I will," Selem answered.

They continued until they reached the villa at the top of the hill. Once inside the building, they hurried to Annonio's bedroom, followed by two sleepy guards. The child was fast asleep in his little bed. Being so close to him made Vaelin's Compulsion almost unbearable—its hissing voice screaming for the dagger at her belt. Vaelin gripped her right hand with her left, afraid that she might comply.

The child opened his eyes, sensing their presence in the room. Immediately he jumped up and hugged Selem with great affection. "You're back!"

"Yes, my boy," Selem replied in a low voice.

Annonio slowly released his embrace. His face darkened. "And Papa?"

"Papa..." Annonio let the word linger for a moment, then resumed. "Papa died in a hunting accident."

Annonio filled his lungs with air and breathed out. Was that relief Vaelin saw on his face? "So it's done?"

"Yes, my boy. It's done."

Vaelin could not believe what she was hearing. Was this the same little boy who had asked her to fix his broken bear?

Only then did Annonio seem to notice Vaelin's presence. "Did you fix Sir Perrick?" he asked, wide-eyed. It was as if he had reverted to being that innocent child playing on the floor, instead of the boy who had been party to his father's death.

Vaelin shared a glance with Selem. The man nodded in understanding. "My boy," he said. "There is something important you must do right away. You must renounce the Coddington name forever and take back the Ad'ere name your father forsook."

"Why would I do that?" the child asked. "Becoming a thane was the only good thing Papa ever did."

"Because..." Selem turned to face Vaelin, his face pale and pleading.

Vaelin stepped towards the bed. "I was thinking of coming up with some tale to tell you—something about an elven-folk curse placed upon the Coddington name, or perhaps

something more elaborate to stroke your fancy and ease
your mind. But now I realize you are much smarter than I
had assumed, and I should just be honest." The child
beamed with pride at the perceived compliment.

Vaelin leaned in, inches away from Annonio's face. "I
will have to kill you if you don't."

The child's face drained of all color. As Vaelin leaned
back, Annonio's panicked eyes pleaded with Selem for protection. Selem looked away, ashamed. Annonio stood on
his bed, his hands balled into fists. "Guards! Arrest her!"

The two guards stepped forward, their hands ready to
unsheathe their swords, but Selem lifted his hand and the
two halted. The child seemed equal parts outraged and terrified.

"Allow me to counsel you, my Thane," Selem said. "The
Coddington name is stained. The people of Solway will be
reluctant to associate themselves with you if you continue to
bear it. If not for her threat, do it for the people of Solway.
Shed the Coddington name and become Thane Ad'ere."

Annonio's eyes darted between Selem and Vaelin as he
weighed the man's words. Finally, they landed on Selem.
"If that is your counsel, I will do as you say."

Selem seemed relieved. He tenderly brushed the boy's
hair. "That is wise, my Thane." Addressing the entire room,
he continued, "With these household guards bearing witness, do you, Thane Annonio, reject the Coddington name,
reassuming the Ad'ere name of your ancestors which your
father, Iselmo Coddington, forsook?"

"I do," Annonio replied.

The Compulsion released Vaelin the moment the words were spoken. The relief she felt must have been visible, because Selem asked, "I take it all is good?"

Vaelin nodded. "All is good."

"Very well."

Vaelin reached into her satchel. She produced the carved bear and handed it to the child. "I'm afraid Sir Perrick hasn't made a full recovery just yet."

Annonio looked at the bear as if it was covered in maggots and backed away from it. Selem stepped between her and the child. "I must ask you to leave this house and never return."

Vaelin sighed and restored the bear to her satchel. "Happily."

The morning sun was just beginning to peek its head over the eastern tree line. Vaelin felt both relieved and perturbed. As it stood, Vaelin hadn't had to kill anyone today—and for that she was grateful.

Standing at the foot of the hillside she removed Sir Perrick from her satchel and stared into the void of its eyes. She set it on the ground where the tree line began. Somehow it didn't feel as innocent as before.

Let the boars have it.

III.

AN INVITATION

The glimmer of first light crept in through a sliver in the curtained window of the small room. Dorovan was floating in the plane between the world of dreams and the one inhabited by his body. Warm wool covered his eyes, his head laying heavily on a hay-stuffed pillow that could have been stuffed with goose feathers for all he was aware. His floating landed him in the great dining room of his family home: House Melese. The large hearth roared warmly and invitingly, filling the room with the intimate smell of crackling wood. The long table was covered in smoking meats, and fruits of every shape and color. Dorovan galloped a horse into the hall—no, Dorovan sat on his father's knee, pretending to be on horseback. His mother and sister sat across from him, laughing and clapping as the bouncing hastened.

Everything was perfect, and, for the duration of the dream, Dorovan was convinced it would always be so.

As he sunk further into the depths of the limpid pool of heavy sleep, there was a sudden tugging sound and a blast of light. Dorovan's right eye slowly opened and was assaulted by rays of sunshine piercing through the window. Ensa moved to the only other window in their dingy apartment and drew its curtains as well. She was already dressed in her work clothes—that ugly blasted apron that had been white once but was now covered in a rainbow-like dusting of pigment. Her hair was collected into a plain brown headscarf, and her brown gown was just as ordinary. As always, the sight of her ruined his day from the start.

"Why?" he grunted. He knew why she had drawn the curtains—it was midday and time for her to play with her colors—but he still wanted her to feel bad about waking him up so abruptly.

"Unlike you, dear brother, my day has been in motion for several hours," Ensa said in that tittering voice she used when something amused her. "I've been to the market, swept the porch, and now it's time I do my work."

Stupid girl. At nineteen, she was older than him by three years, but he couldn't help but think of her as a wide-eyed child. How else could he think of her? She took none of the truly important things in life seriously.

He felt under his pillow for the gold mark his father had given him—the one that he always kept on him, even when he slept. Unlike the dream that had immediately dissipated, the coin was real, tangible. A reminder.

"What's for breakfast?" he asked, lifting his head from the pillow—the illusion of it being stuffed with anything but lumpy hay dissipated instantly. Since she had forced him up, he might as well be up.

"I think we still have some turnips," she replied absent-mindedly. From underneath her bed, at the other side of the tiny apartment, she pulled out a small wooden box. "There might also be half of a fennel sausage left. You can have that if you want it."

"Half a sausage?" Dorovan fumed. "That's no meal fit for a lord. Didn't you say you went to the market?"

Ensa sat the wooden box atop a small wobbly corner desk. "A lord!" she chuckled. "That's funny." Dorovan narrowed his eyes. "And I didn't go to the market for food. I had to buy a new brush. My other one was too worn, and Mastro Ovello always says you might as well use a branch if your brush isn't crisp."

"I would be a lord if you put as much effort into regaining our estate as I have!" Dorovan got the whole thing out in one breath and much louder than he had intended. He felt his ears reddening.

"Oh, please," Ensa scoffed, "can't we go a single day without you bringing that up?" She lifted the box's lid. Inside were several glass jars neatly aligned, each one containing fine powders in every color imaginable. Ensa picked up a jar of reddish purple and examined its almost empty contents.

"It's like you don't even want to be a noble again," Dorovan accused as he stood from the bed. He picked up a pair of gray-blue trousers from the floor—the nicest ones he owned, although they were starting to wear at the thighs—and hastily put them on over his pantyhose. He placed the gold mark in his pocket, keeping the reminder of a better life close. "I am trying to find a suitable husband for you, a lord or even a duke—" Ensa cackled at that "—and you just sit here all day playing with your stupid colors."

"Playing with my *stupid colors* could lead to a great career. Guild colorists can make incredible wages."

"Are you hearing yourself? *Wages.*" He made the word sound like a swear. "We should be the ones paying others to do things for us. As a lady, you could get your own col- orist to... color things for you." He was sure she had ex- plained to him what exactly a colorist did, but he didn't care to recall that information.

Ensa turned towards her brother with an insipid look. "Has it ever dawned on you that maybe I want to be a col- orist because I enjoy the work? Because it fulfills me?" She let the question hang in the air for a moment, then she shook her head and returned to her vials. "No, of course you wouldn't understand fulfillment. You do nothing but run around playing the lordling all day as if you knew the first thing about being a lord. Little Lord Dorovan and his game of pretend."

Dorovan felt the heat that already reddened his ears ex- pand into his cheeks. His vision narrowed onto his sister— he wanted to hurt her. Swiftly, he grabbed the vial of purple from her hand and smashed it onto the ground. Ensa stared at him with her mouth agape.

"Why?" was all she asked—her tone not dissimilar from Dorovan's moments earlier. Dorovan picked up his shirt and his belt, to which an unassuming sheathed rapier was looped, and bolted out of the small apartment. About half- way down the creaky wooden staircase that led from their porch to the street, he realized he had left his feathered cap behind—there was no turning back now that he had enraged his sister. Pulling the shirt over his head, he walked to a nearby gray puddle in an indentation of the cobbled street and looked at his murky reflection. He moved his hair this way, then that, and then realized there was nothing he could do to salvage the unkempt brown curls—he really wished he had grabbed the feathered cap.

He hated to give anyone more excuses to think lower of them—of him. Their parents had died when Dorovan was only five. He remembered almost nothing about them except for the feeling of nuzzling his face into his mother's chest when he was sad or scared and smelling the clean scent of herbal soap in her brown hair. They had been Lord and Lady Melese, who had presided over House Melese—a beautiful sandstone mansion in the Ederat, the northernmost district of Sol Forne. While their origins were humble, their father, Vincero, was a decorated hero of the Red Coast war. Their mother, Palima, was said to have been the life of many a party with her poetry.

After their untimely deaths, the circumstances of which still eluded Dorovan and Ensa both, their uncle Asello had assumed control of the estate. But Asello was an avid gambler and drinker who had wagered the mansion and all its contents away—including all of their father's service medals, and their mother's poetry. What had been left of House Melese now was just a building taken over by the Transportation Guild. The courtyard where he and his sister used to run around as children was now crowded with burly workers loudly assembling carts and carriages. The garden their mother had kept was now home to a stable filled with a vast selection of workhorses and mules. Once, a stout woman had even offered Dorovan work there. In response, he spat in her face, which had cost him a bruised jaw and a bloody lip.

Each time Dorovan walked by the old home hurt more than the last, and his dream of one day regaining House Melese faded with each visit. And it wasn't as if Ensa was of any help. No, the foolish girl was intent on her stupid craft.

Pigments. The way Ensa spoke of coloring garments and curtains for lords and ladies soured his stomach with anger. He couldn't think of anything more embarrassing. If she would just dust herself off and keep up her appearance, she would surely get a husband in no time. She could be pretty if she tried.

Dorovan fastened the belt around his waist and made his way into the back alley of the three-story apartment he now called home. If he entered the city center taking the main street everyone would know which district he was emerging from. Unlike his sister, Dorovan would keep up appearances. As far as anyone was concerned, he was a lord on his way to a leisurely morning stroll through the richest markets of Sol Forne.

The alleyway twisted and turned, splintering into tens of different directions. Dorovan followed the same path he took most mornings—which would lead him across town and into the Effore, the newest and most affluent district in the city. Only then would he travel the main street all the way to the market. Perhaps he would strike up a chat with a lady's pretty handmaid—they always laughed at his jokes and told him he had pretty eyes. It was easy for him to talk to lowborn girls, though he made sure to keep his interactions brief. As he pressed on, the alleyway transformed from oppressively narrow to large and inviting. The edifices changed from a dirty dark gray stone to a bright sandy shade of yellow brick, and the cobbles underneath made way for bright marble.

Finally, the alleyway opened into the large Plaza d'Edo, one of the many fountained squares that spotted the face of the Effore like beauty marks. At the center of the fountain was a colorful marble swan with outstretched wings as if it had just landed in the mouth of a large marble clam. Water jetted from both the back of the clam and the mouth of the swan filling the air with a gentle bubbling sound. The grand cathedral known as the House of the Gods dominated the plaza with its tall, twisting spires. Scattered about the space were several benches that appeared to sprout out of the gray-veined marble paving like plants. Some minor lords and ladies perched on the benches deep in conversation, while others smoked their cigarettes and read books. These were his people—those who knew how to enjoy the finer things in life, a world away from the desperate rats that lived in his district.

Dorovan flattened his shirt, although no one seemed to be paying him any mind. As he did so, he noticed small flecks of purple dotting his sleeve. Anger and embarrassment threatened to redden his face again. He wiped at his sleeve in two quick motions hoping no one would notice. The color vanished easily, thank the gods.

Dorovan nodded his head as he passed a well-dressed man, receiving a disinterested nod in return. He gave more flourishing bows to ladies young and old, quickly kicking his left leg back as was custom. Recently, many of the younger male nobles were sporting wigs colored with blue and fuchsia powders—he would have to find a way to acquire one of those wigs, then perhaps put Ensa's powders to good use. The women, on the other hand, wore flashy headscarves of bright, colorful silks piled upon their braided hair and threaded through with strings of gems and pearls. Many of the younger ladies wore yellow dresses, this season's color for those looking to marry. Blue gowns were for those already married, while red gowns were for those open to a good time—not many red gowns around in the daytime.

From the plaza, he turned south and headed towards the market holding his head high like a flag in a parade. "Dorovan," a familiar voice called out. "Dorovan!"

Dorovan cracked his neck loudly in irritation and stopped to face the source of the incessant calling: Captain Velden, dressed as always in hideous dark blue leather armor. Sure, it was nicely fitted for the old man, but no one wore armor in the plaza unless they were guards, and Captain Velden was no guard.

"It's *Lord* Melese," Dorovan corrected the man as he had many times before. "*My Lord* will also do."

The old man grinned and gave him a curt bow. "Of course, of course. *Lord* Melese." He didn't sound particularly serious, thanks in part to that unrefined Vizenian accent of his, but Dorovan was beyond caring what the man thought. In fact, he was past this man carrying any weight in his mind whatsoever.

"I've told you countless times, I am not interested in joining your little blue group."

"You have, but you've yet to provide me with a proper reason."

Dorovan continued to walk towards the market. To his disappointment and irritation, the old man followed. "Must I have a reason to not do something I don't wish to do?"

Captain Velden laughed although Dorovan hadn't intended it as a joke. "Of course not. But allow me to sell you once more. You wish to be a lord, no?"

"I *AM* a lord." Dorovan wanted to scream it into the old fool's face but, in fear of being heard by anyone nearby, he resigned himself to hissing it out between gritted teeth.

"My apologies. You *are* a lord. But you are also very young, with many choices ahead of you. Many paths you could take." Captain Velden leaned in as if letting Dorovan in on a secret. "Why not choose to be something greater?"

"Greater? What could be greater than being a lord? A count? A king?"

"What about a hero?"

Dorovan looked sternly at Captain Velden, but he saw no jape in the man's face. A hero? Was he serious?

Velden took Dorovan's silence as consent to resume his pitch. "Lords and ladies may be respected by other lords and ladies—held in high regard even—but they will never truly be loved. Not by the royals in Vizen, nor by other lords and ladies, and definitely not by those who serve them. A hero, however, is loved by all, highborn and low. A hero commands respect. A hero can go on to become a lord while retaining all that love when they do. Like your father did. Now there was a man who loved his country! At your age, he would have joined up with the Blue Scarabs in a heartbeat!"

"You don't know my father," Dorovan snapped.

"But I did, we both served in—"

Dorovan halted and pointed an angry finger in Captain Velden's face. "You *don't* know my father. And you *don't* know me. Now, once and for all, leave me in peace. I have no intention of joining your blue bugs."

Just for a moment, Dorovan could see a crack in the man's ever-present serenity. "The *Blue Scarabs*," Captain

Velden made sure to enunciate every word, maybe in hopes that they would finally stick with Dorovan, "will always be looking for fit young men and women who wish to serve their country for a greater purpose. When your eyes finally open, young lord, and you see the threat that looms at our doors, you know where to find me. I'll be waiting."

Dorovan shook his head and carried on towards the market—this time Captain Velden did not follow. Not one day went by that Dorovan wasn't pestered by that nuisance. What could possibly make him think that he would want to join that ridiculous militia of his? Dorovan wasn't some poor sap that needed to risk his life for a handout from the royals. He was a lord. Lords didn't beg.

The rush hour at the market was just ending, much to Dorovan's delight. The higher class did not bother themselves with patronizing the market early in the morning—that was a servant's job—they only came out to the market to breathe in the fresh air and maybe purchase a pastry or piece of fruit as a snack. Looking at all the beautiful produce that filled the baskets and crates, Dorovan's insides began to shift uncomfortably in hunger. If Ensa had bought food this wouldn't be an issue. *That useless girl.*

A merchant loaded a basket of apples atop a rickshaw—they were lumpy and sad little things, no doubt the remaining few no one had wanted. When the merchant released the basket, an apple dropped onto the ground and rolled towards Dorovan, stopping at his feet. The merchant watched the apple roll away with a shrug—it wasn't a big loss to him.

Dorovan stared at the apple for a few moments. Part of him wished he could reach down and grab it. Take a bite of it. His stomach protested as he turned to walk away. The life of a lord was one of sacrifice. Even a small thing such as picking up an unwanted apple from the ground could set back all of his plans and progress. He reached into his pocket and felt the gold mark that sat there. If he ever was to spend it, he could purchase an entire orchard of apples with it. What good would a lumpy apple be to him?

Half a fennel sausage started to sound really good.

Three young men lounged at the far end of the market square—lordlings and minor nobles by the way they conversed. There was a way that men of the noble class carried themselves that set them apart from the common folk. Each word they spoke was thought out, savored, weighed, and only then uttered. Dorovan lacked their skillful way with words. He hadn't received their level of education and that, he was aware, was his greatest hurdle in being perceived as the lord he knew he was. He watched the men converse for a few moments, then stopped himself when he realized he had been imitating the men's mannerisms.

He sat at a nearby bench to continue his observation—not for himself, mind you, but for Ensa. The fool girl needed a husband. That was the quickest path for them to rejoin the noble class. But not just any man would do. Not the one on the far right—he was by far the richest looking, and most pompously dressed. A man like that would never settle for his sister. The one in the middle, however... He had a slender frame, much smaller than the other two, but he had a way of carrying himself that spoke of ardor and dependability. His lips glimmered with olive oil, and his soft jaw was freshly shaven. Atop his head was a frizzy powdered wig covered in lavender and yellow powder. Dorovan imagined this young man taking one of the sapphire rings from his fingers and sliding it down one of Ensa's. Their eyes would meet, and then they would share a kiss, his lips tasting richly of olive oil.

Dorovan licked his lips. Yes, this man would surely do. Dorovan stood from the bench and walked to the three men. Their eyes immediately fell upon him and suddenly Dorovan felt like the smallest ant that had ever crawled through the market. He opened his mouth to speak, but what came out instead was the stuttering sound of his stomach twisting in hunger and nervousness. The three men shared a look and then burst into laughter. Dorovan joined them as if he were, in some way, part of the joke. The three men then turned and headed towards the plaza, looking back a few times, their glances ripe with mockery.

Dorovan walked to the apple that still sat in the middle of the square. He felt tears well up in his eyes, his neck and ears turning hot. His stomach convulsed with bile. He lifted a foot and stomped on the shriveled fruit, smashing it into a white-brown pulp. He wished he was that apple.

"If you stomp on it any harder, you'll make a hole in the ground."

Dorovan lifted his head. To his bewilderment, in front of him stood Lady Lenora ca'Salviati. The Salviati House was one of the richest and most powerful in Sol Forne, owning most of the newest and most beautiful buildings in the Effore, as well as many of the vineyards that surrounded the city. The patriarch of the family, Lord Pendro ca'Salviati, was the head of the city's Noble Council. They weren't the sort to mingle with the common folk, or even the lower nobility for that matter, especially not in the market. What was Lady Lenora doing out here? Talking to *him*?

"M-my Lady," Dorovan floundered, stumbling into a clumsy bow.

"And your name?" she asked. Her voice was a bite of honeycomb after a cup of bitter orzo. Her full lips glistened in the sunlight and her round cheeks were dotted with yellow and orange pigment resembling freckles. A yellow headscarf covered her head—yellow, Dorovan noted, like her dress.

"Dorovan, my lady," he managed. His head was still low—why was his head still low? He was a lord and she was a lady. They were supposed to be equals. So why couldn't Dorovan lift his head? "Ca'Melese," he added, but it sounded like an afterthought.

"Can you use that?" she asked. Dorovan finally looked up. Her finger pointed to the rapier sheathed at his belt.

"Yes, my lady," he replied.

"And are you good with it?" she asked, tilting her head like a cat pondering which leg to pluck first from a spider.

"I am, my lady," he bluffed. In truth, the rapier had only been used once to scare off a drunken brigand that had broken into their home at night. But Dorovan wasn't about to tell Lady Lenora that. "Would you like me to show you?"

Lenora giggled, her eyes bright and the color of wine. "Eager to please. I like that." She held out her open hand and her attendant placed a piece of parchment in her palm. Only then did Dorovan realize the woman was escorted by an armed retinue. Two men in dark uniforms flanked her, while three others kept their eyes towards the market.

She handed Dorovan the parchment, but he dared not look at its contents without direct permission from her. "An invitation," she explained, "to a grand showcase of skill I am hosting at the Salviati home tomorrow. Will you make it?"

"I—of course! I will, my lady," Dorovan answered, struggling to rein in his enthusiasm.

"Good," she said with a smirk that could melt iron. Dorovan's heart threatened to punch through his chest as Lenora reached out her hand, placing it tenderly on his face. It felt cool and smooth against the heat of his cheek. Oh, gods, his cheeks better not be red.

"Won't you show me your skills and be my hero?" she asked.

Dorovan couldn't muster a single word. All he could do was nod. She seemed to find that amusing—the cat watching the legless spider wriggling to escape. She retrieved her hand. "See you then, Dorovan ca'Melese," she said, then turned to go, her guards following closely behind.

No longer troubled over his sister's mood, Dorovan sprinted back home. The Benine District, where he lived, felt claustrophobic in its density compared to the open-air plaza he had just left. The sun was shielded by the tall buildings, dimming the streets even in daylight but doing a poor job of concealing their disrepair. Peasant laughter and yells infested the air. Dorovan shoved passed his neighbors, eager to be rid of them soon.

He dashed up the wooden steps and barged through the door of the apartment. His sister was still bent over the pile of purple pigment, sweeping it into a vial with a small brush. On any other day, the sight would have irritated him, but today was a good day.

"You will not believe what just happened to me," Dorovan began, struggling to contain his exuberance. "Guess!"

Ensa remained silent. Dorovan's prompt was suspended in the air like dust.

"Seriously, guess!"

"How foolish of me to expect you to return with an apology," she replied coolly. "I'm in no mood for a guessing game, Dorovan."

Dorovan rolled his eyes. He walked over to the small dresser between their two beds and opened the top drawer. Inside sat the half sausage his sister had offered him earlier next to a browning onion that made the drawer smell ripe and insipid. He pulled the sausage from inside and took a bite—it was tough and flavorless.

"Dear sister, I'm in a good spirit, so I'll offer an apology for breaking your... purple." He waited for a moment in silence, expecting a word from Ensa that never came. Irritated, he swallowed the dry sausage and quickly glanced around the room for a pitcher of water to wash it down. He took the wooden pitcher that sat on Ensa's desk with both hands and drank deeply. "You'll be relieved to find out that I have found our salvation! We no longer will need you to marry a lord because an unwed lady has taken interest in me. Not just any lady, mind you. The Lady Lenora ca'Salviati! Can you believe it?" Dorovan took another pause, expecting a reaction from his sister, but she remained focused on the trail of pigment on the floor. His irritation ripened, threatening his excitement.

"Did you not hear me?" He was aware he sounded petulant, but the foolish girl must have grown deaf. "Lady Lenora of House Salviati invited me to a showcase of skill at her family home. Tomorrow! She seemed rather forward for a noble lady, but that's no mud on my boot. Can you imagine if our Houses combined? How powerful we would be! Are you ignoring me?"

Ensa swiped angrily at the puddle of pigment with a loud grunt. "Gods!" she cursed. Red bloomed on her hand where a remaining shard of glass cut her. "Where did I go so wrong that you don't know when to shut your gods-be-damned mouth?"

Dorovan stared at his sister, dumbfounded. Everything he had wanted to say dissipated from his mind. Ensa stood then moved to her desk. With tweezers, she plucked the small granule of glass from her palm. Tears ran down her cheeks. Dorovan dropped what remained of the sausage atop the dresser. From the bottom drawer, he produced white gauze, which he set on the desk in front of Ensa. His sister's eyes met his for just a moment, red and bitter.

"It hurts?" he asked with the pitiful voice of a scolded child.

"I'm not crying because this hurts," she said. "I'm crying because I'm scared for you."

"Scared? Of what?"

Dorovan saw a frenzy behind Ensa's eyes as if she had more to say than one mouth could fit. "These people you're trying so hard to impress, they don't see us as what we were. They only see us as what we are, and we are nothing to them. The best we can do is move on from the life we once had—the life we could have had—because it's not one they will simply let us reclaim. It just doesn't happen. I've told you time and time again, but you won't listen. And besides, mother and father were killed by that life. Why would you ever want to return to it?"

Dorovan's hands trembled—whether with anger, sadness, embarrassment, or something else, he wasn't sure. Ensa gently dabbed at the cut with a strip of gauze. Dorovan just... stood there, frozen.

"I remember when you were little and you would cry because you missed them so much," Ensa continued. A distant smile formed on her face. "You would climb into my bed and nuzzle your face into my hair until you fell asleep. I knew then that I had to find a way to create a better life for the both of us. But somewhere along the way, you began to sabotage our progress. I just don't understand—"

"You're the one who doesn't understand," he exclaimed loudly, surprising even himself. "I am tired of being a worm. A rat. A leech! I want to take what's mine by birthright. You ask why? Because it's mine, and I won't let go of it. This entire time I thought the key to regaining our name was through your marriage, but it looks like I don't need you anymore." Dorovan glared at Ensa's box of pigments. "I can do this on my own, and, when I do, I won't spare you a glance for you will be just another worm."

"Dorovan, calm yourself," Ensa said.

"Mother and father would be ashamed to see what their daughter has done to this family."

"Out!" Ensa shot up to her feet. "Get out of my home."

"Gladly, worm." Dorovan stormed out. If Ensa refused to be a Melese, then she was no sister of his. At the base of the steps, Dorovan realized he had once again forgotten his cap. He sighed and took the path that led to the Effore—perhaps the peaceful air of the plaza would calm his mood.

He passed a poster hanging on the wall of a cramped alleyway. The notice called for day laborers to help with the repair of the city's eastern wall. Dorovan unsheathed his rapier and assumed a lunging stance. He had never taken formal lessons in fencing or sword fighting but how hard could it be? You just held your blade firmly, swung it when you wanted to hit something, and tried not to get hit in return.

With a few quick flicks of his wrist, Dorovan slashed at the poster, sending shreds falling to the ground. He smirked, imagining the pieces of parchment to be bits of blood and flesh. Tomorrow he would show Lady Lenora what he was made of. Tomorrow would be the day he would become a lord again. Dorovan sheathed his rapier before anyone could see him—it wasn't proper to wield a sword in the city streets, and the last thing he needed was for someone to mistake him for a common thug.

A thought perturbed him: where would he spend the night? What would he eat? Dorovan realized that his sister did have one thing right: lords and ladies would not show him kindness. And why should they lower themselves so? For all they knew, he was a nobody. Until he had his estate and title returned to him, Dorovan could not ask any of them for aid.

The idea that hit him was like a punch to the gut. His stomach soured at the thought—or was that simply hunger? Yes, surely hunger was fogging his brain if it made him think of such a foolish plan. Yet, once Dorovan reached the plaza, he found himself walking towards a group of three blue-armored men. Captain Velden's eyes widened with delight upon seeing Dorovan approach. He lifted a hand and the two other men walked away in eerie unison.

Captain Velden nodded his head in greeting. "Lord Dorovan," he said, giving "lord" great emphasis.

"Captain Velden," Dorovan greeted. In truth, he was
simply stalling—maybe, given enough time, he would realize
what a terrible idea this was.

"To what do I owe the pleasure?" the old man asked,
shattering the awkward silence Dorovan had created.

"I—" *This is a terrible idea! What am I doing?* "I don't
like to do this, but recent circumstances have left me no
choice." Dorovan swallowed nothing, his mouth drier than
that damned fennel sausage. "I need lodging, just for tonight."

Captain Velden's forehead creased in wonder. "That's
quite a change in tone since this morning."

Dorovan cringed. "I am willing to work if that's what it
takes. I just need a place for the night—and a meal."

The old man grinned knowingly. "My dear boy, do not
worry about work or any other such thing." Velden slapped
Dorovan's back amicably. "We will lodge you in the Blue
Scarabs' guest quarters, and you shall dine with us this evening. Come, my son, let me show you where you'll be staying."

Captain Velden led Dorovan across the plaza with a firm
hand on the boy's shoulder—perhaps he was worried Dorovan would change his mind and flee. Dorovan considered
that possibility strongly for just a moment. But the promise
of a free meal was too tempting to resist.

The Blue Scarabs' lodge was an unassuming white brick
building with no frills or adornments. The walls were flat,
and the windows were simple squares with black iron slats
across them. While the door was made of beautifully

smooth ashewood, there were no engravings or carvings anywhere to be seen. The only piece of adornment, if that's what it could be called, was the engraving of a scarab beetle just above the door, faded blue pigment doing its best to stand out against the white brick. The building was indeed nothing special, yet Captain Velden beamed at it with what Dorovan assumed was pride.

Velden pushed the door open to let Dorovan inside. Sunlight struggled to illuminate the interior through the slatted windows, and it took Dorovan a few minutes to adjust himself to the darkness. The walls were fitted with a few maps of Hovardom and a large shield bearing the royal coat of arms—the Talessi green sparrow sigil on a red field. The rest of the walls were blank. Other than a few lit sconces, the foyer was entirely devoid of decoration—even the air inside felt austere and sanitized.

Velden pushed Dorovan onward through the foyer and into a bland hallway. "This building used to be a brothel until the king outlawed the practice last year and we seized it," Velden explained. "It serves a much greater purpose now, wouldn't you say?"

Dorovan shrugged—he wasn't entirely convinced.

"Many think of us as simple soldiers, but we're no such thing. Aye, we don armor and wear swords at our belts, but we weren't formed only to fight. We were formed to heal our great nation and bestow its bounty onto the rest of the world."

Having heard this pitch from Captain Velden many times before, Dorovan simply nodded. The old man led him into a small dark room with six beds lining the wall.

"This is where you'll spend the night. We currently don't have any other guests, so you may pick any bunk."

"Thank you," Dorovan said unconvincingly.

"Of course. Any child of Hovardom is welcome in our lodge. This way."

They reached the end of the hallway, which opened into an expansive mess hall. Rows of dozens of wooden tables spanned the length of the entire hall. "Have a seat, son," Velden said, and then snapped his fingers. A man and a woman, both in their middle years, rushed into the hall. "This is Lord Dorovan. Please bring him something to eat." The two nodded and left the hall at a quick pace.

"Sit, sit," Velden repeated when he realized Dorovan hadn't moved. The wooden chair was hard and stiff on Dorovan's backside—it was not made for comfort. Soon, the woman returned carrying a bowl that she set in front of him. A hot brown stew greeted him, thin wisps of steam rising from it. It was hard to say what it contained exactly besides a few orange carrots, but the smell of meat and onion was enough to make Dorovan feel faint. The middle-aged man reentered the hall and handed Dorovan a spoon. He didn't need any permission—he dug in and began to eat voraciously. It was too lightly seasoned for his taste, but that hardly mattered.

Captain Velden nodded, and the couple left the hall. Velden walked to the other side of the long table, chuckling to himself.

"What?" Dorovan asked. He hated not being in on others' jokes.

"I was just thinking about how long I've been trying to get you in here, and then here you are, asking me for a place to stay." Dorovan held no mirth in his face. "Oh, lighten up! It's a bit funny, don't you think?"

Instead of replying, Dorovan returned his attention to the soup.

"I promise, I won't try to recruit you while you're here," Velden responded, clapping his hands together. "But I do ask one thing of you. When they return from training or patrol, ask any Blue Scarab their name and why they joined. Their answers might surprise you. Will you do that?" Velden leaned forward. "A hot meal and a bed to lay in, in exchange for a simple question?"

Dorovan sighed deeply. He knew there had to be a catch, but there was no backing out now—not while his belly was full and warm.

"All right," he said.

"All right," Velden mirrored. "I'm afraid that duty calls and I must attend a few meetings. Feel free to explore the lodge. We have a library stocked with more histories than you could ever read in a single lifetime. Farewell Lord Dorovan ca'Melese." With a curt bow, Velden left Dorovan alone in the hall.

Once he finished his meal, Dorovan returned to the guest bunks. He sat on the cot closest to the door—that would allow him a speedy exit should he need one. Just like the chair in the mess hall, the cot was rigid and offered little to no comfort.

Dorovan unsheathed his rapier and held it in front of his face, examining its blade. He stood and swung it about, hitting a pretend adversary over and over again—first their legs, then their head. He imagined their head falling to the floor and rolling at his feet. He placed his foot on the imaginary head and raised the rapier in victory.

"You got 'em," a young man's voice said.

Dorovan quickly lowered the blade, the imaginary head vanishing underneath his foot, and turned to the door. A man and a woman stood there observing him, both of them in heavy blue armor. Both had shaved their entire heads bald, eyebrows included. Dorovan's ears and cheeks felt hot and red.

"Is it customary to just walk into others' rooms here?" Dorovan asked, embarrassment lending his words a frenetic slur.

The two shared a look. "Our apologies," the woman said. "The door was open. We were merely glancing in when we saw you... What exactly was it that you were doing?"

"And what business is it of yours?" Dorovan felt his grip on the rapier's hilt tighten.

"Steel yourself," the man said. "We didn't mean any offense. I am Lieutenant Leano, and this is Renna."

Dorovan still felt hot indignation throbbing in his neck, but his breath relaxed. He sheathed his rapier and introduced himself. "I am Lord Dorovan ca'Melese, here by invitation of Captain Velden."

The two did not appear at all impressed by his title, although it was hard to tell with the lack of hair cloaking their expressions. "A lord, eh?" Leano intoned. "We have many lords and ladies here." Renna shot him an admonishing glance that no lack of hair could hide. "We have many who *used to be* lords and ladies here," she corrected. "Now we are all Blue Scarabs."

Dorovan was confused. "What do you mean they *used* to be lords and ladies?"

"When they joined the Blue Scarabs, they forfeited their titles, their Houses, and their family names," Renna explained. "We call it 'the Obligation.'"

"But—" Dorovan was dumbfounded. Why would anyone ever freely give up their noble status?

The two seemed to understand Dorovan's unspoken question. "Because," Renna began, "what is a House without a homeland? What purpose do titles serve when you don't have a home? We joined the Blue Scarabs because our eyes were opened to the forces that threaten Hovardom. And I don't simply mean outer threats, like Sazisan threatening our borders, but the threats from within."

"Corruption, greed, immoral living," Leano listed. "This is a battle for the lifeblood of Hovardom, and we, the Blue Scarabs, have placed ourselves at the frontlines."

Dorovan examined the floor beneath his feet. He couldn't wait for this conversation to be over. Renna touched his shoulder gently and Dorovan lifted his head to meet her eyes. They were green. She would have been pretty had it not been for the lack of hair. "I used to be an enchantress," she said.

Dorovan shrugged out of her touch and backed away in apprehension. Enchantresses were not at all present in Sol Forne like they were in the north. He had once heard from a group of excited urchins that an enchantress was making her way through the market. The stories Dorovan had heard of witches and dark enchantments were enough to make him decide to return home that day, although he heard later from those same urchins that the enchantress had looked like an ordinary woman in her middle years.

"Still am, really," Renna continued, smiling reassuringly. "But now, instead of practicing my trade for my own gain, I do it for our country. We all sacrificed something to be here, not because someone made us, or even asked us to. We did it because it was what needed to be done."

Captain Velden was strange in his devotion to Hovardom, but these two took things to an entirely different degree. Why should he care about his homeland? What had his homeland ever done for him but strip him of what was his? And what were these supposed "threats from within" that had concerned even an enchantress enough to cause her to exchange her craft for a soldier's life? Dorovan was hesitant to ask.

"I think I would like to be left alone," Dorovan said. Renna smiled and backed towards the door. "As you wish, Lord Dorovan." There was not a hint of mockery in either the words or the deep bow she gave him.

As she left the room, Leano bowed as well. "Keep your wrist light," he said.

"What?"

"While holding your rapier. You're very rigid. Keep your wrist light and relax your arm."

Dorovan closed the door. He would not suffer any more prying eyes or unsolicited advice. He unsheathed his rapier once more and slashed the air, this time making sure not to stiffen his wrist. Perhaps the bald man did know what he was talking about. Dorovan grinned, imagining the performance he would put on tomorrow for Lady Lenora—a performance so captivating, it would win back his name and, if he was lucky, her heart.

IV.

THE DUCKLING

It wasn't the stone slab of a cot that kept Dorovan up most of the night, nor was it any sort of anxiety over Lady Lenora's showcase of skill. No, what kept Dorovan awake was the silence. Nights in the small apartment he had shared with his sister were filled with all sorts of sounds—noisy drunkards stumbling home, moaning alley cats, and the frenetic clattering of the occasional fistfight. Those city sounds had been the backdrop to many of Dorovan's dreams. But here, in the Blue Scarab lodge, the silence was deafening. It couldn't actually be that quiet on the street outside—the area was well-known for its taverns. Perhaps it was a feature left over from the building's previous use as a brothel—insulated walls so that no one could hear the goings-on inside.

But it wasn't just the lack of street noise that gave Dorovan pause. He was already tucked into his bunk when the Blue Scarabs had returned to the lodge, their footsteps hitting the dark stone floor in perfect synchronization. They headed for the mess hall where they shared a quick, quiet meal, and then retreated to their rooms. A veil of stillness had suddenly fallen over the halls—not a furtive footstep, nor a snore, nor a wheeze.

Dorovan could hear the pulsing of his racing heart in his head. He simply had to survive the night. Tomorrow, he would become a lord again. Tomorrow, everything that had been stolen would be restored to him. He reached into his pocket where his father's gold mark sat secured, and held onto the coin dearly, conjuring dreams of his family's former glory.

The next morning, Dorovan was offered some stew to break his fast. He declined—his eagerness had him almost shaking. Also, he wanted to avoid running into Captain Velden at all costs. He knew the man would have all sorts of questions about his stay and what he'd learned from asking the other Scarabs about their reason for joining. A cool breeze greeted Dorovan as he exited the lodge, the bright yellow sun a harbinger of a beautifully warm mid-Spring day. He immediately made for the Effore, which was much closer from here than his usual route through the back alleyways of the Benine. North of Plaza d'Edo, past the House of the Gods, was House Salviati: a beautiful blue-marble villa surrounded by a blue and yellow colonnade, each column snaked by twisting marble vines bearing stone fruits.

A knot formed in Dorovan's throat—a flicker of uncertainty. *What am I doing here? I don't belong here.* No! He swallowed that thought like sour wine. These were his peers. Lady Lenora had approached him because she had recognized his status. She would have never done so had he been just some unassuming commoner. A feeling of calm resolve eclipsed Dorovan's hesitance.

He approached the front gate of the estate. A spectacled man with a thick red wig stood there, seemingly waiting for someone. When he saw Dorovan, his attitude changed instantly to one more cautious and restrained. "What?" he asked curtly.

"I'm here for the showcase," Dorovan said, oozing confidence—you had to be firm with the help, or so he had once overheard some lordlings say.

The man dismissively examined Dorovan from head to toe and then did so again for good measure. "You?"

How dare this simple-minded servant question him? He ought to put him in his place! Not just yet. First, Dorovan must regain his titles. Then, he would enjoy watching this servant grovel for forgiveness.

Dorovan cleared his throat. "Lady Lenora herself invited me." The man arched an eyebrow. Perhaps that was not the right thing to say. However, after one more examining glance, the man cracked a smile—a smirk, not quite mocking but...

"Ah," he intoned. "You're the boy."

"The *boy*?" Dorovan repeated, indignant. "Mind your tongue when you speak to a lord."

The man's smirk only turned more enthusiastic, almost combative. "Right this way," he said, opening the gate for Dorovan to walk through.

Dorovan felt his face flush with heat. He needed to cool his temper—Lady Lenora shouldn't see him red in the face. This was a good day; he wouldn't let some servant ruin it with his insolence.

The servant closed the gate behind him and led Dorovan through the colonnade, towards the back gardens of the estate. Manicured hedges lined the inner perimeter of the columns, purple and white flowers blooming fragrantly throughout. The hedges then turned inward towards the fountain at the center of the great garden, the polished statue of a *mer* emerging from the water, weightless, as if in flight. Several lords and ladies drifted about the grounds lazily, some with fantastically colored drinks in hand, others eating grapes and honeycombs from small plates. All of them wore the latest fashions, their lush silks and laces ballooning in the slight breeze.

Dorovan breathed deeply—this was it. This was his moment. He took a step towards the path leading to the garden, when a gruff mustachioed man grabbed him by the arm and dragged him away.

"Pardon me! What do you think you are doing?" Dorovan protested, attempting to retain a modicum of properness.

"I could ask the same of you," the man said through his mustache, his voice like a lumberman's saw. "What were you thinking, joining the guests in that way?"

"I am a guest, you fool!" Dorovan attempted to shake out of the man's grip to no avail. "Let me go, you... you... you have very strong fingers."

"You? A guest? Pfwa!" The man's sudden laughter sounded like wood being split. "Keep up the japes and they'll love you."

"The japes? I demand an explanation!"

"There, that's the one!" That melodious voice could not have reached Dorovan at a better moment. The gruff man halted suddenly and bowed his head as Lady Lenora approached them flanked by two lovely ladies dressed in yellow and a handsome young lord, his white wig dotted artfully with orange pigment.

Dorovan smiled and joined the gruff man in a bow, albeit not as deep, as befit a lord. "My lovely Lady Lenora," Dorovan greeted. "Your beauty eclipses even the sun." The two ladies giggled and whispered to each other while the lordling rubbed his chin in amusement.

"Dorovan, right?" she asked.

"Yes, my lady," he said, grinning.

"Are you prepared to put on a good show for us?"

"I am, my lady. However, there seems to have been some sort of miscommunication and this brutishly strong man has been dragging me to gods-know-where. I don't mean to cause a fuss, but would this happen to be your man?"

The ladies giggled again. Not Lenora, though. Her face remained graceful and unmoved, however, there was a curious cast to her eyes. "Captain Anone is one of my father's men. He's not known for his gentle disposition, isn't that right?" That last question was for Anone himself.

The captain let go of Dorovan's arm and lowered his head. "No, my lady."

Dorovan rubbed his arm where the man had grabbed him—it would definitely bruise. "Thank you, my lady."

"Now, lead young Dorovan to the stage. We will be starting soon."

"The stage?" Dorovan asked. The bemusement in the young woman's eyes narrowed into something else. She seemed irritated, although why she would be was beyond him.

"The showcase, remember?" she said as if asking a child. "You will be performing for us today, won't you?"

Dorovan felt so stupid. How could he have forgotten? She had invited him to show his prowess with the rapier, foremost. Only after the showcase would he join the other guests in their mingling. "But of course," he said with a gallant bow. "I will put on the best show you have ever seen."

Lady Lenora smiled. "Of that, I have no doubt." As they walked away, the two women chittered like hens as they snuck furtive glances at him. The handsome lord peeked back at him as well and flashed a bright-toothed grin.

"This way, please," Anone said, summoning all the politeness he was most likely capable of. Dorovan followed him to the stage: a courtyard of beaten dirt surrounded by a short cushioned marble wall that functioned as seating for the audience.

"So, what sort of tricks are we showcasing today?" Dorovan asked. "I can catch wooden circles with the tip of my blade. Or perhaps they want me to spear some fruit and feed it to the ladies."

"Today we melee."

The answer was so curt and direct that it put Dorovan off balance. "What do you mean, melee?"

"Melee," Anone repeated, handing Dorovan a sack. As soon as Anone released it, Dorovan just about toppled over under the weight of its contents. "You know what a melee is, right?"

"Of course I know what a melee is, you imbecile!" Dorovan opened the sack. Inside were pieces of boiled leather armor. "What is this?"

"And you call me an imbecile? That's armor, boy."

"I know what armor is!"

"Then why did you ask?"

Heat—no, fire—spread across Dorovan's face and neck. "What sort of melee are we talking about here?"

"The regular kind. One-on-one. You swing your weapon, and when you hit your opponent, you win."

"I'm not wearing this—this... *thing*." The armor was truly hideous. Not even a spot of color. Faded slashes lining the chest plate spoke of the strength of past blows.

"You might want to at least wear a helmet, 'case you get shaved."

Dorovan dropped the sack and let the contents spill out. "I am not wearing *any* part of this. I am a lord! I don't melee."

"As you wish. I can show you back to the door if that's your choice."

Part of him wanted to do just that—leave with his dignity still intact. No one would see him wear this sort of armor, not now or ever. Cheap leather armor was for hired guards, brigands, and fools who had nothing else to look forward to in life. Sure, his father had worn armor and had became a lord for it, but that had been Vizenian steel. Dorovan fondly recalled admiring it as a young child, his father pointing to the custom engravings on its red surface and explaining what each one signified. Dorovan had always dreamed of one day being able to wear that armor, but thanks to his uncle, reclaiming it would be impossible.

How was Lady Lenora supposed to admire his collarbones and toned calves when they were covered by horrid brown leather? How was she supposed to look into his blue eyes when they were concealed behind a helmet?

But then again, Lady Lenora had personally asked him to be here. To leave without participating in the showcase would surely offend her. Past lords had lost their titles for causing such offense. What would be his fate if he offended the highest lady in Sol Forne? His honor would never recover.

Taking in a lungful of air, Dorovan lifted the helmet from the bag. "I'll wear the damned helmet."

"Good," Anone said. "Now we have to get you a proper weapon."

"No," Dorovan blurted. "That's where I draw the line. I keep the rapier."

"Son, are you certain about that?"

"The things I can do with this may surprise you," he boasted.

"I sincerely doubt it."

Half an hour later, the guests began to seat themselves along the marble wall, still lost in their vivid conversations. The two ladies and the lord that followed Lady Lenora sat across from Dorovan, watching him and cooing quietly amongst themselves. Dorovan smiled his most heroic smile, and the three chuckled in delight. Lady Lenora had asked him to be her hero. Dorovan had decided to embody that fully. Everyone he fought today would be defeated in his lady's name.

Captain Anone led Dorovan aside to a far wall. Around him were several others, most of them much older than he. These were seasoned fighters—men with hair on their bare chests, women with long braids that were heavier than the armor Dorovan had refused, and even some errant knights here to demonstrate their worth. Only one of them seemed similar in age to him: a thick-armed girl about twice his size, a short sword at her hip, and a large fresh scar running down her chin.

Dorovan felt sick. What was he getting himself into? He still had time to make a run for it. He knew where the exit was—no, it was too late for that. He had committed to this melee, and he would see it through.

Dorovan shifted closer to the thick-armed girl. "So, this melee," he began, unsure. "It's all pretend, right?"

"What do you mean, pretend?" she asked blankly.

"It's all fixed, right? The winner is decided in advance and we all just play along."

The girl gave him a sideways glance. "See this?" She pointed at the pink and puckered scar on her chin. "I got this at last month's showcase. Almost took my whole jaw off, that one did." She pointed to a nearby man sharpening a long-bladed knife on a whetstone. His black eyes, intent on the blade, made Dorovan shiver.

"He did?" This was madness. "Why are you back here?"

"Because I either fight here or in some tavern's dark basement, and the Salviatis pay more."

"You're getting paid for this?"

"You're not? Oh..." Dorovan could be mistaken, but it seemed to him as if she was suppressing a laugh.

"What was that?"

"Nothing."

"Nothing?"

"You'll see."

Dorovan had the sudden urge to excuse himself when suddenly Lady Lenora approached the stage along with her mother, Lady Elma. She was not nearly as beautiful as her daughter, but there was something in the way she carried herself that commanded awe and respect. The guests stood at the sight of the two women.

"Please, everyone be seated," Lenora said, and the crowd obeyed. "We are here to celebrate the season with our first springtime showcase. I see many familiar faces, so I'll be brief. I wouldn't want to bore you all." The crowd chuckled. Dorovan joined in as well. The thick-armed girl shook her head. "Two by two, these fearsome warriors and heroes will fight for your amusement. Only one will be victorious in the end. Who will they be? Only fate shall decide." The crowd clapped and cheered daintily, and Lady Lenora took a seat on the wall beside her mother.

Captain Anone walked to the center of the stage and cleared his throat. "I call upon the first two fighters, Blario the errant knight, and Erje the killer." The crowd erupted, obviously favoring Erje's name.

Erje dropped the whetstone and sheathed his long knife at his belt. Unblinking, he headed towards the center of the stage. Why would the crowd be cheering for such a fiendish man? A younger man than Erje sighed deeply and headed for the stage. Unlike Erje, who wore boiled leather, Blario was in full steel armor, the blue cross of the errant knights engraved on the chest plate. Nervous did not begin to describe how Dorovan felt. He grabbed onto the hilt of his rapier in a white-knuckled effort to hide his quivering hand.

"On my word," Anone announced. The two fighters faced each other, and silence descended upon the yard. "Begin!" Anone yelled, and immediately ran for the marble wall, hopping over it in a single swift motion.

Blario unsheathed his longsword and lunged for Erje. Had Dorovan not known better, he would have thought the man intended to kill the other. Erje, knife still at his belt, easily dodged the heavy knight and circled him. The crowd laughed as if it was the funniest thing they had ever witnessed. Dorovan did not think any of this was funny—not anymore.

Another heavy swing from Blario that Erje calmly dodged. Then another, and another. Blario began to pant visibly, as the crowd continued laughing and cheering at the show. Blario spat. "Stop dodging, you slippery son of a—"

Dorovan never saw Erje unsheathe his weapon—suddenly it was just there, in his hand. Erje tripped the tired knight, who fell onto his hind with a heavy metal clank, and immediately pounced on him like a cat on a mouse, knife to his throat. The palm of his left hand lay flat against the hilt of the blade—a slight forward motion would easily send the tip directly into the knight's throat.

"End match!" Anone called out, and the crowd cheered as Erje stood from the defeated knight and made his way back to where the rest of the fighters stood watching. He picked the whetstone from the ground and returned to sharpening his knife as if nothing had happened.

Anone helped Blario to his feet. "That was too quick!" someone in the audience complained.

"Our undefeated Erje does not like to waste time," Anone replied, to the audience's laughter. Erje did not seem to notice his name being used. Dorovan shivered again. He sent a prayer to the gods that he may never find himself at the wrong end of Erje's blade.

Blario clambered over the marble wall and was escorted towards the estate's exit by a servant. "I know the damned way," Dorovan heard the knight hiss.

Anone cleared his throat, the grating sound immediately recapturing the audience's attention. "Next up on the stage—" Lady Lenora lifted her hand and Anone headed towards her. She whispered something in the man's ear, and he nodded fervently. Returning to the center of the stage, Anone resumed his announcement. "The next two fighters that will face each other are a special treat, courtesy of our very own Lady Lenora." The audience clapped gleefully. "One of her favorite warriors, the bloodthirsty Alizia—"

The thick-armed girl raised her fist, and the crowd cheered. Lady Lenora smiled and nodded her head in favor.

"—will face off against this showcase's *duckling*—" At the sound of the word the entire audience began to loudly quack and flap their elbows. "—Dorovan the lordling."

Dorovan's heart sank. In a panic, his eyes landed on Alizia. The look she gave him was that of pure pity. Nevertheless, she walked to the center of the stage and stood next to Anone. She whispered an obvious complaint to the man. He shook his head and responded inaudibly. It appeared as if she wanted to fight Dorovan just as much as he wanted to fight at all.

As he stood there, unmoving, the crowd began to chant "Dorovan the duckling! Dorovan the duckling!" all the while quacking and flapping their imaginary wings. Heat rose in his face, neck, and ears, and his vision began to narrow, the edges of his periphery warping as if swimming underwater.

Anone approached him and took the helmet from the ground—Dorovan hadn't realized he had dropped it. He placed it firmly onto Dorovan's head. "It's time, boy," he said and dragged Dorovan by the arm to the center of the stage.

Alizia's hand hovered over the hilt of her short sword, but her expression was unsure and uncomfortable.

"On my word!" Anone announced. "Begin!" He exited the stage calmly this time.

Alizia slowly unsheathed her sword and pointed it at Dorovan, who just stood there, unmoving. She made a strange motion with her head. *What was that? Some sort of an involuntary tick? Oh!* She was telling him to unsheathe his rapier! He did so as quickly as he could, and the rapier fell to the ground. Dorovan quickly picked it up and pointed it at Alizia. The girl rolled her eyes and shook her head. That irritated Dorovan more than the audience's continuous quacking. *Keep your wrist light,* he reminded himself and swung the rapier at the girl's face.

One moment the rapier was firmly in his hand, the next it was on the ground several feet from him. Alizia rotated the sword in her hand with a flourish. She bowed and the audience cheered. Anone re-entered the stage. "End match! The winner is the merciless Alizia!"

"No!" A single word brought the audience to a standstill. Lady Lenora stood wearing an unimpressed expression.

"My lady?" Anone asked.

"Again," was all she said.

Anone looked from Lenora to Alizia, who seemed just as confused as him. "Again," he repeated, and left the stage.

What did they mean again? Had Dorovan not embarrassed himself enough already? Alizia picked up the rapier from the ground and handed it to Dorovan. "Looks like we're going again, duckling."

"Don't call me that." Dorovan could taste the petulance in his words.

Alizia swung her sword lazily at his chest. Dorovan backed away, missing the blade by mere inches. The crowd resumed its cheering, but Lady Lenora remained standing, observing their fight as attentively as a general studying a battlefield. Dorovan smelled his own fear. The quacking of the audience bored into his skull with blistering scorn.

They want me to be a helpless duckling, eh? I'll show them!

Dorovan lunged for Alizia as rapidly as he was able. The motion must have caught her by surprise because her eyes shot wide. All it would take was a quick step to the left for her to miss the blow, however, she lifted her sword and went in for a parry.

Once again Dorovan's rapier fell to the ground—but not the rapier alone. Blood spewed from where Dorovan's ring and pinky fingers had been cut. The pinky was gone entirely, while the ring finger dangled loosely by a strand of flesh, as if a gentle breeze would send it flying off. Dorovan screamed. The crowd howled. He found himself on his knees clutching his bloody hand. Alizia sheathed her sword and sighed—her face struggling to hide shame... no, embarrassment for Dorovan.

"Once again, Alizia is victorious," Anone announced as he made his way back to the center of the stage. The crowd roared even louder than before. Through his tears, Dorovan saw Lady Lenora. Her face was a mask of coldness, but a rose's thorn of a smile pulled at the corner of her full lips. Anone seemed to notice that smile as well. "My lady?" he cautioned.

The audience quieted. Lenora licked her lips and allowed the smile to bloom. "Well fought, Alizia." The girl bowed her head in thanks. "But we're not done with our duckling quite yet." A murmur filled the audience, like a swarm of confused bees. "This one introduced himself to me as a lord." Mocking laughter filled the air. "Can you believe that? This one, a lord! Lord Dorovan ca'Melese. I asked my father if he had ever heard of such a House, and to my surprise, he had."

Lady Lenora made her way to the center of the stage, beside Alizia and looming over the shaking Dorovan. "House Melese was a House of pretenders, not purebloods like us. His father was nothing but a soldier who won a token battle. So the king gave away our birthright like some kind of servant's prize. As if titles alone can make a commoner equal to our legacies." Lenora turned her icy gaze down on Dorovan. "Thank the gods, Sol Forne was rid of these fakers. Yet, this one still believed himself a lord. And now we have taught him what he truly is. He is this showcase's duckling. And what do we do with ducklings?"

The audience stood and, in unison, cried out, "We pluck them!"

Lady Lenora turned to Alizia. "Break his sword," she commanded.

"As my lady wishes," Alizia said. She picked up Dorovan's rapier and easily snapped it under the weight of her boot. The audience cheered at that as well.

"Take him away!" Anone called out, and a pair of guards lifted Dorovan off the ground. When had they entered the stage? The world around him began to blur and oscillate. The blood from his hand poured down his sleeve.

"Not just yet," Lady Lenora ordered. The guards held Dorovan firmly, his legs hovering a foot off the ground. Lady Lenora moved in close to his face and whispered, "You will never be a lord. You will never be a hero. You will never be anything but the dirt beneath my feet. I need you to know that."

Dorovan looked at her. How could someone so beautiful be so cruel? Her smile was a cold northern wind icing his bones. She nodded and the guards took him away—away from the laughter of the crowd, away from Lady Lenora's gaze, away from any chance of him ever reclaiming his lordship.

The marble ground smacked him in the face when the guards dropped him outside of the estate gates. His blood stained the white stone. The pain in his hand was muffled, overtaken by a dull warmness that made his entire body shiver. He stood, somehow, and wobbled his way through the streets. Lords and ladies he passed placed handkerchiefs at their noses to protect their sensitive selves from the stench of his failure.

With nowhere to go, no home, and no hope, Dorovan walked. And walked. And cried.

V.

A GREAT PERFORMANCE

T he countryside gave way to more countryside, the up and down of the rolling hills the only thing to mark the passage of time between Solway and the next town, Adelton. Vaelin recalled barely anything about Adelton other than that it indicated Sol Forne was a day's journey away. To her surprise, a tall stone fortress greeted her where the town had once stood. These humanfolk were so different from the elvenfolk she had lived among thousands of years before. When elvenfolk built a structure—whether it be a town or a monument—they did so intending it to remain standing for all of eternity. Vizen, for example, now the great capital of Hovardom where the royals resided, was once known to her as Lyelwyen, a port city-state of the Arish nation.

Whereas elvenfolk had built for longevity, humanfolk structures were a temporary sort. Vaelin could appreciate that about humanfolk—unlike the elvenfolk, who had believed that their dominion would last forever, humanfolk recognized that everything was in flux. Maybe change was in their nature. Or maybe it was something they learned when they set foot on the continent eight hundred or so years ago and had to adapt the vast abandoned cities left by the elvenfolk for their purposes.

On the other hand, this constant building and tearing down was incredibly unhelpful when it came to remembering where things were. One decade they built an entire city and then the next century it was gone. Who had the time to keep track of all that?

A small gate at the front of the fortress was propped open but heavily manned by soldiers in blue armor—the sweat on their bald heads glistened in the sun. Visible within the fortress were small wooden houses and larger buildings of the same style. Clearly, Adelton still stood but had been swallowed whole by the enclosing fortification.

"What in the gods are you supposed to be?" a bald soldier asked when she reached the gate. Not just bald, but smoother than a naked mole. His armor was wiped spotless, and his boots were free of any mud or dirt that Vaelin could see. The soldier waited at a small desk—a piece of parchment splayed in front of him.

"You humanfolk and your ever-changing hair fashions," Vaelin said, shaking her head. "Can't say I'm particularly fond of this one."

"This ain't no *hair fashion,*" the man scoffed. "Now, whatever you are, what business you got in Lornaros?"

"Lornaros? Isn't this Adelton?"

"*Was* Adelton," the man corrected. "There was some civil unrest here a year or so ago during the eastern migration after the Albadonian fires. The Blue Scarabs seized the town, returned the peace, and named it after the king's grandmother, Queen Lorna, the Elderqueen. Now, what is your business here?"

"Just passing through. Need a bed. And a bath too, if I'm lucky." This was the first she had heard of this Blue Scarab group and she wanted very badly to hear more about them and what they were doing there. But if there was one thing Vaelin had mastered over the centuries it was learning to discern when to not ask further questions.

The man reached for a quill and dunked its tip into a wide ink bottle. "Name?"

"Vaelin," she replied, arching an eyebrow.

"Surname?"

"It's just Vaelin." The man wrote with a slow and unsteady hand. "What is it you're doing?" Vaelin asked.

"This here's a ledger," the man explained, his tongue sticking out of the side of his mouth as he sounded the name. "Everyone that comes into Lornaros needs to be accounted for... for accounting purposes." He stopped abruptly and went to scratch hair that wasn't there. "Vaelin? How many L's that got?"

"Just the one," Vaelin replied. The man took his time with the last three letters and then handed her a small iron coin. Three numbers were engraved onto it: 6 4 4.

"If you're caught without that you'll be in big trouble, so make sure you don't lose it." Vaelin nodded and placed the small coin in her bag. "And don't forget to return it on your way out. Welcome to Lornaros," he said like an actor stiffly repeating memorized lines.

Lornaros. Changing the names of towns on a whim was just another humanfolk absurdity. But Vaelin had learned to expect such surprises. Even humanfolk children could adapt in unpredictable—even dark—ways, as Vaelin had recently discovered. She recalled the way the child, Annonio, had smiled upon hearing of his father's death, and wondered briefly what would become of the people there. No, best not to dwell on that. Better to adopt the humanfolk way—to move on while embracing the flux. Vaelin only wished her nature could be as quickly adjusted as a town's name.

Adelton—no, Lornaros—was very similar to how she remembered it all those years ago, save the surrounding structure. Most houses were made of light-brown wooden slats and had hay roofs. The only building that seemed to have been upgraded since her last visit was the inn at the center of the town. *The Brass Jug* had been refinished with painted bricks, following the fashion of Sol Forne.

The strumming of a mandolin and a floating tenor voice beckoned her to enter—she never could resist a bard. Several Blue Scarab soldiers reclined about the inn in small clusters, most of them eating or resting while off duty. A few other patrons sat at the bar on the western side of the building, quietly enjoying a snack or glass of wine—this close to Sol Forne, the wine would be of incredible quality. At the opposite end stood a lanky middle-aged singer in a frilly coat, gently strumming a mandolin and singing, his eyes never leaving the ceiling.

> *"And while my quiet heart rejoices to the One,*
> *The fire-scorched throne I embrace.*
> *And though still my hand plays only for thee, One,*
> *I wish that mine words might abate.*
> *May these fires of yours, One, abate.*
> *May mine chant-song the True One elate."*

While she wasn't quite sure what the words of the song were supposed to mean, Vaelin was enraptured by the

man's tremolo. He could have sung about cleaning chamber pots and Vaelin would have listened to him with equal
interest. A Blue Scarab spat on the floor in front of Vaelin's
feet, returning her to the present.

"Shove your True One," the soldier cursed. The singer
lowered his eyes from the ceiling with a startled expression,
as if exiting a trance. The Blue Scarab stood, his chair slamming to the floor behind him. "If I hear you sing about that
blasphemous shit again, we're going to kick you out of here
squealing, you hear?"

"Steel yourself, man," another soldier said, tugging the
other man's arm, clearly not sharing his companion's offense. The singer lowered his eyes, fearfully, and walked up
to the bar—not quite fearfully; he was disappointed. Only
then did the soldier pick up his chair and sit back down, his
angry gaze following the singer all the way to the bar.

Vaelin sat a few stools away from the singer. The other
patrons at the bar eyed the man warily.

"What did I tell you about singing those kinds of songs?"
the old barkeep said, shaking his head.

"You did warn me, aye," the bard replied with a heavy
northwestern drawl—woodsfolk by the sound of it. "But I
did my duty and that's what matters. The True One's flame
will not touch this town."

The barkeep sighed. "Look, that one's always getting irritated over something. Just make sure you don't go angering any of my other patrons. Here." The man set a small
cup of wine in front of the singer.

The singer nodded. "If the True One sets a helper in
your path, don't hesitate to follow... or drink their wine in
this case."

"I liked your song," Vaelin interjected. Both the barkeep and the singer faced her, their eyes widening in confusion.

"You... Wait a moment," the barkeep said, squinting as if recalling something. "I know you. You're that elf that visited when I was a boy and my mother kept this inn. You look..."

"The same?" Vaelin suggested.

"Well-traveled. And perhaps a bit ripe," the barkeep replied.

"I could use a room and a hot bath, that's true."

"If you got pieces, I can have a bath drawn in your room when you're ready to retire."

"That sounds lovely. In the meantime, could I trouble you for a glass of your best? And the singer's next one is on me."

The barkeep reached under the bar and pulled out a dusty bottle. He wiped the dust off the label and read it. "This one's from fifty-nine. A great harvest that year."

"Sounds like the one for me," Vaelin smiled. The barkeep uncorked the bottle and gave it a deep sniff, his face brightening. The man poured it into a wide-brimmed glass and set it in front of her.

Holding the stem, Vaelin drew small, gentle circles in the air, sending tiny waves of red splashing against the side of the glass—when she stopped, droplets like small waterfalls cascaded slowly downward, reuniting with the rest of the wine. The barkeep watched her with an approving nod.

The dark smell of leather was only slightly overtaken by a floral note, like the smell of a hyacinth crushed between the pages of an old book. She took a sip and coated her mouth with the room-temperature liquid. Sweet, savory, and pungent in all the right ways. She found herself smiling—it had been too long.

"You seem to know your wine," the singer said.

"That, and much, much more," Valin replied, taking a second sip.

"My song," the man said, as if something was bothering him. "You said you liked my song."

"In truth, I mostly enjoyed the way you sang it. The way you seemed to trap the sound in your throat and let it rattle about your chest—I could never do that. I even took lessons once. Turns out some people are made to sing, and others to listen."

The singer nodded with poorly concealed disappointment.

"You seemed to believe every word you sang," Vaelin added. "I hear that is what makes a good performer. Conviction."

"Every word I spoke is true. There is a great fire hovering above us and, like a swollen river slamming into an unsecured dam, it's waiting to wash us all away. I've seen it with my own eyes." The man had not touched his glass and was instead staring into it as if wishing he could hide inside if the flames suddenly erupted.

Vaelin eyed the man curiously, then finished her wine. The barkeep was quick with a refill. "A fire, eh? What do you mean by that?"

The man moved onto the stool next to Vaelin. He lowered his voice close to a whisper—in fear of being overheard by the irate soldier, Vaelin assumed.

"Almost a full year ago, late at night, I sat outside my home unable to sleep. My wife, two daughters, and my mother all slept inside soundly. At the time, I was working in Albadone on this structure called a *bore*. This large contraption dug into the earth, sucking up its innards." The man took a pause, perturbed by the words he was speaking. "No one liked the idea of it, but the wage was good. We were warned by... practically everyone that the *bore* was no good—some went as far as to call it evil. But we ignored the warnings. We were simple workers fulfilling a contract. We should have listened."

The man's eyes welled with tears, but he carried on. "That night, I saw it. Well, first I heard it—the sound of the earth screaming. Then, the sky turned red, and the fire fell from above onto my home. It was.... Oh, True One, it was so fast. My family were.... They didn't feel a thing. Never even woke up to scream, thank the True One. I stayed and watched everything burn, even as the fires raged around me. I prayed for the flames to take me too, so I could join my family in death. But I was left behind."

Wiping his eyes and taking a quick swallow of wine, the man steadied himself. "The next morning, as the fires raged on, I heard the True One speak to me as if he was standing right in front of me. He told me that what I had witnessed was the beginning of a great burning that would leave nothing in its wake. I heard the song then, and I knew that it was meant for me—that the places I sang it would be spared when the fire visited. So, I sing this song of *Warding* wherever I go." Turning his mandolin upside-down, the singer revealed the circular rune of *Warding* etched in the instrument. "My daughters loved it when I sang them to sleep, and my wife always told me it's what I am best at. So I sing because it's the easiest way to spread the message the True

One tasked me with, as traveling singers are always welcome at taverns, inns, and courts."

Vaelin nodded. The entire kingdom had heard of the Tragedy of Albadone. So many lives lost, humanfolk displaced, and, as Vaelin was uniquely aware, it had been a huge toll upon the Cycle of Nature. The singer had obviously gone mad from what he had witnessed then. Who could blame him?

"Your wife was right, you do have a beautiful voice," Vaelin said.

"Thank you, but to me what matters most is that everyone else in the world hears the song of the True One, lest they succumb to his ire."

"A commendable aspiration," she said, taking a sip of her wine. "What is your name, singer?"

"Pardon my rudeness. It's Mynde."

"Nice to meet you Mynde, I am Vaelin."

"Vaelin..." he said pensively. "An old sounding name. And what do you do, Vaelin?"

"I'm a traveler, much like yourself. I've been on the road all my life, even before there were roads."

"Where does your road lead?" the man asked.

Vaelin smirked. *Maybe he's not as mad as he looks.* "I don't know that my road leads anywhere in particular. At least not at the moment. Besides, I've heard it said the journey is what's important, not the destination."

"Aye, that's true. But without a destination in mind, a journey it is not. It's just aimless wandering, like being in an impenetrable forest, thick with foliage, surrounded by more of the same on all sides. You can enjoy your time there, but eventually you'll want to see the sky."

No, not mad at all. "There's an old saying that your people have in Albadone. I'm not sure if it's used anymore. It went something like, a nobleman can teach you the meaning of words, but a poor man can teach you the meaning of life."

Mynde smiled wide. "I have heard that one, though in a slightly different way. You've been to Albadone?"

"I have, many times over the course of the centuries."

"Centuries..." Mynde shook his head, pondering the word. "So, the barkeep said it right, you're an elvenfolk of some ageless sort."

"A djinn, actually, but that's a common mistake."

"A djinn! Incredible!" The man took another sip of his wine, mulling something over in his head. "If I may ask, in your time upon the True One's earth, what is the most important lesson you've learned?"

"So, you require payment for the pearl of wisdom you've bestowed upon me, eh? A wisdom for a wisdom?"

Mynde laughed. "Don't the wise know that one who gives generously should also collect judiciously? If that's how you'd like to look at it, so be it."

After a deep drink, Vaelin said, "Always listen to every side of a story before making a judgment. Sometimes your final judgment might mirror your first reaction, and that's fine too. Instincts are important, but what's even more valuable is inquisitiveness. Take these Blue Scarabs." Vaelin waved at the rest of the inn where the blue armored soldiers were lazing. "I know that one stopped you from singing but I get the impression his companions don't feel the same way. Rather than religion, they seemed to be motivated by other... convictions."

"True, but conviction alone does not make folk right," Mynde added.

"Couldn't the same be said for you? You seem to have conviction to spare."

Mynde pondered the question for a moment. "I suppose it could."

"So what is their conviction?" Vaelin asked, nodding her head towards the Blue Scarabs.

"They claim to be helping bring security to the *Red Road*." Quietly, he added, "But from what I've seen of them, they're just bullies with big swords." The barkeep cleared his throat admonishingly. Mynde lowered his gaze.

"Some people use conviction to do what's right, while others use it to do what they want. Intention is often lost to time, just like... well..." Vaelin chuckled to herself.

"Just like what?" Mynde pried.

Vaelin moved her face closer to the singer. Mynde moved in closer as well. "The gods that Blue Scarab is so concerned about—I've met them. Well, I've met two of them: Yssic and Aelfe."

Mynde's eyes widened. "The Nameless were real gods?"

Vaelin snorted into her wine. "They were real elvenfolk, most definitely. I was actually Contracted by Yssic to entertain Aelfe on his name day celebration—an elven tradition, similar to the birthdays you humanfolk celebrate. They were kings and also complete opposites. Yssic was a notorious socialite and Aelfe was, well... let's say he was very stoic. Yssic fancied himself profoundly talented at gift giving, yet had never seen Aelfe crack even a smile at any of his previous name day offerings. That's where I came in."

The barkeep was doing a poor job of concealing his interest in her story, his hands busily wiping the same spotless glass again and again.

"I was the gift, you see," Vaelin continued. "Back then, I wasn't as careful about the Contracts I accepted. Yssic told me I'd be fulfilling whatever wish Aelfe might request for that evening. He seemed to suspect that Aelfe's interests would be of a darkly peculiar sort, so he warned me to brace myself. He was partly right.

"After the party, I met Aelfe in his quarters and explained who had sent me and why. He asked me to leave, but I explained that I would need to fulfill at least one wish for him before I could go, even if it was relatively insignificant. He was quiet for long enough that I was about to suggest I mend some pants of his, when he suddenly walked over to a large wardrobe and opened its doors. The shelves were absolutely overflowing with pigeon whistles."

"Pigeon what?" said the barkeep, no longer maintaining his farce of being busy.

"Whistles," replied Vaelin. "You're lucky you didn't have to listen to him explain the damned things. It was a hobby-craft where reeds, wood, and other such materials were fashioned into an instrument that was then saddled to the tail of a pigeon. It was then played by the wind rushing past when the bird was in flight. The skill of the craftsman was determined by how clear the tones were and how many reeds were incorporated."

"And he collected these... bird instruments?" asked Mynde.

"He made them himself. And he told me about each one, in detail. I've lived entire centuries that were not as long as that evening. Eventually, I had to remind him that I was there to grant a wish of his. Do you know what he wished for?"

Both men shook their heads in rapt unison.

"The nut from a Pilata tree. He explained the tree was very rare and that the nuts were highly prized in whistle-making for the strength and thinness of their shell walls. Yssic nearly shook himself to death laughing when I told him what Aefle's one wish had been."

Mynde let out a laugh that was hardier than his scrawny form seemed capable of and Vaelin joined in.

"Enough!" a voice cried out. The Blue Scarab that had yelled Mynde off the stage stood loudly. Most soldiers groaned and returned to their conversations, while a few others tensed tentatively, ready to intervene if necessary. The angry soldier approached the bar.

"You really will let anyone in here, even a shadow beast, huh?" he barked at the barkeep.

Vaelin narrowed her eyes. Conviction was one thing, but discrimination she had no time for. "I can go where I please. I am a free folk."

"You won't be for long if you don't hold your tongue, shadow beast."

The soldier's companion grabbed his arm once more. "Let them be, Deven. We're not here to start any trouble with travelers."

"She started the trouble! They both did, him with his blasphemous songs and her with her... Just look at what she is."

Vaelin stood. She barely reached the bald soldier's chest, but she held her ground, staring deeply into his dark eyes. "Barkeep!" she called out. "I think I'll take that bath now."

"If you give her a room," the soldier told the barkeep, "you are going to have trouble."

"Deven, that's enough," the other soldier scolded. Deven shrugged out of his companion's grasp and trudged closer to Vaelin—too close.

"See, if you would have just let me have my bath..." Vaelin shook her head. "But you just had to drag others into your business."

"Are you threatening me, shadow beast?" the man spat. His hand moved for his sword.

Vaelin's hand met his a half-second after, the man flinching at the almost intimate touch and lack of distance between them now. He jerked his arm in an attempt to unsheathe his sword but Vaelin's slim fingers held it firmly in place without much effort. The man's face purpled with rage and exertion, then grew pink from the embarrassment of having been so casually rendered harmless.

"How are you—"

Vaelin didn't give the man a second longer to finish his words. "You might fashion yourself some type of champion in that fancy armor of yours, but all I see in front of me is just another man forcing others to abide by his ways." She let her words hang in the air for a few moments then withdrew her hand. "Remove your hand from the sword."

Deven licked his lips. The soldier slowly lifted his hands to show he intended no harm. Only then did Vaelin back away.

"That's better." Turning to the barkeep she added, "Now, about that bath."

It took Deven a few moments to regain his composure, even as his companions pulled him away from the scene. None made any effort to confront Vaelin, either because they feared her or, more likely, because they had orders to not start squabbles in town. The barkeep showed Vaelin upstairs to her room. It was surprisingly spacious, with a window that overlooked the street and a comfortable-looking bed. She had spent the last few years sleeping mostly in grassy meadows, under trees, in barns, or, at best, on a lumpy cot in some drafty spare room. The prospect of a proper bed was enticing.

Two young girls dragged in a copper tub with some effort. Following them was a plump woman with a bucket in hand containing a brush and a bar of soap. Their eyes widened at the sight of Vaelin.

"See, I told you I met an elvenfolk," the barkeep smirked. He introduced the three as his wife Helonia and daughters Reda and Sonfeia. Vaelin introduced herself with a smile, her fangs sending the girls to hide behind their mother. She handed the barkeep his payment and a little something extra for the two girls, and the family left the room. Moments later, Helonia and her daughters returned with buckets of steaming water which they dumped into the tub.

Finally alone, Vaelin disrobed and immersed herself in the warm bath. She lathered herself with the lightly scented herbal soap and then scrubbed her back, legs, and feet. Once properly clean, Vaelin leaned back and allowed herself a moment to unwind. But her mind rejected that simple pleasure, instead ruminating on the near tragedy of her last Contract. Sure, she had been able to bypass spilling blood that time, but how long would it take until there was another victim of her Compulsion? Another notch in the belt that strangled her every waking moment. She had lived with the Compulsion for so long that she could barely remember her life without it. It was a parasite—the unwanted companion she carried with her wherever she went. One that only reared its head when she least expected it, impossible to predict. But there was hope.

I have found what you've been seeking for so long.

Could Myssa have meant what Vaelin hoped? Much of Vaelin's life had been dedicated to this purpose. Could her search have reached an end? If it had, she would finally be able to end her Compulsion—her enslavement to the Hunger. There would be no more near misses, no more Contracts to go wrong. But most importantly, she could fix the harm that had been done to the Cycle of Nature and ensure that she would never inflict damage upon it herself by failing a Contract or succumbing to the Hunger.

She submerged until only the top of her head stuck out of the water. The heat soothed her skin and made her feel like she was one with the tub—a feeling similar to that of being in her old prison. Even after all these centuries, it was still hard at times to think of herself as free. She wasn't truly free—not yet.

The bed was not nearly as comfortable as it had appeared, but she made do—it wasn't like Vaelin was going to get much sleep anyways. She didn't need sleep, but she enjoyed the peace of nighttime and the stillness of resting in its calm.

As the sun began to rise, and the street below filled with the morning sound of townsfolk heading to their business, Vaelin stood from the bed and put on her clothes. Downstairs, the barkeep was already at his post, setting small plates of green olives across the bar top. He greeted Vaelin with a warm smile.

"Where to now?" he asked.

"To Sol Forne," she replied. "I have business there."

"Beautiful time of year to visit. Haven't been in quite some time. The season of festivals begins very soon, so I might take the girls there in a month or so. But only if I can find someone to watch this inn. Sometimes I feel as if I am bound to this old place." There was no sadness in the statement—it was merely a matter of fact.

After a few more goodbyes—southern goodbyes seemed to last forever—Vaelin left the inn and made for the city gate. Ahead of her, she saw two Blue Scarabs emerge from a dim alleyway. The shorter one looked around furtively before clapping the taller man, who Vaelin now recognized as Deven, on the back with a nervous laugh. Upon meeting Vaelin's gaze, he turned abruptly, the hand on Deven's shoulder now dragging him in the opposite direction. For a brief moment, Vaelin could see a look of satisfaction on Deven's face before they were lost in the crowd.

Then she heard it, a soft lilting sound trickling out of the alley the two soldiers had left—the sound of a single mandolin string being plucked. She followed it into the shadows. Mynde lay on the ground, breathing heavily. As Vaelin neared the man, she noticed blood pooling underneath him.

"Mynde!" Vaelin called out, kneeling in front of the man.

"Oh, Vaelin," he said, grunting. "I hoped it would be you who found me."

"You're hurt," she said. Mynde's hand held onto what looked like a stab wound in the left side of his ribcage. Blood bubbled around his hand.

"Aye, I am."

"I must get you to a healer."

Vaelin reached under the man to pick him up, but he placed an arm on her shoulder to stop her. "It would be of no use. I hear my family calling my name. It's my time."

Vaelin nodded. The bleeding showed no sign of stopping, and based on the coloring of Mynde's face, he had lost too much blood already.

"Did Deven do this to you?" she asked.

The man grinned miserably. "And what will you do with that information? Avenge me? No. No more blood should be spilled." Mynde coughed a spray of crimson. Vaelin lifted the man's head to aid his breathing. "You said you are a djinn," he said weakly.

"I am."

"Could I make one wish before I am returned to the True One?"

Vaelin considered it, unsure. She felt no Hunger, but she could make an exception for the singer.

"I was headed to Sol Forne, to sing so that the True One may spare the people there." Mynde gestured at his instrument. "Would you take my mandolin and play my song in Sol Forne?"

Vaelin smiled. "I am no singer."

"That is not the most important part of a great performance, is it?"

Vaelin nodded. This she could do without striking a Contract. This was a favor for a friend. "Your wish is my command."

Mynde smiled. His breath stilled.

Vaelin returned to the inn and informed the barkeep of Mynde's death. Together, they returned to the body and wrapped it in a blanket. There was a Death Hall in town, but Mynde deserved an Albadonian burial. The barkeep agreed to help Vaelin transport the body out of town.

"Token, please," said the Blue Scarab at the gate, holding his hand out. Vaelin returned her iron coin to the man, who inspected it and marked something down on his parchment. The innkeeper presented a silver coin to the man, who nodded. Before they crossed the gate, the Blue Scarab called out, "Hold on! His token too," pointing at Mynde's body. The absurdity of the request made Vaelin laugh.

They took the body into a sparse woodland about a half mile away and leaned it against a sturdy tree.

"Just like that?" the barkeep remarked.

Vaelin nodded. "Albadonian woodsfolk still hold to the old ways. They believe in returning their bodies to the Cycle of Nature. His flesh will feed wolves, wildcats, and birds, and his bones will nourish the earth."

"If I ask you who did this, would you tell me?" The barkeep's face was stern and rigid. Vaelin shook her head. Not only had Mynde requested no more blood be spilled, but Vaelin herself had seen the consequences of responding in such ways. Sure, she could seek Deven out, but at whose feet would that chain of events eventually land? She was a traveler and would be moving on soon. She looked at the barkeep and thought of his two daughters and his wife. There was always someone left in town to pay.

Cradling the mandolin, Vaelin began to strum an old tune she had learned centuries past and sang the few elven lyrics she remembered.

"Not a lover's scorn, nor an enemy's victory,
Shall compare to the tears shed from the loss of a friend."

When she stopped, a deep silence landed between them. "I thought you said you couldn't sing," the barkeep said, almost regretfully, as if his sudden words would break the spell.

"Conviction is the key to a good performance."

VI.

THE OBLIGATION

Renna's scalp itched terribly. Though her head had been shaved clean—just one of the many requirements of the Obligation—she would never complain.

Today was a day of study. Captain Velden had brought up on multiple occasions their master's interest in *Binding*, so Renna had been researching its less conventional uses. The Toropanese had quite radical ideas on its capabilities, even theorizing that one might be able to use *Binding* in conjunction with *Transference* to join one's soul to another's body.

Tomorrow would be a trial day. Renna wasn't the most adept with the sword, or any other weapon for that matter, but, like everyone else, she would also participate in the training. Had she this training in Twineback, perhaps she would have been more able to defend her people against the invaders. At the very least, she wouldn't have been so helpless.

"You're still here?"

Renna lifted her head from her book. When had it gotten so dark? The single candle she had on her desk struggled to illuminate the large office. Leano leaned on the door, shaking his head with a handsome grin. She really wished she could have seen him with hair—he must have been quite striking.

"I lost track of time," she explained.

Leano entered the room and folded his arms. "Are you trying to go blind in here? I can barely see my own nose."

"I'm almost done," she said, returning her eyes to the page, and—Leano grabbed the book from under her and tossed it across the room. This foolish man and his blatant disregard for her things! "Now why would you do that?"

She turned to face him, and nearly collided with his chest—how did he move so quickly and so silently? He placed his hand underneath her chin and tilted her head up to face him. She felt her face grow hot—*How dare he make me flounder like some child?* He knew exactly what he was doing!

"It's dinner time," he said.

Her stomach rumbled loudly, right on cue.

They both stared into each other's eyes and then burst into laughter. Renna shoved Leano's shoulder and untensed. "You could have just said that without making such a scene."

"That's no fun," he shrugged. "I like watching you squirm."

Oh, so he enjoys tormenting me, eh? The nerve! Oh, he drove her mad! She wanted to kiss that stupid beautiful face so fiercely. But relationships with other Blue Scarabs were prohibited and, as a senior in the lodge, she needed to set a good example for the newer recruits. Leano should as well, as he was recruited in Ausserwud around the same time as she was. He should have known better, yet he was intent on making her blush. He was very aware of the effect he had on her. She would show him one of these days—once she figured out how.

It had been just over four years since Captain Velden had found her and taken her in. Until then, the only town she had ever known was her birthplace of Twineback to the far north-eastern border of Hovardom. Her family were masons by trade and she had been brought up to assume the same work herself. Around her eighth year, Mother Selna, Twineback's local enchantress, had begun to seek her out for long conversations that seemed to be about nothing in particular. At first, her parents had not approved of this special attention. But eventually, they had understood what was truly happening. Mother Selna was growing old and needed someone to replace her. Whereas everyone else who looked at Renna saw the mason's girl—her future set before her firm and unyielding like the stone material of her family's trade—the old woman saw hope for the future.

She apprenticed under the enchantress for twelve years, until the woman passed. Renna was raised to full enchantress as a result. She became Mother Renna, and, for the first time in her life, she felt at home in her identity.

For the next five years, however, her life had not known peace. Twineback had been subjected to incessant plunder by the Sazisans from the north. When the royals had finally dispatched their army to the region, the citizens of Twineback had thought they were being rescued. Instead, the king had decided that Twineback would be sacrificed so that Hovardom could gain strategic territory on the Red Coast.

As she watched the blood-red cloaks of the royal army keep their distance, using her people as no more than meat shields for the Sazisans to sink their blades into, everything inside of her broke. She saw her friends and family extinguished by sword, spear, and arrow; her town brought to the torch. Her study and all of the tomes Mother Selna had meticulously collected went up in an instant. Only after the single-day assault was completed—and the Sazisans had tired—did the royal army intervene, winning the battle in a matter of hours. The day was won on the blood of the ones she had promised to serve.

With the few survivors, she had managed to escape the butchery heading inland towards Ausserwud. There, she had met Captain Velden and the recently formed Order of the Blue Scarab—or Blue Scarabs as they would become known. They saw her disillusionment and gave her somewhere to belong again, a role that felt meant for her. While it couldn't fix what was broken—like a runestone of *Life*, which could neither heal nor mend—her newfound purpose soothed her, gave her direction.

It took eight weeks of training until she was allowed to don the blue and shave her head in a ceremony they referred to as "accepting the Obligation." The head shaving, Captain Velden explained, was a symbol of unity for the Scarabs—a way to shed the past and begin anew as a unit. A way to bind them to each other. "*The Blue Scarabs are one body,*" Captain Velden had said on her initiation day. "*To be a body, each member must shed what they used to be. Today you are no longer Mother Renna, the enchantress from Twineback. Today you are Renna, Blue Scarab of Hovardom.*"

Renna had heard other participants in the ceremony talk about the guilt they felt at shedding who they had been up until then. But Renna felt no such loss. She had already been stripped of her old self like a snail plucked from its shell, and had been surviving raw and exposed as a nerve. No, Renna had the distinct impression of gaining something, a new home to belong to. And this time, she was determined to defend it at any cost.

She spent two years in Ausserwud helping Captain Velden set up a Blue Scarabs lodge, gaining the trust of the people by providing her enchanting services at no cost. Since joining the Blue Scarabs, she had wanted for nothing and had no use for extra coin. If she required funds for enchanted materials, books, or poultices, she could simply ask the lodge's treasurer and she was never denied.

Anything they needed, their master would provide.

In her third year with the Scarabs, Captain Velden presented her with the opportunity to go with him to Sol Forne where he had been tasked to start a new lodge, which would extend the scope of the Scarabs' protection to southern Hovardom. She accepted readily. She had grown comfortable in Ausserwud, but a Blue Scarab should never grow complacent and soft. Changing location would present new challenges. And that excited her.

She had never stated it outright but after six months in Sol Forne, she had grown to despise the place. Not the city itself or the location—the ancient Elveshari architecture, with its organic twisting pillars and spires, mixed rather beautifully with the more contemporary Oshemari plazas and fountains. The climate was the envy of the world, temperate during the day and breezy in the afternoons. It wasn't Sol Forne she despised, but the Sol Fornians.

Where northerners could be almost too neighborly and overly involved in one another's lives, these southerners kept to themselves, ignoring each other whenever possible. This extended itself to the nobility, who ruled the city in a distant and disinterested manner. While those with old and important names luxuriated in the upper districts of the city, most peasants lived in squalor in the surrounding slums. Worst yet was that the peasants accepted their place so complacently, never daring to go against what the old custom dictated.

The Sol Fornians were resistant to change. While Ausserwud gladly accepted the Blue Scarabs securing their trade routes to ensure their safety against highwaymen and brigands, Sol Fornians had fought tooth and nail against the Blue Scarabs securing their port. That had left them no choice but to take over the port by force, which hadn't been ideal. While it had been easy enough for an organized militia like the Scarabs to outfight and, on more than one occasion, outbribe the independent security forces hired by the port merchants to defend against them, it had resulted in a tremulous standoff between the merchants, the dock workers, and the Blue Scarabs. The nobles, for their part, had not yet responded to the situation, seeming to lack either the skill or motivation to do so.

Perhaps both, thought Renna critically.

Captain Velden had always been adamant: *"We cannot force unity. Our fellow countrymen must want it. But where that want is lacking, we must act in the best interest of the kingdom."*

The situation at the port had caused a standstill in the waters, between ships unable to dock, and others that could not leave. How could they make the Sol Fornians want the unity they were offering when they were so disinterested and detached from the lives of their fellow countrymen? Captain Velden called it a challenge. Renna called it a dream in a well—visible, yet unreachable.

On the other hand, the books contained in the Academy of Sol Forne and the various city libraries held more knowledge than Renna could ever absorb in a single lifetime. Some were translated from newer Toropanese tomes, while others were purchased from the famed Magstian errant librarians, and others still were as old as the kingdom itself. Captain Velden encouraged her to study and read as much as she could, going so far as to cut her daily sword trials down to every other day in order to give her more time in the library.

"Our master shares your inquisitiveness and passion for the enchanting arts," Captain Velden had explained to her. *"He will do everything he can to ensure that you are well-studied and filled with love and passion for your craft."* Although she had never met their mysterious founder, the fact that he had taken a particular interest in Renna's studies—albeit from afar—filled her with pride. *"Master has a great vision for how you can heal this kingdom. Perhaps one day, you will be lucky enough to meet him in person."*

Renna picked up her book from the floor and set it back on the desk. "Next time please don't shove my tomes about," she scolded Leano. "Some of these are priceless!"

"Of course, my liege," Leano mocked with a bow.

"Am I interrupting?" Captain Velden's voice made the two immediately face the door and salute with a fist to the heart.

In unison, they both intoned, "Captain!"

Velden raised his hand. "At ease, you both." He eyed Renna's desk. "I see you're still studying. Good. The master greatly approves of your commitment to the cause."

"Yes, Captain," Renna replied.

"So much so, he would like to commend you himself." Captain Velden said it so matter-of-factly that Renna barely had any time to react. Leano faced Renna with a startled expression.

"You mean, the master is here?" she asked.

Velden nodded. "He is passing through briefly. But he is very eager to meet you."

Renna's mind felt empty. "With all due respect, why me?"

"Besides the fact that you are more committed to our cause than most other Scarabs, it's your research that has become a point of interest to him."

Renna could only muster a nod. Like trying to catch flies, her words flitted away before she could find the right ones.

"Well?" Captain Velden asked, a bit impatiently. "Are you coming or not?"

Now? Why did Leano have to surprise her right before this meeting? She felt her cheeks growing hotter, but she did her best to steel herself and summon calm.

"Yes, Captain," she said emphatically.

Captain Velden turned and walked out of the room.

"Go with him," Leano whispered, nodding towards the door.

Renna hadn't realized she was standing still, unable to command her legs to move. Leano placed his hand on the small of her back and pushed her gently but firmly towards the door. The touch barely registered to Renna as she followed Captain Velden through several dimly lit hallways, passed the mess hall where other Blue Scarabs were gathering for dinner, and towards the pantry.

Where is he taking me? She had never actually been inside the large pantry—sacks of grain lined the wall, and aged cheeses, dried meats, fresh fruits and vegetables filled the shelves. A strange smell—like sickly sweet mold in a rain-damaged home—cut through that of the food.

Captain Velden stopped in front of a small door—Renna hadn't the faintest idea what was behind it. "I have something to mention before you meet him," Velden said, "I told you that the master was here, but that's not quite the truth. You will understand when you see for yourself." Captain Velden sighed deeply—his sudden nervousness made Renna uncomfortable—and held the door open for her.

Renna entered the dark room. It wasn't just dark—it was like stepping into a void. The sudden cool breeze that caressed her cheek startled her. The smell of decay assaulted her, making her eyes water. She continued to inch her way forward, when suddenly Captain Velden's hands caught her shoulders, halting her.

A few silent moments went by. Something shifted in front of her. The breeze moved in and out as if breathing. Her head felt like it was floating in sap. The sudden dizziness caused colorful shapes to form in her vision. To her surprise, the fuzzy shapes consolidated into what appeared to be a face. No matter where she turned in the darkness, all she saw was him. The master.

His voice was a lick of red-hot fire.

"You must be Renna."

VII.

A Room For The Night

"Mind the door!" Gelsema yelled, hitting Dorovan on the back of his head with a heavily calloused hand. The woman's slaps held nothing back. Instead of working, Dorovan had been staring at the cobbled street beneath his feet for the better part of an hour. He straightened his back with a grimace. Gelsema shook her head, her thin, wispy, white hairs fluttering about like cobwebs. Gods, but the woman was horrid to look at. Her face was wrinkled in frustration like dry, cracked mud. Two black hairs sprouted from a mole at the center of her cheek. Who would have ever imagined that such an unpleasant creature would be the owner of *The Bee and the Toad,* one of the nicest taverns in the Verario District?

Gelsema gave Dorovan a last judgmental once-over, then reentered the tavern. Dorovan should have felt grateful to the woman for giving him employment and a place to stay, but all he could feel was resentment. He resented the work he had to do—watching the door like a fish-brained simpleton—and he resented the woman for her unseemly appearance. But most of all, he resented the lingering pain he felt in his hand—a pulsing reminder of his miserable failure two weeks ago.

The evening after the disastrous showcase, Dorovan had
stumbled aimlessly out of the Effore, eventually collapsing
onto the street—blood oozing profusely from his missing fingers. He had awakened the next morning in a small bed,
Gelsema shoving a spoonful of much-too-salty vegetable
broth into his dry mouth. His right hand had been cocooned in gauze to stop the bleeding. As he had stared at
the wrappings, the lack of his two fingers had finally dawned
on him. While his pinky finger was entirely missing, his ring
finger now ended in a stump one-third of the way. The
shame of being a nameless peasant—of being just Dorovan—
was now something he wore like a brand.

But why should he feel shame? Those nobles had done
him a favor! They had revealed themselves as the conniving
cowards they truly were. They were nothing like his parents.
His father's nobility had been forged in the heroism of battle even before a rank was ever conferred to him. And Dorovan now understood that the value of that heroism would
always be greater than that of a mere title alone. These other
nobles had been born into their names. They had no con-
cept of what it meant to earn something.

He peeked inside the tavern—at Gelsema yelling at a
pretty barmaid—and straightened once again. His job as a
doorman was easy, if boring. In Gelsema's own words:
*"Stand by the door and keep an eye on those who come in;
no ruffians, peddlers, or beggars; no one already drunk is
to be let inside, and anyone too drunk is to be escorted out.
And, most importantly, no Blue Scarabs!"*

Gelsema had begrudged him an ugly old light armor of
boiled leather and a sheathed short sword for his belt. Any
time he attempted to swing the sword—always in the

alleyway, out of sight—his missing fingers made it slide right out of his grasp. Nobody needed to know that. The dull old sword was merely a deterrent and, as such, it was surprisingly effective as long as Dorovan concealed his injury. Only twice before had drunkards challenged him—both times for not being allowed in while already visibly inebriated. Thank the gods, the city guards had intervened both times, arresting the instigators and dragging them off to sober up overnight in a cell.

After the second incident, Dorovan had begun practicing holding and swinging the sword with his left hand. He didn't expect to actually have to use the weapon, but he didn't want to be caught off guard in case. Holding it that way felt foreign, like drinking out of a mug and expecting water but instead getting soured wine. It would take a lot of time to adapt, but, in his current predicament, time was all Dorovan had.

As the sun descended behind the city walls, the crowd heading into the tavern swelled from a trickle to a steady stream. The Verario District contained most of the city's distilleries, wineries, and butcheries, so most of the tavern's patrons were laborers who had closed up shop for the day. Even a few off-duty city guards made their way inside, their shifts having just ended. By the time the sun had vanished completely the place was quite packed, firelight from inside the tavern glowing yellow and orange onto the cobbled street outside. Laughter, cheers, and singing overflowed.

Dorovan wished he could be anywhere else. What was there to be so happy about anyway? Happy peasants embarrassed him. Dorovan's hand ached. At least they weren't happy nobles—those angered him.

"You there," a person asked. The stranger was much shorter than him and wore the most unconventional and unfashionable clothes Dorovan had ever seen—trousers that widened at the calf and a red-tinted leather jacket over a well-worn white shirt with striking blue buttons. A dusty leather satchel hung limply at her side, and strapped to her back was a dingy old mandolin. Her hair was dark and wild, worn loose without a headscarf. Every element of the mismatched outfit spoke of someone who had no care for appearance or custom. But it wasn't just the clothes that stood out—everything about this person was strange. The gray skin may have been a trick of the light, but those ears...

"I'm looking to play a song. Does this tavern allow singers?"

Dorovan dared himself to look into the stranger's eyes—unnaturally black, like the Talmur Sea at night. There were parts of her face that could have been described as beautiful—like those angular cheekbones, and that delicate nose—but the rest felt unnerving.

"Are you all right?" she asked.

"We allow musicians," Dorovan stated, answering her first question.

"Thank you," she replied, making her way past him and into the tavern.

Dorovan watched as the stranger pushed her way through the crowd all the way to the raised stage at the far end. Suddenly, Dorovan felt a hand touch his shoulder. He turned with a start to find Renna, Leano, and two other Blue Scarabs, all still dressed in their spotless blue armor. He was starting to believe the Blue Scarabs were born in that armor and were not able to remove it, like turtles with their shells.

"I'm sorry Dorovan, I didn't mean to frighten you," Renna apologized.

"You didn't frighten me," Dorovan answered, summoning as many shreds of dignity as he could, then instantly deflating once he remembered where he was and what he was doing.

"Of course, of course," she nodded. Behind her, Leano suppressed a chuckle—*What does he find so funny?*

"Are you following me? Did Velden send you? I'd assume that by now I made it clear that I'm not interested in what you're selling."

Renna smiled gently. "Nothing of the sort. We were on an assignment when we saw you standing here and thought we'd greet you. That's all." At this, she pointed behind them. Leano and the other Scarabs held onto ropes tied to a large-wheeled wooden trunk.

"What are you doing in the Verario?" Leano asked.

"I'm working." Dorovan glanced away. "You shouldn't be here."

Renna raised an eyebrow—or she would have if she had an eyebrow to raise. "Why do you say that?"

"My mistress doesn't like your kind."

"Our kind?" Leano asked, suddenly annoyed.

"You know... Blue Scarabs," Dorovan explained, lowering his voice as onlooking peasants eyed the two bald soldiers suspiciously. It wasn't only Gelsema that didn't trust the Blue Scarabs. Since their recent takeover of the port, the general attitude towards them ranged from mistrust to outright hatred. Sol Forne was an independent city with its own customs and culture that differed greatly from those of the rest of Hovardom. To accept invaders under the guise of assimilating with the nation could mean the loss of every-thing that made the city so unique—at least that was the common argument posed by many a tavern patron. But like in any city, nothing could be agreed upon universally, so a vocal minority had recently taken it upon itself to champion the Blue Scarab's cause.

Renna and Leano glanced at each other and sighed in resignation. "The people of this city don't yet understand that we are on their side," Renna said. "In time, they will come to learn that there is tremendous power to be found in unity."

"I don't know about all that," Dorovan said, placing his maimed hand atop the pommel of his sword. "But you better move along."

"Or what, you're going to stop us?" Leano asked sharply.

Renna placed her hand on the man's chest. "Steel yourself, Lieutenant. I'm sure that's not what Dorovan intended." Leano relaxed, his face a mask of calm. Renna continued, "We don't mean any disrespect, Dorovan. I know you have a job to do, as we have ours." She nodded towards the wheeled trunk. "I simply approached you to greet you and remind you that if you ever feel the call to join a greater cause, you will always have a home at our lodge."

"As I already told you and Velden, I am not—"

"Shoo, baldies! Before I call the guards," Gelsema yelled, waving a handkerchief as if swatting a pair of flies. "Guards! Guards!" she cried out, not giving the group a chance to react.

"We heard you, crone," Leano scoffed, rejoining the other two soldiers. Renna nodded farewell to Dorovan and joined her companions in dragging the trunk southward, towards the Portos District.

"What did I tell you?" Gelsema admonished, swinging at Dorovan's head, who narrowly managed to evade the blow. "No Blue Scarabs in *my* tavern!"

"I wasn't going to let them in, mistress," Dorovan explained.

"That sort will be the end of this city, I tell you!"

"So you have said, about a dozen times before."

Gelsema leered at Dorovan. "I also said to not let in any ruffians, yet I just so happen to see some gray *thing* walk into *my* tavern with a dagger at its belt." She pointed inside the tavern—the gray-skinned stranger sat at a stool atop the stage, tuning her mandolin. The crowd quieted, as if awaiting a song—or perhaps they were simply gawking at the strangeness of the creature before them.

"It looks to me like she's about to sing a song," Dorovan said. "Last I checked, bards were allowed inside."

"I want that thing out of here! Now!"

"No need to yell."

"NOW!"

Angering the woman any further would risk her withholding his allowance of food and wine that night. Dorovan entered the tavern and shoved his way through the dense crowd—the stench of sweat and drink almost suffocated him. Right before he reached the stage, the stranger opened her mouth to sing.

The song was unlike anything he had ever heard before. The words were not in Hovardian, and—while Dorovan spoke no other language—he was certain that they weren't in any of the tongues he'd ever heard either. The words flowed out of the creature's mouth like sweet tree sap. It was the melody, however, that froze Dorovan in place. It was both strangely familiar and entirely foreign, like visiting his old family home after it had been taken over by workers and horses. Bits of it stung him with their dissonance, and yet they resolved in unexpectedly satisfying ways.

The bard was no professional singer—her voice cracked at high notes and quivered slightly at the low ones—and he had heard more adept strumming from other bards, but the silence and undivided attention of the tavern agreed with him: none of them had ever seen or heard anything like this.

Gelsema latched onto his arm in a griffin's talon of a grip. "What are you waiting for?" she whispered. Even in her eagerness to rid the tavern of the stranger she had taken on a surprisingly reverent tone.

Dorovan was pulled out of his captivation and headed up the stage. He placed his hand atop the stranger's strumming hand, bringing her song to an abrupt halt. She looked up at him—the whites of her eyes were whiter than anything he had ever seen when contrasted with the inky blackness of those irises. Dorovan's spit turned to sand.

"You have to go," he said, in an almost whisper. But it was no use—the tavern was so still that even those standing at the back had heard him.

The stranger said nothing, only sighed and stood, returning the mandolin to her back.

"Let her play!" someone in the crowd yelled. Other shouts and whistles of disapproval filled the tavern. As the stranger made her way off the stage and through the crowd, patrons threw the ends of bread loaves, loose olives, and even splashes of wine from their cups at Dorovan. Gelsema appeared worried as the crowd grew rowdier. She quickly made for the stage and ordered Dorovan to "Be gone."

Dorovan quickly ran off the stage towards the back kitchen. Unrestrained patrons kicked and spat at him as he passed. Atop the stage, Gelsema lifted her arms to grab the attention of the crowd. "Peace, everyone," she yelled in her shrill voice. The crowd quieted somewhat and directed its attention towards the woman. "The doorman is a bit slow of wit. Wouldn't know what good art was if you choked him with it!" The crowd laughed at that. Of course, the woman would send him to the grape presses—make it his fault so she wouldn't have to deal with her own bad decisions.

"As a sign of our sincere apology for interrupting the singer, all ale tonight is half price." A quick cheer broke out.

"And the wine?" a man slurred.

"The wine?" Gelsema's face stiffened but she couldn't back down at this point. "Yes, of course! The wine too. But only your next glass!" Her last few words went unheard as deafening cheers broke out. Gelsema stomped her way to the kitchen. Her expression darkened further when she saw Dorovan standing there—somehow that always seemed to happen when Dorovan was around. "Didn't I tell you to leave? Last thing we need is for someone in there to see the buffoon who tried to ruin their night."

"Then why are you still here?" Dorovan intoned petulantly, immediately regretting the words as they left his mouth.

Gelsema drove her bony finger into Dorovan's chest—even through the leather armor, he could feel her nail digging into his collarbone. "This is the thanks I get for taking your sorry behind in and giving you work? You best find another place to sleep tonight. And don't return until you've learned to show me the respect I deserve."

"This is shit!" Dorovan yelled as he made for the back door of the tavern. The alleyway facing him was narrow and unlit. Dorovan slammed the door and stormed off into the night.

He would show Gelsema when he regained his name! He would have her tavern torn down by his loyal men. He would...

What am I thinking? That had been the favorite fantasy of the previous Dorovan, the naive fool with his pitiful rapier and full set of fingers. He had since learned that he could never become that sort of noble—that he would never even want such a thing. This was his life now—the life of a nameless peasant. Scraping for food and coin, doing favors for drinks, and being beholden to the whims of ugly old crones. This was what he had to look forward to. A thought occurred to him. Hadn't his father been in the same position as he was now when he was a young man?

His father had managed to demonstrate his worthiness through action long before he had proof of it in the form of title papers. What had Lady Lenora called them again? *"A House of pretenders?"* The battles his father had fought in had certainly not been pretend. The lives he had saved had been real. On the other hand, was there anything about Lady Lenora that hadn't been fake, from her feigned innocence to her sweet smiles?

Dorovan could no longer understand how he had confused such swindlers like Lady Lenora for true nobles like his parents. He would show them who the true pretenders were. He would become a man like his father had been, one so dripping in noble virtue, strength, and bravery that the titles these imposters held so dear would seem like chamber pot rags in comparison.

He would become a hero!

Dorovan reached into his pocket and thumbed the gold mark protectively. Beside it, he could feel three copper pieces—not enough to buy himself a proper room for the night. He would rather keep his coin and sleep in an alleyway than waste it on the dingy room that he could afford. He would, however, buy something to drink. If he was drunk enough, even an alleyway would feel like a warm feathered bed. Dorovan made his way through the sparsely populated streets—most people were already at home or in taverns at this hour—his mind set on a glass of wine as he headed towards the watering hole he favored.

The Loathsome Scholar was just across the street from the Academy, so its learned patrons were less rowdy and less likely to start fights—physical ones, that was. Hardly any of them were nobles—those preferred to congregate in the more luxurious drinking halls of the Effore and Tarentia. These were usually the sons and daughters of merchants, landlords, chemists, and such. All of them were insufferably pretentious, but they never paid Dorovan any mind, always too absorbed in their debates and nonsensical diatribes. Dorovan enjoyed listening in on those conversations ranging from radical speeches over the abolishment of the monarchy or debates on whether the Blue Scarabs were Hovardom's saviors or downfall—the last of which were particularly common as of late.

His missing fingers itched—they did so any time his thoughts traveled back to the showcase. Any moment spent alone not busying himself with something meant his mind could wander back to that day in the Salviati family courtyard—the day of his humiliation. Filling his head with the conversations of others, as obnoxious as they may be, helped.

He pushed open the door of the inn and stepped inside. A crowd of patrons sat in a circle facing the center of the hall where scholars usually debated and poets and musicians performed. The audience's eyes were fixed upon tonight's entertainment: the gray-skinned stranger, who stood playing her mandolin and singing.

Dorovan caught the final verse of the song, almost at the exact moment he had interrupted it earlier. The ending reprised the melody from the beginning of the song, but with added weight and intensity. Then, unexpectedly, the song ended unresolved. It was unlike any other song he had ever heard before. It wasn't an ending; it was the unfulfilled promise of more to come.

The audience kept its eyes on the stranger, unsure of how to react. Dorovan found himself in agreement—the song was just... too different; too strange.

The stranger didn't seem to expect any sort of reaction either. She simply strapped the mandolin to her back and made her way to the bar—the eyes of everyone in the hall followed her closely. A few whispered voices spoke to each other, and eventually, the sound of regular tavern conversation rose across the space—although Dorovan could guess that most, if not all, conversations were revolving around the stranger and her baffling song.

Dorovan took a seat at the far end of the bar opposite where the stranger sat. He heard her order a glass of wine—the best they had in stock—and saw her place a silver piece on the bar, to the innkeeper's delight. Was singing in taverns really so lucrative? Dorovan didn't remember seeing anyone pay for the performance. She must be making her living some other way. Then he remembered the dagger at her hip—perhaps she was a hunter or mercenary? Or worse: a brigand! And yet, her short stature and delicate features did not seem to fit that image. Along with the wine, she ordered a bowl of brown olives. Immediately she placed one in her mouth and savored it with a pleased smile.

The innkeeper took Dorovan's order—a local wine named *Sharazi* after the lower House that owned the vineyard, which was surprisingly palatable for how cheap it was. Dorovan placed the three coppers on the bar, advancing himself at least two more glasses.

"That was quite an interesting performance," a woman's voice next to him said. Dorovan turned to see that an unassuming middle-aged woman in a scholarly—and unfashionable—gray gown had taken a seat next to the stranger. "That was High Elven, correct?"

"I believe that's what you scholars would call it," the stranger replied.

"What would *you* call it?" the woman asked.

"I would call it Elren, although it was known as Arish for a time," the stranger said. "It was one of the three major languages spoken in Elveshar."

"*Three* languages in one kingdom?" the woman asked in puzzlement.

"Do you know how many tongues I've heard you humanfolk speak throughout the centuries?" The stranger took a sip of her wine and nodded approvingly.

"I see," the woman said. She suddenly seemed perturbed.

Elveshar? What are these two talking about?

"Cressena, I presume?" the stranger asked.

"That is correct," the woman said. "And you are Vaelin."

"What gave it away?" Vaelin replied, with a grin. Only then did Dorovan notice the stranger's fangs. A chill crawled up his neck.

"Myssa has told me a great deal about you, although you are not quite what I expected."

"Oh?" Vaelin intoned. "And what did you expect?"

"Well, I did not expect to find you singing," Cressena said. "For someone so knowledgeable and... ancient," she seemed to choose that word carefully, "you seem to exude a rather youthful spirit."

"Did you expect me to be some sort of museum artifact?" Vaelin asked, finishing her glass. She pointed at the innkeeper and then at her glass to ask for more. "Either way, I will elect to take that as a compliment."

"Gods! It was not meant as an insult," Cressena said frantically, her eyes wide.

Vaelin chuckled. "Don't worry yourself, Cressena." Vaelin raised her once more full glass and swirled the wine within in a circular motion. "As someone so... *ancient,* I have learned that the young have no exclusive claim on joy and curiosity. Think of me as a good old vintage in a shiny new bottle."

Cressena nodded but did not seem to grasp the stranger's exact meaning. "I have been waiting for you," she said. "For six months."

"It's a long way on foot from Magsta to Sol Forne," Vaelin replied.

"You mean to tell me you traveled that distance on foot?"

"I am not fond of horses or mules. I don't much care to steer—or be steered, for that matter. And ships tend to make me sick."

"Ah, yes," Cressena said as if remembering something. "Myssa said as much."

"How was she, in the end?" Vaelin asked.

Cressena folded her fingers together, her leg bouncing uncomfortably. "She lived a very long life—longer than most—and very full. One day she developed a cough and, thereafter, her health degraded rapidly. It was like watching a beautiful and meaningful sculpture succumb to the inevitability of the elements and time. Chemists did what they could, but nature soon took its course. Even through the pain, Mistress Lonne was still sharp as ever. She never took a break, nor did she stop working."

The stranger smiled fondly.

"She spoke of you very often," Cressena added.

"Did she now?"

"Sometimes as if you were a tome she had once studied, other times as an old friend. And other times... well..." The rocking of Cressena's leg grew in intensity—Dorovan could feel the vibration through the floor, climbing up his stool.

"As a lover?" Vaelin asked.

"I'm sorry, I should not have brought that up." Cressena did not strike Dorovan as the type to have much experience or interest in romantic matters.

Vaelin finished her second glass with a gulp. The innkeeper was quick to refill it this time. "We had a very intimate bond, Myssa and I. But unlike most humanfolk, I don't feel the need to fulfill drives of the sexual sort."

Dorovan choked on his wine and quietly coughed to himself. This Vaelin was scandalously open with her thoughts. Dorovan had heard conversations on the subject of sex before in this very hall, but those had been flavored with innuendo, their meanings masked with playfulness. To hear this one speak openly of *"sexual drives"* was... improper! Cressena must have thought so too, as she shifted in her chair while uncomfortably glancing about.

"However," Vaelin continued, "there are some bonds that transcend those of a sexual nature. You may call them romances—although those usually tend to end up in sex as well, from what I've observed."

Gods! Does she have no shame? Dorovan's cheeks reddened.

"The bond Myssa and I shared was similar to that of lovers. We were companions—partners who shared our lives and what we had. We were like family. At times it felt like we were made for one another, as if we shared the same essence of *life energy.*"

After a pause, Cressena asked, "If you two were so... close, how did your partnership come to an end?"

Vaelin turned towards the woman as if returning from a wonderful dream, her face saddening with the reminder of the reality she inhabited. "It's a long story I don't wish to dive into at this moment," she said. "But I will say this: there's a bond that holds me much more firmly than any humanfolk can ever attempt, Myssa included."

Cressena nodded as if she understood what Vaelin meant. "The Academy warehouses are closed tonight. My office is in the western wing. Stop by anytime tomorrow and I will take you there."

"Do you know what Myssa is keeping there for me?" Vaelin asked.

"The lucerne."

Vaelin nodded to herself as if something had been confirmed to her.

"I am not entirely sure what it is, although I have an inkling. Mistress Lonne stressed its importance and secrecy. Even after you left her, she continued to search for it. She never truly let you go." Cressena stood. "I should head back home before it gets too dangerous to be out."

"Would you like an escort?" Vaelin suggested.

"No need. I'm just around the corner. Good evening, Vaelin. It was a pleasure to finally meet you."

"Cressena," Vaelin called out. The woman stopped abruptly. "Thank you. For being there for her."

Cressena nodded and headed for the door.

This was about as strange a conversation as Dorovan had ever heard. This Vaelin creature spoke like a professor, a chemist, or a historian. Perhaps she was a scholar—that would explain her knowledge of ancient languages. But then again, those ears, skin, and black eyes... The other woman had mentioned something about elvenfolk. Could this stranger actually be a living elvenfolk herself?

Ridiculous! The elvenfolk were creatures of legend. If they truly had existed at some point in time, that was a time long gone. She was most likely a scholar with an unfortunate facial deformity. Perhaps she came from Sazisan in the north. Only someone with hard, gray skin could live in a place that cold. And yet, that dagger...

"So, how much of that did you catch?"

Dorovan's back tensed as he turned his head towards the gray-skinned woman. Vaelin smirked at him as she sipped her wine.

"You didn't think I would notice?" she asked.

"I... I... I'm sorry," was all he could muster.

"And who might you be?"

"I am Dorovan ca'Me—" *No! You are not a lord! You are just Dorovan.* "I am just Dorovan."

"*Just* Dorovan?" She eyed him up and down. "Well, just Dorovan, why did you follow me here?"

"I didn't follow anyone here. Why would you ask that?"

Vaelin chuckled. "Are you going to deny kicking me out of that other tavern as well?"

"I... did do that," Dorovan admitted. "But not by my own accord. My mistress made me stop you."

"I see. So, you came here to apologize?" she asked, picking up an olive and placing it in her mouth.

"Apologize?"

"I'm teasing you, just Dorovan," she laughed.

Dorovan's ears heated. What was this stranger's game? Did she enjoy making him feel like a fool like everyone else? Dorovan gulped down the last of his wine. Suddenly, the *Shirazi* didn't taste nearly as palatable as he remembered.

A sudden *crash* halted most of the chatter in the tavern briefly. Olives were scattered across the floor. The small bowl that had contained them moments before lay shattered. However, Vaelin appeared more inconvenienced than angry.

"Clumsy me," she shrugged. From her satchel, she produced two copper pieces and placed them on the bar. "For the trouble," she told the innkeeper.

"Just don't go doing it again," the innkeeper said, grabbing the broom that leaned against the wall behind the bar.

"If I plan on doing it again, I'll make sure you're the first to know," Vaelin replied. The innkeeper chuckled to herself. Had that been Gelsema, Vaelin would have been led out the door with a broom to the rear. The innkeeper was nice here, which was another reason Dorovan enjoyed the place.

As the innkeeper swept the mess of olives and clay shards, a tremor shook the ground beneath them. The building groaned and Dorovan clasped onto the bar top to keep himself from toppling off the rickety stool. It was the second earthquake they'd had that week. Very unusual for Sol Forne. He turned his attention back to Vaelin. She seemed lost in thought, mouthing something quietly to herself. Something about her demeanor had shifted—she seemed to have suddenly grown dazed and tired.

"Are you all right?" Dorovan asked.

She looked up at him—no, not tired: exhausted. Even so, she managed a fanged smile.

"Thanks for the concern, but I am fine," Vaelin took a sip of her wine. She reached into her satchel and pulled out a pipe.

"No smoking in here, love," the innkeeper said, sweeping up the last stray olive into her wooden dustpan.

Vaelin sighed and placed her pipe back into the satchel. "So much for that." Vaelin then looked at him—*really* looked at him. Dorovan found himself unable to look away from those terrifying black eyes. "Say, Dorovan, you wouldn't happen to be a lord or of the nobility, would you?"

Dorovan felt a sudden stab at his throat. If his ears were hot before, now his entire face felt like it had been kissed by a furnace. *A lord?* Could this creature see Dorovan's destiny with those eyes? Was his destiny to follow in his father's path, and become a noble hero? What else did she see? He stopped his hand before it could reach the gold mark in his pocket.

"I—" he started. *I am Dorovan ca'Melese,* he wanted to announce, but he couldn't—not after what had happened to him at the showcase. He filled his lungs with air and admitted, "I am no lord, nor am I a noble. I would never mingle with that cowardly sort."

Vaelin nodded, appearing strangely pleased. Suddenly, she clutched her chest as if holding back something ready to burst from within. She looked tortured, seemingly keeping a great deal of pain at bay.

"Do you have a place to stay tonight?" Vaelin asked.

Dorovan didn't realize he could flush any further. "What... I... I—"

Vaelin turned to the innkeeper. "I noticed a vacancy sign out front. You wouldn't happen to have a room with two beds?"

"I do," the innkeeper replied, though she seemed a bit apprehensive at the request. "One silver piece a night."

"A bit steep, but I wager those rooms are spacious and clean. Let's call it two silvers and I take the rest of that bottle, eh?"

The innkeeper's eyes widened. "Sure! Let me fetch the key for you."

Vaelin reached across the bar and grabbed the bottle of wine she had been drinking. She removed the cork and poured herself a tall glass. "My oh my, do I love the wine in this city!"

"What was that about? A room with two beds?" Dorovan asked.

"If you had a place to go back to, you would have said so."

"What gives you the impression I'm trying to bunk with you? I don't even know who you are."

Vaelin took another drink and then wiped her mouth with the back of her hand. "I offered you the option. Whether you take it or not is entirely up to you."

"Upstairs, second room to the left," the innkeeper said, handing Vaelin a large key. "Now, no smoking and no mischievous business, understood?"

"I promise all of my business will be as serious as can be," Vaelin replied, taking the key. She picked up her glass and the bottle of wine and headed up the stairs.

Dorovan weighed his options carefully. On one hand, he had just been offered a warm bed to sleep in. On the other hand, this Vaelin character was the strangest he had ever met. And there was also the dagger at her belt. She was shorter than him, which meant he could overpower her should she try to rob him. All he had was the short sword at his belt and the ugly armor he wore—which by this time of night was surely more sweat than leather. And the gold mark, but who would suspect someone like him to possess such a thing?

He drank the last of his wine and stood from the bar, following Vaelin upstairs. He would have to be a fool to turn down such an offer, and Dorovan was no fool.

VIII.

THE CONTRACT

The Hunger was so damn unpredictable. Sometimes it took months to manifest, but other times it took only a matter of days. In the past, Vaelin had tried to find the pattern in it. In a leather-bound journal, she had tracked the intervals between each bout of the Hunger. When that yielded no results, she had begun tracking what she was contracted to do and by whom. Her assumption was that certain types of people, or types of Contracts, affected the lulls between her feedings. However, decades later, that theory had also proved fruitless. She now figured it must be something in the blood she fed upon, but Vaelin could think of no way to prove if that was true. Instead, she had resigned herself to the Hunger's mercurial whims.

It had been about two weeks since her last feeding. That Contract had almost gone terribly wrong, but fortunately, she had managed to turn that mush into a meal. She would have to be more careful with whom she contracted—how many times would she have to give herself that advice before she actually took it?

This boy, Dorovan, seemed like an urchin of sorts. Tired and hungry, his wants would most likely be of the material sort. If she could only convince him to follow her into the room. As she reached the top of the staircase, Vaelin heard the soft thud of indecisive steps climbing the stairs behind her. *Good boy.*

As instructed by the innkeeper, she walked to the second door on the left and opened it with the key she was given. The room had two beds—both much larger than what she had anticipated. The room was clean but quite tight. Separating the uncomfortably close beds was a slim dresser—a single white flower, a lilifrith, poking out of a painted vase sat on top. The flower had been used as a symbol of hospitality and safety for centuries. Its strong, clean, smell was instantly recognizable and familiar.

A large window illuminated the space with the orange glow of candle-lit street lamps. Sol Forne never truly went to sleep. The view outside was rather unseemly—the squalid alleyway behind the building was wet with perennial mud and street sludge; a man splayed across the muck appeared dead until he raised his hand to swat a fly that had perturbed his sleep.

"Which one are you taking?" the boy asked as he shyly rubbed the back of his neck.

"I'll take the left," Vaelin replied, setting the mandolin gently on the bed and sitting next to it. She poured herself a glass of wine and drained it in one gulp. It was good—well worth the extra coin she had splurged to buy it. Dorovan entered the room and sat on the other bed. Although he faced away, he kept glancing at her from the corner of his eye expectantly, as if she would rescind her offer of a bed at any second.

"So," she said, closing the door. "Are you from here?"

"I'm just here for the bed," he responded dryly. "I'm not looking to get friendly with you."

"Understood," she replied. *Rude little fucker. But all things considered, he's right. I'm not here to make friends either.* "In that case..." She downed what remained of the glass in a single swig. "I will bid you goodnight. If you plan on leaving this evening, please don't make too much noise if you come back."

"I think I've had more than my fair share of excitement for one night." Dorovan laid back on the bed, not bothering to remove any of his clothes—strange for someone planning on staying put.

Vaelin removed her boots and jacket and jumped back onto the surprisingly soft bed. She closed her eyes and waited. The boy needed to be asleep, or at least more relaxed before she could begin. He had a sword, and she wasn't sure how adept he was with it—although those missing fingers on his right hand provided her with an instant advantage; unless, that was, he was skilled with his left hand. Better to be safe than sorry.

With her eyes closed she could hear the slimy voice of the Hunger beckoning—equal parts seductive and threatening. Her hand trembled, the tips of her fingers prickling as if stung by nettles. Soon she would have a chance to quiet it permanently. She would feed tonight, then tomorrow she would finally collect the lucerne.

Tonight would possibly be the last time she would feel the Hunger.

It took an hour or so before Dorovan's anxious tossing and turning subsided; a few more moments until his breathing grew shallow. *It's time.* Slowly, Vaelin stood from the bed and crept towards the deeply slumbering boy. Vaelin glanced at the sword still at his hip. She would need to do something about that. If the boy was skilled as a swordsman in any way, feeding off him while he wore it could prove disastrous. She unsheathed Vitra and unbuttoned the front of her shirt, revealing the vicious wound at her chest. Her fingers glided for the sword at the boy's side and, swiftly, released it from its sheath.

Dorovan's eyes shot open. Vaelin quickly tossed the sword onto the other bed to minimize any noise, then placed her hand over his mouth. The boy struggled—they always did. His panicked screams came out muffled and strained underneath her hand. Upon seeing Vitra's dark blade, he shook and shoved, to no avail—she was much stronger than him. But my, did the boy try, wiggling about like a freshly caught fish in an ursa's maw.

"Stay still," she whispered. "This will be over in a moment." Vaelin moved the dagger toward Dorovan's arm. The boy continued to lunge about frantically. The hand she held over his mouth loosened its grip, just for an instance, but that was all he needed to bite her—hard enough to draw blood.

"Little shit!" she whisper-yelled. Dorovan squirmed from under her and dropped onto the floor.

"Help!" he yelled as he crawled away.

"Stop that, please," Vaelin begged, rubbing the bite marks on her hand.

"Why would I?! You are trying to kill me!" he accused. "Help!"

"I wasn't going to kill you, you fool!"

"Then why did you take my sword? Why point that evil-looking knife at me? Why is—" His eyes dropped to her unbuttoned shirt. His face reddened. "Why is your shirt—"

"Don't go getting strange ideas," Vaelin admonished, sitting on the bed. "Will you at least allow me to explain?"

Dorovan stood up slowly—a dog expecting to have a shoe thrown at him. He glanced over at his sword.

"Pick it up," Vaelin conceded. "So you'll know I mean you no harm."

Dorovan's eyes bounced between her and the sword. In a quick, but clumsy, motion, he picked up the weapon in his right hand and pointed it toward her in what he must have thought was a threatening manner.

Right-handed. Not a swordsman at all.

"Who are you? What do you want with me?" he squeaked.

"Settle down." She sighed upon realizing he had no intention of settling. "My name is Vaelin, as you know. I am a djinn."

"A what?" he asked.

Vaelin raised a brow. "Usually, humanfolk have at least some sense of what a djinn is. Your parents never told you tales of djinn when you were a child?"

The boy shook his head, a pitiful look on his face.

"Well, to make a long story short, a djinn is a being of pure *life energy*. Long ago, I was enslaved inside an object and forced to fulfill the wishes of anyone who summoned me from it. Since then, as you can see, I've freed myself from that object. But only partly. I'm still compelled to fulfill people's wishes. I must fulfill those requests or... something really bad will happen." There was no sense in delving deeper into what the consequences of dying meant for her or the world at large. That would go over his little human-folk mind. Best to keep the story simple.

The boy remained standing, sword still pointing ahead, although his stance had relaxed somewhat. He blinked at her as if he couldn't understand the difference between her foot and her head.

"Did you understand any of what I just said?" Perhaps she needed to make her story simpler still.

"I think so," he said at last. "Then why the dagger?"

"The Contract must be sealed with a blood pact. I usually prefer to contract first and explain later to avoid folk rejecting me out of sheer skepticism. But here we are. So, Dorovan, will you allow me to form a Contract with you?"

The boy licked his dry lips. "What happens if I say no?"

Vaelin shrugged. "By refusing you leave me with two options. I either go look for someone else to contract or I pin you down and contract you by force. I have to say, the latter is not my favorite but I will do what I must to survive."

"You're in pain?" he asked. Something in his mind seemed to fall into place.

"I don't do this for fun."

Dorovan nodded to himself. "You said you would fulfill a request?"

"I did."

"*Any* request?"

Vaelin narrowed her eyes. "As long as it's not impossible, yes." Vaelin felt impending disappointment at the boy's question. In her experience, the wishes that followed such an inquiry were typically of a disqualifying sort, causing harm to others or crossing other moral boundaries.

Innocent wishes simply didn't require that kind of reassurance before being shared.

The boy lowered his sword. "What if..." He took another moment to truly think about it.

This ought to be terrible.

"What if I needed work and a place to stay?" he asked.

Oh. That could have gone much worse. "I could do that for you. But you might want to be a bit clearer than that. What sort of work are you willing to do?"

Dorovan looked around the room as if looking for something. "What about here?"

"The inn?"

"Yes." Dorovan lifted his sword again, his request now a threat. "Get me a job and a place to stay at this inn and I won't tell anyone that you tried to harm me."

Vaelin laughed. "That's not quite how it's done, but good effort. As I said, my enslavement demands we strike a blood pact. Only then will I be able to fulfill your wish." Vaelin twirled Vitra in her hand as she approached the boy.

Dorovan assumed a fighting stance. "Don't you dare come any closer!" he threatened.

"Don't be stupid, boy. Do you want to forge a Contract with me or not?"

Dorovan's eyes floated around the room in indecision.

Three raps at the door cut through the silence, making them both jump. "Hello?" a voice called out—it was the innkeeper. "I heard some noise and yelling so I need to ensure everything is in order here."

"Everything is good, thanks," Vaelin replied.

"And the boy?" the innkeeper insisted.

Vaelin turned to Dorovan, who was still pointing his sword at her face. The two locked eyes—Vaelin nodded to assuage him.

"All's good," Dorovan finally replied.

"All right then," the innkeeper said. "Please try to be mindful of the other guests." In silence, they listened for the woman's footsteps to disappear.

"I take it you agree to forge the Contract, then," Vaelin confirmed.

"I—I do," Dorovan replied.

"Good, now please put that thing away."

Dorovan cautiously sheathed his sword, and Vaelin walked up to him. His eyes were fixed on her dagger. When she lifted it towards him, he flinched unconsciously. "Calm yourself!" she hissed. "You won't feel a thing."

She grabbed onto his wrist and pulled his balled-up fist towards her. "Open your hand." He did so as if it pained him. She placed the blade on his palm, barely touching it, and let it glide gently across—like running a feather atop the surface of water. He only realized that she had cut him when blood began to spill out of the thin wound to pool in his hand. Still holding his wrist, she placed his bleeding hand to her chest and began to move it about, spreading the blood across her wound. The boy blushed—humanfolk could be so strange about certain forms of bodily contact.

The waves of dull heat that flowed through her body made her knees buckle. The room became brighter, the colors sharper. The Hunger had been satiated once more. She released the boy's hand, but he retracted it from the wound at her chest very slowly. Vaelin rebuttoned her shirt.

"What is that?" he asked, his voice sounding both perturbed and fascinated.

"This is an etching of *Sealing*. It is what enslaves me."

"But how—"

"I don't have time to explain, boy," she said, not unkindly. It was hard to be unkind with the almost euphoric feeling that came from feeding. "As agreed, please clearly state your wish."

Dorovan nodded, holding onto his bleeding hand. "Right. Is there a way I have to state it?"

Vaelin shrugged. "People usually begin with 'I wish'."

After a short pause, Dorovan stated firmly, "I wish to have work and lodging at this inn."

"Your wish is my Contract," she replied with a nod.

"Now what?" he asked.

"Now, I will fulfill your wish. Wait here."

Already the effects of the feeding had begun to overtake her. The night sounds outside—the uneven clicking of drunken boots on cobblestones, the meowing of a cat two streets down, a fight in some plaza—all felt much sharper, closer. Southward, towards the sea, Vaelin felt a pulse of *life energy* of a magnitude she hadn't experienced in years. Just as quickly as it had appeared to her senses, it was gone.

Her awareness of the boy was intensified, his quick and steady heartbeat could have been her own. On the ground floor, Vaelin could hear footsteps that she recognized as the innkeeper. Vaelin exited the room and headed downstairs, her bootless steps soft on the wooden floorboards.

The innkeeper was delivering two glasses of wine to the last two patrons of the night—a man and a woman who, from their muted garbs, appeared to be clerks or researchers of some sort.

"Still hard at work at this hour of the night?" Vaelin asked the innkeeper as she returned to the bar.

The innkeeper eyed her apprehensively. "What is that boy to you?"

Vaelin smirked. "A dear old friend."

"I could have sworn you were strangers when you met earlier in the evening. Must have imagined it." The words dripped with sarcasm. From behind the bar, she produced a bottle and poured out a dark, heavily herb-scented, liquor into two small glasses, handing one to Vaelin before downing the other herself.

"Concerned for his well-being?" Vaelin asked, taking a sip of the fragrant liquid.

"I've seen too many stupid pretty boys like him get taken advantage of to not be at least slightly suspicious of a stranger, especially one that looks like... you. This city takes folk like him and wrings them dry."

"Well," Vaelin smiled, "I have a proposition for you."

"I'm not interested in whatever your services may be. Got no one I hate and no one that hates me." The woman eyed Vitra with distaste.

Vaelin chuckled, mostly to pacify the woman. "Nothing of the sort. You seem in need of help taking care of this inn."

"I manage."

"All by yourself?"

"I manage," the innkeeper repeated.

"If you'd rather do better than 'manage', the boy upstairs would like to inquire about some work."

The innkeeper set her empty glass down and tilted her head. "Why didn't he ask me himself?"

"He's shy," Vaelin said.

"No place for shy boys in this business," the innkeeper answered, shaking her head.

"But I'm sure that under your wing the boy would ripen into quite the charismatic young man," Vaelin persisted. The innkeeper narrowed her eyes, probably wondering if that was meant as a compliment.

Vaelin began to feel nervous. *Please make this easy on me.* She leaned in. "I feel for the boy. That's why I offered him a bed. One like that, with no family, no place to go... It breaks my heart. Not only would you find time to rest by splitting the labor with the young man, but you would be offering him an opportunity to stay off the streets—make something of himself."

The woman thought quietly for a moment while intently staring into Vaelin's eyes. Vaelin caught herself holding her breath. Just a little push more. "He has experience too! I saw him working as a doorman at *The Bee and the Toad* earlier tonight. He did a wonderful job of kicking me out," Vaelin added with what she hoped was a winning smile.

"*The Bee and the Toad*, you said? That's Gelsema's place." The innkeeper seemed to be considering the offer seriously after all. "Is he Guild?"

"Doubtful."

"All right." The innkeeper poured herself another glass. "But he starts at first light. Pay is lodging, food, and whatever coin patrons leave on the tables. I expect him to be available to me at all times of the day."

Relief from the Contract being fulfilled washed over Vaelin like a cool bath in a scorching summer. "Thank you, mistress. You shall not regret this."

"I better not," she said, sipping her drink. "I'm looking forward to taking some rest in the near future."

"As you should," Vaelin replied, turning towards the stairs. Then she paused and turned back. "Can I ask what changed your mind?" Vaelin knew she was talented at convincing people, in large part because she always sought to improve her skills.

"I lied to you earlier. There is someone I hate. Not enough for..." The woman gestured at Vitra, "Not enough for that sort of thing, but enough to deprive an old woman of her doorman," the innkeeper concluded with a wry grin.

Vaelin tried not to feel too stung that the innkeeper's reason had so little to do with her skills of persuasion as she climbed the stairs. When she entered the room, Dorovan sat up from the bed. "So?"

"You have work and lodging," Vaelin replied. "You begin at first light. And thus, our Contract is fulfilled." Vaelin reached into her satchel and pulled out some cloth and herbs that were twined together with a string.

"Just like that?" he asked.

"Just like that," she repeated. Pointing at Dorovan's still bleeding hand she said, "Give it here."

He reached his palm towards her, and she rubbed some of the herbs onto it. He winced—ashenroot stung, but not terribly. "My blade won't cause infection, but it never hurts to take precautions. You never know what sort of filth your hand will touch working at an inn." After cleaning the wound, she wrapped the cloth around his palm.

"So that wish," he said, "it wasn't just nonsense. We made a blood contract, and you went and fulfilled it. That was blood magic!" It sounded like it might have been a question, but the boy's tone implied something else.

"Can we do it again?" Dorovan asked, a strange glint of determination in his eye.

"No," she replied, laying down on her bed. "I only forge Contracts when I must feed."

"But..." he trailed off. "That wish was nothing. It was merely a test to prove the truthfulness of your words."

"A test," she chuckled. "Doesn't work that way. You made a wish, I made the wish come true, and now the Contract has been fulfilled."

"That's not fair," he said in a petulant way that pricked Vaelin's nerves. "I wouldn't have asked for that if I knew I could ask for anything!"

"What's done is done, boy," she said, curtly.

"You *must* do it again," he commanded frantically, moving closer to her. "Please." He added politeness as an afterthought. "Please!" he pleaded again.

"You're beginning to irritate me," she said, not bothering to open her eyes. "Don't make me rethink allowing you to sleep in this room. Now, goodnight. I have a long day ahead of me, and so do you. First light, she said."

Dorovan remained standing next to her bed for a few moments, then retreated to his side of the room. In the silence of the night, Vaelin didn't need her increased awareness to hear the boy's soft whines.

"It's not fair. It just isn't fair."

IX.

THE ACADEMY OF SOL FORNE

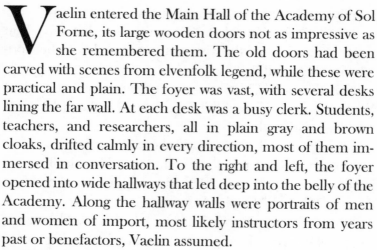

Vaelin entered the Main Hall of the Academy of Sol Forne, its large wooden doors not as impressive as she remembered them. The old doors had been carved with scenes from elvenfolk legend, while these were practical and plain. The foyer was vast, with several desks lining the far wall. At each desk was a busy clerk. Students, teachers, and researchers, all in plain gray and brown cloaks, drifted calmly in every direction, most of them immersed in conversation. To the right and left, the foyer opened into wide hallways that led deep into the belly of the Academy. Along the hallway walls were portraits of men and women of import, most likely instructors from years past or benefactors, Vaelin assumed.

Vaelin approached the desk with the least busy-looking clerk. The short balding man's nose was sunk into a large tome. With a pen, he was scratching notes in the margin of the pages as he read. His gray tunic was much too long for someone his size. A brooch in the shape of a blue scarab beetle adorned his collar. Vaelin shuddered at the sight.

"Excuse me," Vaelin said, "I am looking for someone."

The clerk looked up at her and stared with wide eyes. "Have we met?"

What a strange question. "I can't say that we have. My name is Vaelin. I am looking for Cressena. She's a researcher here."

The clerk continued to examine Vaelin with some degree of recognition. *Maybe he does know me. But how could he?*

"Do you have an appointment?" he asked as if snapped from a daze.

"I do." *At least I think so.*

"In that case," the clerk stepped from behind the desk, "allow me to take you there." He motioned for Vaelin to follow him and headed down the hallway to the right. Abruptly, the man stopped dead in his tracks.

"Are you all right?" Vaelin asked.

The clerk pointed to one of the portraits lining the wall. In faded oil, Vaelin observed a painting of... herself. Her depiction wore a flowing white tunic while riding astride a white horse. When had she posed for that? She looked at the signature—it read 'Inis Montevi.' She somewhat remembered having posed for a painter by that name some hundred years prior. But that had been in Efray. How had it made its way here?

"There was no horse when I posed for it," she said, narrowing her eyes.

"But how—" The clerk seemed utterly dumbfounded.

Vaelin read a small label beneath the painting. "*The Pale Death Rises.*" Vaelin shook her head. "Tasteless." As embarrassing as the painting was, it had been a simple Contract. Recalling Montevi's spiteful temperament, it could have been considerably worse.

It took a few moments for the clerk to regain his composure. A myriad of questions was no doubt floating through his mind, but he kept them to himself. The painting must have been quite a landmark within the school, as several other patrons of the Academy shot Vaelin alarmed glances as they passed. Usually, she was gawked at in suspicion or disgust. It was new for her to be stared at as if she was a character that had just walked out of a storybook.

She still didn't enjoy the attention.

Walking through the halls of the Academy, Vaelin was reminded of just how expansive the building was. A true city within the city. The Verario, Sol Forne's center-most district, was almost entirely occupied by its opulent Main Hall, which encircled the Academy's other buildings like an embrace. Its orange-brick exterior contrasted with the yellow brick and white marble style of its surroundings. Paired with its twisting spires, it was an ideal example of ancient Elveshari architecture.

Similarly to the kingdom's capital, Vizen, Sol Forne had been built around pre-existing Elveshari buildings. While the elvenfolk favored sprawling open-aired cities, the humanfolk seemed to prefer densely packed buildings fortified by walls. The Academy, however... no humanfolk could have ever built anything quite like it. It stood much the same as Vaelin remembered when it was first erected, other than some larger windows that had been added to the main hall. Why change perfection?

Whereas the Vizenian Royal Tower had been converted from its original purpose as a library, the Academy of Sol Forne had always been used as a house of learning, even by the Elveshari. At age ten, Elveshari children had been sent to the Utenke Mioni—which loosely translated to *the farm of knowledge*—to study for one thousand and one days. To repay the school for its teachings, every ten years each elvenfolk would bring one new book to fill its halls.

Whatever happened to all of those books? Vaelin wondered. She remembered the thousands upon thousands of books lining the shelves of the Utenke Mioni. A common nickname for the school's large library had been *the forest*; the shelves had been referred to as *the trees* and the books, *the leaves*.

After the Great Return, what had happened to all that written knowledge? Vaelin cursed the lapse in her memory. She could hardly recall those dark years. The population of the continent had vanished and, along with it, her major source of feeding. Only the Remnant had stayed behind, so Vaelin had been forced to contract her over and over for the greater part of a century. The woman had a name, but Vaelin would never speak it—not after how that relationship had ended.

Cressena's office was the first just to the right of the staircase on the second floor. The clerk opened the already unlocked door and asked her to wait since the woman Vaelin was there to see was not in at the moment.

"I think I'll be just fine on my own," Vaelin said, annoyed at the man's lingering presence. With a final glance that rode the line between inquisitive and embarrassed, and a half smile, the clerk left the office.

It seemed too large to be only Cressena's office, but, perhaps, the woman's work was important enough to warrant such a space. Several desks were scattered around the room, one with two surprisingly well-preserved elven gowns draped across it. Vaelin ran her fingers across the fabric, remembering having worn something very similar centuries before. Books were piled high in every direction, making it almost impossible to see the walls of the space. Still more books were piled open atop the desks, next to vases, parchment scrolls, and other interesting artifacts. Most of the artifacts were not from Elveshar but rather from Oderlen, the land the humanfolk had left behind when they migrated to the continent over eight hundred years prior. Besides the gowns, the only Elveshari artifacts present were two vases, both covered in dark brown-on-brown clay paintings of the Four Rulers of Elveshar—Yssic, Aelfe, Ydeon, and Omeol—which many of the humanfolk had adopted as their Nameless Gods. Vaelin knew they were only 'nameless' because the elvenfolk believed names were to be spoken, never transcribed, lest they be cursed.

Vaelin had tried and failed to explain these concepts to the humanfolk, but once the mistaken belief had become part of a religious dogma, she had surrendered those efforts. Her words would never be appreciated by people for whom the truth had become sacrilege.

"Are you enjoying what you're seeing?" Cressena trudged into the office carrying a heavy-looking wooden box. The jangling of the keys hanging from the hoop at her belt followed her every step. She placed the box atop a precarious stack of books and stopped to catch her breath.

In the candlelight of the prior evening, Vaelin had not been able to take a good look at the woman. Cressena was several years shy of middle-aged—by Vaelin's, admittedly poor, estimation. At the center of her oval face was a very typical Sol Fornian aquiline nose. She wore a headscarf with yellow and blue florals embroidered across it, a stark contrast to her plain brown tunic. Smudged ink at her elbows hinted that this tunic had either not seen a wash in quite some time or had been the victim of repeated mishaps with ink—Vaelin got the sense the latter was true.

"I'm not one to dwell on the past, but I have to admit you have quite the collection," Vaelin said.

Cressena retrieved a crowbar laying on a neighboring desk and began prying open the nailed top of the box.

"Allow me," Vaelin offered, unsheathing Vitra. Cressena stepped aside, her inquisitive dark eyes falling upon the black dagger. Vaelin sliced the top of the box as if she was skimming the cream off of a fresh mug of milk.

"That dagger," Cressena said, eyes wide. "Is that obsidian?" Vaelin smirked and handed the dagger to Cressena. "No, not obsidian," she corrected herself. "It's much lighter than that." As gently as one might handle a kitten, Cressena examined first the blade, then the pommel, running her finger against the cross-shaped etching of *Binding* carved into it.

"May I?" she asked, pointing the dagger towards the box.

Vaelin smiled wide. "Of course."

Cressena gripped the dagger—for a scholar, she seemed strangely comfortable with a weapon in hand—and ran it against the box's lid. Nothing happened, not a scratch or scrape. Cressena raised an eyebrow and attempted it again and again, running the dagger across the wooden lid, to no avail. "How in dirges—" Cressena ran the blade against the palm of her hand.

"It won't work," Vaelin said, lifting her right hand to show the woman the etching of *Binding* that was branded on its back.

Cressena glanced at the pommel of the dagger and then back at Vaelin's hand. "I've read about this," she said, intrigued. "Unfortunately, my knowledge of enchanting is limited, but I've heard of Extransforial Etchings."

"It's not exactly the same as Extransforial Etchings, though it is a similar process." Vaelin reached for the dagger and Cressena handed it back. "Extransforial Etchings involve creating a seal by injecting the flesh with ink made from enchanted black earth. This," she raised her hand once more, "is more direct—more secure. I am directly *Bound* to that dagger. Even if someone else was to create a similar etching and then attempt to take over the *Binding,* they would never succeed. That dagger will only be *Bound* to me. Because I am a djinn, I am a being of pure *life energy,* even though I currently have a corporeal form. While you humanfolk are limited to creating links between *life energy* and the enchantment—the black earth within an Extransforial Etching, for example—I am not, for I am the link, the etching, and the source of *life energy,* all in one."

"I see," Cressena said, though her lack of expertise was apparent. There was, however, a spark there—something that reminded Vaelin of her old companion.

"Myssa used to give me that look," Vaelin said.

Cressena blushed and lowered her eyes to the box. "I'm sorry."

"Don't be. I'm used to being studied." *Used to being a specimen, to be exact.* She hated when strangers set their probing eyes upon her, regardless of whether their motives were positive or negative. Yet, Myssa's inquisitiveness had somehow endeared her to the woman. It was a contradiction, she knew. Perhaps that was a part of love—allowing one person the privilege of exposure.

Cressena raised the lid of the box and set it aside. From inside she produced a piece of mildewed parchment. The musty smell of old leather pervaded the office. Cressena set the parchment on the desk and unrolled it skillfully. The writing that covered it was mostly faded by browning water damage, but the little that was legible was in Elren. The halfway-rotted illumination of a fox standing on a treasure chest confirmed to Vaelin that the text was a copy of a story she was quite familiar with. She had heard it recited often in the taverns of Lyelwyen.

"This is our newest acquisition," Cressena said. "We believe it is part of a holy text of some sort—"

"I don't mean to interrupt," Vaelin interrupted, "but I did come here for a reason."

Cressena looked up at Vaelin, tilting her head. "Oh my!" Cressena sounded anxious as she carefully rolled up the parchment and placed it back into the box. "My deepest apologies, Vaelin. How inconsiderate of me! And here I was blathering about religious artifacts."

"It's quite all right," Vaelin smiled.

Cressena placed the lid atop the box, then searched about the desk. "Now where did I put those keys?"

Vaelin coughed to get Cressena's attention and pointed at the keys hanging from the woman's belt. Cressena blushed a deep crimson. "Of course! There they are." With a nod, she led Vaelin out of the office and down a long hallway.

After walking silently for a few moments, Vaelin chuckled to herself.

"You wouldn't happen to be laughing at me?" Cressena asked. "I know I can be somewhat pomace-brained at times."

Vaelin grinned. "Not at all! I was simply reminiscing about that 'ancient holy text' of yours."

"You've seen it before?" Cressena asked, her eyes wide and bright with curiosity.

"It's a story I'm surprised made it into writing."

"A story? Would you mind telling it to me?"

"Eh, I doubt you'd enjoy it," Vaelin said.

"It's not about enjoying it," Cressena explained. "It's about the preservation of a historic document."

"Very well, then," Vaelin said. "It's the story of an elvenfolk man who was known far and wide for boasting about his ability to make love better than any creature upon the True One's earth. His boasts made their way to the forest kingdom, where they were heard by the great and powerful fox king. The fox king challenged the boastful man to a contest of love-making. Each would have to seduce and make love to as many members of each other's species as they could. The loser would have their manhood taken and locked away forever.

"The elven man happily agreed to the terms, certain that no elvenfolk in their right mind would ever bed a fox. But, as soon as their agreement was struck, the fox king transformed into a beautiful elven man. As it turned out, the boastful man was correct in his thinking that no elvenfolk would ever bed a fox as that, unfortunately, included him as well. Thus, he lost the bet as the fox king was able to seduce and bed several elvenfolk, including multiple nobles. The elven man's manhood was then taken and locked away forever."

Cressena grimaced, her cheeks and ears blooming red once more. "You were right. I don't care much for that story."

Vaelin laughed heartily. "You look surprised."

"I didn't expect elvenfolk to have had such a... distasteful sense of humor."

"Did you expect them all to be stoic and lifeless like the structures they left behind?"

"No, but—" Cressena vigorously shook her head. "It's just not what I expected, is all."

"Misunderstandings arise when you assume things," Vaelin said. "That's why I only ever expect to be surprised."

"At least the story cleared something up for me. I've seen depictions of foxes on several ancient trunks and boxes."

Vaelin nodded. "Elvenfolk depicted the fox king atop containers they wanted to keep locked away from prying eyes, as if to say 'the fox king will keep its contents safe.' "

They continued down hallway after hallway for a while. The deeper they progressed, the more skimp and sparse the décor became. Finally, they reached a spiraling staircase that continued down below the earth. The brick walls bid them farewell in favor of more rustic stone ones. Two lit sconces illuminated a large red wooden door at the far end of yet another hallway. Cressena unclasped the roll of keys from her belt.

"We are here," she said, trying to find the correct key in the faint glow of the flames.

Vaelin's heart began to beat like an anxious drum. An end to her life of enslavement was just behind that door. She should have felt relief, but all she could feel was fear. *Fear at what, exactly?* Freedom presented infinite possibilities. Possibilities that disrupted the routine imposed on her for centuries. Possibilities were terrifying.

Cressena unlocked the door and held it open for Vaelin, who made her way inside. The warehouse was vast—no, enormous! Light from the sconces illuminating the antechamber struggled to fill the cavernous space. Cressena picked a torch from a nearby stack and held it over the flame of a sconce, setting its wrapped tip ablaze. The woman entered the warehouse, Vaelin following closely behind. Rows and rows of shelves containing tomes, crates, and artifacts extended seemingly for miles into the darkness.

"The first time I saw it, I couldn't breathe," Cressena said. "Still to this day, I have barely skimmed the surface of the Academy's warehouse. Sometimes it makes me sad knowing that no matter how much time I spend here, I will never be able to study all of it. But the more I study, the more time those who come after me will save."

Vaelin felt a sudden rush of esteem towards the woman. "That sounds just like Myssa. You must have been a good assistant."

Cressena turned abruptly to face away from Vaelin. *Is she blushing again?*

"It's this way," Cressena said, leading Vaelin through the vast stacks of the warehouse. Uneasiness grew within Vaelin. By now, she should have felt her own *life energy* reflecting back at her from the lucerne, yet all she felt was silence. Could the artifact have weakened after centuries spent apart from her? Even the dormant *life energy* she had previously felt towards the port felt stronger down here.

They continued walking for several minutes in silence. Possibly sensing Vaelin's growing wariness, Cressena eventually said, "We're almost there. Myssa made sure it was far from the entrance. She didn't want to risk anyone removing it. Although, if I'm not mistaken, she's chained it up, so I don't see how anyone could—"

Cressena froze.

"What is it?" Vaelin asked.

"I don't understand," Cressena said, her voice trembling.

Vaelin walked around the woman. A pile of heavy chains was heaped on the stone floor, broken. Vaelin felt the stab of a deeper, darker, fear than she had felt in centuries.

"It was right here!" Cressena's voice sounded panicked. "It was chained up right here. There was no way anyone could have taken it! Not without the key."

Vaelin picked up one of the chains—it was incredibly heavy. Where the broken links had been sheared apart, she could feel the residue of an enchantment—the *life energy* of it hanging in the air like the echo of a faraway song bouncing off the walls of a quiet city.

"A *Power*-imbued weapon did this," Vaelin said through gritted teeth.

"I'm so sorry," Cressena cried. "I don't know how this would have been possible. Only I and two other clerks have access to the warehouse."

Vaelin dropped the chain onto the floor. It landed heavily, the metallic sound reverberating through the massive space.

Expect to be surprised, I said. What a damned fool I am!

"Take me to these clerks," Vaelin said, struggling to maintain a level tone.

After locking the door of the warehouse, they returned upstairs and paced through the long hallways back to the main hall of the Academy. The same clerk that had greeted Vaelin when she first arrived gave a start upon seeing her again. Cressena asked him about the warehouse, but he informed them that he hadn't entered it, nor had he let anyone inside in weeks.

Cressena led Vaelin through other corridors without saying a word. The woman's perturbed eyes were focused on the floor in front of her. Vaelin's heart was beating incessantly as her hands shook. She felt lightheaded and scattered. Vaelin hoped that this other clerk would have an answer to the lucerne's whereabouts. If they didn't... Well, Vaelin would rather not think about that just yet.

They reached a small office in a hall of the eastern wing. A woman sat inside transcribing the contents of a small piece of paper into what looked like a ledger. She wore a plain brown tunic similar to Cressena's, although hers bore no ink stains at the elbows. Her face was wrinkled, though not entirely from age—those wrinkles told the story of someone who loved to laugh. Today, however, was not a laughing sort of day. The woman looked up at Cressena and Vaelin with a cold expression.

"Yes?" she asked, her voice like the moan of a bored house cat.

"Mistress Veta," Cressena greeted with a curt nod. "I have a question for you." Cressena's voice took on a meek tone around this woman, and she stood at the threshold of the office, seemingly not daring to enter. Veta rolled her eyes and returned to her work.

Vaelin pushed herself in front of Cressena, stepping into the office. "Veta, was it?" Vaelin asked. "The warehouse. When was the last time you visited?"

Veta looked up at Vaelin, her face creasing with disgust. Perhaps those weren't laugh lines at all. "Did I say you could enter my office?"

"No, but I took your lovely disposition as an invitation."

Veta looked at Cressena, who in turn looked away, abashed. *Not one for jokes, this one*, Vaelin thought.

"Someone stole from the warehouse," Vaelin said.

"Impossible," Veta declared, her tone dismissive.

"Apparently not. We were just there to retrieve an item, which seems to have been taken by force."

"Cressena!" Veta yelled. The woman outside just about jumped at the sound of her name. "This is absolutely unacceptable! Who is this... this... *thing* that you let into the warehouse, who now makes such ludicrous accusations? The Board shall hear about this."

"Veta, I'm sorry, I—" Cressena stuttered.

"Why are you apologizing?" Vaelin asked. "Listen, *you*. This is a matter graver than you can imagine. An extremely dangerous artifact has been removed from the warehouse. An artifact that belongs to me. Whether it was stolen or not, that's beside the point. It was there, and now it's not. So the question stands: have you entered the warehouse recently, or have you let anyone inside?"

"I don't care for your accusing tone."

Vaelin met the woman's nasty stare with equal venom. If this woman continued to ignore the urgency of the situation, Vaelin would have to resort to physical threats. Something in Vaelin's eyes must have communicated her intentions to the woman, for her features softened into a light scowl. "I go into the warehouse once a month to take inventory," Veta relented, pointing at the ledger she was filling out. "And no, I did not let anyone else inside. It's against the Academy Board rules. Cressena should know about that. Now, go, before I call the Academy guards and have you escorted out of my office by force."

"You take inventory? Mind if I take a look?" Vaelin asked.

"Out!" the woman screamed, slamming her hands onto her desk.

Cressena grabbed Vaelin by the arm and dragged her out of the office.

"The Board will hear about this, Cressena!" the woman yelled after them.

The two walked back to the main hall. If Cressena appeared worried before, now she was panicked. "We shouldn't have gone to Veta. She's much too stern and precise to have done something like this."

"That ledger of hers, we could have used that."

"Forget it! I'm in huge trouble already. We're not supposed to let anyone into the warehouse. I've done something punishable by suspension. The Board will have me flayed."

Vaelin grabbed hold of Cressena's shoulders, firmly but not unkindly. "Listen, Cressena, I know it might not seem like it to you, but this goes beyond you, me, or the Academy. Even this city, for that matter. That object has power that, in the wrong hands, could threaten this whole world."

"What are you talking about?" Cressena said, narrowing her eyes.

"You, there," a man's gruff voice called out.

Vaelin and Cressena turned towards the front doors of the Academy. The balding clerk scurried up to them like a beetle flanked by two soldiers in Blue Scarab armor. "She was the one asking about the warehouse," he said, pointing at them.

"Thank you," one of the two Blue Scarabs said. He had a nose rendered crooked by years of fistfights. The black hair atop his shaved lumpy head was beginning to sprout fresh. "You two must come with us."

The other Blue Scarab, a woman with a long gaunt face, grabbed Cressena's arm and tugged on her brusquely. Crooked-nose grabbed Vaelin's shoulder, but she immediately shrugged out of his grip. "What's this about?" Vaelin asked.

"The Blue Scarabs have a few questions for you," the man answered while attempting to grab Vaelin again.

"I don't think so." Vaelin shoved the man away.

"Very well," the man replied, unsheathing his sword and pointing it at Cressena's throat. "Captain said there would be only one of you, so I have no use for her." Scholars and teachers stopped in their tracks around them and watched the scene with shock. Some ran outside the Academy to avoid any possible bloodshed, while others hurried off to call the Academy guards.

But there would be no bloodshed today, not if Vaelin could help it.

Vaelin unsheathed Vitra and the man grinned. "What do you think you'll do with that little thing?" he mocked.

"Why don't you see for yourself?" Vaelin winked at Cressena. The woman looked utterly terrified, but, to her credit, she was holding it together as best as she could.

"Enough of these games," the other Blue Scarab lamented. "Come with us or she gets it." The man moved his blade closer to Cressena's throat to accent the threat. Vaelin was almost convinced he meant to harm her.

She closed her eyes and inhaled deeply, focusing her attention entirely on the chant of *Power*. Instantly, a surge of strength coursed through her as she embodied the essence of *Power*. She felt as if she could run through a thick wall unscathed.

Vaelin must have appeared as a blur of light and color to the Blue Scarabs as she sliced the sword in two with Vitra. One more heartbeat and Vaelin had pulled Cressena behind her and away from the two Scarabs.

The man watched his blade fall to the floor with a hollow clang.

Vaelin released her awareness of *Power*, feeling its essence retreat out of her to return to the Cycle.

"What just happened?" crooked-nose asked in amazement.

The other Blue Scarab unsheathed her sword and swung it at Vaelin. Vaelin parried it with Vitra, and half of the woman's sword joined the other severed blade on the floor. The two gaped in utter bewilderment.

"Now that that's done with," Vaelin began, returning Vitra to her belt. "Explain to me exactly what you're doing here and what you want with me."

"What are you?" Crooked-nose asked, sizing her up and down.

"Always that unimaginative question. Are you human-folk that boring? And besides, I asked you to explain first." A dark suspicion solidified at the forefront of her mind. These Blue Scarabs knew something about her. Well, not these ones specifically—these were the muscle, sent to wrangle her. Someone else with more brains knew something about her connection to the lucerne. They had expected her to be here to retrieve it.

"I'll come with you," Vaelin said suddenly.

"You will?" the two Scarabs and Cressena asked in unison. "I mean, of course, you will!" crooked-nose added.

"But you must promise to not bother her ever again. She was simply giving me a tour of the Academy and has nothing to do with me."

"We don't take orders from the likes of you," the Blue Scarab woman spat.

Vaelin took a few steps until she was inches from the woman's face. The woman's breath reeked of sardines. "You touch one hair on her head and my blade will know your heart."

The woman attempted a defiant stare but was unsuccessful. Vaelin's stare, on the other hand, remained firm and unyielding. The Scarab lowered her gaze and nodded.

"Now that we have an understanding, please lead the way," Vaelin said. Crooked-nose and sardine-breath walked Vaelin towards the front doors of the Academy. Rather than looking like two soldiers escorting their captive, they appeared more like Vaelin's retinue. Vaelin glanced back at Cressena and gave her an appeasing nod—the woman's demeanor was that of a tangled ball of yarn. Following these two soldiers could be a terrible idea, but these Scarabs had known where to find her and the lucerne. Could they know what the object was capable of?

That bald clerk must have let them into the warehouse. That brooch he was wearing...

Vaelin admitted that she had underestimated the influence of these Blue Scarabs. She had seen militant forces rising in the name of a cause hundreds of times before—some causes more just than others. Some looked to an imaginary past to dictate how they should live and act. Others looked to either a bleak or a hopeful future. The one thing all of these groups had in common: they never lasted long—at least, not by her standards. But clearly, that didn't mean she should dismiss their ability to interfere with her plans.

She hoped that by following these two she would find out where the lucerne had been taken to. That, or she was in for a sorry surprise.

I only ever expect to be surprised.

X.

IN THREE DAYS' TIME

The unassuming Blue Scarab lodge was tucked between the Tarentia and the Effore Districts. While the presence of the bald, blue-armored soldiers was heavy in the area, Vaelin noted that many of the citizens of Sol Forne eyed them with distrust. Not all, however, did so. Some folk, mostly peasants, tipped their hats or flashed pleasant smiles at the soldiers. Blue Scarab brooches were pinned on their collars to show their support for the cause.

The etching of a scarab beetle over the doorway of the lodge glimmered mildly in the mid-morning sun. Crooked-nose and his companion escorted Vaelin inside. The interior was quite bare, to Vaelin's surprise. Perhaps these Scarabs were trying to foster an austere image for the common people, which was ludicrous considering that their lodge stood between two of the most affluent districts in the city. Likely, their entire venture was being funded by some well-off benefactor that stood to gain something substantial from their operations. Who were they trying to fool with such homely headquarters? Well, the peasants wearing those brooches seemed very taken by their front. Whatever these Blue Scarabs were selling was gaining some ground.

The shifting tide of public opinion did not concern her at the moment. What mattered instead was that this group had something to do with the lucerne's disappearance, and she needed to find out what that was.

The two soldiers led her down a flight of stairs into a dimly lit stone hallway that reminded her too closely of a dungeon. To the opposite side of the staircase was a small vacant cell filled with leashes, empty bowls, and splintered bones—a kennel. Barred doors that led into cramped cells on each side of the hall confirmed her suspicions.

"In here," Crooked-nose barked, pointing to a cell at the far end of the hallway.

"I'd rather not," Vaelin protested mildly, crossing her arms.

"It's only for a few moments while I fetch Captain Velden."

"I think I'd rather stay on this side of the bars. Better yet, I'll wait upstairs."

The female soldier sighed. "It's embarrassing enough to return here with only half our swords. Please, at least help our captain see that we've done a good job in capturing you." The woman suddenly looked away, too embarrassed to even meet Vaelin's eyes.

Crooked-nose grinned pitifully. "I promise you, he only wants to ask you some questions and then he'll let you go. Gods strike me down if I'm a liar! And besides, with that dagger of yours, you'd be able to escape easily if it did come to that." The other Scarab shook her head at her companion's words.

"You do make a compelling argument," Vaelin said. "Very well, I'll comply."

The two looked utterly delighted as Vaelin stepped into the cell. The fact that this captain of theirs had sent these two incompetent buffoons to fetch her made her feel somewhat more confident that capturing her was not a very serious matter. As soon as she settled on the small wooden stool at the center of the cramped cell, Crooked-nose closed the barred door, locking her inside. The two soldiers left in abashed silence. Vaelin would wait for this captain of theirs and hopefully learn something useful about the lucerne's whereabouts. As the soldier had said, it wouldn't be a problem for her to escape the cell if it came to it.

And so, the hours passed. Hours didn't bother her normally—her life had been filled with them; what were a few hours more? But these hours were haunted with the specters of her unanswered questions. She had felt so close to the end of her journey. She had been in the same city as the lucerne for the first time in over one thousand years. Over one thousand years since gaining physical form. Over three thousand years since she had been *Sealed* to the lucerne. How many hours had filled those years? Too many to bother counting. Yet, the anticipation and anxiety that filled these few were making them feel substantially longer.

She closed her eyes, focusing her attention on the *life energy* that surrounded her. If the lucerne was still close enough she should be able to sense it. She stretched her awareness to its limits. As if in response, a pulse of *life energy* called out to her from the south. She recognized it as the same brief pulse she had heard right after her most recent feeding. Could this be the lucerne? The artifact's *life energy* had always felt familiar to her, like an echo. The energy she sensed now felt foreign.

A single set of footsteps descended the staircase into the small dungeon and continued through the hallway before stopping in front of her cell, breaking her concentration. The captain—or so she assumed—was an older man whose sturdy and dignified demeanor made him appear much younger than his years. Only his wrinkled knuckles and calloused hands betrayed his age. The ghost of a smile barely pecked at the sides of his mouth. He eyed Vaelin up and down with an inquisitive gaze. Unlike other humanfolk seeing her for the first time, there was no fear in his look. But there was danger there—she could see that plainly.

"I was warned someone might come for the artifact," he said, skipping over pleasantries. "I just never would have imagined it would be someone like you."

"What did you imagine?" she asked dryly.

He brandished a smile. "My name is Captain Velden. This Blue Scarab lodge is under my administration. As such, you are my guest."

"Wolf spit!" Vaelin cursed. "Do you keep all your guests in cells?"

"Precautions had to be taken. I hear you've disposed of two of my Scarabs' swords with ease." He eyed Vitra at her belt—the two soldiers from before must have told him about it. "I know someone in Vizen who would pay a king's bounty for such a thing."

"Or you could simply take it, as you did with the lucerne."

"The lucerne?"

She narrowed her eyes.

"Is that what it's called, then?" he asked.

Vaelin stood, knocking the stool to the ground, and gripped the bars with white-knuckled fists. Her patience was wearing thin. "Tell me where it is."

"You're not really in a position to make that sort of demand."

"I think I'm exactly where I need to be. Tell me what you've done with it. Now."

The faint smile Captain Velden wore must have been a trick of the light because, without making so much as a single motion, the man's face transformed into something grave and hollow. "I think our master will be very pleased to know you are in Sol Forne. His array of interests includes ancient artifacts, rare materials, and... peculiar specimens. He will be in Sol Forne in three days' time for Leper's Day, and I'm sure he would be more than delighted to make your acquaintance."

The man pulled a ring of keys from his belt and unlocked the cell door. Vaelin took a step back from the bars as Captain Velden pushed them open and moved aside. He met Vaelin's confused glance with a sort of grim mirth. "What's the use of keeping you in here when you have that dagger of yours? My men might have been exaggerating, but they mentioned that thing managed to slice through their swords like a chemist's blade slicing through tender flesh. I'm sure it could easily free you from this cell."

Vaelin walked out of the cell dubiously. "That, it could."

"A marvelous weapon," Captain Velden complimented, eyeing the dagger greedily. He made for the stairs at the end of the hallway. Vaelin followed. "As far as the artifact is concerned—the lucerne was it?—I'm afraid I cannot comment on its whereabouts. Those who took it were under direct orders from our master, orders I am unfortunately not privy to. However, as I mentioned, our master will be in Sol Forne in only three days. Return to this lodge on that morning, and I'm sure you will find the answers you seek."

He gestured towards the staircase, indicating for Vaelin to climb them first. She walked upstairs and made her way towards the front door of the lodge.

"One more thing," the man said, betraying his age as he struggled with the last few steps. "I want to make it clear that all we do is for the greater good of Hovardom. If, for instance, our master does not wish to speak on the matter of the lucerne, it would be best to not press him on it."

Vaelin hoped her smile was as unpleasant as it felt to wear. Her insides boiled with indignation. "I'm sure your master will be understanding."

Captain Velden wrinkled his lips, but not in any way that could have been described as a smile. "Understanding. Yes. He is."

❦ ❦ ❦ ❦

It hadn't been fair.

The djinn woman hadn't explained the contract thing well enough! If she had, Dorovan would have never wished for something as mundane as a job and a place to sleep. He would have wished for something more exciting—something that could benefit his quest for heroic virtue.

Complaints aside, Dorovan made himself available downstairs in the inn's tavern at first light, as he had been instructed. The innkeeper was already at work, signing off on the delivery of a brand-new cask of wine. She spoke to the courier with the intensity and preciseness of someone who had had a full night's sleep, which, considering the time of day, would have been impossible for her. Yet, there she stood, not one wild hair peeking from under her plum-colored headscarf, face clean, apron washed, and dress pressed.

Dorovan stood to the side awaiting her. He wore his sword, although he was unsure that he would need it for whatever this woman had planned for him. His head felt light, not from the drink he had imbibed the previous night, but from a lack of sleep. He had been tormented the entire night by regretful fantasies of what could have been. To have an actual magical wish like the kind from the wishing trees of legend drop into his lap only for him to squander it made him queasy.

"There you are," the innkeeper blurted as if scolding him.

Dorovan straightened his back—something about this woman's disposition made him want to obey and please her, whereas his previous employer's acerbic nature had only made him want to misbehave.

The innkeeper introduced herself as Arvana Tirinvo, a third-generation member of the Hospitality Guild. She made sure he took note of the wooden Guild seal hanging behind the bar—two snails crawling up the sides of a full glass of wine. Dorovan made his introductions, careful to not divulge his last name. Certain names carried weight in Sol Forne, and the last thing he wanted was to lose this job immediately because of that recognition. Noble families, even those long gone, were not hired by guild workers.

Some would say that the guilds and nobles had been in a never-ending feud for control of the city since its inception— the Noble Council managed the city's laws and expenditures, the Guild Union managed the labor, while merchants and traders, on the other hand, inhabited a sort of unregulated gray area between the two.

Arvana eyed Dorovan's sword distastefully. "Hand that over."

"Why?" he said, defensively placing his hand over his belt.

"Because I said so," she said, impatiently. "I am your employer now, and what I say goes. You will not be needing any weapon since you will not be working the door. That position is already filled."

"And what exactly will I be doing?" Dorovan asked, removing the sheath from his belt.

"You will be a runner. You will serve drinks and food to tables when I am too busy. But mostly, you will keep the place tidy. This is a respectable establishment patronized by a scholarly sort—eyes to me when I'm talking to you! The reason I haven't hired any help is that I can't trust anyone to uphold my same standards. By hiring you I am making a gambit. You understand? Move this cask to the back and then return for more instructions."

No, not much different from Gelsema at all.

Dorovan handed the woman his sword, re-fastened his belt, and made for the cask. The large wooden cask stood atop a small wheeled platform which made it easy to carry to the back room of the tavern. Back at *The Bee and the Toad*, the cask wagon had been missing a wheel. Dorovan had watched grown men struggle to carry full casks on that thing. He was thankful this one functioned properly. With only a bit of trial, he managed to wheel the barrel to the back of the tavern.

As it turned out, the functioning cask wagon was the only true difference between this tavern and Gelsema's. The back room looked just about the same, even worse in some respects. It was cramped and surprisingly messy, with unclean plates and glasses from the prior night dispersed about. For all of Arvana's talk of a respectable establishment, the back room spoke of neglect. Dorovan found where the casks were stored—shoved in a far back corner between crates of sad, limp carrots and sacks of fragrant ground barley. He rolled the cask in front of the others, then tilted the wagon forward. The cask slid down the short plank at the front of the wagon and joined the rest with a dull thud.

"Notice anything back there?" Arvana asked when Dorovan returned to the main hall.

"No," Dorovan lied.

"Perhaps we should invest in some spectacles for you." Arvana cracked a sly smile. "Your assignment for the day is to tidy up the back room. The cook will arrive in the afternoon. Try to not leave him too much to clean. He's already busy as it stands." Dorovan nodded broodingly and returned to the back room.

By the time the cook walked through the back door into the kitchen, Dorovan was only halfway done with the cleaning. He had started with the cooking station, which was now quite tidy, but the storage room remained in disarray. The cook—a lean young man only a few years older than Dorovan—shook his head and folded his arms. "You're the new help? Well, not much help, are you? You'd think only a noble would be this bad at cleaning."

Dorovan ignored the comments and kept to his task. It was dark outside before he was fully done. Perfectly on cue, Arvana ran through the back door yelling for Dorovan to come and help her with the patrons that had started to populate the hall.

"Not even one spare word of praise," Dorovan lamented.

Arvana looked at him as if he had said the most inane thing imaginable, and tossed him an apron wear. "I'll praise you by paying you. The work isn't even close to being done, boy."

She did not exaggerate. The rest of the evening made cleaning the back room feel leisurely. Patrons had filled the main hall to bursting—a famous monologist from Efray, in central Erwynne, had come to Sol Forne, and it seemed like every damned student in the Academy had shown up to hear him speak.

Dorovan did not catch much of his monologue, but what he did hear had sent his eyes rolling. It was a long-winded speech about the virtues of serfdom. Everyone knew they did things differently in Erwynne, but this man's speech made the place sound downright treacherous. For any offense, whether they were crimes of injury or insult, any person could be taken into serfdom for a period of time as penance, regardless of their class. And this monologist was praising the system!

That can't be right. Dorovan must have misunderstood something while running drinks and food to the tables.

When the speech was done, a bard took over the stage, but the crowd rapidly dissipated. The monologist left to go perform at a different establishment, followed by a crowd of hangers-on. Though Dorovan thanked the gods for the lighter workload, Arvana wasn't eager to have him enjoy the small respite. She instructed him to clear all the tables of used glasses and set all the dirty dishware in a tub of salted water to soak in the back.

By the time this last task was completed, Dorovan's apron was drenched in water, sweat, wine, and food scraps. Dorovan returned to the main hall of the inn to find Vaelin slumped at the bar, drowning in a glass of red. Immediately, he felt something he couldn't place overtake him—it wasn't quite anger, but it was close. Part of him knew she wasn't to blame for how lousy this tavern job had turned out to be, but he couldn't help but place some of the responsibility onto her. She should have been much clearer about the contract ritual. Up until the end, he had thought it was all one big joke. How was anyone supposed to take her words seriously without some sort of proof?

Arvana patted Dorovan's back, heavily but not unkindly. "Watch the bar," she ordered, immediately heading for the back room. Dorovan made his way behind the bar with a huff.

"Enjoying the work?" Vaelin grinned.

That only added salt to Dorovan's festering mood. "You look terrible," he answered.

"And I feel it as well!" She gulped down the last of her wine.

"What happened?" Dorovan asked. He wasn't the least bit interested, yet he had asked almost instinctively. There was something about standing behind a bar that made one want to invite others to converse—or perhaps it was merely a last attempt at gaining another wish.

"What happened is that my enslavement has been prolonged by at least three more days." She shook her head. "It felt so close. I could still feel its energy lingering in that space. I was only a day or so late."

Dorovan nodded as if understanding. "Say, is there anything I can do to help?"

"Not unless you know where the Blue Scarabs hide their ancient artifacts."

"What sort of artifacts?"

Vaelin looked up at Dorovan. The creature's strange dark eyes seemed incapable of tears, yet the sadness they bore was one very familiar to him. "It's strange," she began, "after all this time I only have an idea of what it's supposed to look like, but the more I think about it the less I can actually see it."

That was a feeling Dorovan understood well. What he could recall from his childhood about his parents, and his brief time as a noble, now seemed vague and unreliable. He had memories that were dreams, and dreams that were memories. How was he supposed to determine what was real and what was but a wish? "Maybe, if you allow me one more wish, I could wish for you to find this artifact."

Vaelin looked up at Dorovan with an unreadable expression. Her eyes darted back and forth between his mouth and his forehead as if determining which was the origin of such a stupid thought. "I told you, I do not need to contract again so soon after feeding. And even so, I would not strike one with you again." Her words had an intensity behind them that startled him.

"Calm yourself," Dorovan said with a forced smile. "It was merely a joke."

"I did not care for it." Vaelin pointed to a bottle behind the bar. "Hand me that bottle, will you? I don't think I'm much for company this evening." Dorovan handed her the bottle, which she uncorked easily. Vaelin set a coin on the bar and stood. "I bid you farewell, Dorovan. I hope your future holds pleasant surprises." With those final words, the djinn left the bar and headed upstairs, bringing along the freshly opened bottle of wine and her glass.

It was late in the evening before Arvana returned to the bar. She neither paid him, as she had said she would, nor praised him. Instead, she simply dismissed him and told him to get a bowl of stew from the kitchen and some sleep, and to return at first light for more work. When he inquired about payment, she simply laughed and walked away.

His lodging was in the cool and musty basement where Arvana and some of the other staff also had bedrooms—*bedroom* was kind; these were more like cramped stalls filled with sacks. The sacks had been stuffed with hay to at least provide some level of comfort, although Dorovan sorely missed the luxury of the bedroom he had shared with the djinn the night before.

He almost had a mind of returning to that room, at least for this night. It would be easy enough to pull off—the extra sets of bedroom keys were kept in the basement, hanging from a hook by the staircase. He could quietly climb back up, unlock the door, lay in the extra bed, and slip out in the morning before the djinn woke up. Especially since she had brought a fresh bottle of red wine upstairs with her—after finishing that, it would take the earth splitting to wake her.

A sudden thought made Dorovan sit up in his dingy sack bed. What was stopping him exactly? Climbing up the stairs and entering the djinn's room would be easy. Except, instead of going to bed...

What am I thinking? It's not right! A hero would never... Dorovan laid back down, shaking his head. But this idea continued to blossom, keeping sleep away from reach. He saw the plan so clearly. He would unlock the door of the djinn's room, unsheathe her dagger, slice his palm, and make another wish before she awakened. It was so simple—but he had to be quick about it.

At some point in the night, his plan fermented from a fantasy to something real. He was going to do this. He was going to go through with it and wish for what he truly wanted. No, what he needed.

Softly, he crept out of the room and towards the stairs. He slowly removed the ring of keys from the hook and then clenched them in his fist, careful to not let them jangle about. Up the stairs, through the dark and empty main hall, and then up the second flight of stairs—he stopped in front of the bedroom door. His heart felt as if it was thudding against his ribcage. This was crazy. Was he truly going to go through with this?

He found his hand inserting the long master key in the lock, and turning it.

He pushed the door open and peeked inside: Vaelin slumbered in bed. For just a moment, he froze. But not because of any indecision. He was... excited. Everything he had ever wanted awaited him in this room. He simply had to reach out and take it. For once in his life, something would be easy.

He closed the door gently behind him and padded softly into the room. Vaelin was deeply asleep, a trickle of drool adorning her wine-blue mouth. Dorovan took in a deep breath and reached for the dagger at the djinn's belt. It released from its sheath almost too easily. The blackness of the blade made the room appear a touch brighter than it was. He wrapped his unbandaged hand around the blade and closed his eyes. With a swift motion, he slid it across his palm and waited. Like the first time, he felt nothing at all—no pain or sting, just the cold edge of the blade.

But then something strange happened. Or rather, nothing happened at all. No blood appeared on his palm. Upon closer inspection, there was no cut either.

What in everlasting dirges?

Dorovan repeated the motion again, and again, sliding the blade across his hand and then his arm with increasing gusto. No matter how many times or in what manner he wielded it, the blade would not cut his flesh.

His excitement shattered into sharp panic. His hands shook. What to do? Had his plan been foiled? Dorovan looked around the room for something—what exactly, he really wasn't sure. But then, miraculously, he saw it.

The wine bottle Vaelin had purchased earlier that night lay empty on the floor. Dorovan set the dagger onto the bed next to Vaelin, then picked up the bottle. It was sturdy glass. There would be no way to smash it without waking Vaelin. Then, he noticed the empty wine glass atop the dresser.

Dorovan set down the bottle and picked up the glass. This, he could easily destroy without much noise. He placed the glass gently onto the floor and then rested his heel against its stem. With a small shift in pressure, Dorovan felt the thin glass split. He bent and retrieved one of the shards, wincing as he ran it across the span of his uncut palm. He pressed onto the skin to draw more blood. Once enough of it had pooled, he closed his eyes and drew a fluttering breath.

This was it.

With no time for modesty or embarrassment, Dorovan shoved his bleeding hand down Vaelin's shirt and smeared it about, declaring, "I wish for you to make me into a hero."

A tight icy hand locked onto his wrist. Dorovan looked down at Vaelin. Her eyes were wide and aghast.

"What have you done?"

The panic in her voice frightened him.

XI.

A Violation

Vaelin felt the rush from the feeding run up and down her body like chills. It was like covering a freshly painted wall with another unnecessary coat. She shoved Dorovan away from her. The boy landed roughly on the other bed. Vaelin sat up and looked at her chest. The never-healing wound had consumed the blood as it always did during a feeding. Yet this feeling was nothing akin to the refreshing euphoria she usually experienced. She felt unclean, burdened.

"*You...*" she seethed, forcing herself to look at the boy. "You've violated me against my will. How dare you?" His dumbfounded expression—as if he had no idea of the damage he had done—enraged her. For the first time in a very long time, she was willing to kill a person. All restraint was gone, and the torrent of her fury threatened to drown her.

She stormed towards the boy and pushed him onto the bed by his throat, her nails digging into his flesh. "You filth! You have taken from me the one freedom I still possess—the freedom to choose who I contract. Without that I have nothing. You scum! You filth!!"

"I—I'm sorry," the boy apologized pitifully.

"There's no amount of sorry that can fix this. What you have done is akin to rape." At that word, Dorovan's eyes widened in horror. Perhaps he did understand.

No. I will make him understand.

Vaelin lifted Dorovan by his shirt. He dangled limply in her grasp, his strength seemingly dissipated. Her breath had grown torrid and rough. She felt at the edge of tears, though she was not able to cry. She felt spent. She looked into the boy's blue eyes. Tears streamed down his crimson cheeks. He was terrified, she realized.

Then, she felt it, like a whispered reminder prying her memory. *"I wish for you to make me into a hero."* The wish was now imprinted into her mind, echoing over and over again. The Contract had been forged and she had been *Sealed* to it—*Sealed* to the boy.

She slowly lowered the pathetic child until he was seated back on the bed. He trembled as he sobbed freely. Vaelin sat across from him on her bed and breathed in and out, attempting to steady herself, not daring to lift her eyes and look at the boy. The disgust she felt was going to make her sick.

Several minutes went by before she broke the silence. "I want to kill you. But even that is a choice I am not able to make."

Dorovan wiped the tears from his face. "I'm sorry, I just—"

Vaelin lifted her hand to shush him. "I am not finished speaking." She shook her head, finally meeting his eyes. "You wished for me to make you a hero by taking my free will. Does that sound heroic to you? Do you even know what you are asking?"

This time it was his turn to avert his gaze.

"You wouldn't know the first thing about being a hero. I've met people like you before. You're not unique. Just another drop of piss in the ocean of time. But what's been contracted cannot be undone. I *will* make you a hero, or we will both suffer greatly."

Dorovan looked up, both confused and grateful. The sudden brightness in his eyes almost made her laugh. "Really? Oh, thank you—"

Vaelin picked up Vitra, which lay on the bed behind her, and calmly sliced across the palm of her hand. Dark blood began to pour out. She quickly snatched Dorovan's arm and pointed the dagger at his hand—the same he had just used to perform the Contract. "What are you doing?" Dorovan yelped. The boy was much weaker than her, so Vaelin easily etched the two lines needed to complete the etching of *Sealing* on his palm. Then, while embodying the properties of *Sealing*, she placed her bloody hand atop his and interlocked their fingers. As hard as he tried, Dorovan could not release himself from her bloody grip.

"What are you doing?" Dorovan asked again in a panic.

Vaelin smiled. "As I said, I will make you a hero. But I do not trust you to have a hero's heart, so I require some form of assurance. In the same way I am *Sealed* to your Contract, you are now *Sealed* to my fate."

Vaelin let go of Dorovan's hand, and the boy crumpled onto the bed. He stared in dread at the three bloody lines on his hand. Vaelin returned Vitra to its sheath.

"What? Does that mean—" Dorovan asked thinly.

"Yes, dear boy. If I perish because you are not able to become a hero, you shall follow me in death."

Dorovan stood abruptly, blood draining from his face—pale fear took a hold of him. She couldn't help but relish in his panic.

"What is it, Dorovan? Do you not like it when others impose their will on you?" This was maybe going too far, but at this point, she was willing to push her lesson, perhaps her revenge, as far as she could.

Dorovan bolted out of the room and down the stairs. The innkeeper stood outside the room in her nightgown, candle in one hand and the other raised as if she had been about to knock. "I've had it with you and your noise, gray one! Begone from my inn!"

Vaelin huffed—this was added injury to her already terrible night. Without thinking, she reached into her satchel, pulled out her coin pouch, and tossed it at the innkeeper. Vaelin was surprised by how adeptly the woman caught it. The innkeeper weighed it consideringly—there was more than enough in there to secure the room for a couple of months. Before the innkeeper could contribute a word, Vaelin shoved passed her and out of the room.

Vaelin ran downstairs into the empty main hall, but Dorovan was nowhere to be seen. She exited the inn and looked around into the deserted streets—a peddler dragging a covered cart across the cobbles was the only person in the area. An orange tabby washed itself at the edge of a dark alleyway. The torchlit glow of the city did its best to hide the stars above. The black sky was an uncaring void.

"Dorovan!" she called out. The stupid boy was going to cost her her life. She realized her fists were balled and calmed herself. She focused on her senses, heightened by the forced feeding. The boy's scent lingered on the street—

he smelled of booze, roast, and, worst of all, boy. She followed the scent south until she found him walking aimlessly, sobbing bitterly into his sleeve.

For a moment, she felt pity for him, but that moment didn't last long before her pity morphed once more into rage. She knew, however, that further violence would drive Dorovan away, and she could not have her contracted person—as unwilling as the Contract may have been—disappear. This boy needed to be coddled. She took a deep reluctant breath and joined him.

"Surely, you must understand my anger," she said.

The boy sniffled and wiped his face on his sleeve. She couldn't believe the pitying feeling had returned. "I do," he said. "I'm sorry."

Vaelin sighed. "For hundreds of years, I've been a slave to others' wills, never being able to make decisions for myself. It has cost me every relationship I've ever had. I thought that imposing my will upon you would make me feel better about this situation... and it really, *really* did."

Dorovan scowled silently.

"I can't heal what you've done with another impulsive decision. Therefore, I am willing to release you from my *Sealing.*"

Dorovan looked at her, his eyes glistening with tears. "Really?" He looked hopeful. That pissed Vaelin off.

"Sure," she begrudged.

"But what if I don't succeed in my wish?"

"Then I, alone, will die. And then there's the catastrophic damage that it will cause to the Cycle of Nature, but you humanfolk have made it abundantly clear that you have no concerns about that."

Dorovan thought about it for a moment. He looked at his bloody palm as if it would reveal to him a deep secret. "No. Keep it."

"Don't be daft, boy. Let me release you."

"I'm serious!" he said, with a hint of not-quite-obstinance. He sounded like a child who had never gotten the attention he thought he deserved.

"You don't seem to fully comprehend the extent of this *Sealing.*"

"If I fail, you die, which means I die as well. Seems pretty simple to me."

Damned child! If he wished to drink his own poison, then so be it.

"And besides," he continued, "perhaps the fear of death is what I need to push me towards my goal. I *will* be a hero."

Vaelin smirked. He sounded determined. She wondered briefly what death would feel like.

Then, thoughts of the lucerne returned to her. In three days she would have to meet with this mysterious Blue Scarab master. Her smirk wilted into a grimace.

"A hero... What a wish... Well, a hero we shall make you in three days."

"Three days?" he exclaimed. "That's all we get before we—"

"No," she swatted. "We have about a month before I am too weak and depleted to do anything. In three days, however, I have an important meeting to attend, and the last thing I want is to be contracted when I attend it."

Dorovan nodded. "I understand. In that case, when shall we begin?"

Vaelin stopped walking, Dorovan halting at her side. She looked around at where they had ended up. The port was filled with fishing boats bobbing up and down in the smooth waves. Out in the distance, several ships were anchored, their sails furled. The only people about were a few Blue Scarab soldiers, out on patrol. The smell of sea salt reminded her of Myssa.

A large wooden board had been raised nearby. An idea infected Vaelin, as she made her way to the board. *Job postings. Of course!* She scanned the weathered sheets for any job that might inspire some sort of heroic deed. Dorovan smiled and joined her, understanding what she meant to do.

Dorovan ripped a flier off the board. "What about this one?"

Vaelin took the flier from the boy and read: '*Help needed to stave off miscreant night robbers.*' She raised an eyebrow. "Night robbers?" she questioned. "I thought you wanted to be a hero."

"What's more heroic than stopping robbers?"

"Many, many things. I don't think this is the right one for us."

Vaelin went to place the flier back on the board, but Dorovan snatched it out of her fingers. "We're taking this job," he said. There was that petulance again.

Vaelin felt her nostrils flare in irritation. "As you wish. If not a hero, I will make you into a fine watchman. At least then you'll be able to make an honest living. Right up until we both die." Dorovan's ears turned red. "The flier has an address on it. We'll head there first thing in the morning."

Vaelin turned back to return to the inn. There was enough night left to at least get a bit more sleep. Dorovan folded the flier into his pocket and jogged up to join her. "What about my job at the tavern?" he asked.

"As far as you're concerned, your job is becoming a hero now. For lodging, I've paid that innkeeper enough for the both of us."

Dorovan nodded to himself. "I didn't much care for that job anyways."

Vaelin chuckled. The boy stared at her as if wishing to be included in her mirth. "Didn't care for the job, eh? Well, what makes you so certain you'll enjoy what it means to be a hero?"

At that, the boy went quiet. He didn't speak for the rest of the night.

Try as she may, Vaelin could not bring herself to fall asleep. Between thoughts of the lucerne, and the constant reminder of what Dorovan had done, she found herself haunted by sleeplessness. She had erected a facade of peace with the boy because she needed him to be near in order to fulfill his forced Contract. But that didn't mean she had forgiven him.

No. Not even close.

Simply the sound of his breathing in the bed next to hers was enough to add to her sleepless torment. She wanted to hurt him—badly. She wanted him dead. What he had done was unspeakable; unforgivable.

Vaelin rolled over, facing away from Dorovan. She would do what she had to do—like always.

XII.

To Catch A Thief

A rvana was not nearly as displeased as Dorovan had expected her to be when he informed her he would no longer be under her employ—she seemed strangely relieved. She returned his sword, paid him three copper pieces for his work the day before, and dismissed him. It was as if he had immediately vanished from her thoughts and worries.

Vaelin waited for him outside, appearing sullen—her mind elsewhere entirely. Dorovan was still coming to terms with what he had done the night before. None of it felt real, stalking into Vaelin's room, pressing his red palm to her chest, making his wish...

"Let's go," Vaelin said coldly, before heading towards the address indicated on the flier.

The job poster was surprisingly cheery for having been robbed of as much grain as he claimed. As he escorted Dorovan and Vaelin to his storage warehouse he detailed every expense for his son's upcoming sixth birthday—fire-throwers, jugglers, and even a mime. He was so wrapped up in his unrequested elaborations that he didn't even seem to notice Vaelin's appearance. It had been a good year for him, he said proudly, despite the recent mysterious disappearance of grain from his stores.

"Had all the grain been there, I would have really been able to splurge!" he lamented. "I could have rented a couple of long-necks for the children to ride. But alas, with my stores being depleted and these damned Blue Scarabs blocking the port, the price was just too steep. Maybe next year."

As they made their way through the Portos District, they noticed porters and sailors lounging lazily about the cobbled streets—it seemed like no one was in a rush to go anywhere.

"I must admit I am somewhat perplexed," Vaelin said while getting a good look at her surroundings. "Why not hire guards?"

The man cackled. "As if I'd be able to find a single trustworthy man in this entire city. Damn Guild Union! Rondhill—where I'm from—now, there's a place where you can trust your neighbors. Nobody is out to stab you in the back or stick their nose where it doesn't belong. Here in Sol Forne, it's an entirely different story. The folks here wish for your downfall so they can pick up the scraps of your success. I've seen it often enough. There's no true difference between the lowest urchin and the highest nobility here. They're all scum. Show me a street rat I can trust, and I'll consider hiring a Sol Fornian to guard my stores. No, the one thing I trust Sol Fornians to do is turn on each other. That's why I'm hiring you two to catch the thieves rather than to guard my stores."

Vaelin glanced over at Dorovan with an unreadable expression. Dorovan, however, felt heat rising in his face.

How dare this outsider speak so lowly of Sol Fornians?
Seeming to take note of his simmering indignation, Vaelin
raised a hand, as if to calm him.

"The way you speak, you're lucky I'm not from here.
Actual Sol Fornians might not take the insult as passively,"
Vaelin warned.

The man looked at them both, perhaps really seeing
them for the first time. He shuddered visibly at the sight of
Vaelin. "Yes. Not from here," he repeated to himself. The
man finally halted in front of a tall building with a wide
wooden door large enough for two wagons to roll in side by
side. "This is the place."

Vaelin entered the thin alleyway to the building's left, between the warehouse and a mender's humble shop. She
walked to the far end of the alleyway, where it was interrupted by a tall stone wall. She examined the window several feet above. The opening was covered by a wire mesh, a
portion of which had clearly been cut and pried apart.

The man shook his head. "I know what you're going to
say. It's obvious they're entering from there. I can see that
plainly."

"Then why not close the window, or use iron bars that
can't be easily cut?" Vaelin asked.

"Grain cannot be stored in a closed room. The heat and
humidity would ruin it. The mesh is for keeping out birds,
not thieves." He explained it as if it was the most obvious
thing. "Usually, the grain is only here for a few days until I
can ship it out, but since the Blue Scarabs took over man-
aging the port, incoming ships have been stuck at sea. No
one is coming in or going out, at least until they give us all

the go-ahead. Till then, my stores are stuck here gathering must."

Vaelin nodded. "Show us inside."

The man pulled a ring of keys from the depths of his pocket and thumbed through them for the correct one. Vaelin leaned towards Dorovan and whispered, "Go check with the mender next door. Maybe they've seen something."

Dorovan didn't argue but knew that speaking with the neighbor would be a waste of time. If Vaelin had been from Sol Forne she would have known that, whether the mender next door had seen anything or not, they would never say a word about it. The peasants of the city kept to their own business to a fault. It wasn't as if their lives were particularly interesting anyway. Compared to the nobility, who loved to chitter on and on about themselves and everyone around them, the peasants could be downright stubborn with their tightness of lip. Dorovan took it merely as an opportunity to stretch his legs and headed for the mender's small shop while their temporary employer loosened the padlock at the entrance of the warehouse and escorted Vaelin inside.

The mender's shop was much smaller than any of the neighboring buildings, and, by its appearance, much older as well. It probably looked almost identical to when it had opened a half-century earlier, Dorovan estimated. Not to say it was dirty or unmaintained. Not at all—in fact, it was surprisingly well tended. But no amount of cleanliness could hide the rot in the wood boards that made up its exterior. While the building and its owner had seemingly done a decent job of ignoring the passing of years, time had chosen to not reciprocate.

The mender was a wiry, leathery man in his late years who lounged in an old chair in front of his door. An old hound snoozed softly at his side. The man sipped on a mug of milk. Dorovan could not recall the last time he'd had milk. While wine and olives were as easy to come by in the city center as seawater and sand, milk on its own was often a luxury. Transporting it from surrounding farms, in the summers especially, required the use of carved ice bottles that were etched with runes to prevent them from easily melting. This made milk prohibitively expensive for anyone not in close proximity to the farm where it was produced. This essentially meant that only nobles and some of the wealthier merchant families could enjoy it regularly.

"Can you believe it?" the old mender asked, noticing Dorovan's dumb stare. "Since the ships stopped sailing, they're practically giving the stuff away! No sense turning it into cheese if they can't ship it away, I guess." He took another sip of the milk, leaving a foamy white mustache at the top of his naked lip. "Haven't had proper cow's milk since I was a boy. And, back then, only once."

The man licked his lips and met Dorovan's gaze. While his body seemed old and frail, his gray-green eyes were filled with youthful zeal. "Ever had cow's milk, boy?"

Dorovan shook his head. "Only goat's milk, but that was a long time ago."

"Here." The man smiled as he held out the cup to Dorovan.

Dorovan didn't have to be asked twice. He took the mug and took two steady sips—enough to get a good taste, but not enough to offend the old man. The flavor was bold, yet clean—like fresh green grass billowing in the morning breeze, or the smell of rain after a storm, or the—

"Are you going to give that back?"

Dorovan opened his eyes—when had he closed them? The taste of milk was still faint on his tongue like a cherished memory. He handed the mug back to the man and nodded in thanks.

"Have you seen anyone?" Dorovan asked.

The man raised an eyebrow both at the strange question and the abrupt change of topic. "I've seen many here. It's a busy street, in the mornings especially."

"I meant, have you seen anyone enter the next-door warehouse? Particularly through that window?" Dorovan pointed at the open window to the side of the building. The man smirked knowingly, not bothering to turn and look, then shook his head. "Are you certain?" Dorovan confirmed.

"Of many things, I am. Especially to not stick myself into others' business."

There it was—that Sol Fornian lack of cooperation. "Those who broke into the warehouse also stole grain from it. Doesn't that worry you? These ruffians could do the same to you!"

The man laughed softly. "*Ruffians!* Where did you learn to talk like that? Do you think you're some sort of knight? No, whoever stole from that warehouse would not steal from me."

"How are you so certain?"

The man shifted in his seat and leaned forward as if what he was about to say was of the utmost importance and secrecy. Even the sleepy hound opened its droopy eyes and lifted its head, as if it was a fellow conspirator. "Boy, they would not steal from me because I am not a problem. Nor am I a threat. Do you understand my meaning?" As Dorovan stood there silently, the man scanned him with his alert gaze. "No, you wouldn't understand. You a noble, boy?"

Dorovan swallowed—the answer to the question stood on a tightrope.

"At least a minor noble, I'd wager from your attitude. From your clothes though... You got relatives in a House, at least," the man continued, easing back into his seat. "If that's the case, I've said all I mean to say to the likes of you. Good day." The man took a sip of his milk and settled his gaze on the still ships at the horizon.

Dorovan wasn't quite sure what the anger he felt was directed towards. He was insulted at having been perceived as a noble and yet he was sharply aware of how much he would have longed for such a misunderstanding just weeks before. "Can't believe I gave a noble boy my milk," the man grumbled to his dog as Dorovan turned and headed for the warehouse.

The warehouse's interior was much larger than it had originally appeared. *Dreadhall* mushrooms glowed blue and purple in lanterns along the walls, giving the space an eerie coldness. Dozens of large sacks of grain were stacked neatly about the space—the back row had an empty stretch where Dorovan assumed the stolen sacks would have been. There was an open second floor to the warehouse accessible by a wooden ladder that led to the window above.

"How did these robbers manage to lift these sacks up there and out of that window?" Dorovan asked.

The merchant gave a start at the sudden intrusion of Dorovan's voice.

Vaelin pointed to the edge of the second floor, by the window. "What do you see up there?"

Both Dorovan and the merchant squinted. "I don't see anything," Dorovan said.

"Look closer," she insisted. "Rope burns are fraying the wood at the edge of the second floor. This was a very meticulous job with two, maybe even three or four, people involved."

The merchant nodded in displeasure. "I don't care how many there are. All I care about is seeing them brought to justice."

Vaelin turned to Dorovan. "Did the mender say anything useful?"

Dorovan shook his head.

"Figures! These Sol Fornians look out for each other. I would wager a barrel of vintage that the man is in on it! BAH! Never liked that man anyways! There is no loyalty between merchants here, unlike in Rondhill. There, we merchants run the city. We watch each other's backs when it comes to dealing with these lowly street scum."

If Dorovan had any barrels of vintage, he would have wagered them all on the merchant complaining just as richly about Rondhill if he was still there. Not that Dorovan had ever been to Rondhill, but he couldn't imagine that a city run by merchants would be at all interesting, and this particular man seemed to savor dissatisfaction the way others would a hobby.

"We'll stake out the warehouse tonight," Vaelin told Dorovan. "While you were gone, he told me the last time he was robbed was two days ago. With the current blockade, they'll likely strike again soon."

"And what if they don't?" Dorovan asked.

Vaelin narrowed her eyes briefly, then resumed a neutral expression. "Then we will return and stake out the warehouse tomorrow."

Dorovan huffed quietly. Taking on this job was starting to not seem like the heroic endeavor he had expected it to be. Given Vaelin's scowl, she could clearly tell that he was holding back his complaints. He wouldn't give the djinn that satisfaction.

"I will lock you both in to arouse no suspicion that anyone is inside," the merchant explained. He eyed Vaelin warily. "You two best not betray my trust. If I find out a single sack of grain has left this building tonight—"

"Spare us the threats, merchant," Vaelin interrupted, holding up a hand in distaste. "After we're done, you will no longer have a thief problem."

That seemed to placate the man. Without bidding them another word, he exited the warehouse and replaced the padlock outside.

Vaelin sprawled herself across two sacks of grain.

"What do we do now?" Dorovan asked.

Vaelin squirmed around atop the sacks, struggling to make herself comfortable. "We wait."

"But we didn't bring any food and it's several hours before dark," Dorovan complained—he almost annoyed himself.

"You should have thought about that before dragging us on this heroic adventure," Vaelin mocked.

Dorovan walked up to a sack of grain and kicked it hard, hurting his toe. But he would not admit to any pain in front of the djinn. He limped to the opposite side of the warehouse, careful not to place too much pressure on his foot, and sat on the floor with his back to the wall, giving out an exasperated sigh.

Vaelin chuckled darkly. "What made you this way?"

"What do you mean?" Dorovan asked, doing his best to not sound annoying.

"You huff and gripe about everything you do, even when nobody is making you do it. I've lived a life longer than you can imagine, and I have never met anyone as displeased about everything and nothing as you are."

"I don't huff and gripe about *everything.*"

Vaelin laughed.

"Quit that! You don't seem so pleased to be here either!"

Vaelin's laughter halted abruptly. "Must I remind you that I am not here of my own volition? I'm only here, following you around, because you wished for it."

"So, if I decide to leave right now, you won't protest?"

Vaelin sat up. "While I would love nothing more than to leave this maleficious warehouse, my Compulsion to fulfill your wish would not allow it. Perhaps we both know that the heroic thing to do is to uphold our word to that scummy merchant. And that's what you wished for, right?—for me to make you into a hero."

Dorovan sighed.

"There you go again," Vaelin snickered.

Dorovan stood abruptly, ignoring his aching toe's protests. "Fine! We'll stay and catch these robbers in the act, are you happy now?"

"Happy? You want to talk about happiness?" Vaelin rose and paced up to Dorovan. He almost flinched when she stopped inches from his face, her hands balled into fists. But he stood his ground.

"You know what makes me happy?" she continued. "Agency—which is something I don't usually have much of. But the little I do possess, I use by personally selecting the people I contract. And you, puffing, whinging, little Dorovan, took even that away from me. And now you have the nerve to ask me if I am happy? I would strangle you until the air left you, if I could."

The two stared into each other's eyes for one endless, uncomfortable, moment. Dorovan felt unable to escape the pull of those dark wells. Then, something shifted in Vaelin's demeanor. Her fists relaxed as she moved away from Dorovan, sitting back down on a nearby sack of grain with her head in her hands. Dorovan caught his breath, only then realizing he had been holding it, and his heartbeat steadied. His toe still pulsed with pain, but his shame at being yelled at superseded it. He leaned back against the wall and stared at the floor. He felt he should apologize, though he wasn't sure where to start.

"Why do you want to be a hero so badly anyways?" Vaelin asked, breaking the thick silence.

"My father," Dorovan began, to his surprise. Not many people other than he and his sister knew this story. "He was a soldier during the First Red Coast Expansion. One night, while their camp was quiet and asleep, they were ambushed by the Sazisans. As they were slaughtered in the darkness—soldiers, generals, and captains alike—my father organized the remaining troops and led them against the ambush."

Dorovan wished he could have seen it. Indeed, he had imagined it so often he almost felt he had. His father's deeds filled him with so much pride. "If it hadn't been for him, they would have all perished. The only surviving general was a Sol Fornian noble. He was so taken by my father's heroism that he promised him an estate and a name in Sol Forne. Thus, House Melese was founded." Dorovan realized his fingers had been tracing the imprint on the gold coin in his pocket as he spoke.

When he lifted his gaze, Vaelin's eyes were intent on him, following the story with much more interest than he would have assumed.

"Do you understand now?" he asked. "If I can learn to be a hero like my father was, then the nobles will have no choice but to reinstate my name and acknowledge how far they've strayed from what their duties should be."

Vaelin shook her head and looked down at her feet. "You can't be serious."

"Of course I'm serious! Why wouldn't I be? That merchant was wrong. There is a difference between the nobility and the lowest street urchins in this city. The nobility is worse! They fatten themselves on the perks of their status while avoiding the obligations of their role. But I care, and I will restore the role of a noble to its former glory!"

Vaelin chuckled again.

"And what is so damned funny about that?" Dorovan fumed.

"I only laugh because your wish may have fucked us both."

"Not if you can—"

"—You wished for me to make you into a hero, yet all I see before me is a petulant child. You want to be a hero? Then go be one! But you must first let go of whatever notions of heroism you think you already know. No one is stopping you but yourself."

"Maybe I misjudged you," Dorovan said, shaking his head. "You seemed well-traveled, so I thought you surely would have met a hero or two in your lifetime. Yet, you clearly know nothing about what it means to be one. You've done nothing but complain all day while acting like you're somehow better than I am." Dorovan approached the wooden ladder and climbed it, the wood groaning under each step. He struggled to get a good grip on the ladder with his bandaged hands, so he wrapped his arms around the steps instead.

"Where are you going?"

"Where does it look like? Door's locked and the only way out is that window up there."

Vaelin jumped to her feet. "So, you're quitting this job? Very heroic indeed."

"There you go, mocking me again." Dorovan rolled his eyes as he hoisted himself onto the second-floor platform.

"You make it easy."

"You know nothing about me—about what I've gone through. My name is all I have left of my parents. If I don't fight for that then what kind of son am I?" Dorovan turned to the window.

"Wait!" Vaelin called out.

Dorovan looked down at the sliver of alleyway below, realizing he would need to find a rope to get down.

Vaelin continued, "I have lived a long, long life. I have seen an entire civilization vanish before me in the blink of an eye. I may never have had parents, but I have cared for and lost people dear to me more times than I wish to remember." After a brief pause, she added, "Your wish to be a hero is a commendable one. I'm simply worried you wished it for the wrong reasons."

"What makes you say that?" Dorovan asked, finally turning to confront Vaelin below.

"Selflessness is at the core of what it is to be a hero. You can't be a hero for your own gain or advancement, but for that of those around you. Unfortunately, my Contract relationships do not allow me to be selfless, so my deeds aren't necessarily heroic except insofar as the intentions of the one who contracts me. But I have seen heroic deeds performed many times before, by many different people, and for many different reasons. You're right, I know something of what it means to be a hero. Even though I am not given that chance." She stopped and looked away, a puzzling expression on her face.

Dorovan sat on the edge of the second floor, his legs dangling over the side. "Selflessness," he said, hating the word as soon as it was spoken.

"I don't know if it's something that can be taught, but I will try my best," Vaelin assured.

The two locked eyes. Dorovan took a deep breath, then nodded. "I will not change my goal."

"I'm not asking you to. Only to keep an open mind. Like selflessness, there are many aspects of being a hero that you may not like."

Dorovan nodded again, this time to himself. "What if I can't learn?"

"The first step is to be willing to learn. I know you are willing, deep down. Think about it: you claim you want to become a hero to gain a title, but you could have simply asked me to make you into a noble. I'm sure that occurred to you."

Dorovan realized he not only hadn't considered such a request, but it would also have seemed distasteful to him. An image of the smiling Lady Lenora flashed through his mind.

Vaelin continued, "That is because you know that to achieve your true goal, you must change who you are and become better. To me, that sounds like a willingness to learn."

The djinn made a good point. He no longer had a strong desire to simply have his name reinstated. And even if it was reinstated, with the way he now knew the nobility conducted themselves, carrying a title alone would not have honored his father's legacy—his family's legacy.

A metallic sound rattled on the wood boards behind him. He turned to face the window—a three-pronged climbing hook tied to a rope lay in the middle of the platform, inches from where he sat. Something tugged on the rope outside, pulling the hook towards the window. One of the prongs bit firmly into its frame.

"What was that?" Vaelin asked.

Dorovan struggled halfway down the ladder before losing his grip and falling back onto the grain sacks below. He stood clumsily and whispered, "They're here!"

XIII.

A HEROIC DEED

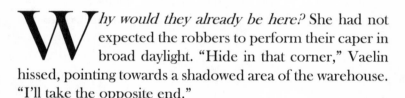

W hy would they already be here? She had not expected the robbers to perform their caper in broad daylight. "Hide in that corner," Vaelin hissed, pointing towards a shadowed area of the warehouse. "I'll take the opposite end."

Dorovan unsheathed his sword.

"What are you doing?" Vaelin asked.

"We can't let them escape."

"Put that thing away this instant!" she commanded, pointing at his sheath. "We don't know how many there are, if they're armed, and with what." Dorovan seemed to realize his hastiness was a mistake and returned the sword to his belt. "Now, hurry and hide. I will give you a signal when it's time to act."

Dorovan nodded and quietly scurried for the corner Vaelin had pointed to. Vaelin positioned herself at the opposite end of the room. The boy was naïve. That did not excuse what he had done to her, but she was beginning to understand that, other than being retold these supposed heroics committed by his father, no one had instilled in him firm moral guidance. The boy wanted to be a hero—a commendable yet childishly idealistic effort.

Above, on the second-floor platform, Vaelin could hear feet shuffling, her keen ears picking out three distinct pairs. She couldn't see the platform from her hiding place, but the intruders would become visible as soon as they neared the sacks. One of the three came into view—no more than a child, the boy looked like a street urchin with his dirty loose-fitting pants and shaved head. Something felt off about this.

From the other side of the room, Vaelin could see Dorovan standing within the spilled shadows of his hiding spot, his features only barely illuminated by the *dreadhalls*. Dorovan placed his hand on the pommel of his sword and inched forward. The boy was about to do something stupid—no real surprise there.

The young thief skillfully wrapped a fishing net tightly around one of the sacks, then attached a rope to it with an intricate sailor's knot. He tugged on the rope three times—a signal—and then stood back as the sack was hoisted towards the platform above. Once it had raised a few inches off the ground, Dorovan unsheathed his sword. Vaelin felt a surge of panic—surely the boy was not going to attack a defenseless child.

She couldn't be too careful.

Vaelin lunged out of her hiding place. Dorovan took that to mean he should do the same. The child spotted them instantly and yelled, "We're had!" The sack fell to the ground and burst open, spilling grain across the wooden floorboards. The two that stood on the second floor had let go of the rope and were now climbing out of the window.

Dorovan pointed his sword at the child's throat. The child backed away, arms raised pleadingly, before tripping backward over the other sacks. "We caught you, scoundrel," Dorovan said with a smirk.

Vaelin rolled her eyes. She placed her hand on Dorovan's blade and lowered it. "The child is unarmed," she pointed out.

"Good," he said. "That means he'll stay put until we hand him to the city guards."

Vaelin shook her head and studied the thief. She wasn't sure if he was more scared of having been caught or of her appearance. "What's your name?" she asked.

"Varsco," the child replied, steeling himself—he seemed to possess more calm and sense than Dorovan, despite being several years younger.

"Well, Varsco, your companions seem to have deserted you. Not very nice of them."

"I would have done the same," he said, puffing out his chest. "We all know the risk we take."

"How many of you are there?" Dorovan asked forcefully, lifting his sword yet again.

"Will you quit that?" Vaelin demanded. "And sheathe your sword. There's no reason to have it out."

"And what if his companions return with reinforcements?"

"Somehow, I highly doubt that. Now, put that thing away." Dorovan obeyed with a scowl. Vaelin returned her attention to the child. "Why were you stealing this grain?" she asked.

Varsco narrowed his eyes as she met Vaelin's gaze. "I won't tell you a thing, demon."

"I am a djinn, not a demon. My name is Vaelin, and I'm not here to hurt you."

"Can you say the same for this one?" Varsco asked, nodding towards Dorovan.

"This one won't either. Isn't that right, Dorovan?"

Dorovan folded his arms. "I don't understand why we're not calling the guards right this instant."

Vaelin elbowed his arm. "I said, isn't that right?"

Dorovan rubbed his bicep where she had nudged him and nodded distastefully.

"Now that we've got the introductions out of the way, will you tell me why you're stealing from this warehouse? And in broad daylight, when everyone can see you? Doesn't seem very smart."

"At night the guards patrol the streets. In the day, it's the Blue Scarabs, but they're too busy minding the port to care about a warehouse. It's safer to come in the afternoon when people are resting."

"That makes sense," Vaelin agreed.

"The child has confessed. Now let's bring him to justice," Dorovan said.

"Who're you calling a child?" Varsco protested. "You're what, three or four years older than me? Even so, I'd wager I stopped wetting myself long before you."

Vaelin chuckled to herself, but Dorovan did not take the insult lightly. He stepped towards Varsco and shoved him. The child landed atop the grain. Vaelin grabbed Dorovan's arm firmly. "Enough!" she exclaimed.

"He started it," Dorovan said, that slimy petulance returning to his voice—he seemed intent on proving Varsco right about himself. Vaelin simply glared at Dorovan and released his arm. She then offered Varsco her hand and helped him back to his feet. "Were those two friends of yours? Family?" Vaelin continued.

Varsco looked suddenly sullen. "My brother and my sister."

"Do you have other family?"

Varsco lowered his eyes and nodded slowly.

"Is this about the blockade?"

The child lifted his head. "Mama says we can't even afford olive oil anymore since the Blue Scarabs took over the port. Everything is too expensive. Everyone is always so hungry."

Just as she had suspected. This wasn't a crime of greed but one of need. Had this family not resorted to stealing, they would no doubt have succumbed to their poverty. Suddenly, the lavish party being thrown by the warehouse owner filled her with disdain and disgust.

Vaelin reached into the lining of her satchel and pulled out a gold piece. The child's eyes went wide—as did Dorovan's. She held it out for Varsco to take, but the child simply stared at it as if reaching for it would sully it somehow. "For you," she prompted, and Varsco finally obliged. Once he touched the coin, Vaelin cupped his hand with both of hers and met his eyes. "You must promise me that you, your family, and everyone you know will never steal from this warehouse again."

The child immediately nodded. "I promise. I'll tell everyone to leave this place alone."

"Good," Vaelin said, letting go of the child's hand. Varsco stared at the coin in disbelief, then quickly pocketed it. "Now, don't go losing that on your way out the window."

"We're letting him go?" Dorovan asked in astonishment.

Vaelin sighed. *Is this boy truly incapable of learning?* "Go on," she told Varsco. The child didn't need to be told twice. He nodded in thanks and ran to the ladder, making his way up and then quickly out of the window.

Dorovan shook his head as he watched the child disappear. Then, suddenly, he grinned. "Oh! I see what you're doing!" he exclaimed. "Now we follow him back to his little rat hole, where we'll catch his family of thieves."

"No, Dorovan!" she said, much louder than she had intended—or maybe she had. "Now we leave him and his family alone."

"But... but they're thieves!" Dorovan exclaimed.

The boy was beginning to truly irritate her. "If you want to catch criminals and toss them in a cell, you should have wished to join the city guard. But no, you wished to be made into a hero, yet you keep allowing your simplistic notion of justice to taint the way you act."

"We were hired to catch these criminals!" Dorovan yelled. His face was turning red as a summer melon.

"If they're only criminals then you are only someone who forces contracts onto people while they sleep." The words had the intended effect. Dorovan's eyes met the floor. "We were hired to stop this warehouse from being a target, and we did just that. With that gold, that boy's family will be able to buy all the food they could ever need until the blockade is lifted, and beyond. They will not need to steal from here again. Don't you see that there are multiple paths to justice, paths that do not always involve punishment?"

To his credit, Dorovan seemed to ponder over Vaelin's words. "And what do we tell the merchant?"

"What *do* we tell the merchant, Dorovan?" A test.

Dorovan thought about it for a moment, the full redness of his face slowly fading. "Well, we shouldn't lie, right? That wouldn't be heroic."

"That's true. But there are many different ways of telling the truth."

Dorovan grunted. "I wish you would speak straight for once."

"I may not speak plainly, but I never lie, boy. We will tell that rapacious merchant the truth, but it won't be a truth he'll like."

And so, Vaelin and Dorovan made themselves comfortable atop the sacks and waited for morning. Vaelin was used to spending long stretches of time without the need for food or water, but Dorovan was still a growing boy. When his hunger pains made themselves known to her through their grumbling, Vaelin told him to stay put. She climbed the ladder and jumped out of the window onto the street below. In a nearby tavern, she bought some bread, a few slices of hard cheese, a small clay jar filled with pickled figs, and a bottle of wine. When it came time to pay she realized with some embarrassment that her satchel was now empty of coin. Instead, she bent down and produced a couple silver pieces from a small pocket in her shoe. The vendor wrinkled his nose as he accepted them. Vaelin would have to find a way to make some coin soon or perhaps seek one of her many hidden caches in the area.

She returned to the warehouse and shared her bounty with Dorovan. The boy ate greedily, only thanking her as an afterthought once the food was gone. Vaelin uncorked the wine and took a pull, her face pinched—when drinking from a glass, one got a full sensory experience, while drinking straight from a bottle all smell was obfuscated; a good way to drink bad wine, she supposed.

An hour after first light, the merchant unlocked the padlock at the front of the warehouse and opened the wooden doors. Vaelin and Dorovan had been up for a few hours already. The sacks of grain were too uncomfortable and lumpy to be slept upon continuously. Once inside, the merchant squinted, his eyes adjusting to the softer light within.

"Well?" he insisted, upon seeing them.

"No villains were here tonight, nor will any robbers disturb you again," Vaelin said.

"What do you mean?" the man asked, raising a suspicious eyebrow.

"I mean what I said," Vaelin answered firmly.

The man took a few steps inside the warehouse. At the sight of the busted sack of grain, his face creased with anger. "What's this? What have you done to my grain?" He turned to face Vaelin, only then seeing the bottle of wine peeking from her satchel. "And drunk on the job too? This is what I get for trusting anyone in this damned city. Out! Out, I say! Never show your ugly faces around me again!"

Vaelin nodded politely at the man and then turned to leave. "Let's go grab some proper breakfast."

Dorovan followed behind her. "I thought you said we wouldn't lie," he complained.

"I didn't lie," Vaelin answered.

"But you said no robbers were here tonight when we both know that's not true," Dorovan said.

"When your entire life is beholden to others' whims, you tend to pay close attention to the words people use. I never said *'robbers.'* I said *'villains.'* Stealing food from those who have more than they need in order to feed one's family is in no way a villainous act. To an extent, one may even consider it heroic."

"Stealing is never heroic," Dorovan stated firmly.

Vaelin shook her head. "Believe what you will. Either way, it looks like our Contract is not yet fulfilled."

"Even after we let that thief go?"

"I let him go. You would have had that child imprisoned."

Dorovan stopped and widened his arms in frustration. "Well, considering we're still contracted, perhaps that *was* the heroic thing to do."

Vaelin narrowed her eyes and continued walking. This was going to be more difficult than she had originally thought. It wasn't just about teaching the boy heroism anymore. It was about changing him. The boy may have the willingness to learn, but did he possess the drive to unlearn everything his life had taught him thus far? Vaelin wasn't so sure.

"This place will do." Vaelin stopped in front of a tavern between the Portos and the Verario Districts called *The Olive Pit*. The smell of herbed meat had attracted her to this particular establishment. The inside was candlelit and intimate. Four rabbits were roasting over the hearth fire, a young girl turning the spit.

"Yes," Dorovan agreed. "This place will do just fine."

A surprising amount of patrons were inside for this time of day. Most of them wore painted armor and had the look of travelers from out of town. A few others had gathered around these armored strangers, listening intently to their boasts and tall tales.

A young boy hurried up to the two of them and asked what they would be drinking. "Unfortunately we're not currently selling wine," the boy said, in a surprisingly proper fashion. "All's we got... all we *have* is ale."

"That will do, then," Vaelin said. "Two ales, one of those beautiful rabbits, and perhaps some olives and bread."

"That we can do," the boy replied with a grin, then hurried off to see to their order.

"Unfortunate about the wine," Vaelin said. "I was hoping to try some at every establishment in the city."

Dorovan grimaced. "I can't believe my fate is in the hands of a drunkard."

"You're complaining about free breakfast? Because that's what you're about to get. And besides, I don't get drunk. I get inspired."

The drinks and food arrived soon after. The ale was palatable, nothing special like those Sourrock darks, but it did pair well with the rabbit. The mixture of spices that coated its crispy flesh was fragrant but skimp—most likely another victim of the blockade.

Dorovan enjoyed his meal in silence—at least, he seemed to enjoy it. It was hard to tell with him. During the meal, he stole more than one glance at the other end of the tavern, where the armored men and women were conversing. Vaelin hadn't been paying them much attention, although they were quite rambunctious.

"—when I came to," said a young blonde-haired man who was already in the middle of his boastful tale, "the

Reaverlord's curse had taken its hold over me. I was weakened and decrepit—could barely stand!"

"What happened then?" a bright-eyed young woman asked, eating up his words.

"The beautiful woods witch healed me and then enchanted my armor at no extra cost."

"Tell them how she healed you, Yugo," another one of the armored men chided.

Yugo reddened, unexpectedly. "I don't know if this is the place."

"Please tell us!" the young woman begged with a smile. "How did the woods witch lift the curse?"

Yugo smirked and took a pull from his ale. Before he could say anything, the other man brusquely interjected, "She bedded him and healed him with her magical cunt."

All of the armored men and women joined in boisterous laughter, while Yugo appeared almost embarrassed. The young woman and the other Sol Fornians listening to the story didn't seem as amused.

Yugo cleared his throat, hoping to win back the audience. "When I was returned to my normal self, I took my newly enchanted armor to Vizen and entered a warrior's tourney. I came in second in the melee. I would have done better had the winner not wielded an enchanted sword that could sever limbs at the bone as if they were nothing. Had I not possessed that enchanted armor, I would have surely lost an arm. But, alas, my shield had succumbed."

Errant knights. Vaelin shook her head. She had met their kind many times before. A crass bunch of mercenaries, not noble enough to be knighted by the king, yet not humble enough to have any sense of self-awareness.

Dorovan seemed enraptured by the young knight's words. *This can't be good.*

"Ignore that one," Vaelin said to Dorovan. "His kind is only good for telling tales and warming armor."

"That man fought a *Reaverlord*," Dorovan said.

"That should impress me?" Vaelin asked.

"How many *Reaverlords* have you fought?"

"None, for I have never been contracted to fight one."

Dorovan stood and walked over to the knights' table. *Stupid, stupid boy.* Vaelin reluctantly followed him. The last thing she needed was to let the boy be seduced by some story-weaving, no-good, errant knight.

"Ser Yugo?" Dorovan asked the young man. "Is 'ser' the proper term? I've never met a knight before."

The young man smiled, his teeth straight and bright. His armor was smooth and pristine, like something from out of a portrait. A large blue cross was painted across his and all of his companions' chests. "An errant knight is unanointed, so there is no need for the honorific. You may simply call me Yugo."

"Yugo," Dorovan repeated, "I'm Dorovan. I liked your story. How did you kill the *Reaverlord?*"

"Well, I didn't kill him myself. My companions did. I was a bit late to the showdown, as I was locked in combat with two or three of the *Reaverlord's* underlings."

"How many was it? Two or three?" Vaelin asked, stepping forward.

Yugo's smile slowly vanished at the sight of her. "And what might you be?"

"A man as well traveled as you must have heard of djinn, no?"

Yugo's smile returned, even brighter than before. "I'm afraid I haven't."

Dorovan shoved himself in front of Vaelin, seemingly annoyed that she had taken over his conversation with the errant knight. "I am on a quest to learn what it means to be a hero. You wouldn't happen to have any advice?"

Yugo swatted Dorovan on the shoulder. "Dear boy, you came to the right person, for I am adept in the art of heroism and chivalry." Two of the accompanying knights snickered amongst themselves. Yugo shot them an arrow of a glance.

"Could you teach me some of what you know?" Dorovan asked.

Vaelin sighed and reached for Dorovan's arm. "This is a bad idea—"

Dorovan shrugged out of her grip. "Please, Yugo."

"Of course, of course! How can I refuse? Dorovan, was it? Being a hero is simple! All it takes is to do the right thing. Whether it be rescuing a damsel in distress, or dueling against a villain, heroic deeds always call out to those who have dutiful and pure hearts."

Vaelin wasn't sure if she should laugh or sick up. This young fool was a parody of a hero.

"How did you learn to become one? Could you teach me?" Dorovan asked, his questions stumbling over themselves to escape.

"Well," Yugo continued, scratching his perfectly defined jaw, "I'm not sure it's something that can be taught."

At least he's got that right, Vaelin thought.

Dorovan looked disappointed. Yugo patted Dorovan's shoulder again in a friendly, albeit patronizing, manner.

"How about this: I am in Sol Forne on errant knight business. I was hired for a job and I could use a local as a guide. These labyrinthian districts are quite difficult to navigate, I must say. Maybe if you follow along you'll learn a thing or two about what it means to be a hero."

No, Vaelin thought. *Never in a million years.*

"That sounds wonderful! Thank you so much," Dorovan declared emphatically.

"No!" Vaelin countered. "There is no way we're going with this..." Vaelin couldn't find the word to describe how this errant knight made her feel—or, rather, she would not say the first thing that came to her mind.

"Are you, perchance, the boy's guardian?" Yugo asked with a mocking tone.

"She is not," Dorovan quickly interjected. Then to Vaelin, he added, "You don't have to come along. Maybe Yugo here will make me into a hero and our Contract will be terminated without you having to lift a finger. Wouldn't that be nice?"

"Somehow I highly doubt that," Vaelin deadpanned. "I'm coming with you if anything to ensure this *valiant* errant knight doesn't lead you into trouble."

"As you wish, fair djinn," Yugo said with a nod. "Perhaps your kind has something to teach me as well."

Dorovan didn't seem as enthusiastic as the young knight about Vaelin joining. "So, when do we begin?"

"There's no time like the present," Yugo said, taking a final swig of his ale. "Let's be on with it!"

XIV.

OFFICIAL ERRANT KNIGHT BUSINESS

There, Queen Altima stood, beautiful as ever, a pale rose in her hand. Both I and my opponent got down on one knee, as is customary—although I placed my sword tip down into the ground, which is more proper; my opponent laid his sword across his lap like a simpleton. Our battle had raged on for what felt like hours after all the other melee participants had been vanquished. Just me and this brute. Well, I do not jest when I say the queen herself locked eyes with me, which made my heart quicken. In that instant, I knew she wanted me, but neither of us would ever act on this attraction for she belongs to our king, may the gods bless him. I do not regret locking eyes with her, though it did cost me the victory, for my brutish adversary hit my shield with his enchanted blade, destroying it instantly. Swiftly, he struck my arm, numbing it. Had I not been wearing enchanted armor, I would have surely lost the limb. The melee was called in his favor."

Yugo shook his head at himself, reminiscing with a fond smile. "For just one instant, I thought the queen was going to bestow me with her white rose even though I had lost— that's how deep her attraction to me was! Alas, she gave the rose to my adversary and named him the melee champion. I was still commended for my valiance and bravery and was given a spot at the banquet table. All night the queen watched me with those... queenly eyes of hers. She was begging me to make a move on her, but I would not dishonor her or our dear King Petar, may he live forever."

Dorovan was entirely enthralled by the young knight's story as they made their way down the marble streets of the Effore. Was this truly the life of an errant knight—to travel far and wide across the country on quests and participate in tourneys for kings and queens? That sounded wonderful to him. Though his intent was still firm on reinstating the Melese noble name, becoming an errant knight didn't seem so bad either. Perhaps there was a way to do both. He could become the first noble to work as an errant knight—show these lazy Sol Fornian aristocrats what a heroic lord does for his people. His head was already populated with the beautiful tear-stained faces of the damsels he would save, the general sounds of the streets morphing in his mind into the cheering of his admirers.

Vaelin, on the other hand, didn't appear particularly taken by Yugo's story. She had huffed and scoffed throughout, her arms folded across her chest. Hadn't she complained about his huffing and puffing just the day before?

"What exactly is this job we're heading to?" Vaelin asked after Yugo's story finally was over.

"Right to the point! I like that," Yugo replied. "Today we are settling a contract dispute."

"A what?" Dorovan asked.

"The man who hired me recently purchased that tavern we were just in, *The Olive Pit*, from a noblewoman who lives in this richer side of town. Unbeknownst to him, the tavern was built upon sinking land. I saw it myself—given a few more years, that basement will be entirely submerged in water, and the tavern will do more for fishes than folk."

"So what exactly have you been hired to do about it?"

"I was just getting to that. You see, the contract stipulated that a scholar, banker, or accountant would inspect to ensure that the building had been properly maintained and cared for before the sale could be conducted. Yet, the inspector failed to notice the foul conditions of the basement. Doesn't that sound suspicious?"

"I suppose," Dorovan begrudged. Suddenly, this errant knight's quest didn't seem as exciting as he had originally expected it to be. "So you're going to go find this inspector and ask them about it?"

"Precisely. If they were paid off by the original owner to keep the situation hidden, then we have a breach of contract on our hands." Yugo paused for a moment to gauge Dorovan's reaction. "I know this isn't the sword-slashing sort of heroism you probably expected, but mediation is a big part of what an errant knight does. It's crucial to a functioning society that contracts are respected."

Dorovan looked over at Vaelin, expecting dissent—especially in the face of a contract-based job. But what he found on her face instead was determination. "Looks like you may learn something yet from this errant knight," she said.

"You had doubts?" Yugo smirked. At Vaelin's raised eyebrow, he quickly added, "Don't answer that."

Dorovan huffed. What could a contract dispute possibly teach him about heroism?

They soon reached Plaza d'Edo with its bubbling, shimmering fountain and its to and fro of nobles and upper society. Dorovan had always looked at them with envy, wishing he could have their lives—wishing to return to the life he was born for. But for some reason, all those nobles he saw now looked so... bored. Their conversations sounded vapid and droll, and their lounging about appeared vulgar and meaningless. How had he never noticed their listlessness before? When House Melese was reinstated, he would show them all how a true noble ought to conduct themselves.

Then, Dorovan spotted Captain Velden, standing out like a pine tree in a vineyard with his dark blue armor and shiny bald head. He was speaking serenely with an angry group of merchants. Dorovan looked down in fear of being seen and approached yet again by the man.

The captain looked over at the three of them, to Dorovan's chagrin. Strangely enough, however, the Blue Scarab barely gave Dorovan a cursory glance. Instead, his eyes landed on Vaelin. For a moment, Captain Velden ignored the aggrieved merchants entirely, smiling at Vaelin in an unreadable way. The djinn locked eyes with the bald man and nodded knowingly.

What was that about? Did Vaelin have some unknown ties to the Blue Scarabs? Dorovan continued to ponder this as they approached the bank, which stood in a back alley of the Effore, hidden from the public eye. Other than in marketplaces, Sol Fornians considered monetary transactions to be a private matter, so no banks were to be found in public settings. Dorovan knew where this bank was very well, as it was located near a tailor's shop whose window he frequently admired on his walks.

"Thank you for guiding me, Dorovan," Yugo said, heading for the bank's unassuming entrance.

A guard at the door stood in his way. The clean-shaven guard wore a white powdered wig, white-painted leather armor, and a long, clean, white cape, making his appearance just as pleasing as anyone else in the noble district. "State your business, errant knight," the guard said, with no hint of malice. Just a man doing his job.

"I am here on official errant knight business," Yugo declared. "Contract dispute."

"And are you a Guild member?" the guard asked.

"Yes, yes, I've paid your damned dues," Yugo scoffed, pulling out a piece of parchment from within his chest plate. The parchment was stamped with the seal of the Sol Fornian Errant Knights' Guild—a vine climbing around the length of a sword.

"You may enter, then. But you must leave all weapons outside."

"Fair enough," Yugo agreed, unfastening his sword belt. He turned to Vaelin and handed her the belt and sheathed sword. "Stay out here and keep an eye on this, will you? You too, Dorovan. Remove your weapon."

Dorovan nodded and removed his sword from his belt, also handing it to Vaelin. She held both swords as if they were week-old fish. "Don't take too long," Vaelin said, with a hint of annoyance.

"This should take but a moment." Yugo nodded to the guard, who moved aside to let him and Dorovan inside.

The bank was cramped and dark, the ceiling strangely lower than it ought to be for such a tall building. For all his height, Yugo had to bend over slightly to fit, which, in his armor, could not have been comfortable. The faint smell of tobacco smoke pervaded the air, which was strange as it was seen as impolite to smoke inside buildings unless they were taverns—and even then, only in the seediest of establishments. At the end of the small room was an opening into a much larger area where a thin gray-mustachioed man in scholar's robes sat at a desk. Behind him were tall shelves spilling with envelopes, papers, and ledgers.

"Hello there," Yugo greeted. "My name is Yugo and I'm here on official errant knight business."

The mustachioed man regarded Yugo with a blank and almost perturbed expression. "All bank business must be preceded at least three days by formal notice. Have you filed such a notice?"

"I have not, but my business is quite urgent," Yugo stated.

The banker returned his attention to the papers on his desk. "No notice, no business. Good day."

Yugo sighed. "We find ourselves at an impasse. I had hoped to not get my hands dirty." From his boot, Yugo produced a long knife. Dorovan jumped at the sight of the weapon. Yugo climbed over the divider and into the larger area of the bank.

"Help—" The banker began to shout, but Yugo knocked him off his chair and onto the floor with a kick.

"What are you doing?" Dorovan asked, standing still as if paralyzed.

Yugo climbed over the banker and placed the tip of the knife at his throat. "You don't yell and I won't have to hurt you, understood?"

The banker nodded rapidly.

"My client recently purchased a property called *The Olive Pit* in the..." He turned to Dorovan, "What was that area called again?"

Dorovan stared at Yugo, dazed, the question bouncing through his mind. "The Verario," he answered in an unsteady voice.

"The Verario! Thank you Dorovan," Yugo said. Then, returning his attention to the banker, he continued, "I know you sealed the contract, declaring the tavern to be safe, knowing full well that its basement was in danger of flooding."

"I— I did," the banker said, trembling. It almost sounded like a question. Dorovan looked away, finding the sight of the man too pitiful to bear.

"And why would you do such a thing?" Yugo asked.

"Sh-she made me!" the banker exclaimed, now panicked.

"The seller?"

"Yes. Amela ca'Pottara. She made me ignore the damage."

"She made you? How so?"

The banker licked his lips and sighed. "House Pottara owns this bank, though you won't find their name on any of the books. They make me do things sometimes, like change numbers or names in the ledgers—"

"Falsifying documents for their gain," Yugo interrupted. The banker nodded. "Well, I've heard all I needed to hear." He stood and held his hand towards the banker to help him to his feet. He brushed the man's shoulders in a mock cleanup and then asked Dorovan, "Do you know where to find this House Pottara?"

Dorovan nodded, still in disbelief at what was happening around him.

"Let's go pay them a visit, then. But first," he turned to the banker, "you're going to rescind your inspection approval on this contract." Yugo pulled out a rolled-up piece of parchment from beneath his chest plate and set it gently upon the banker's desk.

The banker eyed the document as if it was a death sentence addressed to him. "I must protest as the breaking of an inspection seal will raise all sorts of legal queries."

Yugo lightly touched the man's shoulder. "And to that, I say that I don't give a god's bullock."

The banker sighed in resignation and unrolled the parchment. "So be it." With a rounded finger-length knife, he broke the seal upon the contract. He then plucked a quill from a jar of ink and signed his name over the broken seal. "There. It's done."

"Many thanks," Yugo said, rolling up the parchment and returning it behind his chest plate. "Lastly, I am going to need a gold piece from you."

The banker's gray eyebrows shot up. "A gold piece? Whatever for? You're going to charge me for my own assault?"

"For assurance. To make sure that you are telling me the truth and not hiding your culpability in all of this. The gold piece shall be returned to you upon completion of the contract dispute."

"Doesn't sound like I have a choice," the man scoffed. Yugo did not have to answer. The banker unfastened a coin pouch from his belt. At least twenty gold pieces shimmered within. Dorovan had never seen that amount of gold in his life. The banker handed Yugo a coin and then quickly re-fastened his pouch as if Yugo would snatch more of his precious gold if given the chance. "Now leave me be," the banker said. "You've done enough already to ruin my reputation. Your guild will hear about this, I tell you!"

Yugo smiled at the man, placed the coin into his pocket, then vaulted over the short wall separating both sides of the bank. Dorovan followed the errant knight to the front door. His head was light, and his chest felt stuffed with cloth. Was this how every contract dispute was conducted? Perhaps that was why they never made it into songs and tales. But even if this was common practice for errant knights, Dorovan felt something was wrong. A heroic deed shouldn't leave him feeling embarrassed and guilty. At least he didn't think so.

"All done?" the guard outside asked.

"All done," Yugo confirmed, leading Dorovan outside.

Vaelin returned their swords. "Did you get lost in there? That took some time."

"Apologies. Legal matters often take longer than physical ones," Yugo answered. "But I got what I needed. The banker understood our concerns and broke his seal of inspection. Now we have legal recourse to go to this Pottara place to sue for the cost of repairs. Dorovan, lead the way!"

Dorovan sighed. "This way," he said.

Yugo flicked the gold coin he had just taken from the banker towards the guard, who caught it mid-air. The guard stared at the piece incredulously. "For your trouble," Yugo said, then followed Dorovan down the eastward street.

As they walked, many passersby smiled and nodded at Yugo, who saluted back. He truly was exactly how Dorovan had always pictured knights to be. Yet something about the young man's methods unsettled him. He wondered if these people would still greet him had they known that Yugo had just beaten up a Sol Fornian banker. Would they still smile if they knew he was headed to a noblewoman's home to force her into paying a peasant?

"What is it?" Vaelin whispered—when had she walked up to him? He shot her a questioning glance. "You seem off-kilter, dazed. What happened back there?"

"It's—nothing! Don't worry about it."

"Is this sort of heroism boring you?" she asked with a sharp-toothed grin.

"No, it's just—"

"Someone was wronged by a minor noble. There's no injustice greater than one done by a person of means. You wish to be a noble in this city, so never forget that."

"No, it's not that, it's that..." Dorovan thought back on the banker's pitiful face as Yugo leaned over him in his pristine armor. Vaelin was right: an injustice had been committed by the Pottaras—even Dorovan could recognize that—but did that justify Yugo's violent methods? Dorovan wasn't so sure. But then again, he didn't want to appear indecisive to Vaelin. Indecisiveness didn't seem heroic.

"Let's just go," Dorovan resigned.

House Pottara was a modest noble house when compared to the others in the Effore. It was built in the Vizenian style rather than that of Old Oshemar like the other homes on the street. Its roof was flat instead of slanted, and its windows were square and long rather than tall and arched.

"Not the grandest I've ever seen, but I wouldn't complain about it," Yugo admired the home.

The three of them were approached by two armed guards at the front gate. They wore an outfit very similar to the bank's guard, although they had the Pottara family crest embroidered on their chest and cape—a vase overflowing with red wine; to Dorovan it almost looked like blood. "What business do you have here?" a guard asked.

Yugo unrolled the contract parchment and held it open for the guards to see. "This contract has been retroactively rescinded by the banker who inspected the property listed. I am here to sue the Lady Pottara for the damages to the property."

The guards glanced at each other with stupefied looks. "And who might you be?"

"I am an errant knight. And before you ask—yes, I am signed with the local guild," Yugo said, showing the two his guild seal.

"And your crew?" the same guard asked.

Yugo turned to face Dorovan and Vaelin as if he had forgotten they were with him. "The boy is my ward. I am showing him what it takes to be an errant knight."

"Bit young to have a ward, aren't you?" the other guard asked.

"I look young for my age—at least that's what I've been told," Yugo replied with a self-flattering smile.

"And the gray one?" The guard pointed at Vaelin in distaste.

"She's..." Yugo let the word hang, unable to think of a reason why Vaelin would be with him.

"My sister," Dorovan blurted out.

Vaelin shook her head with a look of embarrassment.

"Of course," Yugo stated, unsure of the lie. "That's my ward's... sister."

"You and the boy may enter." The guard then turned to Vaelin with suspicion. "The... *sister* will have to wait out here."

"Fine by me," Vaelin said. "Be quick about it."

One of the guards opened the iron gate and escorted Yugo and Dorovan through and into the house itself, while the other stayed behind with Vaelin. The main hall was dark, the small windows and the fire in the hearth doing a poor job of illuminating it entirely. Two wide sets of stairs snaked around the hall, leading to the second floor above. In front of the hearth, a woman in scribe's robes was feeding books and loose papers to the flames in a mad frenzy.

Another woman paced across the hall, carrying a crate of papers with her and setting it down in front of the hearth. She was tall and slender and wore riding pants and boots. A pale gray scarf covered her head—not very fashionable, to Dorovan's surprise.

The guard cleared his throat, and the woman in riding clothes started at the sound. "Oh, Pevente!" she exclaimed. "You brought help, thank the gods! Take those two to the office. There's plenty more there."

"No, Lady Amela," the guard replied. "This errant knight has come here to sue for payment on a rescinded contract." Yugo displayed the broken seal upon the contract to punctuate the statement.

Lady Amela looked at it distractedly and then turned back to the hearth, throwing the papers scattered on the floor into the fire. "As you can see I am quite busy. I don't have time for this today."

The guard turned to Yugo and Dorovan and nodded towards the door as if his Lady's word had been final. Dorovan had already seen how Yugo reacted to dismissals, so he braced himself for a possible outburst. Yugo pushed ahead of the guard and walked up to the woman. "I only need your signature right here."

For all her franticness, Lady Amela turned to face Yugo with a startling coldness in her eyes. "And I said I am busy."

The room appeared to grow dimmer to Dorovan. Even Yugo took a half step back at the woman's icy tone, but he quickly steadied himself and unsheathed his usual grin. "It will only take but a moment, my lady."

"Pevente!" the woman called out. "Get the knight and the child out of here!"

The guard firmly grabbed onto Yugo's arm with one hand, drawing his sword with the other. "You heard the lady," he said.

Yugo slammed his armored elbow into the guard's gut, sending him doubling over to catch his breath. "Looks like I was wrong, Dorovan. An important rule to remember is that matters are very seldom as simple as they appear." Yugo unsheathed his sword and pointed it at the coughing guard. The woman in the scribe's robes dropped several sheets of paper with a high-pitched yelp. Lady Amela ran quickly into a room on the other side of the hall, slamming the door shut behind her.

Things were happening around Dorovan so fast that he was not able to comprehend his own actions. "Dorovan!" Yugo called out. Dorovan wasn't certain what sort of expression he wore, but whatever it was made Yugo grimace. "Your sword!" Yugo barked.

Dorovan clumsily unsheathed his sword with his left hand and stared at it—the prospect of actually using it for any reason made the weapon feel entirely foreign in his hand.

"Keep an eye on him," Yugo commanded. "I will procure that signature." There was something about the way he smiled when he said those words that raised the hairs on Dorovan's arms. Yugo ran up to the door of the room where the noblewoman hid. He tried for the handle but the door was locked from within. He slammed his heavy armored boot into the door, smashing clean through it. The knight withdrew his leg, then rammed the door with his shoulder—the door gave way instantly.

As Yugo vanished into the room, Dorovan realized he had been distracted away from the guard he was meant to be watching. He faced the man, but it was too late: sheets of parchment and papers glided through the air blocking Dorovan's view. It took a moment for him to understand that the guard had furtively picked up the nearby crate and tossed its contents into the air.

Before the last of the papers had landed on the marble floor, the guard had the tip of his sword pointed at Dorovan's jaw. "Drop it!" he commanded. Dorovan threw his sword at the guard's feet. The guard sent the sword sliding away towards the far end of the hall with a kick.

"What's going on here?" The other guard appeared at the door, his sword drawn. Vaelin stood beside him, shaking her head—Dorovan couldn't tell if her disappointment was aimed at him or the guard. Knowing her, it was probably both.

"Watch the boy!" the guard commanded. "The knight is after Lady Amela!"

At that moment, Yugo returned to the main hall, rolling up the contract parchment and placing it into his chest plate. It was as if Dorovan had vanished, as the guards' attention was diverted entirely to the errant knight. They approached him, swords drawn. Yugo stretched his arms up toyingly. "No need for aggression, you two. I got what I came for, and now I'll be on my way."

Yugo took a few steps forward, but the two guards closed in on him. "I don't think so," one of the two said. "You're in deep shit barging in like you did, breaking property, and attacking a noblewoman. The Noble Council will have your head!"

"Errant knights aren't immune to the law," the other guard added for good measure.

"Dear guards, if you check on your mistress in the other room, you will find her maybe a bit shaken, but wholly intact."

"Lady Amela!" the guard called out. "Are you all right?"

No reply. In the time that it took the two guards to glance at each other and then back at Yugo, the knight's sword was already in his hand. In another breath, the sword had already sliced through the right shoulder of one of two guards—Dorovan could have sworn he saw a flash of white flame upon impact. Yugo extracted the sword with ease and turned to slice at the other guard, who managed to parry his attack. The guard's sword bent from the impact.

Dorovan watched the scene in utter disbelief. Yugo had gone from the ideal of what Dorovan had thought a hero was supposed to look like to... a madman.

Vaelin unsheathed her dagger and bolted towards Yugo and the struggling guard. She shoved the guard aside—the poor man fell to the floor in a daze—and lifted her black blade to meet Yugo's. The sword rang acutely against the dagger, like a ship's bell. Both Yugo and Vaelin's eyes widened in confusion.

"Enchanted blade?" Vaelin asked.

"Of course," Yugo replied, his brow furrowing. "After losing the royal melee I vowed to never be surprised like that again. Though, you seem to hold a few surprises of your own." Yugo swung his sword at Vaelin, the heat from his enchanted blade caressing Dorovan's face. Though her dagger was much smaller than his sword, she parried the blow as if it were nothing. "Why did you attack me?" Yugo asked. His teeth were gritted behind the smile he wore.

"You attacked me, just now," Vaelin smirked. "I was simply stopping you from killing these men. Dorovan," she called out to him. "Go check on the noble lady." Dorovan snapped from his daze and ran towards the smashed door across the hall, if only to leave the violent scene behind him.

The small disheveled office was eerily silent, so much so that Dorovan could hear his own blood pumping in his head. Tomes and ledgers had been pulled from the shelves that lined the opposite wall, their pages ripped out. Lady Amela sat on a small leather couch, her back turned to Dorovan. Her hand was firmly pressed against her cheek, as she sobbed.

"My lady," Dorovan said quietly. At the sound of his voice, the noblewoman turned towards him with a start. Her tear-stained cheek had swollen where she had been struck by Yugo. Dorovan backed away into the main hall, preferring the violence out there to the crying woman's accusatory eyes.

"So?" Vaelin asked. She stood a few feet away from Yugo, who circled her like a hungry wolf, the sword glinting in his hand.

"She's hurt," Dorovan said. "I think he struck her."

Yugo smirked. "So? She's a noblewoman. She'll put some cool gold pieces against the bruise and the swelling will go down."

To Dorovan's surprise, Vaelin chuckled at that and then returned the dagger to her belt. Yugo lowered his weapon and tilted his head in confusion. "You got what you came for," Vaelin said, moving aside. "There's no reason to keep this up."

"You sure? I'm having so much fun," Yugo said. While his tone was filled with mockery, his face betrayed his relief. Vaelin gestured for the front door, as if guiding a child. Yugo nodded and calmly walked towards the exit, though he kept a firm grip on his sword. Upon passing Dorovan, Yugo winked at him with a wry smile.

Dorovan couldn't believe what he was seeing. This man had wounded a guard and even attacked a noblewoman! This behavior was worthy of legal recourse—surely the djinn could see that.

Vaelin kneeled over the bleeding guard, examining the wound. "Thankfully the sword's enchantment of *Power* seems to have cauterized the wound as it created it," she explained. "Let's see if I can help a bit more."

Vaelin placed her hands over the man's wound. The sudden smell of burned flesh would have been enough to make Dorovan sick had he not already been disgusted by the events that had transpired.

"There," Vaelin said. "The wound is now fully cauterized and you should feel some relief. You may feel some pain in it later tonight, so don't strain it too much!"

The guard seemed to have regained a bit of color to his face. He moved his arm and opened and closed his fist in surprise. "Thank you," he said wearily.

Dorovan gaped at Vaelin, unable to explain how she could have performed such a miracle.

Lady Amela walked out of the room and back to the main hall. Her step was unsteady and her cheek was purple where it had been struck. The uninjured guard hurried to her side and offered his arm. "My lady! I am so sorry. We have failed you."

The noblewoman kneeled and picked up a stack of papers. "We'll deal with that later. Help me with these. That's all that matters now."

The injured guard stood and joined the woman and the other guard in picking up the loose papers and tossing them into the flames of the hearth. Dorovan felt redundant, as if he were an unseen intruder—all things considered, he was. He turned to face Vaelin, but she had already taken her leave. He walked across the hall and picked up his sword, returning it to its place at his hip.

Vaelin stood outside by the front gate, lighting her pipe in the afternoon heat. The sour stench of the smoke reminded Dorovan of a skunk. "Why did you let Yugo go? Shouldn't we have stopped him?" Dorovan inquired.

"Because he did what he came to do," Vaelin replied, blowing a cloud of smoke around her head.

"So what?" Dorovan asked, heat rising in his cheeks. "He struck a noblewoman! And almost cut her guard in half."

"Who unsheathed their sword first, Yugo or the guard?"

"The guard, I guess. But only because–"

"That gave Yugo recourse to defend himself."

"But he struck a noblewoman!" Dorovan repeated, indignantly. How was this djinn not understanding the wrongness, the arrogance, of that action?

"He struck a rich person who had scammed a peasant out of their livelihood," Vaelin said as if it was obvious.

"He also kicked the banker when we were inside," Dorovan added.

"The entire thing could have been handled with a bit more finesse, but ultimately Yugo did what was necessary to sue the lady for reimbursement."

Dorovan shook his head. The smoke and heat of the sun made him feel sweltering. Nobles didn't scam peasants! That just wasn't a thing that happened. Nobles didn't need to scam anyone!

Again, the image of Lady Lenora's predatory smile flashed through his mind. He hadn't been scammed by her, not truly at least. She had merely invited him to a test of skill. The one who had lied to him about being qualified for such an event was only himself.

"You don't seem to agree," Vaelin remarked. "How would you have dealt with the situation? And I don't mean Dorovan, the flustered boy. I mean Dorovan, the hero."

"I–" Dorovan began, then stopped to think. What would he have done? Would he have just let the noblewoman escort him out of her home without making further demands? "What would *you* have done?" Dorovan asked when he couldn't conjure a satisfying answer.

Vaelin emptied her pipe of the bits of ash that remained within, placed it into her satchel, and then started down the road away from the Pottara home. Dorovan followed. "A hero always seeks to do what's right—always strives for justice," she began. "The noblewoman must pay for the damages to the tavern, that much is obvious. It's the path to justice that is not always so clear." Vaelin sized Dorovan up and down quizzically. Dorovan noticed that was a thing she did when she was about to test him. "Tell me, what did you notice about Lady Amela? Anything out of the ordinary for a lady to be doing in her home?"

"Well, she was burning all of those papers," Dorovan answered.

"Yes. Did you take a look at any of the pages scattered about?" Vaelin asked.

"I— No, I did not."

"Had you been a bit more observant, you would have noticed that those documents were almost all ship ledgers." Vaelin paused. Dorovan waited for the djinn to continue, but something in her words stood out. Vaelin smiled at seeing the realization on his face.

"Could this have something to do with the Blue Scarabs and the port?" Dorovan asked.

"Right on target, Dorovan."

Dorovan blushed at the unexpected compliment—he immediately regretted doing so.

"Not to speculate too freely, but I assume Lady Amela has been scamming more than just tavern owners. Whoever it was she was scamming, she is deeply afraid of being found out. Now, Dorovan, did you notice anything else about Lady Amela? Anything else that stood out to you as strange for a noblewoman?"

Dorovan replied immediately, "She was wearing clothes made for riding horses, rather than a gown."

"Again, you are precisely correct. Why would a noblewoman wear riding clothes in her own home while burning evidence of her crimes?"

"She intends to flee." The realization hit Dorovan like a cold slap. Lady Amela truly was a scammer. "I don't understand. Why would a noblewoman need to scam a peasant?"

Vaelin chuckled. "Heroism isn't the only way to gain nobility, Dorovan." The way she said it, like a sister scolding her little brother, irritated him. But the djinn was right—Lady Amela, like those others, didn't deserve the nobility bestowed upon her. The Pottara family was tainted by crooks. "So, I ask you again, how would Dorovan the hero have handled that situation?"

"Call the Blue Scarabs and have them arrest Lady Amela?"

"No need to call the Blue Scarabs. If Lady Amela's hasty actions and outfit are any indication, the Blue Scarabs are already on their way."

Dorovan shrugged. "I give up. What's the answer?"

"Unfortunately, Dorovan, there is no clear answer. A hero can have a strict moral code they adhere to, but ultimately it all comes down to the choices they make at the moment they are presented. While getting that tavern owner their money back is the heroic thing to do, Yugo's choices left a lot to be desired."

"You're just talking in circles, making it sound like being a hero is both the most obvious and most contradicting thing." To Dorovan's further irritation, Vaelin smiled knowingly at his words.

"All right," the djinn said, halting abruptly. "I will stop speaking in circles. Had I been contracted to perform this job, I would have started by bribing the banker to break the seal—knowing that they are already susceptible to bribes—either by finding out something about them they don't wish others to know or by learning their price. Then I would have gone to the Pottara home and, being faced with the situation we saw inside, I would have allowed the guards to escort me out. I would have then sought the house's stables, cut their horses loose, and moved them to another location, to prevent the lady's escape. I would then await the lady at the empty stables."

Vaelin paused momentarily, allowing Dorovan to see where the thread of her story led. "Once there, I would again approach the lady with the contract: her signature in exchange for her horse's whereabouts. As we've seen, the lady is quite frantic, so I am quite certain she would sign. I would then lead her to her horse—"

"—and watch her ride off?" Dorovan interrupted. "What about the ship ledgers and the Blue Scarabs?"

"The Blue Scarabs may not be that different from Yugo. Their justice isn't my justice. In this scenario I was contracted to seek reimbursement for the tavern owner, not to have the lady arrested for her crimes against an army to which I bear no allegiance and, frankly, do not trust."

Strangely enough, those words made sense to Dorovan. "We have no way of making the noblewoman pay for every one of her scams," he said. "What matters is making her pay for the one we are aware of."

Vaelin looked at Dorovan with a surprised expression. A wise smile brightened her eyes. "I think we've earned ourselves a drink," she said.

XV.

EXTRANSFORIAL ETCHINGS

Renna's flesh prickled in anticipation. She was seated at the center of a small room tucked within the belly of the Blue Scarab lodge. The flickering candlelight cast unsteady shadows around the otherwise empty room. What was about to happen here would be the culmination of all of her recent studies. She didn't remember much of her meeting with the master—the particulars had vanished from her mind like an early morning dream—but what had remained was a drive the likes of which she had never felt before. Discovering the many properties and applications of *Transference* and *Binding* had become an obsession.

She had immersed herself in Toropanese writings. It was unclear why, but the Toropanese seemed to have built their entire culture around *Transference*. They even believed that if the family of the deceased covered the funeral pyre with runestones of *Transference* placed in a spiral shape, the soul of their loved one would be shifted into another being.

Whether the *Transference* of a person's soul was possible or not, the crowning achievement of Toropanese enchanting was what they called Extransforial Etching. Toropanese enchantresses imported black earth from the

Womb of the World—the great mountain where all of *life energy* was said to have originated—and used it to create runestone etchings beneath their skin. Because of the enchanting properties of black earth, this created a direct link between the person and *life energy* itself. It was said that Extransforial Etchings removed the need for chanting. The possibilities that opened were immense.

Thus, Renna found herself sitting in this room, waiting to receive her own Extransforial Etching. The Etcher, as they were called, was an old woman with swirling tattoos weaving up and down her dark arms. It had been surprisingly difficult to convince her to etch Renna. She had insisted that to be Etched, one must complete some sort of initiation or ritual intended only for her folk. Thankfully, the woman was in dire need of coin so she could go visit her ill son in Landsmeet. Otherwise, Renna wasn't sure they would have been able to compel her without resorting to force.

The Etcher sat on the cold stone floor while whispering the seven chants over a small sack of black earth. Her eyes were shut tightly, creasing her already wrinkled face. Once finished, she started over again, repeating each chant six more times. It was unclear why she chanted, as the Etchings upon the woman's arms should have removed their need. Renna surmised it had more to do with ritual than necessity.

From her sleeve, the Etcher produced a small vial of clear liquid. She uncorked the vial and drank its contents—no, she swished them in her mouth and then spat them back into the vial. She pinched a bit of black earth and placed it into the vial before recorking it. She shook the vial vigorously for quite some time until the black earth and the liquid were fully mixed. She then retrieved a gold needle from a pocket at her chest. The woman stood slowly, her joints cracking like kindling, then made her way towards the candle that lit the room. She heated the needle, then placed its tip into the vial.

Renna had been told not to utter a word, but she was bursting with questions. She wanted to know the ins and outs of every aspect of this enchantment. All she could do was watch attentively—perhaps then she would be able to replicate it and Etch upon someone else.

The woman walked over to Renna and, without warning, began the Etching. Pain sprouted up Renna's arm as the woman poked the hot needle into her flesh. Beads of black and red peppered the areas where the woman pricked. The entire Etching lasted well over two hours. By the end of it, Renna's arm felt like it was on fire—sharp ghost needles marched from her shoulder to her wrist like ants.

When the Etching was finally completed, the Etcher nodded emotionlessly at Renna, then placed the gold needle over the flame again. "It is done," the woman said, returning the needle to her sleeve. She then kneeled over the open sack of black earth on the floor and fastened its strings. The woman reached into her other sleeve and pulled out a handkerchief. She handed it to Renna, who used it to wipe the blood and earth from her arm.

"Make sure to bandage your arm and use enkroot extract or any other herbs to stave off infection on it twice a day, for at least the next month," the woman said.

"Thank you," Renna accepted, genuinely.

The Etcher stared at her blankly. Unexpected grief bloomed in her eyes. "Nothing to be thanked for. I have betrayed my people's secrets. I am the bearer of great shame." With that, the woman picked up her sack and walked to the iron door. She knocked twice and the door was opened by a Blue Scarab on the other side, who then escorted the Etcher out.

Renna remained seated, looking over the fresh dark spiraling etchings that climbed her arm. It was strange how unrecognizable her limb looked with just a few added drawings. Did she feel any different? Not really, which was disappointing. She had expected to feel *life energy* coursing through her body, yet no such feeling was apparent. Had the Etcher done something incorrectly? Was the ritual the woman had mentioned actually required for the Extransforial Etching to take effect? Renna would have to perform an enchantment to test it out.

She reached into her pocket—ever since the attack on her people, she always kept a runestone of *Life* there. She held the purple runestone in her fingers. The pulsating *life energy* within runestones had always reminded her of the distant rustling of wind through trees, but this felt... different somehow. It wasn't a distant sound at all—Renna felt the runestone *speaking* to her. No, not quite speaking, but it did have a sort of voice. It sounded gentle, like a parent encouraging their toddler to walk. Renna touched the triangle etching of *Life* on the runestone and pulled at it with her own *life energy*.

Suddenly, the etching cracked. But the essence of *Life* that was within the runestone hadn't been returned to the Cycle—while Renna couldn't see it, she could feel it hovering in the air right in front of her. Releasing the essence from a runestone was something that should have only been possible through rigorous enchanting, yet Renna had simply willed it. She felt the essence of *Life* enter her—invade her. A dull, discomforting pain sat within her like a new organ straining to fit where it was never meant to be. She focused her attention on the pain in her arm and directed the essence of *Life* into it. Immediately, her arm felt soothed, and the pain of holding the energy disappeared.

The Extransforial Etching had worked. Renna now possessed a direct link to *life energy*. But the sensation that accompanied it would take some getting used to. The excitement that she suddenly felt made her laugh loudly. A Blue Scarab soldier entered the room. "Are you all right?" she asked.

Renna felt slight embarrassment at being caught laughing, but that feeling was immediately superseded by her bright excitement. "I am better than all right," Renna said, standing from the chair and leaving the room. She wanted to skip down the hallways like a child, but she maintained her composure.

Captain Velden was waiting in her office, leafing through Renna's notes. She felt a slight rush of panic—her notes were a mixture of enchanting observations, personal anecdotes, and original poetry. Not all of it was meant for prying eyes. "Captain Velden," she said immediately, hoping the man hadn't seen too much. "What brings you here in the middle of the day?"

Captain Velden looked up from the notes with a warm smile. "I was simply too eager to hear about this experiment of yours. So, tell me, how did it go?"

Renna pulled back her sleeve to show the man the Etching. Captain Velden leaned forward to inspect it, his face like a boy analyzing a shiny insect. "It's quite striking," he marveled. "Does it work?"

Renna removed the runestone of *Life* from her pocket and handed it to Captain Velden. "I managed to release that runestone's essence without enchantment."

Captain Velden observed the now gray runestone, but it was clear from his expression that he wasn't sure what it meant. "How does a spent runestone help us?"

"It's not spent," Renna corrected. "With this Etching, I was able to release the runestone's essence without chanting or performing any sort of ritual and utilize its power by holding it within myself. The applications for this are numerous. I may be able to perform enchantments much faster and without the need for enchanted materials."

Captain Velden nodded to himself, unable to conceal the apparent worry that lined his forehead. "Do the Toropanese know of these applications?"

"Possibly, but they seem to only use Extransforial Etchings for cultural reasons, such as ceremonies and the like."

"Good," the man said, still preoccupied. "What is the next step, then?"

"The next step?" Renna asked.

"In what way will you use what you have learned to further our cause? I need to know that your time and our resources are being well utilized. Our activities in Sol Forne are starting to require as many hands as we can get. The nobility is sending emissaries out to hire mercenaries from surrounding villages. I can think of several other uses for you."

"You don't think it will come to battle, do you?" Renna asked.

"You worry about your work, and I will worry about the nobles."

Renna disliked the way Captain Velden spoke at times. He could be encouraging one moment, and entirely patronizing the next. She sighed. "I have a few ideas."

Captain Velden nodded and turned to leave. "Please put your ideas in writing and submit them to me by week's end. I shall evaluate your report and choose the best course for you."

"Why this sudden hastiness?" she asked, immediately regretting the question.

Captain Velden stopped, then turned slowly. His face was blank but beneath it were tendrils of queasiness. "Because," he started, then sighed. "Because the master is coming here tomorrow to celebrate Leper's Day with us, this time in the flesh."

A sharp prong of panic stabbed through Renna's chest. *Tomorrow?* The air in her office felt hot, suffocating. Captain Velden wasn't being hasty without reason. He was hoping to use her to impress their master. Renna loved to feel needed, but not knowing what she was needed for felt particularly overwhelming.

"I see," was all she could muster.

Captain Velden placed his hand on her shoulder. Suddenly, he was back to his warm and encouraging self. "Do not dwell on it. The master is a great and patient man. Whatever ideas you have on how to use these Etchings, I am sure he will find a good application for them."

Renna nodded, a bit surer of herself. Captain Velden released her shoulder and left the room without another word. Renna looked down at the spiraling shapes that covered her swelling, irritated, arm. Somehow, she knew that they were a key—but a key to what, she wasn't quite sure yet. *No use in being idle*, she thought. *Time to work.*

XVI.

Leper's Day

After drinks and a meager meal of boiled sausages purchased from a peddler, Vaelin discovered there were only two coins remaining in the emergency stores hiding in the lining of her clothes. She placed the two coppers in a delighted beggar's cup. It was certainly time for her to replenish her funds. She sat on a bench and removed a small journal from her satchel, its pages a blotted yellow-brown from age, and began to flip through it, stopping only when she reached a header marked "Sol Forne." Of the eight caches she had hidden in the city over the years, only two remained uncrossed.

Vaelin sighed. *Due Tower or the port. Not the most auspicious of choices.*

"What are you reading?" Dorovan asked, hovering over her.

Vaelin closed the journal. "A list of locations where I've hidden pieces about the world. When you get to be my age it's good to have written reminders—not that you'll ever get to be my age."

"Pieces? You mean you've got coin just lying about the world and you still choose to wear *that?*" The boy sounded astonished.

"I just so happen to like what I'm wearing. It's comfortable and it makes movement easy. I don't dress to please anyone but myself. Besides, coin isn't everything. Sure, you can use it to buy good wine, but a good conversation is often free of charge and just as satisfying." Vaelin returned the journal to her satchel and stood. "I think our best bet is the cache I left at the Due Tower," she said. "The port is crawling with Blue Scarabs and I'd rather stay away, at least so long as I have the option."

"The Due Tower is quite a ways from here," Dorovan said.

"The walk will do us some good. We may even encounter someone in need of heroics along the way." *And the sooner I am rid of you the better,* she added mentally. Vaelin did not wish to admit it to herself, but she had begun to feel the unwelcome tug of the Compulsion. Ever so slightly, its slimy voice beckoned her to give in and give up. She would need to fulfill this Contract as soon as possible. At this rate, she would only last one more week, or two at the most, before succumbing.

As they walked northeast through the city, towards the Due Tower, Dorovan stopped abruptly and pointed to an alleyway headed in an entirely different direction. "This way is better," he said

"Are you certain?" Vaelin asked.

"How long did you say it has been since you were here last? The city has most likely changed since then. Believe me, this way is better."

Vaelin wasn't so certain but she acquiesced and followed the boy. The alleyway narrowed around them and darkened as they continued along, the tall buildings bending at an angle and obscuring the sky above them. The muck-drenched marble streets were cracked and in disrepair. Dorovan led the way by walking quickly and with intent, his head downcast. It was obvious something about this route made the boy uncomfortable.

Dorovan suddenly bolted and ducked behind an empty rain barrel. Vaelin's hand instinctively hovered over Vitra, although she didn't notice anything amiss around them, only a young woman and a colorfully dressed older man walking past.

"What is it?" she asked the boy.

Dorovan peeked out of his hiding place and then continued to lead the way as if nothing had happened.

"Are you going to explain yourself?" Vaelin asked as she caught up to him.

"It's nothing," Dorovan dismissed.

"Are you certain? You seem distressed, like a cat in a dog kennel."

"Do you want to go to the Due Tower or not?" Dorovan exclaimed, his face doing an impression of a sunset. The boy truly wore his emotions on his cheeks.

"Very well," Vaelin replied. Dorovan guided her silently. The alleyway eventually split in two. On one side, the path opened up into the plaza they had crossed earlier that day. Dorovan halted just before the split and glanced in that direction. At a sudden trot, he took the other path and accelerated his step.

Before following the boy, Vaelin looked out across the plaza. Captain Velden, the Blue Scarab she had met a few days prior, strolled aimlessly with a pleasant smile on his face, his arms clasped behind him.

"Will you hurry?" Dorovan hissed, irritated when she joined him around the corner.

"You sure seem to be hiding a lot today. You know that man?" she asked.

"What man?" he replied, almost too quickly.

"The bald man in the blue armor. One of the Blue Scarab leaders. Captain something."

"Velden. Captain Velden." Dorovan sounded resigned, as if there was no point hiding that he knew of the man.

"You're avoiding him?"

"He desperately wants me to join his Blue Scarabs. Not sure why he keeps pestering *me* of all people."

You are young, desperate, and alone. These sorts of militant groups always prey on the malleable minds of disaffected youths. Vaelin kept the thought to herself. "And you do not wish to join them?"

"Are you kidding? To join their little band I would have to give up my name and title. And shave my head, as if that weren't enough already."

"But you do not have a name or title to give," she said as a matter of fact. To her surprise, Dorovan seemed more hurt than angered by her remark. "You do well not to join them. Groups like those thrive on control. And I don't think you'd look good bald."

Dorovan almost smiled. He carried on at a normal pace, following as the alleyway bent eastward. "He gave you a look earlier," he said.

"Who did?" Vaelin asked.

"Captain Velden. When we were walking through the plaza with Yugo, he nodded in your direction. Have you two met?"

Not exactly a subject Vaelin wanted to broach, especially not with Dorovan. He was far from earning her trust. "He has something that belongs to me. Rather, he knows the person who has it. I am to meet with him tomorrow so I may retrieve it."

"What is this thing you're trying to retrieve?" Dorovan asked.

There was no real harm in telling the boy about the lucerne, but nothing was gained by it either. "It's very personal. Let's change the subject. Why did you hide behind the barrel? Captain Velden was nowhere in sight."

Dorovan sulked. "Perhaps we should walk in silence."

Vaelin smiled. *You keep your secrets and I'll keep mine.*

Past a few older buildings on the outskirts of the city proper, the Due Tower finally came into view. It wasn't tall like the towers in Vizen, but what it lacked in height it made up for in width. One hundred people could stand shoulder to shoulder in a line starting at one end and just barely manage to touch the other. The city hadn't had walls or towers when it stood during the time of the elvenfolk. Those had been built during the civil war some seven hundred years ago, when the kingdom had required defense against itself.

"Well? Where is this cache of yours?" Dorovan asked, crossing his arms.

Vaelin squinted up at the tower. She had caches hidden at several other towers, so she had to straighten them out in her mind. "In the dungeon. No, that was the tower of Vijan in Maegold. In Vizen I hid the cache in the kitchens, so..." Vaelin bit her lip struggling to remember. She placed her hand on the weathered stones that made up the base of the tower. "Oh!"

In the long shadows of the late afternoon, it would be hard to make out, but she clearly remembered marking one of the stones facing eastward. She ran her fingers across the stones, finally touching one at knee level that had a worn carving of a ' *V* 'upon it. Vaelin grabbed onto the stone and pulled as hard as she could. After some slight wiggling, the stone finally budged and slid out. Vaelin reached into the small opening and pulled out a mildewed sack of coins.

"You weren't lying," Dorovan said, eyes wide at the small but full sack.

"Tonight, we shall drink well." Vaelin poured the coins into her coin purse and dropped the frayed sack onto the ground. "It will be dark by the time we reach the inn," she said, mostly to herself—a reminder that tomorrow would be the most important day of her life. And yet, she had not been able to complete her final Contract. For the first time in a while, she was stumped. She had no idea how to make Dorovan a hero. The boy did try—she had to give him that at least. Unfortunately, heroes weren't made of 'at leasts.' She had a sense that he was missing something in his heart.

"Listen," she said, turning to Dorovan. "Tomorrow I must meet with Captain Velden at the Blue Scarab's lodge to retrieve what belongs to me." Dorovan grimaced at that. "You don't have to come with me. I would much rather go alone. Stay at the inn, and I will meet you once I am done." Dorovan agreed with a sigh of relief.

As predicted, it was dark by the time they reached the inn. Along the way, they passed people who had begun to decorate their homes with white tattered sheets hanging from their door frames. Stone circles were set out in the middle of the wider streets in makeshift fire pits.

"Is all this for Leper's Day?" Vaelin asked.

Dorovan nodded.

"I've never heard of this festival. I don't think it was celebrated the last time I was here."

"Years ago," Dorovan began, "even before my parents were born, there was an outbreak of leprosy in Sol Forne. Many died. So the Noble Council rounded up everyone that was afflicted with the disease and their families and burned them in the old city, where the Ederat District now is. The outbreak ended, the city was saved, and now we have Leper's Day. Tomorrow night they will throw those rags into bonfires to ward leprosy from ever touching Sol Forne again."

Vaelin shook her head. "A tragic history repurposed as a celebration."

"It's not a happy story, but many believe that, had the Noble Council not done what they did, the whole city would have died."

"You said they did it where the Ederat now is. Funny how the nobles now live where so many lost their lives at their behest. That's the way of things with humanfolk, you embellish hard truths with festivities. It makes the tragic histories easier to accept—like spicing and salting an undesirable cut of meat."

"It's just a dumb festival," Dorovan said. "Another occasion for everyone to drink more than usual and get into fights."

Even the inn's entrance was covered in tattered white sheets. Dorovan entered, but Vaelin remained outside watching the torn strips sway in the southern evening breeze. She pulled out the bag of herb from her satchel and pinched small amounts of the stuff into the bowl of her pipe—she wouldn't need too much this evening; just enough to take the edge off the pain blooming in her chest.

A dumb festival. She smiled, hoping to have a reason to celebrate tomorrow other than Leper's Day.

As she had hoped, Dorovan decided to remain at the inn the next day. Vaelin suspected the encounter with Yugo and the noblewoman had shaken him more than he wanted to admit. She gave him some pieces to purchase himself some breakfast.

She had barely slept that night due to her fervent anticipation—even wine and herb were of no help—which left her with a nervousness louder than the Compulsion, and a headache to boot. After having a slice of sweet egg bread and a mug of too-bitter orzo coffee, she was quickly on her way.

The last thing Vaelin had wanted was to be under the Compulsion of a Contract when it came time to meet with the leader of the Blue Scarabs. But, today was the day, and Vaelin had yet to turn Dorovan into anything resembling a hero. There was nothing to be done about it now.

Sol Fornians all over the city were dressed in white bandages wrapped around their bodies. In the nearby market many more street vendors were setting up cook pots and grills, and assembling chimneys made of brick for smoking fish and baking pastries. At various booths, artists laid out their brushes and color pallets of sickly shades of gray and green for painting the faces of those celebrating. The festivities hadn't quite begun, yet there was a palpable sense of vibrancy and excitement all about. Maybe Vaelin would be able to join their grotesque celebration if her meeting didn't take long, but there was no point in roasting a rabbit before it was caught.

Few were gathered where the Blue Scarab's lodge was. Those that were there were mostly Blue Scarabs themselves in their customary uniforms. Not one bit of Leper's Day decoration could be seen. A soldier stopped Vaelin at the door. "Woah! That's quite the Leper's Day costume you've got on. It really looks like you're gray and diseased," the man remarked with approval.

"I am here at Captain Velden's behest," Vaelin dead-panned.

"We have many important guests coming today. I don't think—"

"Oh, there you are!" Captain Velden approached the lodge from behind Vaelin and nodded his head in a salute. His tone was filled with anticipation, as if he had been waiting for her for quite some time. The guard at the door saluted with a fist to his chest.

"This is for you." Captain Velden handed Vaelin a small piece of parchment folded in half. "Our master is quite excited to make your acquaintance today."

"What's this?" Vaelin asked, feeling the smoothness of the expensive parchment between her fingers.

"An address and a time. This evening we will be holding a feast there. You, as well as the master, are the guests of honor." Velden looked her up and down. "Please be sure to wear something appropriate."

"Where is the lucerne?" Vaelin asked, annoyed.

Captain Velden smiled sincerely. "The master would like to meet you first. It's not often a being as ancient as the elvenfolk makes itself known."

Vaelin recoiled slightly at that. How much did this man know about her?

"I'm not the person to play this game with," she said, holding out the parchment for Velden to take back.

The captain did not budge. "We would never dream of wasting your time," he said. "Now, if you'll excuse me, I have many preparations to make. I will see you this evening and introduce you to the master personally."

Vaelin grabbed the man's collar. "Give me what I came for!" she barked.

The guard at the door quickly unsheathed his sword and moved towards them. Captain Velden held up a hand to stop him. "I expected you to be more patient than this." The man smiled in an attempt to diffuse the tension. When Vaelin did not reciprocate, he sighed. "What you've been hoping to find will be there. You have my word."

Vaelin wanted to punch the man in his smiling mouth, but, looking in his eyes, she could tell he would yield nothing further to her from either pleading or violence. If they were going to force her to play this game after all, she would not allow them to set the rules. She was going to ruin this feast.

Vaelin let go of Captain Velden's collar and turned to leave. "Be punctual," the man called out behind her.

❧ ❧ ❧ ❧

"Back so soon?" Dorovan had barely finished breaking his fast on sweet egg bread and orzo coffee when Vaelin walked through the door. "Did you find your... thing?"

Vaelin sat across from him, distractedly fingering a small piece of paper. "I've been invited as a guest of honor at a feast this evening." She made the words 'guest of honor' sound sickening. Dorovan brooded with envy, but he did his best to not let it show. "A feast doesn't sound so bad," he said.

"They want me to dress appropriately," Vaelin spat.

Dorovan couldn't help but chuckle at the djinn's dismay. "As they should. If this is an event attended by the noble class, it's obvious you are expected to show some sort of decorum. Those clothes of yours are an eyesore."

To Dorovan's surprise, Vaelin looked hurt. "This is no good. I am not certain another day away from your Contract will do me—do us—any good. I am already feeling myself slowly slip away, like climbing a mountain of gravel."

Dorovan found himself with no words to respond. He felt partly guilty for not being able to complete this damned Contract. At the same time, he blamed the djinn for her inability to make him a hero. For someone so old and so boastful of her experiences, Vaelin seemed entirely inept. Either the teacher couldn't teach, or the student couldn't learn. Or, perhaps, they were both at fault.

Maybe now it was finally time to worry. He was just as much at risk of wasting away as the djinn.

"Where is this feast going to be anyways?" Dorovan asked, mostly to break the silence. Vaelin handed him the small note. His eyes widened when he read its contents:

House Salviati - seven o'clock.

His face must have turned green by the way Vaelin looked at him. The name was enough to conjure a myriad of emotions, from anger to envy to disgust, all at once.

"You know that name, don't you?" Vaelin inquired. "What can you tell me about this House?"

What was there to say—that the young lady of this House had humiliated him publicly, costing him his pride and his fingers? "They... they're the richest House in the city."

"Anything more?" Vaelin pried. He could tell that she knew he had more to say. Those black eyes studied him closely.

Dorovan shook his head with intensity. "They're not good people."

Vaelin chuckled. "By now it should be clear to you that few of these nobles are." Vaelin slapped the table as she stood. "Seems I must find myself a gown, then. I will return tonight after this banquet."

Dorovan's body felt heavy, yet his hands light and useless as he watched the djinn head out from the tavern. He had felt the same way the previous day, when he had caught sight of Ensa walking towards him accompanied by an ostentatious and colorfully dressed man—and then again when he had seen Captain Velden in the plaza. Even earlier, when he had watched Yugo assaulting the guards, he had felt frozen in place like a craven statue. People threw around words like "coward" lightly—he had been called the word a few times himself—but was this what it felt like to truly *be* one?

He sickened himself. The problem was him, not the teacher. This wasn't how a hero was meant to behave—

where simply reading a name would strike him with paralyzing fear.

Dorovan watched Vaelin walk further into the street outside, the door to the inn slowly closing. Before it could completely shut, Dorovan ran up and stopped it with his foot. *What am I doing?*

Among all of the dark, sinking, thoughts of fear and doubt, he had found a beacon of certainty—a willingness to learn, Vaelin had called it. Perhaps it was time to make that a reality. If his cowardice was holding him back from becoming a hero, the time had come to face it.

"Please," he begged Vaelin when he reached her across the street. She looked at him in confusion. He licked his dry lips before continuing. "Please, take me with you."

He expected Vaelin to deny him, but instead, her eyes softened and she nodded. "We will have to find some clothes for you as well, and get you bathed," she said, eying his soiled white shirt. "I won't be the only one made to look appropriate."

The relief Dorovan felt was an ocean breeze in the thick honeyed heat of summer. He suddenly wanted to cry for some reason, but he held in the tears. "I know of a great tailor nearby."

"Lead the way."

Outside his shop, the tailor was wrapping giggling children in tattered strands of white cloth as their wealthy parents looked on in amusement. Upon seeing Dorovan, the tailor's smile quickly faded. Countless times Dorovan had stood in front of his shop, staring at the wonderful clothes he wished he could own. The tailor no doubt assumed he was here once again to loiter about. Then the man's eyes widened—at first from Vaelin's appearance, and then because of the heavy sack of coin in her hand.

"I'd like to purchase something nice for my friend," Vaelin announced. Dorovan was taken aback by the casualness with which she called him "friend."

The tailor was quick to dismiss the children as he led them both into his cozy shop. It was the first time Dorovan had set foot inside the place. The beautiful gowns and suits that lined the walls filled him with an overwhelming sense of anticipation.

"What sort of garment are you looking for?" the tailor asked. Dorovan had never heard him speak so pleasantly.

Dorovan didn't have the faintest idea of how to answer the question. Vaelin jumped in to rescue him from the embarrassment of deafening silence. "We were invited to a banquet. A very formal and... *appropriate* sort of affair." She rolled her eyes loudly.

The tailor moved towards a far wall where several lovely suits of the latest fashion hung. "And what's the occasion?"

"We are to meet someone important at a fancy House. Dorovan, what was the House called again?"

Dorovan's throat felt dry as he uttered the words. "House Salviati."

The tailor laughed as he inspected a purple vest. When his laughter was met with no reaction, the tailor turned to face them nervously. "You're serious? You two? House Salviati?"

"You know the House?" Vaelin asked.

The baffled tailor looked at Dorovan as if to ask, "*is she serious?*" Dorovan shrugged. "She's foreign."

"That much, I gathered. Well, none of this will do." The man waved the suits away as if they were rags. "I have just the thing." The tailor disappeared through a door at the back of the store. A few moments later he returned with the loveliest suit Dorovan had ever seen. With light blue and gold vines climbing up its sides, then blooming into ruffles where they ended at the sleeve, the curd-white suit was everything Dorovan could ever wish for. He reached out and touched it, the delicate velvet material as soft as a lamb's ear beneath his fingers. Filigreed gold buttons shimmered at the cuffs, complementing the swirling metalwork of the buckle for its cream-velvet belt. The pants were similarly embroidered with pleated frillings below the knee.

"A bit gaudy," Vaelin said.

"Gaudy!" the tailor repeated, indignant. "This is my finest work. It incorporates the newest style for men while also adapting centuries of Sol Fornian tradition. You will not find finer work in the city if you paid four times as much."

"What do you think, boy?" Vaelin asked Dorovan. She did not sound convinced.

"It's marvelous." The compliment spilled out of him easily.

The tailor nodded, pleased. "Foreigners could never understand. Come with me, sir." The tailor flashed Vaelin a warning glance, then walked Dorovan to the back of the shop where he could disrobe. The suit fit him surprisingly well, although it was slightly wide at the shoulders and long in the legs. The tailor made a few marks in the suit with needles and then had him change back into his old clothes.

"This feast is tonight, you say? It will cost you," he told Dorovan when they had returned to the main room of the shop.

Vaelin waved the man's words away. "Coin is of no issue. And throw in some pantyhose and a pair of shoes to match."

"Very well," the tailor said, licking his thin lips. "Return in a couple of hours and I will have this fixed for you." To Vaelin he added, "And for you? A gown perhaps?"

Vaelin eyed the colorful gowns that lined the walls with disdain. "Don't worry about me. I have something to wear."

The tailor examined Vaelin's clothes with distaste and a hint of alarm. "I sure hope you do."

After paying the man, they exited the shop. "What's the fastest way to the Academy from here?" Vaelin asked.

❦ ❦ ❦ ❦

Vaelin didn't bother waiting for the clerks at the front hall to acknowledge her; she knew exactly how to reach Cressena's office. Dorovan trailed her—he had the look of someone plucked out of their environment. Students and researchers shot them curious glances, some even seemed startled, but none did anything to halt them. Folk were less likely to stop you when you appeared to know where you were going.

Once she reached the office, Vaelin knocked on the closed door. No response. She reached for the handle, and the door opened. "Stay out here and keep watch. Alert me if anyone comes." Dorovan agreed and Vaelin slipped inside.

To her surprise, while the tomes and papers were still scattered about, many of the crates and artifacts had been removed—no doubt they had been stored elsewhere. Thankfully, the elven gowns were still there. One was draped over a desk while the other hung from a post. On the desk next to the first gown, a book sat open displaying neatly scribbled notes. Vaelin ran her hand across the soft fabric of the gown. This style of dress had commonly been worn by high caste workers of Elren society, such as healers and builders. While its gray color and sleek build would appear plain to a humanfolk, elvenfolk had an appreciation for minimal and comfortable designs.

Vaelin couldn't help but peek at Cressena's notes. The woman had written that because the dress was made out of a type of rare, highly durable, silk, it must have belonged to someone of high status. That was correct, however, she had also noted that because of its plainness it must have belonged to a priestess. It seemed Cressena had missed a crucial feature of the gown. Vaelin reached down its side, running her hand towards where the skirt widened at the hip. There was a slit so well hidden it was almost invisible. A priestess would never wear a dress made to conceal a weapon. No, this gown had not belonged to a healer, builder, or priestess, but rather to a merchant.

Elven cultures had interesting attitudes towards merchants and peddlers. Most saw the prospect of enriching oneself as distasteful since basic necessities were shared and distributed freely from neighbor to neighbor. Markets, where one could find more exotic wares, were often nomadic and restricted to the areas between cities and villages. Those who left cities to make purchases often covered their faces with masks or veils to retain anonymity. Because of this, those who chose to be merchants often concealed weapons to assure that their anonymous clients would not misbehave. The life of an elven merchant was filled with constant threats.

This gown would do nicely. Vaelin pulled it off the post and carried it towards the door. Before she could exit the room, the door opened and Cressena walked in with a startled expression.

"She's coming!" Dorovan yelled, several moments too late. Along with heroism, the boy would need lessons in timing.

"What are you doing here?" Cressena asked, confused.

"I came to see you," Vaelin lied, perhaps a bit too obviously.

"What are you doing with that dress? That's a priceless artifact from—"

"I need to borrow it." Cressena looked at Vaelin as if she were raving. "May I borrow it?" Vaelin amended, hoping that politeness would win her some favor with the woman. "I require it for a banquet tonight. If you allow me to take it, I will teach you everything about it. I will answer any questions you have about any artifact or histories you want."

It shouldn't have been that easy, but by the look on Cressena's face, Vaelin had struck the right chord. "Very well," Cressena said after a few quiet moments. Vaelin ran up to the woman and hugged her tightly. "Thank you so much, Cressena!"

"But please bring it back in one piece," Cressena begged as Vaelin released her. "I'm already in trouble as it is with the Academy Board for letting you into the warehouse."

"I promise I will bring it back," Vaelin said.

Cressena eyed the gown as if already regretting her decision. She quickly moved to the other side of the office, seemingly in an attempt to remove the gown from her sight. Vaelin took it as a dismissal. She exited the office and closed the door behind her.

Vaelin chuckled as she rejoined Dorovan. "Not much of a lookout, are you?"

The boy simply shrugged. "That's what you plan on wearing?" He didn't look all too impressed.

"Isn't it magnificent? The elvenfolk knew how to make something comfortable, useful, and beautiful."

"I wouldn't call it beautiful. It's... very gray. I don't know how they did things back then, but you must have noticed we favor colors in Sol Forne. We like to stand out."

"I have noticed," Vaelin grimaced. At times, the garbs worn by Sol Fornians were indistinguishable from those of the jesters and tumblers of the southern realms. "Maybe I'll stand out by being understated," she said, holding the gown out in front of her. Dorovan eyed it dubiously, but the boy's opinion didn't matter to Vaelin.

Standing out or enjoying the banquet was cursory. All that mattered was getting her hands on the lucerne. The time had finally come.

XVII.

THE BANQUET

The outfit was incomplete without a wig, but Dorovan felt like royalty, nonetheless. Vaelin had paid for him to be freshly bathed at the inn, and his new suit was the most comfortable set of clothing he had ever worn in his life. The alterations made by the tailor were entirely invisible. *So this is what a proper jacket is supposed to feel like?* The only other one Dorovan had worn had been left behind by his uncle after he had abandoned the family, but that jacket had felt more like it was wearing him than that he was wearing it.

It felt uncomfortable to not have his sword but bringing it to the banquet would not have been proper, so he had reluctantly left it at the inn. He had removed the bandage from his left hand, exposing the small cuts left by the djinn's dagger. They were almost unnoticeable, and Dorovan longed desperately to have at least one presentable hand.

Vaelin, on the other hand, looked... well, she looked fine, he supposed. The gown had an interesting shape, a modest square neckline that melted into a captivating texture of overlapping waves that caught the light of the street lamps with the iridescence of fish scales. Beneath it, she resembled a smooth and graceful serpent. He had to admit that it fit her shape quite nicely as if it had been made for someone of her exact stature and build—perhaps all elven-folk had looked the same. That color, though, like a clouded sky just before a Spring rain, was simply too muted and too bland to be in any way interesting. Yet the djinn acted as if it was the most beautiful thing she had ever seen. She was particularly fond of where the skirt widened at the hip for reasons that were beyond him. The only part of her that stood out from the gray of the gown was her wild raven hair, which was barely corralled into a queue by a shimmering silver band.

Despite his imploration, the djinn had insisted on bringing along her horrid satchel. The leather was worn, milky blotches crawling up one side like a pox. The frayed thinner leather at its rim that had once been adornment waved about like a flag of surrender. It clashed egregiously with her gown, yet there it was, hanging limply at her side.

Dorovan knew he had only been invited to this banquet because of her, but he really hoped Vaelin wouldn't embarrass him. He had spent most of his life observing nobles and their habits—he knew how to act properly.

"Are you ready?" Vaelin asked. He wasn't quite sure that he was, but he nodded anyway.

For the first time in a while, Dorovan was genuinely excited to walk through the Plaza d'Edo. To be viewed by other nobles wearing what, to him, was the greatest outfit ever seen in the city was an exciting prospect. And they did draw many stares, although Dorovan was sure they were mostly directed towards Vaelin. The way the colors of her skin and dress meshed was simply unsightly.

The plaza was thrumming with Leper's Day celebrations. Several small unlit bonfires were scattered about, ready to be set ablaze once the evening dark descended. The nobles and the wealthy strolled about with their children, all dressed in tattered bandages, and some sporting sickly face paint. Peddlers sold candied fruit and other treats from fragrant carts, calling out, sweets! sweets! A band of musicians played a merry tune while acrobats tumbled and flipped nearby. It all looked incredibly fun, but Dorovan didn't envy them—had they known where he was headed this evening, he would have been their envy. It wasn't often that even the richest Sol Fornians were invited to a banquet hosted by the Salviati.

A shiver ran down his spine when they finally reached the front gates of House Salviati. The last time he was here was a memory he'd rather soon forget. His missing fingers suddenly itched terribly. He reached mentally for the golden mark in his pocket, hoping to remind himself that he belonged here.

When Vaelin slipped her arm under his, he felt himself blush. "Are you ready?" she asked again. The words did not hold Vaelin's usual determination—it was as if she was asking the question to herself rather than him. Dorovan nodded and tightened his hold of her arm just slightly. She smiled and they both walked towards the gate.

A pristinely dressed man with a face like an elongated gourd unrolled a piece of parchment across a small table when they walked up. "Names?" he asked, his voice booming and loud. At the sight of Vaelin's face, he shook his head disapprovingly. "While it may be Leper's Day, this is a formal dinner. Couldn't you wait until the night was done to join the festivities?"

Vaelin laughed as if the man had said the funniest thing. "Names are Vaelin and Dorovan," she said.

The man's index finger scanned through the parchment, stopped, and then he crossed a name off the list with a pen. "Vaelin, there you are. I don't see a Dorovan. Are you perhaps listed under a House name?"

The question took Dorovan by surprise. He looked down at his clothes, recalling suddenly that he did in fact look like a noble. He must have taken too much time because Vaelin interjected. "He's my guest for the evening."

The man shook his head. "No guests allowed tonight. Only those on the list."

"I'm sure you can make an exception," Vaelin said.

"No exceptions."

Dorovan sighed—he knew this had all been too good to be true.

"Vaelin! You made it!" a familiar voice shouted from the doorway. Captain Velden walked out of the house and joined them by the gate. For the first time, the man was wearing something other than his blue light armor, though the purple velvet suit didn't complement his hardened, old musculature.

Captain Velden shook his head in disbelief at the sight of Dorovan. "My boy! What are you doing here looking like... like a proper lord!" There was a hint of jest to the small bow he gave. The suit Dorovan wore suddenly felt too tight at the neck and shoulders—suffocating. The getup stiffened with each heartbeat. He wasn't sure if it was from nervousness or embarrassment.

"This man said there are no guests allowed," Vaelin explained.

"This is quite the privileged event," Captain Velden said, with a hint of distaste. "But I'm sure we can make an exception for Dorovan, here."

The doorman rolled up the parchment and sighed, irritated. "Of course, Captain. Whatever you say." By his tone, it was clear this had only been one of many changes the captain had requested.

"Splendid!" Captain Velden exclaimed. "Come, come." He waved them towards the front door of the large house and led them inside.

The Salviati home was impeccably decorated. The foyer had a splendid silver chandelier overhead that looked like the nest of a large bird. A beautiful long rug threaded in gold split in two, leading towards the two different wings of the building. Not a single Leper's Day decoration adorned the home. Two servants stood at the entrance taking coats and purses from the guests to be stored away safely. One of them reached for Vaelin's satchel, but Vaelin held it close to her chest as if it was the greatest of treasures. Dorovan looked away from the scene to spare himself the embarrassment.

Following Captain Velden, the left-hand path opened wide into a high-ceilinged ballroom. The fresco painting that covered the length of the ceiling gave Dorovan the impression that he was looking up into the open sky at sunset. Several people were already inside: nobles mingled while sipping sweet wine and snacked on small morsels brought to them on silver platters by well-dressed servants, while a band of musicians at the far end of the hall played a soft and airy piece.

A servant approached them with a tray of wine glasses. Vaelin selected a glass and took a delighted sip. The servant watched her, silently horrified. Dorovan took a glass as well and sipped at it—smooth and sweet, it was the best wine he had ever had. The servant walked off to tend to the other guests, but his eyes dwelled on Vaelin for a few moments more. Several of the other servants and guests had taken great note of their entrance. Many whispered among themselves, their secretive glances betraying the subject of their conversation.

"Shall we mingle?" Vaelin asked in a joking manner.

"I'd rather not," Dorovan replied. "I don't care for the nobility of this city."

"And yet you wish to join them."

Dorovan nodded at himself. "To show a better way of being noble."

Vaelin smiled. She almost looked proud. "Let's see if they have any olives and bread to go with this wine." Dorovan followed Vaelin up to a nearby table covered in a glittering silver cloth. Several silver trays and bowls were scattered about filled with olives, nuts, jams, fish roe, and much more. Flowering vines snaked between the dishes, giving the table a natural and organic appearance.

Chewing on a handful of date-stuffed olives, Dorovan glanced around the room. The other guests seemed so at ease, as if they came with the decor. He, on the other hand, felt entirely foreign—a rat in the royal kitchen. Thankfully, not every guest had that same relaxed air about them: on the opposite side of the room stood a young woman in a bright purple gown, an embroidered plum scarf intricately braided within her hair. Dorovan swallowed the olive entirely before he could chew it.

He had never seen his sister Ensa look so elegant. So noble.

A brightly dressed older man stood next to her, cupping her hands like a grandfather comforting his granddaughter. It was the same man Dorovan had seen walking beside his sister earlier that day near the plaza. The man said something and Ensa covered her mouth to stifle a laugh. It was all too surreal. Ensa then looked around the room, her eyes landing on him. Immediately, Dorovan turned and faced Vaelin. He could feel red heat searing his face.

What was his sister doing here—she who had wanted nothing to do with nobility? The betrayal that overtook him was unwarranted, though it felt right.

"Attention," a man called out from the opening that led to the adjacent room. Dorovan recognized the red-wigged man as the same that had let him into the Salviati home for his last unfortunate visit. "Dinner will be served momentarily. Please head to the dining room and you will be guided to your seats." The guests trickled into the other room with feigned nonchalance—excited wolves acting as placid sheep. Dorovan and Vaelin trailed behind the buzzing crowd.

The longest table Dorovan had ever seen filled the dining room. While there were about fifty or so guests at this very exclusive banquet, the table could have easily accommodated fifty more. Three large plants that Dorovan had never seen before, whose pale foliage shot up into the air like fountains, were evenly spaced across the table, lending an extra sense of height to the room. Several servants lined the far wall of the space, standing by to tend to the guests' needs.

The red-wigged man stood by the foot of the table, guiding the guests to their seats. More than once, guests that thought themselves more important than they were protested at being placed too far from the head or too close to someone they despised. Despite their objections, all of them took their assigned seats in the end.

"So you're the famed Vaelin," the red-wigged man said sarcastically when it was finally their turn to be seated. He didn't seem very impressed by either of them. His eyes lingered on Dorovan, and for just a moment Dorovan thought he felt recognition in that gaze. But then, the man pointed at the two seats on the left closest to the head of the table and said, "For the guests of honor." Vaelin took the one closest to the head, Dorovan the next seat down. To his chagrin, Captain Velden took the seat to his left.

"The servants here made such a big fuss about us needing to move one seat down to make room for you, boy," Captain Velden said, amicably. "I told them there was no need to get upset. You're of noble blood, are you not?"

Dorovan felt sickened by the question, yet he found himself nodding regardless.

Renna, the bald enchantress, entered the room and sat to Captain Velden's left. She wore an unflattering narrow blue gown with long sleeves and a high neckline that hid all of her womanly features. Along with her shaved head and eyebrows, she appeared neither man nor woman. Renna glanced at Dorovan and smiled courteously, albeit briefly— while Captain Velden didn't seem bothered by having been moved down one seat to accommodate Dorovan, Renna, on the other hand, didn't seem at all pleased. She whispered something into Captain Velden's ear that made the man's forehead crease.

About halfway down the table and across from him, Dorovan saw Ensa take a seat along with her escort. The man must have been a minor noble of some repute to secure such a spot. He seemed abuzz with excitement—a feeling Ensa didn't seem to share. He cracked jokes, making the people around them laugh, yet Ensa's eyes seemed distant, as if she was puzzling something out. Dorovan pushed his chair slightly away from the table, hoping that would make him less noticeable to her.

What couldn't be helped, however, was who sat directly across from him.

Lady Lenora ca'Salviati looked just as beautiful as he remembered. Her royal purple dress covered in shimmering gemstones paled in comparison to her lovely face. An amethyst-colored scarf with swirling floral patterns drawn in violet sapphires framed her face like petals. She was radiant, glowing. Dorovan wished her every ill he could conceive. Next to Lady Lenora sat her mother, Lady Elma. The woman was handsome rather than beautiful—but even if she had been beautiful, that beauty would be a candle next to the sun that was her daughter. Blue scarab brooches were pinned at their breasts. While Lady Elma's orange gown complemented the brooch nicely, Lady Lenora's did not— as if it had been picked for the sole purpose of creating an unpleasant contrast.

Dorovan had been aware of the inevitability of this encounter, yet the sight of the young woman settled in his stomach like a foul wine. Lady Lenora glanced at him with the inquisitiveness of a fox sniffing out a mole. To his horror, Dorovan met her gaze. Death could not come too soon for him, yet his soul felt encased in his icy body, unable to find sweet release.

"Hello," Lady Lenora said, her sharp inquisitiveness softening into something sweeter. "I am Lady Lenora ca'Salviati. And you are?"

Dorovan stared at the young woman in utter bafflement. Two fingers made of searing fire had sprouted where his missing two had been severed. What sort of game was she playing? By the way her eyebrows narrowed, confused by the lack of a reply, she must have been serious.

"The lady asked you a question," Lady Elma interjected, flaring her nostrils at Dorovan as if to sniff out an intended offense. He could even feel Vaelin's eyes to his left heavy on him, awaiting his response.

"Apologies, my lady," he said, lowering his eyes. *What are you doing? If Lady Lenora truly does not recognize you, then you must meet her gaze. She must think you are some sort of noble to be seated so close to the head of the table.*

Dorovan met the woman's eyes again. He felt a chill attack his chest, but he weathered it. He relaxed his face and said, "I am... Lord Do... Lord Donalo."

The two women glanced at each other and then smiled as if an unspoken joke had passed between them. Their demeanor relaxed. "Pleasure to make your acquaintance Lord Donalo," Lady Lenora replied.

"And from which House are you?" Lady Elma asked.

Dorovan could hear the question behind the question. *What House are you from that you are worthy to sit across from Lady Salviati?* "I am... House..." Dorovan found himself drawing a blank. If he named his actual House, he would be immediately discovered.

Vaelin placed her hand on the table in front of him. "He is Lord Donalo o'Lanthi, from Maegold. We met during my travels up north, where he agreed to be my guide across the southern realms."

The two women donned an identical expression of disgust when Vaelin spoke—they truly were mother and daughter. "Commoners should mind their manners when lords and ladies are speaking to each other," Lady Elma said, looking up at the space just above Vaelin's head. "Even if they are requested near the head of the table by our guest of honor it does not mean I, the Lady of the House, must treat them any better than what etiquette demands." Rather than speaking to the djinn, it was as if she was making a declaration for the table.

Dorovan felt something shift in the air between him and Vaelin—a hot wind rising before a thunderstorm. He would not dare look at her in fear of the defiance he might find on her face. He wasn't sure whether to worry that she would say something to embarrass them or that she would hop over the table and strike the two noblewomen.

Instead, to Dorovan's surprise, Vaelin just sighed and looked away, toward the dining room doors. He couldn't help but feel bad for her. If Lady Elma noticed Vaelin's reaction, she gave no sign of it—to her, calling out the djinn's breach of etiquette was just something that needed to be done. Lady Lenora, on the other hand, took visible pleasure in her mother's admonishing words. *How could someone so beautiful be so... ugly?*

"Have I seen you before, Lord Donalo?" Lady Lenora asked, noticing Dorovan's eyes were on her. "Your face strikes me as familiar."

The burning sensation at Dorovan's missing fingers bit into his tender flesh. He hoped the typical redness that rose in his face when he was uncomfortable did not give him away. "Impossible, my lady, as I've just arrived in the city only a few days ago. And besides, if I had seen you, I would have surely remembered someone so... lovely as yourself—if the Lady of the House permits my forwardness."

Where had that come from? Maybe all the years of jealously observing the city's nobility had finally paid off.

Lady Elma nodded with a slight, pleased smile, while Lady Lenora rolled her eyes sarcastically. "My lord, you flatter."

"Maegold, you say?" Lady Elma asked.

"Aye—yes, my lady," Dorovan replied.

"Yet your accent is quite... local."

"Well, you see, I've lived in Sol Forne for most of my youth. I seem to have adopted the local way of speaking."

Lady Elma raised an eyebrow. A rush of stories and excuses flowed through Dorovan's mind like a raging river—he kept reaching his hands into the water but couldn't pull out a single one. He was fumbling as a fish pulled from the sea and thrust onto a dock.

Everyone at the table stood abruptly, with the exception of Dorovan, Lady Elma, and Vaelin. Lady Elma calmly looked away from Dorovan and towards the entrance at the far end of the hall. At the sight of the two men making their way into the dining room, she stood as well, seemingly forgetting all about Dorovan's interrogation. Dorovan could

barely conceal his relief as he joined those standing, more
to imitate the rest of the guests than to show his respect.
Vaelin remained seated, her face placid and unreadable.

The servant in the red wig cleared his throat. "Announc-
ing Lord Pendro ca'Salviati and his honored guest, Master
Eggar o'Tamiar, have joined the party."

Lady Elma approached her husband and kissed him
gently on the cheek. Lord Pendro ca'Salviati was a tall, wide-
chested man some may dare call beautiful. His light curls
framed a sharp clean-shaven jaw; his skin was like a freshly
varnished boat. He looked and carried himself exactly like
what he was: the most powerful man in Sol Forne. Dorovan
had only seen Lord Pendro once before in the Effore, albeit
briefly and not very clearly, as the lord had been surrounded by his private guard. Now that he got a good look
at him, he understood what the rest of the nobility saw in
their de-facto leader. Lord Pendro was a noble through and
through.

Master Eggar, who followed Lord Pendro into the dining
room, on the other hand, did not look noble in appearance,
but his demeanor was that of someone who had seen his
fair share of banquets. He was somewhere in his mid-twen-
ties, and much too young to be the leader of the Blue Scarabs, Dorovan thought. His obsidian-black hair was long and
smoothly tied behind him, and a thin mustache perched
over his upper lip. He wore a congenial smile as if he was a
father tending to his daughter's wedding guests. He smiled
even wider as Lady Elma placed her arm around his and
led him to the honored spot at the head of the table.

The rest of the present guests held their silence and
watched the two men take their seats. Only when their

bottoms hit the chair did everyone sit down, and Dorovan with them.

Red wig took his place next to the table with hands clasped behind his back. Lord Salviati cleared his throat. "Let dinner be served." Red wig nodded and clapped his hands twice. Scores of servants entered the dining room, placing silver bowls of a blue-green soup in front of each guest. Dorovan eyed his soup inquisitively: he had never seen food of such a color before. There was also no steam rising from the bowl. *A cold soup?* After each guest had been dealt a soup, other servants poured wine from decanters into everyone's cups—starting with the guests of honor.

Dorovan turned towards Vaelin to comment, but her eyes were locked on the man at the head of the table, her expression uncharacteristically severe. Sure, she had been angry and stern before, but this expression held behind it a gravity the likes of which Dorovan had never seen on her. Master Eggar still held a pleasant smile as he reached for his spoon. As he did, everyone else at the table followed suit—while Dorovan knew the ins and outs of how nobles carried themselves publicly, tableside decorum was new to him; he already found it rigid and rather uninviting. The cold soup tasted faintly of cucumbers and herbs—it was decent, but not something he would have ordered for himself. Vaelin ignored the soup and went straight for the wine.

"I forgot how much I enjoy Sol Fornian cuisine," Eggar said, breaking the silence in the room. He raised his glass of wine. "My compliments to the cooks."

"My lord, you flatter," Lord Pendro replied, nodding his glass towards the man.

"Please, call me Eggar. Or master if you prefer. I am no lord."

Lord Pendro seemed at a loss for a brief moment—perhaps he was seeing how the word "master" tasted on his tongue—then smiled and settled on replying, "Many thanks, Eggar," though his tone was tentative.

"Where is the lucerne?" Vaelin interrupted. The almost-tasteless soup slipped down the wrong side of Dorovan's throat. He felt the eyes of the entire room fall upon them in anticipation.

The lord and lady of the house glared at Vaelin murderously. The lady was about to admonish her for the interruption when Eggar suddenly raised his hand. For an instant, Lady Elma seemed to take the gesture as an affront, at least until she remembered who had made it. "Vaelin." Eggar said the word as if it were a greeting rather than a name. "It is my greatest honor to be in your presence. Words cannot describe the pleasure."

"I wish I could say the same," Vaelin retorted. "But your presence is neither pleasant nor is it truly a *presence*, is it?"

Lord Pendro's chair loudly screeched behind him as he stood with all the intensity of a dark storm. "How dare you speak to my guest of honor with such insolence?"

"There, there, Lord Pendro," Eggar said with a chuckle. "She did not mean to offend. Please don't forget that Vaelin should be treated as a guest of honor as well. She brings your House much esteem by gracing it with her presence."

Lord Pendro's eyes jumped from Eggar to Vaelin, to his wife, and then back to Eggar with much bewilderment. He slowly sat back down and took a pull of wine to compose himself. After swallowing he said, "If you say so, Eggar. But who are these two that you made us add to the guest list in such an unorthodox manner?"

"Vaelin is, in my estimation, the longest living creature still alive today." Eggar said the words with such nonchalance that they took a few moments to impress with the rest of the guests. Lord Pendro and Lady Elma shared a glance of equal alarm and confusion and then turned to examine Vaelin as if they could parse something from her features. Lady Lenora's eyes, however, were fixed upon Dorovan—to his horror, he saw recognition in them.

"I don't understand," Lord Pendro said. "You're saying this... woman is the oldest living creature?"

"Those are the exact words I used, aren't they?" For the first time, Eggar's tone betrayed a bite of annoyance.

"Where is the lucerne?" Vaelin asked again, her intensity much less subtle this time.

"That will have to wait, unfortunately," Eggar replied, his face returning to his signature pleasantness. "We haven't even seen what the second course is."

"No!" Vaelin replied, a touch too loudly. The entire room chilled. "I've waited lifetimes already—enough lifetimes to see everyone in this room be born and die twice over. I'm through waiting. Give it to me, now!"

Eggar's smile faded once more. He took a napkin and gently dabbed it over his mouth, though there was nothing there to clean. "I hate to put it so plainly, but you must simply wait your turn."

"Wait my turn? It's mine! Would you tell the lord of this House to wait his turn to use his own chamber pot?" Vaelin asked, slamming her fist onto the table. The nearby glasses rattled anxiously. "Why would you possibly need it?"

Eggar smiled. "Now, that's a good question. What do I intend to do with an ancient artifact that my most trusted enchantresses inform me practically oozes *life energy*? I intend to find out how it works and, when I do, I intend to replicate it."

Vaelin's eyes widened in horror. "Replicate it?" She laughed mirthlessly. "You don't know what you're dealing with. Return it to me this instant! Misusing the lucerne could have catastrophic consequences."

Eggar didn't seem to give Vaelin's concerns any serious weight. "No, I do not intend to misuse it. The enchantresses in my employ are some of the most powerful and knowledgeable in the entire world. I have learned from my mistakes in giving simpletons free rein over my investments. It can, indeed, be quite catastrophic." That last seemed like a declaration made for the entire room.

Lord Pendro cleared his throat. "I hate to steer this... quite interesting conversation elsewhere, but as the lord of this House, I might start taking offense if some items are not discussed first."

Eggar turned towards Lord Pendro, distant annoyance in his eyes. "Very well."

"We must discuss this blockade situation in the port. It simply will not do. The guilds are becoming a nuisance to bribe, and I have many shipments that must leave port as soon as—"

Vaelin stood from the table and reached into the side of her long dress, pulling out her dark dagger. How that had fit in there without leaving a single outline in the thin material, Dorovan hadn't the faintest idea. As fast as blowing out a candle, the blade was at Eggar's neck. Lady Elma screamed in panic while Lord Pendro stood from the table and ran to the other side of the room, calling for the guards. Captain Velden shifted uncomfortably in his seat but did not otherwise make a move. Renna, on the other hand, was already on her feet, one of the decorative table knives in hand.

"I'm done with this farce," Vaelin said. "Return to me what is rightfully mine, else I will slay this body and follow the fading trace of *Transference* you leave behind to wherever you actually are."

Renna quietly asked Captain Velden, "How does she know?"

Several guards ran into the room with drawn swords. "Tell them to stay back, or this vessel dies," Vaelin commanded.

Lord Pendro held his hand up towards the guards, motioning them to keep their distance. The lord demanded, "What does she mean by 'vessel?' And *Transference?*"

Eggar smirked. "I'm afraid she is correct. I was not able to attend this banquet in the flesh, so I have resorted to using an intermediary to stand in on my behalf. I don't mean to offend."

Offended did not even begin to describe the fire-red anger that bloomed in Lord Pendro's face. "You dare use the witches' incantations to appear before me? What sort of insolence is this?" He ripped the blue pin from his chest and shoved it onto the table. "We have been supporting your little militia even through this blasted blockade, and you cannot even dignify us with a real meeting?"

"Our little militia is the future of this country, Lord Pendro. In the end, it will be the only thing standing between you and the complete annihilation of all you hold dear. Never forget that."

Lord Pendro recoiled from the bluntness of those words, but something in them seemed to ring true to him. He nodded and asked, "Shall my guards intervene?" He regarded Vaelin with sudden strange calm, his face losing redness as if a fever had broken.

"No need." Eggar shifted his head slightly to look at Vaelin while avoiding the blade at his neck. "Allow me to save you some trouble, djinn. I am currently in Vizen, comfortably seated in the guest chambers in the fifth ring of the great Royal Tower. The lucerne is on its way to me. It's in a carriage and it left out of the Old Gate not even an hour ago. If you run to it now, you may still catch it."

Vaelin stared into Eggar's eyes, hoping to find a lie in them. Ten heartbeats later, she and the dagger retreated from his throat. "If you are lying, I will kill you. The real you."

"I know," he said.

Vaelin faced Dorovan and nodded. "Let's go."

Dorovan tried to stand, but a hand cemented him to the chair. He looked up and, to his surprise, Renna towered over him, her grip much stronger than he would have imagined. "Dorovan stays here," she said firmly. Both Vaelin and Eggar stared at the bald woman with equally probing expressions. Facing Eggar, Renna continued, "The djinn and the boy are connected. I sense a thread of *life energy* between them, possibly a *Sealing* enchantment. It may be worth keeping them apart for assurance."

"How did you—" Vaelin began to ask, before being interrupted by Eggar. "I told you, I employ the very best."

"Are you going to be all right?" Vaelin asked Dorovan.

He nodded, although he suddenly felt very afraid, partly due to the situation he found himself in, and partly for being reminded of being *Sealed* to Vaelin. If she did not fulfill his Contract, they would both die. As each day passed, this possibility became a more palpable fear.

Vaelin nodded back and then quickly fled the dining room. Dorovan felt a faint tugging towards her, like a longing. He suddenly felt more alone than he had in a long while.

"Well," Eggar said, breaking the silence. "Shall we proceed to the second course?"

XVIII.

SURROUNDED

Bonfires flashed past as Vaelin barreled through the streets of Sol Forne, headed towards the western gate. Her elven-made gown had been sewn for this exact reason, and she couldn't help the small rush of satisfaction she felt at being able to give it purpose. At times, she had to elbow her way past clusters of tightly packed people near the fires. Merriment enveloped her, as lively music and laughter filled the air. Many removed their bandages and cast them into the flames—each time someone did so, the rest of the crowd cheered uproariously. Leper's Day seemed like a great time, but that was not what occupied Vaelin's mind.

The celebrations grew more rambunctious and crowded as she exited the richer districts and crossed those with heavier concentrations of common folk. Several times she bumped into drunk revelers who wanted nothing more than to fight. One even went as far as to grab her arm and pull her aside. She shoved the man to the ground and carried on. It took her a considerable amount of time to finally reach the Old Gate District—more than she had wished.

The western gate was wide open, the *Red Road* beyond leading away from Sol Forne and towards a stretch of country to the northwest. Vaelin was already winded, but she ignored her body's protests. What was harder to ignore was the tug of the Compulsion pulling her back towards Dorovan. It felt like standing at the edge of a vast precipice—part of her wanted to fall, but she knew better than to follow that alarming instinct. If all went as planned, she would take back the lucerne and return to help the boy within the next hour or two.

As she ran through the mostly deserted road—only a few bored city guards and two exhausted farmers on mule carts populated it—she thought back on the strange dinner she had just fled. And Eggar. When the man had entered the room, she had instantly felt the residue of *life energy* clinging to him like mildew on old clothes. Who was the real Eggar that hid behind the puppet he had sent in his stead? Another mystery was Renna, the bald woman who had sensed her and Dorovan's *Sealing* relationship. Only an enchantress of masterful skill and with incredible ties to *life energy* would be able to trace that. She also seemed to be acquainted with Dorovan.

Vaelin felt guilty about leaving the boy behind, but she had been left with no choice. She had abandoned him to a nest of vipers, and she hoped there would be enough of him left when she returned. Opening herself to another, even in this small way, gave her a sharp sense of anxiety. After centuries alone, it was not a feeling she was used to. The first time she had felt it was after Avea—her first companion—had fallen ill. Vaelin had possessed a vague idea of what illness was, but to see it consume the first being she had ever cared for, that had ever cared for her... Anxiety had bubbled in her heart like a bloody wound—the bitter anticipation of something she knew was coming, but not when.

Wolf spit! There was no point in dwelling on that banquet. It had been nothing but a setup so that Eggar could send the lucerne away while she was distracted.

Vaelin ran without stopping for the better part of an hour. Her chest felt heavy and tight. She paused to catch her breath, just for a moment—one moment would not make a difference. The cobbled pavement of the *Red Road* that travelers knew indicated proximity to Sol Forne made way for the beaten red sediment that made up most of its length. She could see carriage wheel tracks in the dirt. Had they been too old, the cool evening wind would have covered them already. She could also sense a faint trace of *Sealing* along the path and, further still, a great source of *life energy.* That had to be the lucerne! Hope bloomed in her, pushing away the pain in her chest and legs.

A couple hours more at this pace and she would reach Adelton—no, Lornaros, as it was now known. That town was entirely occupied by the Blue Scarabs, making it the ideal place for the carriage to stop and gather supplies for the long journey to Vizen. That was unless the carriage driver was under order to reach Vizen without making any stops. That would be irresponsible, but Vaelin would not put such a thing past them.

To her surprise, she would not have to wait much longer: the carriage was parked in the middle of the road, the two horses at its head indifferently flicking their tails to swat flies away. Atop the carriage was strapped a barrel that oozed *life energy.* Four Blue Scarabs in full armor surrounded it.

Oh, no.

The realization hit her like a piece of rotten fruit to the face. She had been deceived like a child charmed by a street magician—her eyes so focused on what she was being told to see that she hadn't noticed the rest of what was right in front of her.

Vaelin stopped several feet from the carriage and caught her breath, careful not to appear more tired than she was. The Blue Scarabs regarded her with impatient tension. One of them removed his antlered helmet and took a few confident steps towards her, while still maintaining a safe distance.

"Hello there," the bald man said. "I am Lieutenant Leano of the Blue Scarabs. You must be Vaelin."

Vaelin did not answer, in part due to her lungs' protests—she also had nothing to say to the man. This was a trap, plain and simple. Whatever they had to say, she had already heard it before.

"I think it would be best if you came with us," the lieutenant said.

"Let me guess," Vaelin said between heavy breaths, "you want me to hop into that carriage and join you on a little trip to Vizen."

"That just about sums it up," the man confirmed.

"The lucerne never left the city, did it?" Vaelin did not have to wait for an answer. "Looks like I'm headed back."

"I'm afraid we cannot allow that," Leano said. He made a small gesture with his fingers that Vaelin almost missed, and the rest of the Blue Scarabs unsheathed their swords one by one in a metallic chorus. "You can hop into the carriage of your own volition, or we will be forced to make you."

"Last time I fought off some of you Blue Scarabs it didn't go so well for you."

Leano smiled—the young man was quite pretty to look at, even considering the lack of hair. "One of the best qualities of the scarab beetle is its great ability to adapt to any environment and any foe. We have learned from our mistakes. That dagger of yours is not as big a threat as you think it is."

Vaelin could sense the man spoke true. She closed her eyes and followed the flow of *life energy* radiating from the earth, sky, and plants around her. A leaf in the wind, she let herself be guided by the flow all the way to the soldiers and the carriage. Their swords and armor were enchanted with *Power*. The door of the carriage was enchanted with *Sealing*. Along with the barrel atop the carriage, that had been the trail she had followed.

She shifted uncomfortably. *Run. Run, you fool*, she told herself, but her feet remained planted in the red dirt. Anger seared within her.

At her back, she heard the shuffling of booted feet. She was surrounded. How could she have been so carelessly caught off guard? She inhaled deeply and steadied herself. "Very well," she said in her best attempt at a level tone. Truth be told, she was nervous—whoever had enchanted those swords and armors had done a masterful work of it; perhaps it was that same enchantress from the banquet.

Vaelin reached into the hidden side pocket of her dress and slowly pulled out Vitra. She flourished the black dagger in her hand, feeling its familiar lightness. "Who wants to go first?"

Leano laughed uncomfortably. "Must we?" he asked, failing at a playful tone.

Vaelin readied herself for the oncoming assault. Leano frowned and flashed another one of his hand gestures to the Blue Scarabs behind Vaelin. She felt the movement of the *life energy* embedded within their armor like the sudden shifting of a tide. She ducked out of the way the instant a gauntleted hand reached for her arm. With a swift upper motion, she sliced at the man's hand with Vitra. She knew the blade would not cut through armor enchanted that well. The enchantment of *Power* forced Vitra to bounce back in recoil—the armor rang like a muffled bell.

Another soldier lunged forward to aid their companion in securing her. Vaelin ran towards them, then feinted and rolled at their feet, forcing them to trip and fall to the ground. Fortunately for Vaelin, the Scarab helmet was designed with forward sight in mind, making her harder to see with their peripheral vision. *I can use that.*

Two more Scarabs ran up to her, swords in hand. *Let's see how well those are enchanted.* Through many battles, Vaelin had learned that testing the enemy's skill and equipment was the surest way to victory—or, oftentimes, escape. She easily parried a sword swing from the Scarab to the right. The sword rang sharply against the dagger, *life energy* buzzing up Vaelin's arm like hornets beneath her skin. It didn't seem like he was swinging to kill, merely to make her retreat into the clutches of the Scarab behind her, who quickly tackled her to the ground.

Vaelin squirmed under the weight of the soldier's heavy armor. She still gripped Vitra—if she could only...

Leano walked up to her shaking his head and tsking. "We could have avoided this if you had simply gotten into the carriage as you were asked. Now we will have to force you inside." He nodded towards a pair of other Scarabs who walked towards her and, along with the man who held her, stood her up. The man kept his arms tight around her in a bear-armed grip.

If... only...

In a deft and sharp motion, she swung Vitra low, slicing the man's belt. His sword and sheath dropped to the ground. It took one moment of the man distractedly loosening his grip ever so slightly for Vaelin to slip down and out of his grasp. She quickly took several steps away and caught her breath.

Their armor is enchanted, but not their latches and accessories. Now, to test their weapons.

Her chance came abruptly, as another Scarab lunged towards Vaelin—this time, the swing of the sword was meant to maim or, at least, wound. Vaelin parried deftly, then swung, aiming at the sword's pommel sticking out a few inches below the Scarab's fist. Vitra sliced through it as if through air, and the pommel fell to the ground with a soft thud. The Scarab looked at her sword as if it was the first time she had ever held such a thing.

That's more like it!

The Scarab gripped the sword unsteadily with both her hands trying to make up for the lack of a pommel. She thrust towards Vaelin, lifting her sword for a heavy blow. Vaelin dodged the falling sword easily but, as she moved out of the way, another Scarab was there to greet her blade-first. She ducked under the swing aimed at her right shoulder—the air above her vibrated hotly.

As the pommel-less Scarab readied herself for a second swing, a third Scarab joined the fray. It was becoming near-impossible to fend off her attackers without drawing blood.

So be it.

As the third Scarab approached her shoulder, Vaelin bent backwards, as if to fall to the ground. As she dropped back, she flung Vitra upwards with ferocious speed. It was akin to throwing a dart across a dark room to hit a fly. The dagger stabbed through the Scarab's throat in the hair-thin slit between his helmet and his armor. Vaelin pulled the dagger out feeling no resistance, then rocked herself forward again to face the others. The man dropped his sword and fell to his knees, his hands clawing at his throat—red stained his blue armor like the first signs of sunset in a clear sky.

Vaelin pounced at the opportunity to take the man's sword in her off-hand. She braced for another round of attacks, but instead her attackers were watching their fellow Scarab's death throes with solemn intensity. Even through their helmets, Vaelin could sense their stoic expressions. They all turned towards her in unison. Something in their posture had changed. They no longer wished to simply wound her and carry her away. Even Leano seemed to sense this, for unprompted he said, "Remember, we are to bring her to Vizen *alive.*"

As a response, two of the nearest Scarabs charged at her ferociously.

While Vaelin had always preferred combat by dagger, she had a good deal of experience with the sword. It wouldn't mean much to the humanfolk of this age, but she had been trained by the legendary elven swordsman Avfyel. Over one thousand years had passed since that training, but some skills weren't easily forgotten, especially not by her. Unlike the humanfolk and the elvenfolk that came before them, Vaelin was not confined by the limitations of her corporeal form. She was a being of pure *life energy*. Any skill she learned became as much a part of her as a limb.

The first Scarab hit her sword with a spectacularly heavy swing—an executioner's swing, the kind meant to cleave head from neck in one blow. Vaelin parried the hit—*Power* thundered through the air. With Vitra in her right hand, she split her opponent's sword off at the hilt.

The blade fell to the ground just in time for Vaelin to turn and dodge the oncoming thrust from the second Scarab. Cutting through empty air unbalanced the soldier. Vaelin needed to incapacitate him, but two more Scarabs were approaching with swords drawn. She had no choice but to stab the man through his helmet visor with Vitra. The Scarab fell back to the ground, blood gushing from the opening at the base of his helmet—Vaelin wondered if he had felt a thing.

The next moments were a blur of frenzied parries and counterattacks as three Scarabs encircled her, swinging their swords in a continuous barrage. The exhaustion from having to fight so furiously combined with her long run earlier and the festering ache of the Compulsion—Vaelin knew that she couldn't keep this up for much longer.

After so many hits, Vitra finally managed to break one of the three swords in half. The swordless Scarab backed away, leaving only two still on the attack. From the corner of her eye, Vaelin noticed Leano whispering something in another Scarab's ear—the first she had seen without a sword. That Scarab was gripping something in his hand, but Vaelin couldn't tell what it was, her attention was fully on parrying the steel flurry that threatened her life. Then, Leano whistled a precise command and the two Scarabs retreated several feet away from Vaelin. Something fast and sharp sliced towards her. Vaelin's focus was dulled by the intensity of combat; otherwise, she would have been able to dodge the arrow before it lodged itself into her thigh.

Shit! The impact of the arrow made Vaelin stagger back, but she did not fall over. Acute pain assaulted her senses, adding to the other aches in her body like an anvil atop a house of twigs. Across the road, the archer lifted his loaded bow and readied a second shot. Leano lifted his arm, and the archer lowered the weapon.

"She's had enough," Leano said, then flashed another hand gesture. Two Scarabs strutted towards her. Their sword hands were relaxed at their sides—they could tell she would no longer put up much of a fight.

Vaelin felt her leg spasm involuntarily as hot blood seeped down into her boot. She couldn't help but think about the beautiful gown she had ruined and how Cressena would be punished for it. Years ago, the same thing had happened several times with Myssa. Vaelin had frequently taken things from her office without permission. The difference was that Myssa had known how to side-step trouble—

she had been sly and had always gotten her way. Cressena might need a bit more help.

Why am I thinking about this now? The two Scarabs were nearing, and she needed to find a way out of this. She concentrated on ignoring the pain in her thigh, lungs, and everything, preparing to embody the essence of *Life* to soothe some of her pain. *Fuck, it all hurts.* She thought about the herb in her satchel with longing—*Wait!*

Reaching into the satchel, Vaelin felt the small stone vial within. She pulled it out and briefly considered the almost consumed etching of *Power* on its surface. Once again, she found herself wishing she could use it for something more fun than this, but that was not a choice she had. She extracted the wire hoop from the vial's mouth and blew a large bubble through it. The two Scarabs stopped just in front of her, eying the bubble warily. Their sword hands tensed.

Please don't kill me, Vaelin thought as she plunged Vitra into the bubble. It felt like trying to stab a spoon through an iron shield. But then the bubble gave way, cracking like ice. At first, *Power* leaked from the bubble in strands, then it released fully. The bubble exploded. The sound of *Power* escaping from the bubble was that of one hundred waves crashing upon the side of a cliff.

Vaelin was immediately flung to the ground. The release of *Power* hit her chest, pressing her into the road with the strength of a hurricane. She felt eagle's talons scraping into her chest over and over with red hot fury. Then, as quickly as it had started, it abruptly ended. The ringing in her ears— like being surrounded by an opera of steaming kettles— could not muffle the sounds of cries and whimpers that surrounded her. Vaelin lifted her head, her body trembling in protest. One of the two Scarabs that had been in front of her lay on the ground, the plate of his armor had caved into his chest. The other's helmet was twisted and bent at an unnatural angle. Both lay unmoving. A few hundred feet down the road, the carriage was toppled over, the two horses at its head stomping around and neighing in fear.

The only two surviving Scarabs were the archer and Leano. Both lay on the ground quite a ways from Vaelin. The archer shifted slowly, catching his bearings. Vaelin couldn't help but scream as she got to her feet—the pain that flowed through her was oppressive. Her hair was singed at the front as if she had placed her head in a hearth, and the straps of her dress were holding on for dear life.

The archer stood on uncertain legs. Upon seeing her on her feet, he quickly picked the bow off the ground, loaded it, and aimed it at her. He released, but Vaelin was not going to be caught by surprise this time. She pivoted and sliced upwards with Vitra right as the arrow reached for where her face had been heartbeats before. The arrow split in two and each half carried on behind her.

The archer stood frozen in utter astonishment, but only for a moment before reaching for the quiver at his back. Vaelin limped as fast as she was able towards him. Every step brought pain of an intensity she had seldom experienced in her long life. Not the worst she had ever felt, but close. The soldier kept his eyes on her as he rummaged through the empty quiver, hoping to conjure an arrow from thin air. He turned to look around the area—the impact of *Power* had scattered his arrows everywhere. He bent over to pick one up.

Vaelin hastened her step, flinging herself atop the man's back, and then inserted Vitra in the small opening at the nape of his neck. As soon as she pulled the blade out, the man collapsed lifelessly under her.

Vaelin hated killing, yet she found herself laughing joylessly. The sound of a sword being unsheathed behind her made her laugh even harder. How had she forgotten about Leano? She cut off the tip of the arrow that stuck out the back of her thigh with the dagger, then pulled it out from the front—if she was going to fight one more of these maleficious Scarabs, she would do it without a damned arrow in her leg. A feverish sweat beaded her forehead. She suddenly didn't feel strong enough to laugh. The pain threatened to force her unconscious, but she somehow found the resolve to keep her head high and her eyes open.

"I see now why our master wants you alive," Leano said gruffly. The handsome Scarab stood with some difficulty—his heavy armor made him buckle under its weight. "Whatever that was, that orb... That's the sort of thing that we need to bring this country into the future. We need you."

Vaelin spat on the ground—she didn't look at her spit but, by the metallic taste in her mouth, she knew it was bloody. "You assume I bear any allegiance to this country." She was surprised by the strength behind her words. "I am not a tool to be used by your master."

Leano sighed and charged for her, sword ready to stab. Vaelin quickly parried the hit. He was even faster with his second attack, which Vaelin had no choice but to duck beneath. She rolled away and managed to pick up a sword from the ground. She couldn't feel any *Power* coursing through it—the burst from the bubble must have depleted it.

Vaelin switched to the offensive while she still had any energy left to spend. She swung with the sword in her left, which Leano defended easily. The parry broke Vaelin's sword in half. For an instant, she could see triumph in the Scarab's eyes. He had her—or so he thought.

As Leano readied another blow—one that would without a doubt incapacitate her—Vaelin struck upwards with Vitra aimed at the man's helmetless head. The dagger cut so effortlessly that at times it was hard to know if the blow had struck. This time there was no doubt.

Blood began to pool down Leano's neck as his ear slid cleanly off and fell to the ground. Leano screamed and placed his hand over the bleeding hole where his ear had been. His attack was still coming, but it was stained by pain and horror. Vaelin dodged it easily and, dagger in hand, punched Leano in the fresh wound at the side of his head. The Scarab fell unconscious to the ground with a heavy thud.

Vaelin dropped to her knees and sipped in several strained breaths. She had none to spare for laughter this time. She wiped the blood off Vitra using Leano's dusty cape and placed it in her satchel. She once again embodied the essence of *Life*. The soothing, dulling sensation was almost immediate, like the warmth of a hearth on a winter's day, but also the coolness of a river in summertime. The gown she wore was a tattered and bloody mess barely hanging on by a single strap. Vaelin tore the gown off herself easily. She ripped a strand off the hem and wrapped it tightly around her thigh to halt the bleeding.

I'm sorry Cressena. I will make it up to you.

The dead archer was about her size. She shook her head and spat on the ground, feeling rancor at what she must do. It took much longer than she had hoped to remove the armor from the young man—he looked anywhere between sixteen and twenty to her. His dull eyes looked up at her sightlessly, pleading. *I'm sorry.*

It struck her just how light and comfortable the armor felt on her, even despite its bulk. She was pleased to find out that its inner layer had been enchanted with a runestone of *Life*. Its effects weren't as strong as when she used her own powers, but it soothed her back and chest without any additional effort on her part. What was surprising was just how much *Power* the armor still emanated. She felt invincible wearing it.

As she passed Leano, Vaelin glanced over at the man. His words had struck the deep blow his sword had hoped to. *I am not a tool!* To her surprise, however, she found herself relieved that she had not killed him. She crouched beside his body and selected a rounded stone about the size of a gold mark from the beaten red earth. Holding it in her palm, she pulled Vitra from her satchel and carved the arrow-shaped etching of *Life* onto its face. Closing her hand around the stone, she concentrated on the flow of *life energy* surrounding her, narrowing her perception until she felt the thin thread of energy connecting the stone to the Cycle of Nature. She pulled on this thread, like unwinding a sweater, until she had created a small pocket within the stone that could be filled with the essence of *Life*. When she opened her hand, the stone had taken on a purple luster and its surface was now smooth like a glass bead.

She placed the newly formed runestone of *Life* in Leano's limp hand. *His head will be ringing in the morning. It's the least I can do.*

The horses had calmed a bit, although they were still stomping about and flicking their tails in agitation. She despised using living creatures as tools but wasn't left with much of a choice. In her condition, she could not walk back to Sol Forne before the end of the banquet. She freed the two horses from the carriage. She spanked the behind of the more agitated one that she would not have been able to control, sending it to gallop up the *Red Road* away from the city. The other, she mounted with some difficulty. The poor beast wavered slightly under her armored weight but quickly found its footing. She kicked the horse and raced back towards Sol Forne.

XIX.

A KEY

None of the beautiful dishes set before Dorovan brought him any pleasure. The second course consisted of a thin slice of duck breast floating in a blood-red sauce surrounded by roasted beets and small cabbages. The savory smell made Dorovan salivate but he could not bring himself to taste it. Partly, this was in fear of revealing the missing fingers on his right hand to Lady Lenora. The rest of his hesitance came from the uneasy feeling that had settled in the pit of his stomach like a poisonous weed at the bottom of a well. He just could not bring himself to taste anything lest he heave it back across the table. He nodded graciously when the servant took away his full plate and rubbed the stumps of his fingers lightly as if that would compel them to grow back.

After Vaelin fled the hall, Renna had assumed the djinn's vacant seat. The enchantress had put on the air of doing so to keep Dorovan secure, but it was obvious she had moved so that she could be closer to her master. She eyed Eggar as if he was made of gold, even after Vaelin had revealed that the man that sat among them now was a sort of proxy achieved through magic Dorovan did not wish to understand. Eggar paid him no mind whatsoever. Dorovan was incredibly thankful for that. Having the disemboweling eyes of Lady Lenora and his sister's owlish gaze at the other end of the table was enough for him.

"...so, once we finalize our support to this new child-thane of Solway, and secure that stretch of the *Red Road,* we will have the entire route from Vizen to Sol Forne under Blue Scarab control." The entire table erupted into mild applause. The way Master Eggar spoke of Blue Scarab affairs was filled with such passion and vigor that even a rock would find itself enthralled.

"Very well, but may we speak about the situation at the port, now?" Lord Pendro inquired. Eggar could barely stifle his annoyance.

Lady Elma placed a hand on her husband's arm. "Pendro, stop pestering our guest with business talk." It was meant to be placating, but Lord Pendro took it as an affront. He shoved away from his wife's gentle touch. "I will pester our guest as I please," he declared. "Especially when the discussion surrounds the life and death of our city. Our guest is fortunate I do not question him rudely! Have I not offered him the best wine and food Sol Forne has to offer?" Lord Pendro's eyes remained fixed upon Eggar's. His tone never soured nor rose above the level of normal conversation, but there was an intensity behind his words that had not been there moments before. Renna leaned forward, her knuckles cracking loudly as her hand balled into a fist.

"Dear..." The words flowed out of Lady Elma's mouth as a sigh. Eggar raised his hand in a calming gesture. "Your husband is quite within his rights, my lady. You have treated me with the utmost respect, honoring me with the wonderful cuisine of your city and the richest of wines. And what have I done in turn? Rambled about our achievements, all the while, I am not even physically here. Lord Pendro, I have shamed myself in the eyes of your beautiful wife and daughter, and for that, I apologize."

Trying to determine where the jape was, Lord Pendro narrowed his eyes. Apologizing was not something the nobility of Sol Forne ever did. Apologies between the nobility were seen as a form of mockery—nobles had too much honor to either give or accept them in good faith. It was something only done by peasants. Lord Pendro, seemingly recounting that this quirk was particular to Sol Forne, gave Eggar an acquiescent nod.

"Let us talk business then," Eggar said with a smile. As if hearing a cue, the servants entered the room and removed every guest's plates. The third course had consisted of a fried corn cake, not dissimilar from those regularly sold on the streets by common vendors. These, however, had been topped with poached oysters and a drizzling of sweet orange sauce. Dorovan was tempted to try one of the oysters—he could have used his left hand to pick up the fork—but his stomach had gone from closed to churning as the evening progressed. He would not risk any accidents. After these plates had been removed as well, still more servants entered the hall carrying tiny cups of steaming orzo and small white cakes topped with honeyed berries. The red-wigged servant strolled down the table offering rolled cigarettes to the guests. Soon, the entire hall was covered in the faint grayness of the smoke.

"May we start at the beginning?" Lord Pendro asked after finishing his orzo in a single swallow. "Why the blockade?"

Eggar took a bite of his cake—his face brightened momentarily as he chewed. He followed the cake with a sip of orzo, which he savored greatly. Each of his actions felt slow and deliberate, as if every aspect of the evening was to be relished. "I did miss the orzo you have here. The mud we get in Vizen simply cannot compare."

"So I've heard," Lord Pendro said, impatiently tapping his fingers on the table.

"Tell me, Lord Pendro, when was the last time you were in the Portos District? When was the last time you stepped foot aboard one of your ships? Or spoke to one of the sailors or captains in your employ? When was the last time you held a meeting with the Trader's Guild?" The tone implied these questions to be rhetorical, although from the look on Lord Pendro's face the answer was obvious.

"Vizen also has a port," Eggar continued, "although it's nowhere near as vital to the city as Sol Forne's. Most goods that go in and out of Vizen do so through the *Red Road*, which, as I've mentioned, is now almost entirely under Blue Scarab supervision. Sol Forne's goods come and go through the Talmur Sea. And where do these goods go?" Another rhetorical question. "Why, they go to Sour Rock, in Boglynd. They go to Sinlunea, just south down the coast, from which they are then transported into Erwynne, and then Brindicoplis further south."

"Why are you explaining my city's trade to me as if I don't already know of it?" Lord Pendro's tone had finally darkened, bordering on anger.

"I only do so to set the stage," Eggar explained. "I am very aware that you know all of these things, and yet you haven't worked out the reason for the blockade." Eggar finished his orzo before resuming. "Before trading with any other city in Hovardom, Sol Forne chooses to trade with two foreign nations. Allied nations, sure, but foreign nonetheless. How can it be so?"

Lord Pendro was taken aback by the question as if he had just heard the ravings of a lunatic. "Well, because those foreign nations pay more for our goods than any other city in Hovardom, Vizen included. And it's not as if we didn't try," he added that last thought as if predicting Eggar's response. "We raised the price of wine exports within the kingdom last year to match those paid to us by Sour Rock and Efray. It's how business works."

"I do understand, Lord Pendro. But while you are in the business of coin, I am in the business of uniting a country. I—we cannot have a united country until these dealings are a thing of the past."

"What do you expect me to do?" Lord Pendro guffawed. "Not trade with any other country? Lose profits by lowering the cost of goods in Hovardom?"

"That's a good start," Eggar beamed with a smile and nod. To say Lord Pendro was appalled would be an understatement—he seemed ready to pounce on Eggar and rip the flesh from his face. "The Blue Scarabs will provide their service to this city by ensuring that all outgoing cargo is headed for Vizen without any other stops and that all cargo entering from other countries is confiscated. This policy will be enacted immediately."

"You son of a bitch!" Lord Pendro screamed, standing abruptly to his feet. "You are condemning this city to ruin!"

Eggar didn't seem particularly perturbed by the lord's words or tone. "It's a sacrifice you must be willing to make for us all."

"The king will hear about this!"

"The king!" Eggar scoffed. "The king knows. We do what we must in order to ensure this country's prosperity. We have a war at our door up north. Our enemies are building their defenses around the Red Coast as we speak. We are simply saving Hovardom from what the Sol Fornian nobility has done throughout its history."

Indignant gasps filled the hall. Lady Elma stood next to her husband, her face a mask of dark outrage. "How dare you!"

"How dare *I*? How dare *you* forget your history, Lady Elma?" Eggar countered, crossing his arms with chilling calm. "In the Vizenian War of Ascension, which side did the nobility take? What about during the Hovardomian civil war? And even earlier than that, during the Oshemari Rebellion, did your fathers and mothers not align themselves with the foreign guilds, exiling the Oshemari out of their own city?" Eggar's face curdled, and his voice took on a low tone. "You nobles have hundreds of years worth of history where you took the side of profit over that of your people. When the Sazisans march through Hovardom and knock on your door, will you do the same? I would rather not find out. This is for the good of the city and the future of our kingdom."

"Out!" Lord Pendro yelled, the veins of his red neck bulging angrily. He pointed at the door with a shaking hand. "Out with you, or I will have my guards drag you."

The smile returned to Eggar's lips. "I'm afraid that will not be happening. We have much yet to discuss."

"Guards!" Lady Elma and Lord Pendro cried out in unison.

The doors opened and six Blue Scarabs in full armor entered the hall. Captain Velden stood and patted Dorovan amicably on the shoulder. "Well, wasn't that a fun dinner, boy?" His jovial tone brought a chill down Dorovan's spine. "Scarabs, report!" the captain called out.

One of the soldiers—the only one with a sapphire-blue cape—took a knee and reported. "Captain, we have secured the building. All guards have been taken alive."

Captain Velden and Eggar shared a knowing glance. "Disarm them and allow them to go. Incapacitate any who resist," the captain commanded. The soldier saluted with a fist to the chest and he, along with two other Scarabs, left the hall. The remaining three Scarabs stood guard by the doors.

"We supported you." Lord Pendro's voice sounded thin and feeble. "We allowed you into our city, even after the Guild Union warned us. What have we done?"

Eggar smiled knowingly. "There is something more I need you to do now that you mention the Union. I need you to call a meeting between them and the Noble Council. We'll need everyone on board if we are to reopen the port."

"They will eat you alive!" Lord Pendro shouted, venomously.

"I have a hard time believing that. I'm sure everyone will be just as understanding as you have been." The look Lord Pendro gave Eggar was more tired than angry. "So. I believe we have discussed everything we are meant to, no? How about you let your guests leave to enjoy the rest of their Leper's Day?"

Every guest was glued to their chair, but the air of uneasiness and anticipation that filled the hall was thick. All eyes were on Lord Pendro, awaiting a formal dismissal from the banquet. Lord Pendro, however, seemed intent on puzzling something out, quietly uttering to himself. Lady Elma took it upon herself to stand and address the guests. "Have a good night everyone," she said curtly. It was all the permission people needed to stand and leave the building.

Dorovan stood. "No," Eggar said, turning his head towards him. It occurred to Dorovan that this was the first time he and the man had locked eyes. "Not you."

Renna placed her hand on his arm for good measure, not harshly, but firmly enough to not offer him any option but to return to his seat.

The old man at Ensa's arm seemed to have lost most of his jovial nature by now. He leaned warily onto Ensa, his eyes deep in thought. Ensa's eyes, on the other hand, remained on Dorovan. He knew he ought to look away, but he couldn't help but meet her gaze—the worry in her look knotted his throat.

"I know you," Lady Lenora said once Ensa and the man had disappeared past the hall door. The lady pointed at Dorovan's face accusingly. "You're the duckling!" She laughed darkly. "Of course! What are you doing here, little duck?" Lady Elma glanced over at her daughter quizzically. "Mother, this is my latest duckling. Remember? He claimed to be a lord, though he's nothing but a peasant. Show me, duck! Show us your hand!"

Bitter anger rose to Dorovan's ears, tinting them red. His missing fingers burned like hot coals. He slowly lifted his bandaged hand.

Lady Lenora laughed. "Disgusting! Oh, but what are you doing here? Pretending to be a lord again? You never learn."

"We shall take our leave," Eggar said, standing up.

"Father, aren't you going to punish this faker for impersonating a noble?" Lady Lenora said. Dorovan couldn't tell by her tone if it was a serious suggestion or a jest. "Impersonating a noble is a crime punishable by flogging, don't you know?"

Dorovan decided to pay her no mind, though Lord Pendro suddenly looked at him with a dark fury on his brow. Perhaps, because he couldn't punish Eggar, he would lay down his anger upon the next best thing. Sudden fear welled up in Dorovan's chest.

"Threatening guests." Eggar shook his head. "My, how low has the nobility of this city fallen." Then, to Lord Pendro, he added, "Get me that meeting within the next few days or the Blue Scarabs seizing the port will be the smallest of your troubles." Eggar made for the dining hall doors and out to the ballroom, followed closely by Captain Velden and the rest of the Blue Scarab soldiers.

"Let's go, Dorovan," Renna nudged.

Dorovan stood and followed Renna out of the dining room. Behind him, he heard Lady Lenora snicker. "That was the duckling! I can't believe it."

A few Blue Scarabs lingered about the Salviati home, while the rest proceeded southbound. Dorovan followed the procession like a man headed to his own funeral.

Captain Velden and Eggar were at the head, talking quietly between themselves. Two Blue Scarab soldiers were at the head of the group, with four more at the rear. Renna walked alongside Dorovan—she didn't have to touch him for him to understand he couldn't escape. Quietly, they made their way through the bustling streets. Every once in a while, Eggar pointed at a bonfire gleefully. A child bumped into the master while running away from her friends. Eggar laughed and patted her on the head before sending her back to play.

"You understand what happened back there," Renna said with a smile. It ought to have been a question, but it didn't quite sound like one.

Dorovan nodded sullenly. "I think so. That man is trying to conquer this city."

Renna tittered. "Conquer? How can one conquer what is already theirs? No. Not conquer. He is simply reminding Sol Fornians who they are."

Dorovan was unconvinced. The city had been working just fine until now, he thought. Though, for whom was it working exactly? The nobility and the guilds had a firm hold over the city. Sure, Sol Forne paid its taxes and dues to the royals of Vizen, but other than that it had never truly felt like part of Hovardom. Sol Forne was... well, Sol Forne. The logical part of Dorovan's mind made way for a more petty thought—it had felt good to watch Eggar humiliate the Salviatis in front of their guests. In minutes, Eggar had exposed the nobility and put them in their place. Wasn't that the sort of heroism Dorovan strived to achieve? The nobility didn't deserve their spot at the top of Sol Fornian society. Eggar had only made him believe so more fervently.

Dorovan had expected them to head to the Blue Scarab lodge, but that wasn't the case. They walked for the better part of an hour towards the Portos District. The street dwellers had dwindled to a trickle, and what was left was a smattering of drunks seeking private places to urinate. On the other hand, there were far more Blue Scarabs the closer they got to the port. Vaelin was there, too.

Dorovan wasn't sure how he knew it, but he could feel her presence as clearly as if she were standing in front of him. The loneliness and longing he had felt after the djinn had left the banquet were suddenly replaced by overwhelming relief.

Renna sized Dorovan with a glance. She breathed in deeply and placed her hand on his shoulder. "You can feel it too, can't you?" Dorovan nodded, though he wasn't entirely sure they meant the same thing.

Once they reached the docks, Captain Velden and their Blue Scarab escort left them. Dorovan wondered if he should run, though, if the Portos was as under Blue Scarab control as he had heard, perhaps that wouldn't be wise. Besides, Vaelin was here. That, he was sure of. The djinn would see him out safely, wouldn't she?

The docks were lined with wooden barrels—not just the docks, it seemed like the entire port was covered in stacked barrels, more than Dorovan had ever seen there. The black water of the harbor reflected the orange glow of the city like the shimmering of gemstones. Dots of light from ships in the distance freckled the darkness. Eggar stood at the edge of the wooden dock, looking out to the horizon. "Dorovan," he suddenly called. Dorovan stood unmoving next to Renna, unsure of what to do. The name couldn't possibly be his, the way Eggar had spoken it. The woman nudged his shoulder, and Dorovan reluctantly shuffled up to the master.

"I apologize if tonight has frightened or distressed you in any way," Eggar said kindly. "That was not my intention. I have heard many good things about you."

"You have?" Dorovan could hear the childlike inflection in his words. The seeds of embarrassment were sewn, but Eggar's sudden warm smile removed them.

"I hear you are a remarkable young man, and of noble birth too." Eggar moved closer to Dorovan. "Your father was a war hero, Dorovan ca'Melese. Our country could use more men like him."

Dorovan's face flushed at the unexpected compliment, though the pride he felt allowed him to meet Eggar's eyes. "Yes. He was a hero."

"It's terrible what happened to him. You have my sincerest sympathy. I also lost my parents when I was very young, though I never lost the hope for a better world that they instilled in me. Tell me, Dorovan, what would you say if I told you I could help you reinstate House Melese and all it stood for?"

Dorovan hadn't expected this. "What do you mean?" he dazedly heard himself ask.

Something about Eggar's knowing smile made Dorovan recoil. The man was aware of the power behind his proposition. "As you saw tonight, I hold great influence over the nobility of this city. Oh, they may resist me now, but soon they'll come to agree with my ways, forceful as they may see them. I only push when it's necessary. I match the strength of my actions to the power wielded by my adversary."

"Am I your adversary?" Dorovan tested.

Eggar laughed heartily. "An adversary is just an ally you haven't convinced yet. I am asking you to be my ally, Dorovan. I will not be forceful with you. I will give you options."

Having nobility bestowed upon him—without earning it the way his father had—went against everything Dorovan had recently learned. And it would not solve the problem of the Contract he had made with Vaelin. If he became a noble that way, would a path to heroism still be possible? "What do you need from me?" Dorovan asked. There was no harm in hearing the man out.

Eggar turned back to face the dark horizon. "*Life energy* is a collective force fueled by all living things. We are just as much a part of it as wishing trees, or the ancient Guardians." Dorovan chuckled upon hearing the man speak of such folklore. Eggar faced him with a severe expression, as if he had been entirely serious. "You have met a djinn yet you scoff at wishing trees and Guardians?" Eggar prodded.

Dorovan suddenly felt silly. Of course, if Vaelin was real anything was possible, even wishing trees. As if to echo his thoughts, Eggar continued, "Only over a year ago, an Albadonian would have rebuffed my words the same way you just did. That was, until the *melk*—the ancient Guardians of the forest—returned. There are things in this world that you would not believe. *Life energy* fills all, yet only we humanfolk have the will to harness and control it. But our knowledge and power are still very limited. It has been my life's mission to understand how we can bridge the gap. How we can reap great rewards with minimal cost. I gather you've heard of the Albadonian fire."

"Everyone has."

"At first, I thought of the conflagration as a setback to our mission. But it was a necessary evil, as it revealed to us much about the nature of *life energy*." Eggar abruptly changed the subject by asking, "You have some sort of bond with the djinn?"

Dorovan instinctively reached for his hand bearing the etching of *Sealing*. Eggar moved in close and caught Dorovan's hand in his own. He held it, gently gliding his fingers across the etching in Dorovan's palm. Chills ran across Dorovan's body at the strangely intimate gesture.

"*Sealing*," Eggar said. "But why?" He seemed to show genuine concern.

"I made a Contract with her," Dorovan said. He was about to recount what had happened between him and Vaelin in detail, but Eggar gave the impression of understanding.

"Renna," the man called out. "Please show Dorovan exactly what he can do for us." For a moment, the man's eyes became glassy and distant—he looked as if he was about to sick up.

"Have a seat, master. I will tend to you shortly," Renna said, with some concern.

"I can hold on for a bit longer," Eggar replied.

Renna nodded and flanked Dorovan, guiding him away from the dock. As she led him towards a small fishing shack, the feeling that Vaelin was near intensified. He knew that if he was to open that door, Vaelin would be there awaiting him. A Blue Scarab guarded the entrance to the shack. Upon seeing Renna, he pushed the door open and held it for them to enter. Renna took in a deep breath, steadying herself. "Here it is," she said.

Whatever *it* was, it was not Vaelin.

❧ ❧ ❧ ❧

While it produced no light of its own, the artifact seemed to glow the instant Dorovan neared it. Renna sensed *life energy* bouncing between the two of them like a song echoing through a hillside. Could the boy truly be the key to unlocking the lucerne's secrets? "Touch it," Renna commanded— the words left her mouth as a reverent whisper.

Dorovan drew close to the lucerne with much reluctance. He held onto his wrist as if his arm was nothing but an object to be used—a key. He looked back at Renna pitifully, and she nodded towards the lucerne. She bit her lip in impatience. Dorovan slowly moved his hand towards the artifact—the echoing *life energy* grew louder and more frenetic. It seemed to take him a great deal of effort to do so. The boy grunted. His face suddenly lost its boyish flush and made way for a sickly yellow pallor. Guilt and anticipation wrestled within Renna when the boy's hand finally landed upon the lucerne's surface.

The *life energy* emanating from the lucerne was immediately loudly dissonant—a dissonance unexpectedly reflected by the mysterious *life energy* within the waters of the port—then quieted to a trickle. Dorovan breathed a sigh of relief.

"What do you feel?" Renna inquired.

"I... feel... I..." Dorovan went on repeating those incoherent sounds, as if he couldn't form any sentences with them. Renna felt the link between the boy and the lucerne wavering. She placed one hand on Dorovan's shoulder and the other upon the surface of the lucerne, and opened herself to the flow of *life energy* through her Extranforial Etchings. She was too late. There was not enough resonance for her to have made a difference. Dorovan sighed deeply, then slowly lowered himself to the floor.

"Dorovan?" Renna called out, but the boy didn't respond. She placed her hand above his nose, feeling the air brush against her skin. He was only unconscious, thank the True One. She turned her attention to the lucerne and touched its surface. The pulse of *life energy* within had slowed, though it gradually regained its rhythm like a heart that had just been resuscitated. She breathed out in relief, though tonight had not been a success.

The boy was a key, though an incomplete one. She was closer to understanding how the lucerne worked, but she was still missing something. She picked the boy up from the floor with ease and left the shack.

Master Eggar slouched outside, looking out towards the endless black sea. Beads of sweat crowned his forehead. He turned to her and glanced at the boy. The disappointment in his eyes was too much for Renna to bear. She lowered her gaze in shame. "Master," she said meekly, awaiting an order. But no order came.

XX.

The Compulsion

Vaelin took it easy on the poor horse. Not only was the beast still skittish from the earlier explosion, but her Blue Scarab heavy armor must have been cumbersome on its back. Even so, it took far less than an hour for her to reach the Sol Fornian gates. They were still open due to the festivity within the city. They would probably remain open all night.

Vaelin dismounted and slapped the horse's behind, sending it scurrying away up the *Red Road.* She would have ridden it inside, but upon seeing the outcroppings of lit bonfires pimpling the city, Vaelin realized it was probably for the best that the horse roam free, away from the celebration.

The Old Gates was still brimming with peasants cheering and celebrating. All the children had been brought in for the night, and those revelers who remained were rowdier and drunker than they had been earlier in the evening. Music emanated from somewhere close by, though Vaelin could not see any musicians to speak of through the dense partying horde. Further down the street, one of the bonfires had grown too unruly, setting an adjacent merchant's cart ablaze. Some onlookers laughed at the scene, while others promptly tossed thick wetted blankets over the cart. The speed of it all gave Vaelin the impression that this was a known risk of Leper's Day.

While the *Life*-lined armor she wore had worked wonders to soothe Vaelin's chest, her thigh was sore and tender as she bumped past the tight congregation. The arrow wound had opened further from riding the horse. Her head was pounding like a morning after heavy drinking—the surrounding noise didn't help one bit—and her arms felt awkward in their limpness. She hoped with an edge of desperation that the banquet was still going on. It was late, but perhaps the Salviatis had arranged some captivating entertainment for after dessert. If only she could be so lucky. Being too far from Dorovan had made her aware of just how little time remained to fulfill his Contract. The Compulsion created a longing to be near the person she had Contracted, and, because of the added *Sealing* with the boy, there was no doubt he would also be feeling wary.

As she made her way through the crowds and towards the Effore, she noticed more and more that the people had set their alcohol-fueled rambunctious gazes upon her. She did stand out quite sharply in the full Blue Scarab armor. Several times, people shoved their shoulders into her purposefully. "We don't want your kind here," a man slurred— Vaelin couldn't be sure if this was because of the armor or her appearance. She had no time to stop and ask.

The trip from where the ambush had been to the gates of Sol Forne felt much shorter than that from the gates to the Effore. It was a struggle for her to stay erect and awake, her eyes threatening to stay shut after each blink. A single large bonfire next to the fountain with the gaudy swan lit the center of the Plaza d'Edo. The crowds here were tamer than those in the peripheral neighborhoods of the city. Their clothes indicated that they were also a much richer assembly. Most puffed on cigarettes, the light gray smoke rising and joining with that of the bonfire. Men and women in servant's attire served sparkling dessert wine to the chattering groups. Vaelin took the sight in for a few moments, but of Dorovan, Eggar, or the Salviatis, there was no trace.

She passed the fountain and headed north through a wider street, towards the Salviati home, when a hand grabbed her arm. The grip wasn't forceful, but Vaelin turned around ready for a conflict. Instead, she found a young woman in a lovely purple gown. Her expression was extremely concerned, her teary eyes sparkling like diamonds in the trembling light of the bonfire. Behind her stood an older man in a wonderfully colorful robe. Vaelin immediately recognized him from the banquet, though she could have sworn she had seen him even before then.

"I told you it was her," the young woman said to the man. Then, to Vaelin, she added, "You know my brother. Dorovan."

Vaelin's eyes widened in surprise. "Where is he?"

"They dismissed us from the banquet but kept him there. What would they want with him? He's a hard-headed fool sometimes, but he's just a boy." Tears began to stream down her face. The man offered her the pink handkerchief that peeked out of his robe pocket. "There, there," he said, gently. The young woman dabbed at her eyes.

"Is he still inside?" Vaelin asked, alarmed.

The woman shook her head. "After we were dismissed, I waited for him outside the gates, hoping that he would walk out eventually. He did come out a bit later, but he was escorted by that awful man and several Blue Scarabs. They marched him that way, but I don't know where to exactly. I tried to follow, but they blocked us from doing so."

A terrible foreboding wound itself around Vaelin's chest and tightened. Since their job at the port, she had sensed the energy of the lucerne, but it had felt as if it had been evenly scattered across the port, making it impossible to determine which one of the hundreds of ships or storage shacks it was being kept within. Now, that energy felt clearer, more active. And focusing harder, she could feel Dorovan as well almost as strongly. It was as if the two energies had merged into one.

"Can you help him?" the young woman asked. "He's just a boy," she repeated. "He wants to be a noble so badly, but he hasn't learned what that means yet. These people will consume him until there's nothing left, then toss him out like used bath water. Please..." Her plea trailed off into sniffles.

"I will find him," Vaelin replied. The sudden exhaustion that came over her was enough to make her stagger on her treacherous legs. The woman reached out to help Vaelin stay up, though the heavy armor made that an endeavor. Vaelin's face must have paled, for the woman's eyes widened in concern. "I just need to sit down for a moment," Vaelin whimpered. The effects of the *Life*-lined armor wavered, the sting returning to her chest. She was far past the point of being able to soothe herself using her own powers.

All at once, she was on her back, the plaza quaking around her. For a moment, the young woman's concerned face was all she saw—her mouth soundlessly calling out to

Vaelin. Darkness overtook her swiftly. The pain, however, remained.

❧ ❧ ❧ ❧

Life energy enveloped her like a warm blanket. The ache of her body was a distant throbbing—like sunlight during daytime, it was ever-present though one rarely thought about it. Beyond the blanket of *life energy* that cocooned her—that *was* her—stood an impenetrable oily darkness. The Compulsion. It threatened to slice through her *life energy* with its sharp tendrils. The pain was beyond comprehension, but Vaelin fought to keep herself together, to not lose her connection to the body she had assumed all this time—*her* body.

She laughed, if laughing was a thing that was at all possible in this place that was not a place. How she had grown attached to that pile of meat called *body*!

A poisonous tendril invaded her. *That body is not Vaelin. It would take nothing to let go of it.*

As soon as the thought was conjured, she knew it had not come from her. One of the Compulsion's inky spikes had breached her inner mind, injecting it with its numbing darkness. Vaelin fought to keep herself separated from it, though she knew she would eventually succumb. *Why fight at all? Isn't this what you want? To be free?*

There it was again, that slimy voice. No. She would not give in. There was too much to lose. Unlike other living creatures, which, once their life cycles terminated, would inevitably return their *life energy* to the Cycle of Nature, Vaelin was *Sealed* to the lucerne in such a way that once her body succumbed to death, her *life energy* would be exhausted as if she was nothing but a runestone—cursed to never return to the Cycle of Nature. She could not allow that.

Lifetimes ago, she had seen what happened when the Cycle of Nature was stripped of *life energy*. Famine, sickness, death, and despair had tortured the land. A great cost had been paid to right that wrong—a sacrifice Vaelin had not been able to make. Everyone she had ever known, everyone who had ever cared for her, had willingly surrendered their bodies to the Cycle so that the world would live on.

Vaelin had been unable to do anything but watch, her *life energy* imprisoned within her body for eternity. That was, unless she found the lucerne and freed herself from her prison of *Sealing*.

You will never find it. Give up.

NO!

The lucerne was within reach. She could sense it, even here in this dark pit of despair. How could she give into the Compulsion when she was so close?

You're so close.

Vaelin felt the words vibrate through her. Even the Compulsion halted its invasion at their sound—like an iceberg calving from the face of a mighty glacier.

Who said that? Vaelin and the Compulsion echoed each other.

No reply came. Not verbally, at least. The pressure changed around her as another's *life energy* inundated the space like a tidal wave. The waves came in pulses, like heartbeats, that strengthened more and more after each one. The energy was primordial—nostalgic to her in a way, reminding her of the eons she had spent freely roaming the world. This energy felt similar to her own, though it belonged to another.

Something had roused it from its deep ancient sleep. *Why would anyone do something so cruel?* Vaelin thought, sensing the distress pulsing through the space.

Let me take you away from all of this, the Compulsion suggested. *Let me make it easy for you.* The Compulsion reached out to her once again, this time with all of its strength. Everything became nothingness. Nothingness became everything. The Compulsion was right, this was easy. What did the world ever do for her that she owed it her *life energy?*

A small part of her tried to respond. What was it saying? Its voice sounded so far away...

Everything.

The single word was enough to break Vaelin from the Compulsion's snare. She focused her mind on what she knew was true. The Thinking had placed her upon this rock because it needed her here. *Life energy* was the force that connected all living creatures. The Compulsion was nothing more than entropy. While her life would seem eternal by most standards, the Compulsion was something truly infinite. And inevitable.

She remembered what the world was like before the creatures living upon it discovered they could use *life energy* for their own purposes. All energy had been contained within the Cycle. The elvenfolk had learned how to store this energy and harness it, not realizing until centuries after that the cost of this process was the permanent severing of the connection between that energy and the Cycle of

Nature. This led to the exhausting of a resource that was never meant to have been consumed.

We were joined, Vaelin and the other energy spoke in unison.

Help me, the other said, this time alone.

Vaelin felt its sorrow more deeply than she had ever felt her own. *How? What threatens you?*

I do not know.

Vaelin understood what it meant. It knew it was in danger, though it wasn't aware of what that danger was, like the untamed instincts of a wild animal. *I will do what I can.*

That is all I ask. I too will help you, by holding back what threatens you.

Vaelin was suddenly aware that the Compulsion was no longer encroaching on her—its darkness had receded beyond the horizon like stars fleeing the dawn. The other energy was suppressing it temporarily.

Vaelin hoped the energy could buy her enough time to keep her promise to it. If the Compulsion returned again, it would be to consume her entirely.

❧ ❧ ❧ ❧

Vaelin opened her eyes. Not the false eyes she had possessed in her vision, but her real ones. *Who is to say which eyes are real for a being of pure* life *energy?* The Compulsion had been extinguished, at least for the moment. It would be back, and soon, unless she either completed the Contract with Dorovan or found the lucerne. She still wasn't sure where the artifact was, but the spike of *life energy* she had felt from it before she collapsed had emanated from the port.

An intense determination filled her body, though it was superseded by immense pain in her leg and chest. She lifted her head and realized she was in an unfamiliar bed, in an unfamiliar room. The room was small but the extravagant and colorful decor spoke of wealth. Despite the opulence of the interior, there was a general sense of disarray to the space: books were piled at the base of several shelves as if they had been violently thrown off, the large painting of a *dragon* in flight hung crookedly, and a wilted lilfrith blossom sat on the floor in a small pool of water surrounded by bits of smashed vase.

Her wounded thigh was cocooned in clean gauze, as were her chest and back. The Blue Scarab armor she had stolen was piled carelessly into a corner. A jolt of panic rushed through her—what had happened to the piece of ancient elven gown she had used as bandaging? She sighed. What good would it have done to keep that bloody rag? It wasn't as if Cressena could do anything with it now. Poor woman. How would Vaelin ever make it up to her?

The pale sunlight lent the room an uneasy stillness, as if the space was waiting for something to happen. *Wolf spit!* She was out all night! Vaelin stood from the bed, pain angrily biting into her chest and thigh. A scream at the door made her jump. A middle-aged woman in an apron held her hands over her mouth to stifle her startlement, then ran away. *What is her problem?*

A set of footsteps paced down the hall towards the room. A young woman—Dorovan's sister—peeked in warily. "Good morning," Vaelin grunted.

"You're alive," the young woman said in astonishment, cautiously entering the room.

"And glad to be it," Vaelin replied as she leaned against the bed for support.

"The chemist that cleaned your wounds could not revive you. You died last night. They are on their way now with a cart to carry your body away to be burnt."

"Won't be needing them now," Vaelin chuckled, though the woman's pale face informed her that this wasn't a joking matter. What she had experienced the previous night had been more than just a vision—she had died and had been helped by some other force so that her *life energy* would be returned to her body. The woman gazed at Vaelin expectantly, but Vaelin had no idea how to begin to explain it to her. "What's your name?" she resigned to ask.

"Ensa," the woman replied, closing in on Vaelin to help her stand.

"My name is Vaelin, and I need to get out of here. I need my satchel. And," she added, realizing she only wore the bandaging, "some clothes."

"You need to rest," Ensa said. "You're in no condition to go gallivanting about."

"I need to find your brother." Her awareness of Dorovan had shifted away from the port. "He is close by," Vaelin said to herself.

"How do you know that?" Ensa asked skeptically.

Vaelin glanced at the young woman and prudently said, "He and I share a bond. I have a general sense of where he is, although faintly. Last night, he was at the harbor, and this morning he is somewhere nearby, over there." She gestured vaguely outside of the window.

"I'm going with you," Ensa stated.

"What?"

"If you are determined to go find my brother in your current condition, I will come to ensure you are intact." The way the words were spoken made Vaelin believe she would have no say in the matter.

"It could be dangerous. Since Dorovan was last seen in Blue Scarab custody, I'm afraid their lodge is the best place to begin the search."

Ensa nodded to herself. "That's fine. You are in pain and require assistance, and my brother is in danger. What more is there to discuss?"

Vaelin looked at Ensa in amazement. This was Dorovan's sister? The hardheadedness was there, but this young woman seemed much more resolved than the boy. "Very well," Vaelin agreed. "Now, about those clothes?" A deep groan from her stomach reminded her that she hadn't eaten since earlier the previous day. While she didn't have to eat often, hunger pangs meant her body had been strained to the far edge of its ability.

Ensa seemed to understand Vaelin's dismayed expression. "I will get you clothes, right after I get you a warm meal."

Time was scarce, but Vaelin could not bring herself to protest. Ensa left the room and soon returned with a piping hot bowl of hen stew. Vaelin ate it voraciously, tilting the bowl over her lips at the end, drinking in its warmth. When Ensa returned with the clothes, Vaelin asked for seconds.

Ensa was about the same size as Vaelin, but unfortunately, the contents of the young woman's wardrobe consisted of gaudy, colorful gowns. At Vaelin's grimace, Ensa explained, "I am a colorist. The lord of this house has gowns made for me using the fabrics I've practiced on. Other than the banquet last night, I haven't found an occasion to wear any of them."

Vaelin admired the woman's work—the colors were bright and even across the material—but they would not do for her purpose. "Do you have anything less... formal?" Vaelin asked.

"I have work clothes, though those are not nearly as nice."

"Let me take a look."

The woman's work clothes were brown and unassuming, a slathering of pigment dusting the sleeves at the elbows. While the dress wasn't by any means pretty, it fit comfortably. "I have clothes stored at an inn," Vaelin said. *I will return this to you after I change into them*, she wanted to add, though, after the damage done to the gown borrowed from Cressena, she did not want to make any further promises. She was about to encounter more Blue Scarabs, and that could mean another fight—she only hoped she had the strength to confront them should that happen.

The previous day felt like a strange dream. She was certain she had placed the dagger in her satchel but the relief she felt as she retrieved Vitra from the surprisingly still intact bag was immediate. The familiarity of the light dagger in her hand felt reassuring.

Ensa's eyes glanced at the blade in equal parts amazement and fear. "Will it get violent?" Ensa asked. There was no uncertainty behind her words, just precaution.

"I sure hope not. But I will be ready in case it does."

"You don't intend to simply show up on their doorstep and knock, do you?" The genuine concern in Ensa's voice was endearing. Vaelin didn't wish to admit it but that was exactly her plan—urgency made her abandon all caution. Perhaps Ensa sensed this because she quickly added, "I think I have an idea."

Vaelin looked into the young woman's bright eyes. "Let's hear it."

XXI.

SOLE SURVIVOR

Renna had been entirely too entrenched in her studies to bother breaking her fast with the other Scarabs that morning. Instead, she had fixed herself a simple mug of spiced tea. Bitter orzo was the drink of choice in this part of Hovardom, whereas fragrant teas were favored in the north—just another in a long list of regional differences. While the tea worked wonders for suppressing her appetite, it also made her nerves more rigid. They should have received news from Leano by now, who was supposed to have reached the Blue Scarab lodge outside of Yorne that morning. He had been instructed to send back a messenger once they had reached Lornaros, but none had come yet. Perhaps the earthquakes the previous night had slowed down his unit.

All she could do was immerse herself in the work—there was plenty to spare. The lucerne had immediately responded to Dorovan's presence, the *Seal* between the boy and the djinn was powerful enough for that. Renna had tried to use her Extranforial Etchings to bridge the remaining gap between Dorovan and the artifact, but it hadn't been nearly enough. Something was still missing, and she would not waste time eating or sleeping—or worrying about Leano—until she had found out exactly what that was.

The dormant *life energy* within the port had reacted to the encounter as well, which Renna found endlessly fascinating, though not unexpected. She had no idea what that *life energy* belonged to, nor anything else about it besides what she had been told by Master Eggar—which was almost nothing. Was it an ancient being of pure *life energy* like a wishing tree? Or a powerfully enchanted object that had been lost to the sea? Or perhaps, it was something no one had ever seen before. Whatever it was, she would find a way to gently rouse it from its slumber, and seize ownership of it. The lucerne and the boy were each pieces of that puzzle, as was the *black water*. The highly flammable element had been extracted from the depths of the forest of Albadone. The barrels at the port encompassed all that was left of the resource after the disaster in Albadone. The master's Vizenian enchantresses had informed him of the *black water's* highly resonant enchanting properties, so he had thought it best to bring the supply here where Renna could find a use for it.

The liquid functioned similarly to the black earth found at the Womb of the World—the great mountain where *life energy* was said to have originated—though in a more concentrated manner. Since scattering the barrels throughout the docks, that immense sunken *life energy* had begun to stir. Only a few weeks ago, it had been so faint she could barely perceive it at all. Now, it was as if it was the only thing she could sense within the Cycle.

She could feel it fading back to a distant slumber. Though, judging from its peak the previous night, it would only be a matter of days before they would fully awaken it. But what would happen if it awoke and Renna still had no means by which to *Seal* it to herself? Were the earthquakes that had gone on for hours the previous night the harbingers of what an unrestrained *life energy* of that magnitude could do to the city?—to the Cycle of Nature itself?

She had to purge her thoughts of such reservations and fears. There was no place for them in her conviction to the mission. She would succeed. The alternative was simply unthinkable.

Since encountering the lucerne, Dorovan had grown lethargic. There was a moment, during the worst of the tremors, when Renna had feared he would die. His strength and resilience had surprised her—the boy would make a great Blue Scarab one day—though Renna worried that keeping him too far away from the djinn would only serve to weaken him further. She would have preferred that the djinn remain in Sol Forne to be studied by her, but Master Eggar had insisted that she be sent straight to him in Vizen. He had boasted of the enchantresses and chemists at his disposal that would be able to fully study the djinn, and had emphasized that Renna had other tasks to take up her time. Ignoring the pang of rejection, she chose to trust that the master knew what was best—that he would focus her skills where they were most needed.

The enchantment of *Transference* that anchored the real Eggar to his proxy body had regained its stability after some minor enchanting by Renna the previous night. He had rested for a few hours, then left early in the morning to attempt to meet with Guild Union officials. Before leaving, he had wandered into Renna's office. He hadn't said anything; he had simply watched her work. When she had realized he was there, she faced him and saluted. He only

smiled warmly, then walked away. Renna still wondered
what that had been about. Perhaps he had simply wanted to
be certain that she was hard at work—a toddler that must be
supervised. On the other hand, maybe she had impressed
him enough for him to want Renna to join his enchantresses
in Vizen. Would she take that offer if it was presented?

"The boy is awake."

Renna turned to the door with a start—the quiet air of
her office had gone undisturbed for quite some time. Hearing Tiran's voice was always somewhat startling, as the man
had a habit of walking on feathered feet. "Send him here,"
she replied. Tiran nodded his bald head and turned to
leave. "Wait!" she said. The man halted. "Any word from
Lieutenant Leano?"

The man's mouth twisted in chagrin as he shook his
head. Renna dismissed him with a nod and returned her
attention to her books. Unsettling worries about Leano
flooded her, and it became difficult to concentrate on her
work. She had suggested that morning that a pair of Blue
Scarabs be sent for Yorne to ensure that Leano and his unit
had passed through. Captain Velden had denied the proposition. "*Master Eggar says we need as many hands in Sol
Fore as we can muster,*" he had explained. "*We can't afford
to be short-handed for what's to come.*" Renna knew the
man was right, but would one or two Scarabs really make a
difference?

Renna closed her eyes and took a deep breath. *It floods.
It rains. Let's wash off all the stains. Clothes hung to dry,
we'll have a cry, and say farewell to pains.* Her grandmother
used to sing that rhyme whenever Renna was sad. A sense
of peace filled her upon recalling it. "*Not even a Chant is as*

effective," the old woman used to say. Renna chuckled softly to ward pain from the memory.

Dorovan trudged into the office moments later with the air of someone who had just survived a great ordeal. "Thank you, Tiran," Renna said to the Scarab that had escorted Dorovan. The soldier took the gratitude as the dismissal that it was and left the office.

"How are you feeling today?" Renna inquired, noticing the boy's glassy unfocused eyes.

"I've been better," Dorovan replied. His voice was deep and phlegmy. He still wore the simple gray shirt and brown trousers that he had changed into the previous night. The shirt sagged a bit over his scrawny build, but at least it was clean. "I barely slept last night and, when I did, I had strange dreams."

"Oh?" Renna intoned. "What sort of dreams?"

"It was nonsense," Dorovan dismissed.

"Could be. But that's not always the case. Dreams can be a language the Cycle of Nature uses to speak to us. Those of us who have a greater connection to the Cycle, such as enchantresses, have those sorts of dreams more often than others." Renna pointed at the *Seal* on Dorovan's hand. "You are *Sealed* to an ancient being of pure *life energy*. It's only normal that your connection to the Cycle has been elevated. Your dream could hold more meaning than you imagine."

Dorovan rubbed the scar on his hand awkwardly, taking a few moments to gather his thoughts before recounting the dream. "It was dark, but not like night. It was dark like... like nothingness is dark. I was stuck in this nothingness feeling like I belonged in it. As if I knew of nothing else. My eyes slowly became used to it. Then, I saw something shining in the distance, and I somehow knew that it was Vaelin." The boy shook his head and smirked, as if doubting his own words. "Then, I saw another light—much larger and brighter than Vaelin's. Something about those lights was just..." The boy paused.

"Frightening?" Renna suggested.

Dorovan met her eyes darkly. "No. Not frightening... I should have been thankful for the light, but all it did was remind me of the nothingness that surrounded me."

"Then what happened?"

"Then I woke up as the room shook around me, but I couldn't move. It felt like a great weight was pressed down on me. The weight released eventually, but very slowly. Every time I fell back asleep, the dream would repeat all over again."

Renna nodded as if the boy had provided her with some valuable insight. "We will be headed back to the port as soon as you've had something to break your fast. You need energy. We have much work to accomplish."

Dorovan's tired somberness was replaced by his more typical surliness. "Let me guess, I don't have a choice in the matter?"

"Unfortunately, you do not. You have become an integral part of our plans."

"And what exactly are these plans?" He folded his arms. "Don't expect me to continue cooperating without knowing what I'm getting into."

Renna faced the boy. He hadn't said anything outrageous or entirely out of line, but she had the overwhelming urge to slap him. Like every Sol Fornian she had met, he just didn't understand when it was time to allow himself to be helped. A babe didn't ask its mother why it was being fed.

"That light you saw," Renna said, attempting to make the explanation as simple as possible for the boy, "the one that was greater than Vaelin—we are trying to do to it what was done to her. We want to *Seal* it so we might use it for our cause."

"*Seal* it? Why would you do such a thing?" Dorovan asked, that boyish defiance giving some color to his pallor. His affront seemed genuine.

"If we control it, it can pose no danger to us. We're not entirely sure what it is, but we know it's made of pure, concentrated, *life energy*. If we learn how to *Seal* that energy away, there will be no limits to the power we can wield. Imagine all we could do for our country!" The boy shook his head dismissively, his brow knitted. How foolish of her to have expected him to understand the scope of what they must do. "Give me your hand," she instructed firmly. At least he had enough sense to do so without protest.

Renna ran her fingers over the scars on his palm. The three lines of *Sealing* had been cleanly engraved on his smooth skin. "When she did this, did she chant or do anything specific or strange?"

Dorovan shook his head. "She cut those into me and then explained what it meant." His eyes broadened with recollection. "Her hand was cut too. She held my hand with her bloody hand."

Blood. That was something. Blood was the cost of many types of enchantments and one of the most powerful materials when enchanted. Blood was *life energy*. It was all so obvious to her now. The djinn had created a blood bridge of *life energy* between her and the boy. It wasn't a simple matter—one needed incredibly high amounts of *life energy* to achieve such a thing. Would Renna's Extranforial Etchings be enough? She needed to find out as soon as possible.

"Go to the mess hall and eat something. And be quick about it. We will head for the port soon." Dorovan stood at the door, reluctant to leave. "What is it?" Renna asked, annoyed.

"That man, Master Eggar," Dorovan asked. "Do you believe what he says?"

Renna scoffed. "Why else would I be in the Blue Scarabs? Unlike the royals and nobles who only know how to take from others, Master Eggar has given us a chance to create something better. We would all be fools to not take that opportunity."

"But... what he says about the nobility is..." Dorovan bit his lip, struggling to get something out.

Renna's curiosity was piqued. "You may speak plainly with me. This is a safe place."

Dorovan sighed. "He speaks of the nobility as if he has real power over them. He even suggested he might be able to reinstate my House. But only the royals and the Sol Fornian nobility have that power. He isn't Sol Fornian, so does that mean he is a member of the royal family?"

A chuckle escaped Renna's mouth. "Far from it," she said. "Though he does have ties to them in ways I am not privy to."

"But you still trust him, even though he works for the royals?"

"He doesn't work *for* the royals. He works *with* them. In much the same way, he is working with the nobility of Sol Forne here to create a better Hovardom." The sudden cynical look on the boy's face was enough to irritate her. "You best go get something to eat. We really must be leaving soon."

Before Dorovan could heed her order, a mad rush of boots hitting the floor rumbled as Blue Scarabs spilled through the hallway. Voices were raised in a cacophony of concern and anger. "Leano." Renna let the name slip from her tongue as if it were a wish. Dorovan faced her questioningly, as if she had said something to him. "Go to the mess hall. I will see what this is about." The boy obeyed, squeezing himself through the almost-impenetrable wall of blue armor.

The forest of Scarabs that had collected just beyond her office stood unmoving. "What is the meaning of this?" Renna shouted, but nobody heeded her or made room for her to pass through. "Scarabs!" she commanded, finally grabbing the attention of the soldiers. Those nearest to her quieted down and saluted.

"Disperse!" she ordered, and the soldiers moved away, retreating towards the mess hall and bunkrooms. Many still lingered in the hallways. She had to repeat her order to another cluster of soldiers further down—the loudness of their chatter had trampled over her previous command. Renna spotted one of the lodge guards standing with his back against the hallway and grabbed his attention. "Do something about this!"

The man nodded impotently, overwhelmed. "Of course!" he bluffed, then turned to plead with the crowd to disperse. Renna continued down the hall towards the source of the commotion: Captain Velden's office. The older man and several other Scarab lieutenants surrounded the seated Leano.

Dread swept through her. She held onto the door frame because her legs would have melted under her if she didn't. Leano met her gaze pitifully. The chest plate of his armor was dented and scraped. A torn and bloodied rag was wound around his shin. Leano dabbed at the dry dark blood caked down the side of his face with a wet towel. When he removed the towel momentarily, Renna wrestled down her horror and revulsion at the sight of his missing ear. Who could have done this to Leano?—*her* Leano. Tears threatened to leak down her face, but she held strong.

"Who did this?" Renna asked bitterly. Everyone in the room faced her, their concerned and angry eyes skewered her like spears. As an enchantress for the Blue Scarabs, she had the right to be in this assembly, though some of the lieutenants made their uneasiness at her presence apparent.

"It seems this djinn is much more capable than we had originally anticipated," Lieutenant Reolo said in annoyance, the dark half-moons under his eyes making his face appear more skull than flesh.

"The master did warn us to be careful," Captain Velden replied, levelly.

"The master never told us she was strong enough to take out an entire unit," Reolo countered.

"An entire unit? What does he mean by that?" Renna asked Leano.

Leano looked away, ashamed. Renna couldn't bear to see him this way. Captain Velden placed a comforting hand on Leano's shoulder and answered for him. "Vaelin caught onto our trap and fought off the entire unit we sent to apprehend her. Leano is the sole survivor."

Renna couldn't believe what she was hearing. Leano was the best swordsman the Blue Scarabs had in Sol Forne. Even so, to successfully fight off an entire unit meant this djinn was skilled in ways they were not privy to. She suddenly found herself agreeing with Lieutenant Reolo—Master Eggar should have warned them. "Where is she now?" Renna asked.

Leano shook his head. "The horses were gone when I came to," he said, his voice thin and dry. Had no one thought to give him some water? "If I had to wager, she made her way back here to the city on one of them. I had to walk."

"We must find her, now!" The words were more forceful than Renna had intended.

"And since when do you give orders to your lieutenants?" Reolo nagged.

Renna felt a flush of anger lend stability to her legs. Less than proper comments threatened to escape her mouth, but she took a breath and steeled herself. She didn't care for Reolo, but the lieutenant was right. "Apologies, sir," she said as deferentially as she was able. There was neither smugness nor gratitude in Reolo's acknowledging nod.

"Protocol aside, the enchantress' urgency isn't uncalled for," Lieutenant Merindeo added. The broad Sol Fornian woman had never met Renna's eyes due to some unclear local superstition, so the acknowledgement of Renna's presence came as a surprise. "What are our orders, Captain?"

Captain Velden chewed his lip as he kept a wary eye on Leano. Renna could not tell what was going through the old man's mind. "We already have Scarabs stationed at the western and eastern gates, so no need to deploy more. Bring them orders to interview anyone who leaves or enters, and to keep a watchful eye out for the djinn, although she is most likely already in the city."

"Shall we implement the entry tokens, Captain?" Reolo asked.

"No need to take that measure just yet. We will divert the Scarabs from the Effore to the Portos. Both of your units will have to work together. Nobody goes into the port—not guild workers, nor any other Blue Scarabs save for those under both of your commands." Facing Renna, he asked, "How close are you?" There was a hint of annoyance behind his question, as if he was asking *"how are you not done yet?"*

"Very close, Captain," was all she could reply. She had potentially made a breakthrough in her research, but there was no sense in giving Captain Velden any false hope.

"Today."

"Captain?" Renna was taken aback by the man's succinctness.

"You will complete your experiment today. It has already taken you long enough. We can't spare any more resources for this... fancy." There was that unexpectedly impetuous side of Captain Velden again. The man didn't understand what a toll enchanting every day took on her. There was no reasoning with him when he became this way. It didn't matter—Renna knew she was merely a tool, and a tool didn't question its use. She had been ordered to complete her work, and she would have to do everything in her power to make it so.

"I will get the boy and head to the port immediately," Renna agreed.

"We're all counting on you," Captain Velden said with a smile, as if that was of any encouragement. In fact, the effect was entirely the opposite. Renna felt the spiced tea in her stomach turn to bile. She had asked for this burden, yet now it was proving much too heavy to bear. Could she really complete her work today?

Renna glanced at Leano, but he wouldn't meet her gaze. His eyes were downcast and tired. She became aware that the conversation in the room had shifted away from her, so she turned and walked back towards her office. She flipped through her tomes for something that might aid her work, but it was impossible to tell what might be useful. She was about to do something that hadn't been attempted since... well, since Vaelin was *Sealed* to the lucerne. There were no books that covered anything even remotely similar to that sort of enchantment. As far as she was aware, she was only the second person to ever undertake this. None of the writings would be of any help today. It would all come down to utilizing her intuition and existing knowledge.

And the boy. The boy and his blood were the key.

As she approached the mess hall, Renna began to run through her remaining tasks in her head. She would see how the lucerne reacted to Dorovan's blood. See if the blood could bridge the gap between the artifact and the boy. See if her Extranforial Etchings could be used to assist the process. There was so much that could go wrong. It would be trial and error—and she could no longer afford error.

She hoped Dorovan had already eaten something because there was no time to waste. In the mess hall, several Blue Scarabs were seated in small clusters along the lengthy tables. Most of them chatted quietly amongst themselves. Upon seeing Renna, their conversations either lowered to a whisper or ceased entirely. So, they were talking about Leano. They better not be spreading rumors if they knew what was best for them.

"Dorovan," she called out. There was no response. She didn't see the boy anywhere in the hall. She paced through the room, examining every bench at each table. "Has anyone seen Dorovan? The boy!" She must have asked every Blue Scarab in the large room, and, each time, she had received the same negative reply. She jogged out of the hall and through each corridor of the lodge, peeking into every room she passed. She stopped several soldiers to ask them if they had seen the boy, including the door guard, but nobody had.

Dorovan was gone.

She walked back to Captain Velden's office slowly, like a child who had lost the silver pieces her parents had given her to buy olive oil at the market. She wouldn't lie. All she could do was swallow her pride and ask for help first, and forgiveness after.

All the lieutenants, save Leano, had left the office, leaving only him and Captain Velden there. That would make things a bit easier. "The boy's gone," Renna said, skipping a preamble.

Captain Velden and Leano's expressions could not have been more different. While Leano remained defeated, Captain Velden's eyes broadened with cold contempt.

"He's not in the lodge," Renna added as if it would help.

"So be it," Captain Velden said, dismissively.

"Apologies, Captain, but I don't know if I can proceed without him. I require his blood to make any progress."

"Then you should have spilled it when you had the chance." A chill trickled down Renna's spine at his words. "We don't have the resources to spare to find him. Make it work."

"But, Captain—"

"Make it work!" Captain Velden could be downright unaccommodating at times, but he had never before raised his voice in such a way. Renna shrunk at the man's dismissive glance. All she could do was salute and accept her failure. She turned to leave when suddenly Leano's voice broke the cold silence of the room. "Wait!"

Renna slowly turned to face Leano, maneuvering away from Captain Velden's penetrating glare. Leano untied the torn up bloody rag from his leg and held it out for Renna to take, though she did not reach for it. "What is that?" she asked.

"You said you needed blood. This has the djinn's blood on it. Will this work?" Leano asked.

Renna could not believe it. Even Captain Velden inspected the bloody rag in bewilderment. Renna reached out and took the scrap of cloth. The blood was mostly dry, but there were patches of red wetness beneath the arid brownness. A faint silver shimmer glided unexpectedly through the surface of the fabric. "So? Will it work?" Captain Velden repeated the question.

"I don't know," Renna answered honestly. Leano's enthusiasm began to waver, so she quickly added, "But it's better than nothing. Thank you, Leano."

"I just couldn't leave that sitting in the dirt. I was going to let the hounds get a whiff of it to catch her scent. But perhaps it's best in your hands." Leano smiled at her, handsome as ever. Her heart leapt. "You have what you need," Captain Velden said, interrupting the moment Renna had wished would last a lifetime. "Let's not waste any more time."

Renna saluted and left the office, still unsure that the djinn's old blood would work for what she was trying to achieve. It would have to be enough.

XXII.

A Rescue

Ensa was gathering as many blue fabrics as she could find around the house and folding them neatly into a remarkably long wicker basket. Whether they were gowns, curtains, or tablecloths, it did not matter. The laborious task had even given Vaelin time to locate the house's kitchen and grab something more to eat—the thin stew she was given before had been a nurse's pittance. She had the fortune of spotting some small hens roasting over the open flame of a hearth that had been left unattended by servants who were busy repairing the damage that had been done to the home after the previous night's earthquakes.

The amplifying quakes were proof that the Cycle was weakening the closer Vaelin came to succumbing to the Compulsion. The previous night had almost been the end. How much worse would the aftermath have been if her energy had been allowed to dissipate as it had threatened to?

She plucked a hen from its skewer and ate it in secret, disposing of the bones in the soil of a nearby potted plant before rejoining Ensa.

"So what exactly is your plan?" Vaelin's question was marinated in skepticism.

"I'm a colorist," Ensa stated, as if Vaelin had been able to forget—every corner of the vibrant manor served as a gaudy reminder. "I will present myself as such at their lodge. They seem to favor blue, so I am gathering all the blue material that I have dyed."

"Then what?"

"I will use all this blue as an excuse to enter their lodge on the pretext of sampling a selection of my works to them. Once we are inside, we will find Dorovan, and help him escape."

"And how exactly do you plan on getting him out of there once we've found him?" Vaelin questioned.

Ensa gestured towards the large basket containing the fabric, as if the answer was obvious. Vaelin had to chuckle at the simplicity of the plan. What if they were not permitted inside? What if Dorovan was locked in one of the basement cells Vaelin had been held in? What if they were caught? So many 'what ifs' yet no time to come up with a better alternative. Vaelin realized that Ensa had paused her folding and was staring at her as if puzzling something out. "But what to do with you? It's not as if you can walk to the lodge with me. You will surely be recognized."

"A disguise!" The enthusiastic voice sprang in from just outside the room. The old lord of the house waltzed in layered in more color than Vaelin had ever seen on a single person. It suited him in a strange, outlandish, sort of way.

"Lord Lorenzo, were you eavesdropping?" Ensa scolded playfully, as one would with an eccentric elder.

"One of my very few faults." Lorenzo smiled and bowed deeply.

"What was that you were saying about a disguise?" Vaelin pressed. The idea of dressing up again felt tedious, but, if a disguise was the best plan they had, so be it.

"I was an actor of some renown in my younger years," Lorenzo recited. "I have more props and costumes than I have any use for. What do you fancy embodying today, gray mistress? How about an old maid, stricken by pallor? Or perhaps a young squire disfigured by skin rot? Oh! An emissary from Sour Rock plagued by a terrible case of the pox!"

"Why are all these characters sickly?" Vaelin inquired.

"Well... I hope you don't mind me saying, but your complexion is rather... unnatural," Lorenzo explained as tactfully as he could. "Could we mayhaps hide it with some stage powders?"

"No covering," Vaelin rebutted.

"Very well, then," Lorenzo conceded. "Young squire with skin rot, it is!" The man bolted out of the room with more youthful energy than his stringy limbs seemed capable of. Ensa giggled politely behind her hand, then placed a neatly folded blue scarf atop the pile.

"I'm surprised to find Dorovan's sister in such a place," Vaelin observed.

"This is a very recent arrangement," Ensa replied. She grabbed a pair of trousers, shook her head at their blue-green hue, and set them aside. "My colorist instructor, Mastro Ovello, has recently fallen ill. He has retired to a home in the countryside in hopes that the fresh air will do him some good. As you can probably tell, Lord Lorenzo was his most prominent client." Ensa gestured at the kaleidoscope of a room with a smile. "He couldn't bear losing the skill of his favorite colorist, so my teacher recommended that he employ me instead." A deep crimson painted her cheeks. "Mastro Ovello said I was the best and most promising apprentice he had ever had. Lord Lorenzo seems to agree, as he quickly took me into his home to work for him. I've recently even applied to the Fashionists' Guild, and Lord Lorenzo has offered to pay all of the dues. It's just..."

Ensa paused for a moment. She ran her thumb over an emerald silk kerchief as tenderly as if it was a kitten. "All of this happened after Dorovan left. I really wished he could have been a part of it. He's been so misguided, thinking the world owes him something rather than working on achieving anything himself. This was the life I always wished for him and the life I worked so hard to win for us. He's an ungrateful brat, but he's all the family I have left. I hope he will join me here, when all of this is over."

With a strained smile, Vaelin hid her doubts that Ensa's dream would ever come to pass. Ensa glanced over at Vaelin and the two considered each other quietly. An awkwardness that wasn't there before invaded the room.

"A parcel in hand is a prize quite grand!" Lord Lorenzo sang out excitedly as he trotted into the room with a canvas sack from which he pulled a dusty old outfit and a black wig with a small tail tied at its back. The lordling seemed instantly aware of the knot of uneasiness that had formed between the two women, and he attempted to untie it with caution. "Is the costume still required?"

Vaelin walked over to the man and took the clothes from his hands. "Thank you, Lord Lorenzo. These will do splendidly!"

The man beamed. "They should be about your size. We're of similar height, though I had a bit more meat on my bones when I fit in those. Now all my costumes sag about me like loose flesh."

Vaelin smiled at the man. "I'm sure you still look plenty dashing in them. I will change, then we must be on our way." Vaelin directed that last to Ensa. The young woman nodded as she picked up the basket of blue samples.

❧ ❧ ❧ ❧

The morning air hanging throughout the Effore was streaked with the ashy remains of the previous night's festivities. Cleaners wielding wide brush brooms scrubbed black char marks from the white marble pavement where the fire pits had been. Others picked unburnt strands of cloth from the streets, dropping the rags into baskets tied at their waists. Vaelin doubted the same cleanliness was applied to other parts of the city. More likely the ashes and rags there would remain a fixture until time wasted them away.

The clothes Lord Lorenzo had provided fit her much better than she had imagined they would. The shirt was slightly loose at the shoulders, but the trousers were even more comfortable than her own. Perhaps she would try convincing the old man to part with them when all this was through. Instead of wearing powders or the wig Lord Lorenzo had handed her, she had decided to wear an old winter coat with its hood raised over her head to conceal her hair and complexion. She was thankful that it was a cooler morning than usual, otherwise the coat would have been sweltering. Lord Lorenzo had protested the decision, deeming the choice "unconvincing", and suggesting still more alternatives. He was a sweet man, for a lordling.

Ensa wore a look of quiet determination as she held onto one handle of the large blue fabric stuffed basket. Vaelin held the other handle, struggling to match the woman's faster gait. The wounds sustained the previous day were much more serious than Vaelin wanted to admit. They needed time to heal—time that Vaelin did not have. The two women hadn't spoken a word to each other since leaving Lord Lorenzo's home, each nervously contemplating what she must do once they reached the lodge. The more Vaelin scrutinized it, the more it seemed probable that their plan would snap like old wood. It was barely a plan at all—more of a gamble.

As they neared the Blue Scarab lodge, Ensa's steps became slower and more unsure. "Are you all right?" Vaelin asked, quietly.

"Yes." Ensa breathed deeply to steady herself.

"Would you like me to do the talking?"

"No," Ensa replied, then stopped. She turned to Vaelin and forced a smile. "Dorovan is my brother. I would do this even if you weren't here." The woman's sudden determination was enough to kindle Vaelin's courage.

A few steps later, they reached the door of the Blue Scarab lodge. A guard stood outside in full armor. He had the dizzy look of someone who had stayed awake much too late the night before. The man's relaxed posture relieved Vaelin—word of her battle the previous evening must have not yet reached the city. They would not be looking for her. Good.

"What?" the guard asked brusquely, as if they had interrupted an activity of the utmost importance.

"Greetings, sir," Ensa said pleasantly. "My name is Ciena, and this is my assistant Portico. I am a colorist and I've been instructed by Mastro Velden to sample some of my best work so that he may commission some banners to hang about your halls." Ensa glanced over at the basket to accent her words. Vaelin stifled a grin—the woman was impressively convincing.

The guard looked at the basket of fabric as if not comprehending what he was seeing. "The halls have no banners," he stated flatly.

"Well, of course not," Ensa chirped amicably. "That's why I'm here! When I've done my work, blue banners will fly across every hall, reminding you of all the values the Blue Scarabs stand for. It's not enough to only wear blue armor. Captain Velden said you must be immersed in the color to truly believe in your mission."

The sleepiness seemed to vanish from the man's eyes, replaced with unexpected lucidity. "Captain Velden is in his office. Allow me to escort you."

"There's no need to take you away from your task," Ensa said, smiling brightly. "I was here just last week. I know the way."

The man nodded with a dopey smirk and held the door. As they walked past, Ensa asked, "And what was your name, sir?"

The guard blinked in astonishment. "Apologies, mistress. It's Breto."

"Have a lovely day, Breto," Ensa smiled. The man grinned after them.

Vaelin could not believe that had worked, yet she could not revel in the moment of celebration. Her heart was galloping like a horse. They still had to find Dorovan. He could be in the basement cells where she had been placed the last time, but she doubted that the Blue Scarabs would mistreat the boy in such a way. Captain Velden had shown interest in him. Most likely, he had been given a warm bunk for the night. She closed her eyes and allowed the tenuous *Sealing* between them to guide her.

The basket was too wide to fit through the hallway unless they carried it one in front of the other. Ensa walked at the back, and Vaelin took the lead. She could feel Dorovan somewhere nearby, though she couldn't be entirely sure where. From afar, narrowing down a location had been easy, but now that she was at the lodge, the boy's *life energy* seemed to waft about the building like strong incense.

Vaelin held her head high as armored men and women passed, shooting the basket of fabric curious glances. No one stopped or questioned them. Vaelin hoped Ensa would maintain the same composure and intuition she had demonstrated with the guard. The hallway bent left, then opened into a large space filled with long tables where a few soldiers sat eating bowls of porridge. Vaelin scanned the space, but Dorovan was nowhere to be seen. She could sense a subtle panic in Ensa's breathing. Vaelin tugged on the basket and led Ensa towards the back of the hall. Vaelin placed the basket on the floor against the far wall, and Ensa followed suit.

"What do we do now?" Ensa asked quietly. The poor woman wore an apologetic look, as if this was somehow her fault.

"It's all right," Vaelin reassured her. "I can feel him nearby." Vaelin began unfolding some of the clothes, placing them over a table. Once again, Ensa mimicked her actions.

"What are we doing?" Ensa asked.

"See these Scarabs?" Vaelin nodded towards the soldiers eating at the tables. "They saw us come in here. It wouldn't look right if we left immediately after walking in. We must give the impression that we're doing a task before we move along, as if we meant to be in here all along." Ensa nodded in understanding. Vaelin selected a pair of light-blue trousers and neatly draped them across the table, as if to display them. Ensa did the same with a darker headscarf.

"At my signal, act as if you've forgotten something," Vaelin whispered. "Make it believable. I will then leave as if to retrieve it. That's when I'll-"

"What's going on over here?" The two of them turned towards the voice. A bald armored soldier stood before them with her arms folded.

Vaelin felt the words hit her like a punch to the head. She dared not look over at Ensa in fear of seeing whatever dismay the woman wore. Vaelin was about to speak, but Ensa was a breath quicker. "My, you startled us." Her surprise seemed genuine because it was. "That's what happens when one only pays attention to their work and not their surroundings. My teacher always said that was a fault of mine."

While Ensa's tone implied lightness, the soldier's jaw remained set and her eyes became unyielding in their inspection. "Who are you? What is all this?" The woman took a step towards them, her head towering over them by several feet.

"I am a colorist," Ensa replied, lacking the sureness the story had had with the guard. "Captain Velden called us here to sample my work for some banners he wants made." The last words fizzled out under the dark scrutiny of the soldier. The dagger tucked within Vaelin's pants called for her. She wasn't sure she could take on all these Scarabs in her condition, but at least she wasn't helpless.

"You don't say?" the soldier asked, unconvinced. "I will go fetch him, then."

"Please do," Ensa replied with a smile. "We've been waiting for him."

The woman furrowed her brow and walked away, exiting the hall. Ensa turned, breathing hastily as if she could not get enough air. "Gods! What do we do?" she whispered in a panic. "We're caught. It's over. We–"

"Lieutenant Leano is back!" The shout rang within the hall. Every Scarab that sat eating abandoned their meals and ran from the hall. A stampede of soldiers piled into the hallway and pushed towards the entrance of the lodge. The sound of it all forced Ensa to hug the far wall with her back. Vaelin stretched protectively in front of the frightened woman, her hand hovering over where Vitra was nestled. But soon, they were left alone in the hall, as every Scarab within the lodge clotted at the entryway. This was an opportunity they could not waste.

"Stay here," Vaelin instructed. "I will go look for Dorovan amid this confusion."

"What do I do?" Ensa asked, grabbing pleadingly onto the sleeve of Vaelin's shirt as a child seeking the guidance of a parent would.

"Prepare the basket. If anyone asks, stick to your story. When in doubt, feign stupidity. I will be quick."

Vaelin felt terrible for leaving the woman alone, but finding Dorovan took precedence. Ensa released Vaelin's sleeve and nodded. Vaelin rushed towards the exit of the hall when she was suddenly face to face with the boy she was searching for. Dorovan met her eyes and the two stood glancing at one another dumbfoundedly. Neither could believe that the other was there. Vaelin was the first to shake herself out of her stupor, grabbing the boy by the arm, and dragging him towards Ensa.

"Dorovan!" The young woman threw her arms around the stunned boy. "We found you!"

"What in the gods' names are you doing here?" Dorovan whispered.

"We're here to break you free," Ensa replied, placing a gentle hand on the boy's cheek. Dorovan considered the basket for several seconds, then backed away from the tender touch. His face was strangely unreadable. "Come on! Hurry and get inside. We will hide you under the fabric and sneak you out." Ensa clung to Dorovan's arm, pulling him towards the basket.

"Why would I do that?" Dorovan asked.

Ensa blinked in response to the question. "Because you're being held captive by the Blue Scarabs. We're here to help you escape."

"Why would you think I need your help to leave this place?" Dorovan's defiance was apparent.

Dismay began to build within Vaelin. She stepped between the siblings. "This is no time to mess about, Dorovan. Climb in the basket, now."

"I'm fine here," Dorovan shook his head, retrieving his arm from his sister's grasp. He looked into Vaelin's eyes for a moment, then looked away. He appeared burdened with knowledge. "They don't intend to harm me in any way. I think there is a way for me to end the Contract by helping them with their mission. I choose to stay here."

Vaelin considered the boy's words heavily. What did Dorovan know about the Blue Scarab's mission? She had no time to ask, as someone in the hallway called out for the crowd to disperse. She mined deep within herself and found, to her disappointment, that she still did not truly trust the boy. While the Compulsion had receded from her mind for the time being, standing this close to Dorovan had reminded her that it was still there, lurking within the shadowy depths of herself, waiting to spill out and overtake them both. She could not bring herself to trust him with so much at stake.

"If you do not get in that basket, I will make you," Vaelin threatened.

Dorovan grimaced sourly. "Then make me." The taunt was childish. He nodded farewell to his sister, then turned to leave. Vaelin was left with no choice. She pulled Vitra from her waistband and struck Dorovan on the back of the head with its pommel. She smoothly lunged to catch Dorovan as he collapsed limply and dragged him towards the basket.

"Help me," she hissed to Ensa. The young woman was too startled to speak, though she quietly lifted Dorovan's legs and helped place him within the basket. They bent his knees to make him fit fully. In unison, they began to cover him with the blue fabric they had splayed across the table. By then, soldiers had started trickling back into the hall.

"We should go now," Vaelin said firmly. The two grabbed the handles at each end of the basket, then, on Vaelin's count of three, they lifted it together. Dorovan was light enough that carrying it wasn't too much of an ordeal, however his weight was distributed unevenly towards Vaelin, making their walk a bit of an unbalanced one.

Thankfully, the lingering soldiers that filled the hallway were too immersed in their own conversations to notice them. Vaelin overheard some saying that Lieutenant Leano had returned to the lodge, wounded and defeated. She hoped she would not have the disastrous misfortune of running into the man, otherwise this caper would all have been for naught. Increasing her step and ignoring the protests of her chest and leg, Vaelin hoped that Ensa could keep up the pace.

Vaelin shoved the front doors open with her shoulder, and held them awkwardly so that Ensa could join her outside. A sigh was perched to take flight from Vaelin's lips, when the door guard approached them with a confused look. "Out so soon?" he asked Ensa.

The young woman looked utterly incapable of forming a sentence. Her mouth moved soundlessly as the guard held her gaze.

"There was a commotion," Vaelin interjected. The guard looked over at her in bewilderment, as if he had assumed she could not speak. "Captain Velden had other matters to attend to."

The guard nodded to himself—the man did not seem like the smartest sheep in the flock. "Ah, yes. He must be busy with Lieutenant Leano. What a great mess."

Ensa somehow found the composure to smile. "We must be on our way," she said.

"I hope you will come back soon," the man told Ensa, who nodded awkwardly in reply.

Vaelin tugged lightly on the basket, and Ensa joined her in walking away. They kept a natural pace until they turned the first corner. Out of sight of the lodge, they placed the basket on the ground gently—it felt as if the weight had increased tenfold since they had first picked it up.

"Oh gods!" Ensa whimpered. "We made it! I cannot believe we actually made it."

Vaelin gripped her stinging chest.

"What did Dorovan mean about a contract? Did they do something to him?" Ensa asked between strained breaths.

Vaelin shook her head. The boy was irritating and unpredictable but wanting to help the Blue Scarabs was strange even for him. Whatever had happened to him the previous night had convinced him to stay. That was something he would have to figure out on his own after she had found the lucerne and freed herself. Then, all of her ties to the boy would be gone. Well, almost all of them.

"Ready?" Vaelin asked Ensa. The young woman nodded and the two lifted the basket once more. As they made their way slowly through the crowded streets, Vaelin formulated a plan. Unlike the one they had just stumbled through, this one was clear. She would remove the *Seal* she had placed on Dorovan. It was no longer safe for him to bear it.

Then, she would sneak into the harbor, where the other *life energy* resided. Whatever it was, Vaelin knew it would lead her to the lucerne.

It would have been easy for her to succumb to despair. The end of her journey had felt like a mirage for so long, always visible and shimmering on the horizon yet beyond her grasp. It had never felt this fixed before—this reachable. The best she could do was move forward.

XXIII.

As You Wish

The fire in the hearth caressed his face with a warm hand, momentarily stifling the winter chill at his back. Dorovan turned from it and faced the infinite darkness. The light of the flames didn't extend to the rest of the hall in front of him. In spite of that strangeness, he was aware that he was in his family's manor. Footsteps sounded from the darkness and Dorovan felt a deep anguish wash over him. A figure moved in the murky blackness. As it closed in, it came into focus: it was his uncle Asello, his face contorted into a rictus of misery. Suddenly, Dorovan knew what this was. A memory. A nightmare. This was the day his birthright had been taken from him.

As if in response to this realization, the room began to shift and bulge uncontrollably. Making sense of the dream was like trying to tie a sword into a knot. Asello grew and shrunk, as did the hearth and the darkness surrounding him. The tiles of the hearth began to split and fall to the floor as if they were leaves from a tree. The fire leaked from its stone base like a liquid puddle while, above, its tendrils coiled and snaked around the fraying edges of the scene. Some of it seared Dorovan's hand. He looked at his fingers, noticing that they were still intact—still whole. No sooner had he processed the image than it shifted once more, the two fingers of his right hand vanishing like smoke.

Suddenly, there was light. He was awake. The fuzzy room in which he lay came into focus. Dorovan didn't recognize the space, but it had a familiar smell to it. He reached for the back of his head, where a dull ache pulsed. It felt as if he had been bashed by a club. The area was tender and swollen, but there was neither fresh blood nor the stickiness of a scab that he could feel.

What had happened to him? He recalled fainting upon touching that humming, boxlike artifact the night before. Strange dreams had followed. Then, he was at the Blue Scarab lodge. The enchantress. The commotion of soldiers. And then... *Ah, yes.* Vaelin had been there, telling him to come with her. And his sister, too. What had his sister been doing there? As if to answer his query, the door to the room opened and Ensa walked in. She wore a simple, yet flattering, light blue dress. A headscarf with patterns that reminded him of lavender flowers adorned her head. He had seen how beautifully she'd dressed for the banquet, but to see her this elegant in the daytime was shocking.

"How do you feel?" she asked softly.

Dorovan shifted to sit up against the headboard. When was the last time he had slept in a proper bed that wasn't a hard military cot or stuffed with hay? "The damn djinn struck me on the back of the head, didn't she?"

Ensa nodded. "She said it was too dangerous to have you stay in the lodge."

He gripped onto the bed sheets wishing they were the hairs on top of the djinn's head. "Where is she?"

"Gone."

"Where?"

"She said she had something important to do."

Dorovan closed his eyes and focused his attention upon the djinn. It had become clearer each day that he was fuzzily aware of where Vaelin was in relation to him. But now, he could not seem to focus his mind upon her. The blow he had taken to the back of his head could have dampened his focus. Or... Dorovan looked at the palm of his hand where the *Sealing* rune had been etched by Vaelin. A thin pink line ran through the etching where the djinn's black dagger had recently sliced. What could this mean?

"Vaelin did that after we brought you here," Ensa said, seeing the unspoken question in his face.

"Damn her," he seethed. How dare she make that choice for him? Was the djinn trying to teach him some sort of lesson? Why now? Was this to show him how little trust she had in his ability to be heroic? "Where is she?" he asked again.

Ensa frowned. "I told you, she's gone. I don't know where."

Dorovan stood from the bed and took a few steps towards the door. The room spun around him, and suddenly he found himself being propped up by his sister. "She didn't have to hit you so hard," she said. "You should stay here and rest."

Dorovan knew his sister was right, and, for a moment, he considered just laying down and sleeping the day away. Ensa's touch reawakened memories of her nursing him to health when he was sick as a child; of how she would dab gently at his feverish forehead with a cold damp cloth while singing him to sleep. Dorovan shrugged away from Ensa's touch. "I must find her."

"Dorovan, please," Ensa pleaded. She sounded exhausted. "Please stay here. Let the djinn do what she must. It is of no concern to you."

"Of no concern?" Dorovan realized for the first time how his sister saw him: childish and self-obsessed, completely naive to the needs of those around him. He felt indignation at this perception, but also, he realized, shame. It had only been a few weeks since he had left the apartment they had shared together, but he had already changed so much. Even his goal had changed. No longer did he simply wish to become a noble, and to reinstate his family's titles. Those had been the dreams of a different Dorovan—a boy. After meeting Master Eggar, he was now aware of what a hero truly was. A hero spoke truthfully and put those with corrupted power in their place. A hero identified threats and stopped at nothing to acquire and wield the power needed to defend against them. Dorovan had been given the opportunity to help that man in his mission. He hadn't realized how much he wanted to help until he had seen Vaelin and the basket—knowing he could leave the lodge, he had realized that he couldn't. It was the first selfless choice Dorovan had ever made. Was that not the sign of a hero?

His sister would never understand—to her, he was still the boy who had cried himself to sleep every night after their parents were taken from them. The wide-eyed look she gave him now seemed to only half-comprehend that any change had occurred. Dorovan walked to where his boots sulked by the door. He picked them up and lumbered out of the room.

"Dorovan," Ensa called out. Her voice lacked the scolding tone it always used to have. Perhaps, just now, she did see him as more than just a child.

Dorovan stopped for a moment, though he couldn't bring himself to turn and face her. When she didn't say anything further, he kept walking.

❧ ❧ ❧ ❧

It was as if every Blue Scarab in Sol Forne had collected at the harbor to block anyone from either entering or leaving. The nobility of Sol Forne had started a quiet resistance. Rather than organizing a meeting with the Guild Union as Master Eggar had instructed, they had instead continued hiring mercenary bands from outside of the city to come to their aid. Renna knew the Blue Scarabs had only found this out after intercepting a missive at the western gate about an hour ago. Though Leano was injured, he had been sent to join the soldiers there. How many more missives had escaped their scrutiny? Would Sol Forne soon find itself under siege? Would Leano be able to stand his ground in his condition, if it came to it?

Renna banished these intrusive thoughts. The task at hand was much too important for such distractions. She was permitted through the blockade and escorted to the shack where the lucerne was stored. The ripe fishy smell betrayed the shack's previous use before their takeover. The unassuming black artifact shimmered in the lowlight of the shack as if it, alone, stood in bright sunlight. It no longer sang with resonant *life energy* as it had when Dorovan had touched it the previous night, but it hummed like a deep and distant earthquake. The *life energy* submerged within the harbor still harmonized with the lucerne, though it was much quieter than the night before. The time had come for her to awaken that massive *life energy*, and *Seal* it to herself.

With the bloody rag in hand, Renna moved closer to the lucerne. She felt the artifact tug at the djinn's blood ever so slightly. Renna smiled—this would work! Focusing onto the blood, she felt the echo of *life energy* reverberate through the etchings on her arms. Then, she firmly pressed the rag against the surface of the lucerne.

Instantly, she was flooded with awareness. She understood how this *Sealing* had been accomplished, and how much *life energy* was needed to achieve it. The knowledge of how to *Seal* herself to the *life energy* pulsing in the harbor was at last in her grasp. But also, Renna was disappointedly aware that her body would not be enough. The lucerne had been the culmination of extensive research, experimentation, and perfection. It was alive, in a way she could not explain. Vaelin and the lucerne were both beings of pure *life energy*. Renna was merely human. She did not possess enough *life energy* within herself to accomplish such a costly enchantment.

She lowered the rag from the lucerne, immediately severing her connection to it. She felt as if she might cry. She had come so close to fulfilling her purpose in this mission, only to fail everyone in their greatest moment of need.

"Oh, Renna. You give up too easily."

Renna gave a start at the sudden words that shattered the almost reverent silence of the shack. She turned and faced Master Eggar. Immediately, she averted her gaze in embarrassment.

"I'm so sorry, Master," she said. "It seems that to accomplish such an enchantment, one would need more *life energy* within them than a mere human can contain."

Master Eggar approached her until he stood only inches away from her. She could feel his breath on her forehead. "And that's going to stop you?"

Renna forced herself to look into the man's eyes. They were alight with fiery passion. She was suddenly aware that the question he had asked was an accusation. No, she would not give up so soon. Not after coming so far. But what could she do? She was now certain that attempting such a *Sealing* would destroy her. Unless.

Whoever had built the lucerne and *Sealed* Vaelin to it must have had great stores of *life energy* at their disposal. If she needed more *life energy* within her, there were ways to procure it. She was currently surrounded by it—the lifeblood of Albadone. The *black water*. Eggar smiled at the realization brightening her face.

Before she could detail her plan, Captain Velden sprinted into the warehouse. "Master," he said with a curt bow. "It's the djinn. She's here to see you."

The smile remained on Master Eggar's mouth, though it left his eyes. "I was wondering when she would turn up."

❦ ❦ ❦ ❦

Everywhere one's gaze turned it landed on a Blue Scarab. The image of them jostling shoulder to shoulder in their blue armor perfectly evoked their beetle namesake. Each had a sword at their hip. A few had bows and quivers tied to their backs. But, while their hard faces spoke of the anticipation of the conflict to come, the silence that overtook the space was almost peaceful. The only event to disturb the stillness was when Master Eggar, flanked by Captain Velden and a couple other soldiers, announced himself and walked through the barricade towards the docks.

The consistent brushing of the waves in the light breeze would have been reassuring on any other day. But it wasn't just the silence in the air that Vaelin noticed. The *life energy* that had called her to the port had quieted to an almost-whisper. It wasn't gone, just dormant.

The line of Scarabs ignored her as she paced through the parallel street. So, they weren't patrolling—they were guarding. She walked the entire length of the Portos District, unable to find an unguarded opening into the harbor. With no access to the water, and no workers heading in or out of the port, there was no way to smuggle herself inside. She would have to try a different approach. Ever since stepping foot into Sol Forne she had been sneaking about, often disguising herself to avoid being recognized. This time, she would get what she wanted by being herself.

She walked to the main entrance of the port, where the Blue Scarab presence was the thickest. One of the soldiers wore a blue cape and horned helmet identical to those Lieutenant Leano had worn during their confrontation the previous night. This would also be a lieutenant, then. She approached the man. Immediately, two Scarab soldiers

flanked her with their swords drawn. She raised her hands
and stared squarely at the lieutenant.

"Halt!" one of the two soldiers commanded.

"You, there!" Vaelin called out. "Lieutenant!"

The helmeted man faced Vaelin with a quizzical and irritated look. Then, his eyes broadened in alarm. "The
djinn!" he exclaimed. Then, to the soldiers, "Take her!"

Vaelin allowed the two soldiers to seize her arms with no
resistance. "I am here of my own free will to speak to Master Eggar. Please, take me to him."

The lieutenant's gaze was fixed upon her in revulsion.
Vaelin worried her gamble would flop when he suddenly
addressed the soldiers, his confronting gaze never leaving
her own. The man's eyes glowed with opportunity. "I will
take her to the master myself."

"Is that wise, Lieutenant Reolo?" a woman's deep voice
asked.

Lieutenant Reolo faced the woman with distaste. She,
too, wore the cape and horned helmet of a lieutenant. In
her hand was a tall steaming kettle. "What are you doing in
my zone, Merindeo?" he shot back.

"*Lieutenant* Merindeo," she corrected, narrowing her
eyes. "And since you asked so nicely, I come bearing the
gift of hot orzo." She shook the kettle for emphasis.

Reolo licked his lips, then sighed in resignation. "Apologies, Lieutenant Merindeo. Thank you for the... wonderful offering."

"And yet, I hear that you are willing to abandon your
post in order to escort this... *djinn* to the master." She made
a *Warding* gesture at Vaelin by creating a circle with her
fingers. Vaelin had to chuckle.

Heat rose in Lieutenant Reolo's cheeks. Vaelin wasn't sure if it was indignation or embarrassment. Nevertheless, he faced the two soldiers flanking Vaelin and waved them away. "Take her to the master."

Vaelin did her best to hide the relief she felt. She was escorted through the blockade to the docks. Captain Velden's eyes widened in surprise upon seeing her. "What are you doing here?" he asked, sounding genuinely astonished.

"She said she wants to speak with the master," one of the soldiers announced.

The captain nodded to himself, though a profound confusion creased his brow. He hurried away towards a nearby wooden shack. Only then did Vaelin perceive the low hum of *life energy* seeping from the hovel. It was an entirely distinct *life energy* from the one slumbering within the water. It was uncanny—unmistakable.

It was the lucerne. It was here.

The moment she found an opening, she would free herself from the restraining grip of these soldiers, and then remove her *Sealing* with the lucerne. But that could prove a difficult and lengthy process. In truth, she wasn't entirely sure how it would work. If she rushed things now, her plans could all come crashing around her like a house made of glass.

Captain Velden returned, trailed by Master Eggar and the bald enchantress from the banquet, who shared Captain Velden's confused expression. Master Eggar, on the other hand, looked as if he were meeting an old friend.

"Vaelin!" he greeted excitedly. "How wonderful of you to join us. I hear you turned yourself in. Why would you do

such a thing?" He asked the last as if it were the punchline
to a joke.

Give me the lucerne. She held herself from yelling. All
in due time. She was here for another reason. The *life energy* within the water had called upon her for help. She
could not ignore that.

"You must stop whatever it is you're doing here," Vaelin
stated. She felt stupid for not having more concrete accusations to throw their way.

"What, the blockade?" Captain Velden asked.

Vaelin shook her head, then flashed an accusatory leer
at the enchantress. Vaelin hadn't gotten a chance to take a
good look at the woman during the banquet, but now she
saw the dark etchings upon her flesh. This one was deeply
skilled in the enchanting arts. Whatever the *life energy* in
the harbor feared, this woman must be involved in it.

The enchantress looked almost offended by Vaelin's silent accusation. "What do you know about what transpires
here?" she asked.

"Steel yourself, Renna," Master Eggar cautioned, holding up a hand. "We may have found ourselves an unlikely
ally. Do you feel it too, djinn? The *life energy* that inhabits
these waters?" Eggar didn't wait for a reply. "I do not, for I
lack the connection to the Cycle of Nature that enchantresses, and you, possess. Even so, I wish to wield its power
as one wields a sword. With it, I wish to liberate the citizens
of Hovardom from the shackles of war, death, and sickness.
I have seen the possibilities laid out before us, and the gods
have granted us the tools to achieve them. And here you
are, Vaelin, standing at the cliffside with us. Will you pull
us to the certainty of safety, or push us over the precipice?"

Everyone around her seemed spellbound by the man's impassioned words, though to Vaelin, they sounded rote. Here stood a man that wanted to wield for himself a power he knew nothing about. His goal may have been admirable, but it was also unachievable. War was one thing, but sickness and death, while unpleasant, were vital parts of the Cycle, equal to birth and growth. To unbalance such a thing would cause untold ripples of damage to the world. No, Vaelin concluded, that goal could never be realized. But the power Eggar desired could. And that alone made him more dangerous than Vaelin had previously assumed.

She looked at the enchantress, hoping to see shock or scorn on her face, but instead her eyes glowed with awe for the man, the same as everyone else's. This *life energy* was right to feel threatened.

"Ages ago," Vaelin began, "the elvenfolk too had wished to wield such power. They discovered how to enslave *life energy* and use it to their own ends. As one of the only remnants of that age, I am proof of their folly. They paid for the chaos they unleashed with their physical bodies. You are only repeating their mistakes. You are the one pushing the world over the precipice of disaster."

Vaelin's mouth felt dry. She licked her lips and waited for the reaction of those that surrounded her. Eggar smiled pleasantly. "That is precisely why we need you. You have so much to teach us about the failures of the past, and how to overcome them. Tell us, Vaelin, how may we *Seal* this *life energy* to us while avoiding the consequences you speak of?"

Heat rose in her face. "Would you ask someone fighting to gain their freedom to teach you the best way to enslave another? I have seen countless people destroy themselves by achieving what they desire. Too often, I am the one who helps them achieve it. I try to warn you, so why do you stupid humans never listen? You are fools! Abandon what you are doing here. It will not end well for anyone."

Master Eggar sighed and shook his head. "I will find a use for you, yet. Take her back to the lodge." That last was said to the soldiers, who began to escort her away.

Vaelin struggled under their heavy grip, but she was too weak and wounded to shake them off. She was dragged away from the shack that contained the lucerne. She focused her awareness on the essence of *Power,* preparing to break free from her captors.

"Stop!" It was the enchantress' voice. Vaelin's focus wavered. "We can use her for the *Sealing,*" the enchantress told the two men. Eggar beckoned Renna to explain herself with a gesture of his hand. "The *life energy* within me is not enough to be able to successfully complete the *Sealing* ritual. The djinn, however, is a being of pure *life energy.* Her blood, combined with the *black water,* should be enough to guarantee our success."

Vaelin's revulsion tasted of bile. "No, you cannot!" Vaelin thrashed in the soldiers' grip, sending both flying across the dock and into the water with her *Power*-aided strength. Reinforcements moved in to seize her.

Master Eggar ignored the commotion, pondering Renna's words for a few moments. Then, he nodded. "We do this now."

"This is wrong and you know it," Vaelin threatened as the soldiers backed her towards the water.

"It needs to be done," Renna said, stepping through the line of soldiers and moving closer to the djinn. "It needs to be done," she repeated, this time to herself, as if she needed convincing as well. Renna grabbed Vaelin's wrist. Vaelin felt the essence of *Power* being redirected from her and into Renna, the woman's tightening grip on her wrist threatening to break it. The Extransforial Etchings on the woman's arm utilized Vaelin as if drawing energy from a runestone, and the enchantress knew it. If Vaelin continued to maintain her connection to *Power* she would only be giving Renna more strength.

Vaelin released the connection, nearly collapsing as she did so. Renna nodded to two of the soldiers who held Vaelin up by her arms. Vaelin's only solace was that she was still close to the lucerne—maybe close enough to be able to sever its hold over her. Maybe.

❧ ❧ ❧ ❧

As Dorovan paced through the city streets towards the harbor to the south, he could sense that something was afoot in the city. The Effore marketplace was not as lively as usual. Some stalls were shuttered, while the carts had been removed entirely. That was a bad omen. Marketplaces were the vital organs of the city. When they were not in operation it meant that the city's life was being critically disrupted.

As the marble streets gave way to the cobbled ground of the Portos District, Dorovan could hear the sounds of footsteps and chanting in the distance. The streets of the Portos

were even more deserted than the Effore, so the implica-
tions of such a gathering were alarming. Curiosity got the
best of him. Dorovan turned a few sharp corners until he
reached the outer warehouses, where, only a few days ago,
he and Vaelin had been catching robbers. My, how silly he
felt thinking back on it. Nobles and rich merchants were
having their way in this city, while children were forced to
steal so their families could survive. Vaelin had tried to explain it to him, but it wasn't until seeing Master Eggar's actions at the banquet that Dorovan had understood it. Property did not write songs and stories of the heroes that pro-
tected it.

Turning a last corner, Dorovan was faced with a large
group of armed soldiers. Upon their breasts was the insignia
of the Mercenaries' Guild—a five-point star within a circle
of fire. They were marching south towards the port with
swords and spears in their hands. At the back was a line of
archers, bows loaded with vicious arrows. So. This is what
it had come to. Rather than talking and negotiating, the nobility of Sol Forne had once again hired mercenary bands
to protect their interests. Dorovan felt disgusted at having
once associated himself with their kind. He turned down a
side alley and sprinted towards the port, taking a more direct route than the mercenaries were on. He needed to
make it in time to warn the Scarabs.

❦ ❦ ❦ ❦

In Twineback Renna had performed enchantments that
had required strange costs. To enchant *Power* into a pair of

gloves for a blacksmith that had commissioned them, she had once had to eat twelve dandelion flowers in quick succession before reciting a chant of *Power* twelve times. These rituals had been passed down from enchantress to apprentice for generations, this ancient knowledge all originating from the First Enchantress who had laid the groundwork for how enchantments were performed and discovered many of the most commonly known costs. She had also been the one who had first transcribed the language of the True One, Chanter's Tongue—the words that awakened the *life energy* within all things.

This, however, would be unlike anything she had ever attempted before.

As the two Scarabs held Vaelin, the djinn squirmed about feebly. She had been begging them to put a stop to this enchantment since it began. Upon reaching the dock, the soldiers forced the djinn to her knees. Renna unsheathed the short sword at her belt with one hand, carefully keeping the other on Vaelin's shoulder. She was prepared to absorb any enchantment the djinn may try to embody as she had done moments before. Renna had never thought she would have much reason to use her sword. Vaelin's eyes shot wide at the sight of the blade.

"Wait!" the djinn spoke. "You don't need to use that. There's an etching of *Sealing* upon my chest that never heals. It's what *Seals* me to the lucerne."

Renna's interest was piqued. She unfastened the buttons at the front of the djinn's shirt revealing a bandage stained with old blood. Renna ripped the sticky linens, uncovering the dark wound at the djinn's chest. It was, in fact, in the shape of *Sealing*. Another piece of the puzzle had been revealed to Renna. She sheathed her sword—it would seem she would not need to use it just yet. The wound pulsed, red and feverish, partly covered with scabs and partly raw. It was clear to her what she must do.

Renna placed her mouth to the wound and sucked upon it, filling her mouth with as much fresh blood as she could. She knew how this must look to the others, but she was beyond caring about such menial things. She was afflicted with purpose. Once her mouth was adequately filled with the coppery taste of hot blood, *life energy* had begun to coat her from within. It was electrifying. She felt dazed, yet somehow awakened—strangely focused. But it wasn't nearly enough.

Renna wiped the fresh blood that stained her lips. Everyone stared at her in a mixture of confusion and outrage at what she had done. Master Eggar's face, however, was resolved. "So?" he asked, folding his arms at his chest.

"I need more. I must consume the *black water*," Renna resolved. "I should be able to feel when I have enough *life energy* within me. Then, I will have to etch *Sealing* upon my flesh, just like what's on the djinn's chest."

"You will pay for this mistake!" Vaelin cried out. "Don't you see? The cost is enslavement!"

Renna turned back to the djinn. "What do you mean?"

"I created the lucerne!" Vaelin admitted unpleasantly. "I was happy to please and share my knowledge with other intelligent beings who claimed they could use me to help their world. I created the lucerne by cleaving a portion of my power from myself so it could be used by others. But the elvenfolk discovered they could not directly access that power without my aid. So they selfishly *Sealed* me within that portion of myself." Vaelin grimaced. "At first, I was resistant to fulfill their requests, but I soon learned that I did not have that choice. By separating that power from myself, I had made it unstable. If it wasn't regularly directed, it would dissipate without rejoining the Cycle. You, an enchantress, should know the consequences of removing such a great store of *life energy* from this world."

Renna could hear the truth in the djinn's words. She had spent the past few days studying the lucerne, and while she felt she had only scratched the surface of its capabilities, she could imagine how critical its immense power was.

Vaelin continued, "Whether it's severing a vast *life energy* from yourself or taking one into your body, the cost of moving that much power is to forfeit your ability to choose how it's wielded. Since I can't direct the power myself, I must enact the will of others so that the energy within the lucerne doesn't disappear from the Cycle. These are my Contracts."

Renna's fist shook. What was she doing here? The transcribed teachings of the First Enchantress spoke of an "ultimate cost"—a cost so great it could shatter the world. The first thing an apprentice enchantress learned was to never be so careless as to ignore the cost of enchantments. Wasn't that what she was doing now? And for what? To please Master Eggar?

No. To save Hovardom.

"You know this is wrong," Vaelin begged. "If you take in that much *life energy*, not only will you not be able to control it, but your physical body will also die."

Renna chose to ignore the djinn's pleas. "Bring me a barrel," she commanded. Within moments, the soldiers placed one beside her and removed its lid. Renna took a deep breath. Whether she looked foolish no longer mattered to her. She was demonstrating to her master how far she was willing to go to push them towards success. "Give me your helmet," she asked a soldier while holding out her hand. The soldier obeyed reluctantly.

Renna scooped a helmetful of the thick black liquid and drank it in. It tasted like rich and nourishing earth. And blood. *Life energy* filled her from within. For an instant, she thought it would be too much, that she would burst. She dropped the helmet and fought hard not to gag on the thick liquid—that would surely bring her shame.

She wiped the *black water* from her mouth and chin before opening her eyes. The *life energy* that coursed through her made her tremble involuntarily, as if she was fighting a deep chill. Unsheathing her sword and etching the rune of *Sealing* upon her palm with its tip was the fulfillment of a promise to the blade—no one else could do it but herself. There was no need for chants thanks to the Extranforial Etchings upon her arm, but she uttered the words nonetheless.

When it was done, she dropped her sword and held her bloody hand up high. "We need as much enchanting material as possible to ensure this succeeds," Renna declared. Her voice felt strange to her ears, inhuman. She turned to Captain Velden and added, "I will need barrels of *black water* to be emptied into the port."

To his credit, the captain did not question the order coming from her. "How many barrels?" he asked.

"As many as possible," she replied.

"It will be done." The man nodded and signaled to a nearby soldier to approach. After receiving his orders, the soldier jogged away, returning minutes later with a crowd of other Scarabs. They each positioned themselves behind barrels of *black water*, forming a blue wreath around the docks. *That should do.*

Renna uttered a chant of *Blessing* to herself—a minor chant, simply used to guide the flow of *life energy* towards an enchantress. It filled Renna with assuredness. This was going to work.

She nodded at those manning the barrels, then knelt and placed her hand into the water. Almost in unison, the barrels were tipped over, their sludgy contents spilling into the sea. Sudden exhaustion made Renna feel as if she would collapse into the water. But Master Eggar stood over her, holding her steady by the shoulders. Having the man that had reignited her faith in people hold onto her as she fulfilled her use meant everything to Renna, though the look she saw staring back at her in the rippling sea water was that of fear.

What is all this?

There was no verbalization, though Renna felt the words resonate through her as clearly as if they had been spoken. Renna was instantly aware of not only the *life energy* within the waters below, but also of Vaelin's a few feet away. Renna didn't have to turn and face the djinn to feel the essence of *Power* that she was calling into herself.

What are you doing to me?

Renna could not afford to waste time. She didn't have to say anything, though she made the enchantment a declaration. "I *Seal* you to my will!"

Sickness overtook Renna. She wavered limply in Master Eggar's grasp. She felt every part of who she was shatter into an infinity of shards. She was clinging to them trying desperately to piece those shards together, but the more she tried the further they shattered.

"—an attack!" someone yelled behind them. Renna had no strength to acknowledge it with a look. Shouts filled the port, as did the sound of swords unsheathing. A thud rang loud in her ear. Suddenly, Master Eggar let go of her. She fell forward into the dark sea.

She had no strength to swim. She tried to move her arms, but they were useless. The waves had been rendered black and impenetrable by the *black water*. Her open eyes were greeted by a horrible stinging.

Help me. I am drowning.

She could not speak with her mouth full of water, but her words did not go unheeded.

As you wish.

XXIV.

THE BATTLE AT THE PORT

Dorovan willed his legs to run faster but knew that it still would not be enough. "Mercenaries are coming to attack!" he yelled to the first Blue Scarab he spotted at the port. The man's blank stare in response sent a shock of heat through Dorovan's exhausted body. "Did you not hear me? Mercenaries are on their way to attack you all! Alert your captains, or whoever is in charge."

"Haven't I seen you before?" the man pondered, with the tone of one who is forced to humor an intrusive child.

Dorovan couldn't believe how blatantly the man dismissed his words. Without a thought, the boy broke into a sprint towards the docks. "Come back here!" the soldier yelled after him. Then, "Intruder in the port!" He was not understanding that a single intruder was nothing compared to the catastrophe that was about to be at their door.

In moments, Dorovan had a tail of armored soldiers chasing him through the uneven streets. He made a sharp right when he reached the docks, and headed for the shack where Renna had taken him the previous evening. He saw a long line of soldiers coiled around the water, tossing barrels of black sludge into the sea.

Just before he could reach them, a soldier tackled him heavily to the ground. "No! You're not hearing me!" Dorovan exclaimed, though it came out as a child's yelp. Everyone at the dock turned to inspect the commotion. "There's going to be an attack!"

As if he had summoned them, arrows rained down, landing upon the wooden boards of the docks like a heavy hailstorm. Two hit a pair of nearby soldiers, sending them limply to the ground. Dorovan saw a third arrow bury itself into the back of a crouching man who appeared to be holding onto something blue and listless. As the man fell back, crying out in pain, Dorovan could see that what he released was a person kneeling before the water. Without the support from the man—who Dorovan now recognized as Master Eggar—this person fell forward and disappeared into the dark sea.

A second volley of arrows arrived, one landing in the neck of a soldier struggling to hold a woman down. He crumpled forward on top of her, writhing in pain. The woman wrestled herself from beneath his weight and then dove into the water. It all happened so fast, Dorovan couldn't be certain, but he swore that looked a lot like Vaelin.

As soon as the rush of arrows subsided, the soldier on top of Dorovan stood and ran towards the entrance of the port. Shouts were raised, and every soldier in the vicinity had unsheathed their sword or unfastened their bow. Dorovan stood and ran towards the water. Captain Velden hovered over the twisted body of Master Eggar. The grim point of an arrow peeked from his chest.

Captain Velden looked up at him in astonishment. "Dorovan?"

"We are being attacked by mercenaries," Dorovan informed, realizing a moment later he had used the word *we,* as if he were part of the Blue Scarabs as well.

"Scarabs!" Captain Velden barked out to the nearby soldiers, summoning their undivided attention. They turned to him and saluted in unison. "Report to the nearest lieutenant. Protect the port at all costs." The soldiers raced off to heed his command. "Dorovan, help me with him." Captain Velden nodded towards the wounded man.

Together, they dragged Master Eggar into the nearby shack. The man wheezed miserably the whole way there— he had likely punctured a lung. The lucerne loomed silently on its rickety table. They set Master Eggar gently on the ground. The concern on Captain Velden's face was unmistakable.

"Is he going to be alright?" Dorovan asked. Master Eggar's face was pale and dotted with beads of sweat. He was only conscious in a feverish sort of way.

"Whether this body lives or dies, our master is safe," Captain Velden declared as if the wounded man before them was nothing more than a tool. "Dorovan, my boy, I need to ask something of you." Several thumps sounded against the roof of the shack as the exchange of arrows continued. "The artifact is too valuable to fall into the hands of these nobles. Return it to the lodge. Keep it safe."

Dorovan looked at the black box, its shiny surface like a pool of still water. Apprehensively, he placed his hands upon its sides. Unlike the prior night, there was no reaction to his touch. Though his Contract with Vaelin was still intact, this was confirmation to him that the *Seal* between the two of them had been entirely severed. Did he feel relieved or betrayed? Dorovan realized he did not know.

Lifting the box, he was surprised by how light it felt, as if it was completely hollow within.

"Thank you, Dorovan," Captain Velden said, taking Dorovan's interaction with the lucerne as agreement.

"I'm counting on you, son," Eggar said. Dorovan turned to face the man. He was awake, though his eyes struggled to stay open. Strangely, his voice did not share the strain of his face, as if the voice belonged to someone else entirely. The man smiled warmly, as he always did, though the effect was rendered grotesque on his now pallid and trembling face. Dorovan returned the smile as well as he could, then exited the shack.

❧ ❧ ❧ ❧

Vaelin descended downwards into the blackness of the sea. She could no longer ignore the pain in her thigh as she kicked in the water, but she couldn't divert her focus from embodying the essence of *Power* to soothe that pain. Though Vaelin was an immensely powerful being, even she could not embody more than one essence in her sorry state.

She pressed on, barely able to make out the faint outline of Renna sinking within the deep darkness below. Then, suddenly, there was a heartbeat of *life energy* pulsing from the floor of the bay. Whatever was down there was now awake, and it knew that Vaelin had failed to rescue it. A new current violently thrust Vaelin every which way, making it impossible to maintain a steady course. Renna, too, seemed entirely at its mercy.

Suddenly, Vaelin felt something cold and alive wrap around her torso and legs—felt the rush of water as she was pushed upwards. She hovered several feet above the water, blinded by the abrupt sunlight. The dock met her back as she was slammed into it. Every ache from the injuries she had suffered was amplified. Vaelin wiped the greasy water from her eyes. It took a few moments for them to adjust, but what towered before her was unmistakable in its strangeness.

A *mer* loomed before her—one of the ancient Guardians of the sea.

Enormous silver-blue tentacles emerged from the sea like the masts of a splendid fleet stabbing the sky. One of the tentacles cradled Renna as gently as if she were a doll. Renna stirred and awakened. She did not seem at all startled by what was happening—in fact, she seemed to expect it.

So, the *Sealing* enchantment had worked. Renna had successfully *Sealed* a *mer's* power to her body. Anger surged within Vaelin. She would not stand aside and watch as her enslavement was enacted upon another like her.

Renna pointed towards the sounds of battle coming from the northern end of the port. The *mer* wrapped one enormous tentacle around a nearby storage shed and raised it as if it weighed no more than a pinecone. The *mer* launched the structure, hurtling it towards the fighting. With its other tentacles, it clutched anything else it could lift or tear away from the docks—small boats, carts, crates, large chunks of warehouses—throwing them like projectiles.

Vaelin limped in a panic towards the nearby shack that contained the lucerne, desperately afraid that the *mer* might snatch it too. She opened the door, but the lucerne was not inside. Instead, she saw Captain Velden clutching the dying body that Eggar inhabited. The pale man looked up at Vaelin with a smile that looked more like a grimace. "I take it our Renna has succeeded," he said.

"You need to leave right now," Vaelin declared to Captain Velden. "She will destroy the entire harbor."

"Don't you see?" Eggar asked. A lazy tear ran down his cheek. "She has gifted us the power to command our destiny."

The walls of the shack buckled inwardly. Captain Velden stood, carelessly dropping Eggar's body to the ground and exclaiming wordlessly as dove out of the shack. Vaelin followed him out of the small building as it was being lifted off the ground. In the blink of an eye, the shack soared through the air, landing several moments later with a distant crash. Without wasting a moment, Captain Velden unsheathed his sword and joined a nearby cluster of soldiers locked in combat.

Where had the lucerne gone? It was a question she had been asking herself on and off for the length of a small eternity, but its weight felt suddenly maddening.

One problem at a time.

Vaelin faced Renna—the woman's countenance looked deathly pallid, dark blue and black veins webbing her bald head. The *life energy* the enchantress had taken within her had been enough to perform the *Sealing*, but her body would not be enough to sustain it indefinitely. Vaelin could simply wait for the woman to die, but what effect would that have on the *mer*? Would it follow her in death? It was too risky.

"Hey!" Vaelin cried out, waving her arms wildly to get the attention of the enchantress. "You are going to die! Your body cannot carry such immense *life energy* for so long!"

Wood splintered explosively as a tentacle slammed through the dock next to her. Vaelin jumped out of the way just in time to avoid a large falling plank. "You must release the *Seal*!" Vaelin shouted again. "You are going to kill yourself and the *mer* both!"

She caught the silver flash of another tentacle as it descended in her direction. Vaelin tried to dodge, but it quickly and stickily wrapped itself around her, hoisting her from the dock. There was no use struggling beneath its firm grip, so Vaelin saved her strength. As she was raised, the other tentacles continued their methodical assault of the port, using whatever they picked up as projectiles against the soldiers that had come to attack the Blue Scarabs. Once it ran out of structures, it tore into the docks, using the planks of wood like javelins.

From her current vantage point, Vaelin could see the battle to the north of the port more clearly. The Blue Scarabs had scattered to the flanks, so that the onslaught of debris would not target them, while the attackers had either fragmented or retreated entirely. Piles of wood from destroyed buildings, boats, and freight containers littered the scene. A patchwork of armor shone from beneath the rubble where mercenaries and Scarabs had both been crushed.

This close to Renna, Vaelin could see that the enchantress' condition was much worse than it had seemed from the dock. The whites of her eyes were now entirely red, as dark blood leaked from her right eye like a macabre tear. Renna's lips were purpling as if they had suffered frostbite. Her head and shoulders bobbed about limply with the tentacle's undulations. A look of miserable defeat marred her face as she struggled to cling onto life.

"You know as well as I that you cannot keep this up," Vaelin said gently, as if she was speaking to a friend. "Please, end this now before it's too late."

"All I ever wanted to do was be of service," Renna said between grating breaths. "I just wanted to help."

"You can still help the *mer* by removing this cruel *Seal.* All creatures deserve to live freely."

The enchantress didn't seem to hear a word Vaelin was saying. Even so, the woman wept bitterly. Tears and blood poured down her face. Vaelin noticed a sudden silence had filled the air and realized that the tentacles had halted their destruction of the port. The one wrapped around her loosened its grip slightly.

This was her chance.

Vaelin fought her way out of the slippery tentacle and leapt to the one that held Renna. Though Vaelin's hands struggled to grip onto the tentacle's mucusy surface, she managed to wrestle the sobbing enchantress out of its grasp. Renna grunted defiantly, but she was too weak to offer any resistance. The tentacle beneath their feet jerked abruptly, and Vaelin found herself and Renna falling down into open air.

Renna hit the splintered dock below with a heavy thud. Vaelin landed on her a second after. The *mer*'s tentacles vibrated in agony, sending angry waves splashing about the dock. Though Renna had cushioned Vaelin's landing, Vaelin was aware that she was at the strained edge of her strength. She could only hold onto the essence of *Power* for so long. Soon, she would have to release it.

Beneath her, Renna's breath was ragged, but she lived. Vaelin would not get a better opportunity. She unsheathed Vitra and grabbed Renna's wrist, preparing to break the *Seal* etched upon the woman's palm.

Renna's eyes shot open, red and wild. "NO!" she screamed, and the tentacles came crashing down as if they were the enchantress' own hands. Vaelin, Renna, and the docks were engulfed by the waves and undulating tentacles, and forcefully dragged under the sea.

It was unclear to Vaelin how she maintained consciousness throughout the ordeal. Her ears rang within the muffled quiet of the water. The blue tentacles adapted to the coloring of the sea, becoming nearly invisible. Vaelin squirmed until she was free of their grasp, and swam back towards the surface.

The weight of the *mer* had pulled her deep within the depth of the port. It took several moments of struggle to reach the surface. Vaelin immediately filled her strained lungs with air. The realization that Vitra was no longer in her hand made her urgently dive back down. She caught sight of a quick tentacle retreating into the dark below, but of Vitra—the dagger that had been her most trusted companion for centuries—there was no sign.

Vaelin hoisted herself onto a large floating portion of the smashed dock and laid back for a few moments. The ringing in her ears slowly subsided. The port was entirely quiet, the sounds of battle now a distant memory. Who would continue to battle after what had just occurred? The port itself was a broken shell of its former self. Vaelin looked out at the ships that speckled the horizon like ants on an icy puddle. Perhaps those sailors were now thankful to be stranded beyond the port rather than in this mess.

Closing her eyes, Vaelin focused her awareness on the *mer*'s *life energy*. It was still there, but it was now intertwined with Renna's in an incomprehensible way. Instantly, it vanished from her awareness, as if it had closed itself to her. There was nothing to be done. Vaelin had failed to save the *mer* from a fate similar to her own. The Guardian of the Sea, as it had been known long ago, would remain *Sealed* to Renna's body—at least until Renna succumbed to death. Then, that loss of *life energy* would devastate the Cycle as it had so many centuries before. Before Vaelin could make plans for that dark reality, she would have to save herself.

Where is the lucerne? Vaelin turned her awareness away from the sea and refocused it towards the city. Two things called out to her, ever so subtly. Dorovan, who had Contracted her, and the lucerne. She wasn't certain which was which, but both emanated from the same direction.

Her hip felt naked without Vitra. She looked out towards the sea for one final somber moment, then began the short swim to a portion of the dock that was still intact. Over the centuries, she had lost so many loved ones—the dagger was no different. She didn't have the luxury to mourn it now. Renna would eventually die, and, with her, the *mer*. Vaelin was not certain how long she had until she would need to contend with that disaster.

❧ ❧ ❧ ❧

Dorovan left the battle at his back. He ran to the lodge
from the port, halting only a couple of times to catch his
breath. He had never seen so much spilt blood—so many
lifeless bodies piled upon the reddening cobblestones. The
casualties seemed to be evenly distributed between the Scarabs and the mercenaries, so it was nearly impossible to tell
who was winning. No one seemed to pay him any mind as
he slipped away from the battlefield that had descended
upon his home, his arms wrapped tightly around the lucerne as if it would escape.

A sudden crack, like the sound of a collapsing building,
made Dorovan stop and turn his gaze back to the port. He
couldn't see anything past the tops of the warehouse buildings, but he could sense the newfound confusion in the
shouts of the combatants. A small wooden row boat flew
through the air and landed on top of some unlucky soldiers.
Mercenaries and Scarabs both were flattened by the impact.

Dorovan watched in awe and horror, not quite understanding what he was seeing. People scrambled in every
which way as the sound of smashing wood grew louder. Dorovan turned back towards the city and ran for the lodge,
gripping the lucerne even more tightly. *It's not cowardice*,
he told himself. He simply had a mission to do, that was all.

Summoned by the noise, onlookers had gathered
throughout the streets. Some returned to their homes, but
the great majority remained still, as if the nearby battle was
some sort of entertainment. Urchins, peasants, merchants,
and the occasional lordling were unified in their morbid

curiosity. Dorovan lowered his gaze and slithered through the gathering crowd. Bits and pieces of confused chatter reached his ear—rumors of invasion mingled with conspiratorial talk of rebellion against the nobility. The confusion was dizzying to Dorovan's senses, the labyrinth of people becoming increasingly arduous to navigate—the fracas at the port spreading even with Dorovan's increasing distance from it.

The guard at the lodge entrance allowed him in immediately—the man's distant look betrayed much concern for what was happening at the port. Though he was now quite a ways away, the sounds of wood and stone and flesh colliding carried through the humid afternoon. Dorovan was glad the guard hadn't asked about what was happening there, as he wouldn't have known what to say. The guard's sword was drawn, his eyes darting between every single onlooker as if any of them could be a possible intruder. Strangely, the city guard was nowhere to be seen. Dorovan suspected that the bulk of the mercenaries that were attacking the port had been sourced from a mixture of errant knights, mercenaries from outside the city, and the city guard—who were part of the Soldiers' Guild, and therefore could be paid by anyone to fight, no differently than any other mercenary.

Few people remained within the Blue Scarab lodge. Beyond the guard at the door, only a handful of cooks, smiths, and a few other workers remained. There was a vigilant atmosphere in the lodge, as if everyone expected the stillness to be disturbed at any moment.

Dorovan wasn't sure where he was supposed to stow the artifact. He decided to head for Renna's office, which he found exactly as he had left it that morning. Swollen books sat open as if awaiting their reader's return. Dorovan placed the lucerne on a nearby table, glancing at a book as he did so. He could not decipher its curly script, and none of the images within were particularly interesting—the sketch of a single feather occupied an entire page. He quickly averted his eyes. Nothing good could come from looking at an enchantress' notes, and Dorovan didn't need any more misfortune.

He took a seat on Renna's chair and closed his eyes. A deep weariness nested over him. He suddenly felt more strained than he had ever felt before. All the running had drained him of strength. He considered all the soldiers and mercenaries throwing down their lives for what amounted to a squabble amongst the powerful. Master Eggar was right—the nobility of Sol Forne must be put in its place. There was no room in this city for those that did not desire the best for all of its inhabitants. His missing fingers ached in sympathy with his tired legs.

Was this simply his way of getting his revenge upon them for how they had treated him? No. Dorovan considered it but ultimately snapped that thread. These feelings weren't about him or his family. Not anymore. House Melese was dust—he saw that clearly now. This wasn't revenge, it was simply the right thing to do. But at the cost of so many lives? Was this truly necessary?

Footsteps sounded in the hallway just outside, and Dorovan lifted his head. He hadn't realized he had fallen asleep. How could he be asleep while others were dying? He had only a half-second to ponder this before Vaelin entered the office and all of his blood ran to his feet. Her wet sludge-smeared clothes perspired onto the floor like a sorry rain. She limped unsteadily as she crossed the room to-wards him.

"Dorovan," she named him hoarsely, no surprise in her voice.

"What are you doing here?" Dorovan asked, suddenly alert. "How did you get in?"

"I was looking for—" Vaelin's already gray face seemed to pale as her eyes landed on the black box on Renna's desk. Her mouth trembled as if she would burst into tears. Dorovan knew that this artifact was what the djinn had been seeking ever since she had arrived in Sol Forne. He still did not understand why, but he knew that its destruction meant her freedom. Its destruction would also mean the end of the Contract he shared with the djinn. If that came to pass, achieving heroism would be entirely in his hands alone. And was that not what he wanted—to earn his heroism as his father had? Then why was there such anguish within him at the prospect of losing Vaelin's help? Who else could he rely on to instruct him on such matters? Would Master Eggar be there to fill that absence?

Vaelin touched the box and closed her eyes—it felt as if something passed between the two. Suddenly, Vaelin snatched a gold-headed hammer from among Renna's tools and began pounding the box with it over and over. Dorovan gritted his teeth at the loud clanging sound. As the pounding grew in intensity, her frustration showed plainly.

"Break, you cursed thing!" she yelled out. "Why won't you break?" Vaelin thrust the hammer aside in exaspera-tion and began to rummage through Renna's other tools, in search of something more useful.

In a sudden rush of panic, Dorovan dashed towards the artifact and snatched it. While its destruction meant Vaelin's freedom, it would also mean Dorovan's failure. He had been tasked with keeping the box safe.

Vaelin looked affronted. "Give it here," she said icily.

"So you can destroy it?" Dorovan asked, knowing full well that was her intention.

Vaelin reached for the dagger that wasn't there, her face immediately contorting in loss. Without a word, she lunged for the box, but her exhaustion had rendered her sluggish. Dorovan avoided her with ease and fled the office, running towards the front door of the lodge.

"I'm going to kill you if you don't come back this instant," Vaelin yelled after him miserably.

The front door opened before Dorovan could reach it, and Leano rushed in. His face was streaked with soot and dry blood. His once spotless blue armor was dented from where swords had bitten into it, blood splattered across it like a motley. A ragged bandage wrapped around his head. He seemed perturbed as he met Dorovan's eyes. "Have you seen Renna?" he asked frantically. Dorovan had no time to answer before Leano added, "YOU!" in a booming voice that reverberated through the hall.

Dorovan found himself between the lieutenant and the djinn. Vaelin looked more dismayed and exhausted than anything else. Leano looked hungry for more action. "Step aside, boy," he said, unsheathing his sword in a swift practiced motion. Dorovan obeyed, retreating into a nearby corner. *Coward! Coward! He's going to kill her!*

"I've wished this moment would come," Leano said, smiling and flourishing his crimson-stained weapon. "Draw your cursed dagger and come at me. This time, I will end you."

Vaelin looked defeated already. "Unfortunately, I have misplaced my weapon."

Leano emitted a low impatient growl. "I won't fight you if you're unarmed. There's a well-stocked armory down the hall, to the right. Pick whatever you want."

"I don't have time for this!" Vaelin blurted out. "I am weak and tired. No matter what weapon I wield, you will surely cut me down." Dorovan was taken aback by how plainly the djinn stated the truth. The ferocious guilt over-taking him made his knees buckle.

"Pity. I will take no joy in what I must do," Leano said.

"Don't lie to yourself."

Leano smiled revealing his red-stained teeth, then lunged towards the djinn with his blade. Vaelin dropped to her knees and rolled away from the oncoming swing. In the blink of an eye, she was behind the man. From Leano's wavering poise, Dorovan could tell that the man was tired as well. He hadn't seen Leano at the port, so he wondered in which battle he had fought. Just how many other battles were happening around the city?

The lieutenant pivoted, swinging his sword wildly—the heat from the enchanted blade brushed against Dorovan's cheek like a lick of flame. Vaelin retreated from the swing, realizing too late that she had backed herself into a corner. The worry and resignation that dimmed her face sank Dorovan's heart. Time seemed to slow as Leano prepared his final blow.

This one was sure to kill.

Dorovan was frozen in place, his feet sinking into the stone floor below. His eyes were fixed on the box in his hands—the hollowness within the lucerne suddenly rang true to him. The object meant nothing to Dorovan beyond his desire to help Eggar bring security and power to the kingdom as he had promised. Eggar had made it clear that sacrifices would be needed from all to achieve that. And, surely if it were Eggar standing with him now, he would tell Dorovan that the djinn's sacrifice was a necessary loss in the name of a heroic end. After all, Dorovan was certain that whatever force had been unleashed at the port was Eggar's doing. All the death Dorovan had already witnessed was for that dream.

This is wrong.

Dorovan wasn't certain where his sudden resoluteness originated from but he could feel stability and an overwhelming sense of clarity return to his body. A hero would never agree to sacrifice that which was never theirs to give in the first place. A hero would not sacrifice a friend like this.

"Vaelin!" he called out. The djinn glanced at him. Acknowledgement passed between them in an instant. Dorovan threw the black box to Vaelin, who caught it and held it firmly in front of her, shielding herself from Leano's sword. The enchanted blade sliced through the center of the box as easily as if it was flesh.

Dorovan could not describe what he felt in that instant—it was loss and relief in equal measure. The *Seal* within the artifact had been severed. His Contract with Vaelin had been terminated before it was completed, as Vaelin's enslavement came to an end.

Leano attempted to extract his sword from the lucerne, instead pulling the artifact from Vaelin's hands. The sword did not budge. Vaelin took her chance and slammed her fist into the man's nose. Dorovan heard a wet crunch, and the man dropped to the floor unconscious. Blood oozed freely from the bridge of his nose.

Vaelin breathed raggedly for several moments, then began to laugh. The laughs turned to sobs as she fell to her knees in front of the lucerne. She placed a hand firmly atop the artifact and it instantly vanished.

Dorovan joined her cries, though he wasn't certain why. The finality of what had just occurred made it feel as if he was saying goodbye to something for the last time—a feeling that reminded him of when he'd lost his parents.

Vaelin finally broke the strange solemnity that had overtaken the lodge when she stood and wiped her tears. "It's funny how you can wait for a moment your entire life, and then when it happens it's not at all the way you had imagined it would be."

She faced Dorovan wearing a serene smile. Then, she smacked him on the cheek with all her strength. Dorovan held his swelling cheek in shock, though he didn't protest the act. He knew he deserved more.

"Twice you have wronged me," Vaelin announced. "First, when you forced a Contract on me against my will, and then when you took the lucerne from me. It won't happen a third time. I have decided to never forgive you, Dorovan ca'Melese."

With those words, Vaelin limped out of the lodge and out of Dorovan's life.

❀ ❀ ❀ ❀

Freedom. A foreign feeling, though she was named for it. Vaelin stumbled through the crowded streets of Sol Forne clutching the wound at her chest. She no longer felt the voice of the Compulsion taunting her from the deepest trenches of herself. It was over, yet she felt anxious. Without the Compulsion as her constant companion, she was suddenly so alone. Aimless.

It had been centuries since she had held all of her power within herself. Her physical form was almost inadequate for containing it. But it felt right.

The buzzing murmur of the gathered onlookers was a backdrop to the shouts emanating from all directions. The bells of the Hall of the Gods sounded loudly. The city gates would soon be closed. War had begun in Sol Forne. No longer was the threat isolated to the borders in the distant Red Coast. The Blue Scarabs had incensed the hearth of change. Vaelin's mind lingered on that thought, while her feet led her towards the Academy of Sol Forne. Her first decision with her newfound freedom was to ensure that Cressena, who had so aided Vaelin in her time of need, was safe.

She spared a lingering thought for the boy she had left behind. The betrayal she still felt at his actions stung bitterly. Vaelin had thought he would be better than that—had hoped he would. Though, in that last moment, when Dorovan had made the decision to throw the lucerne, Vaelin had felt the connection between them instantly sever. With that act, Dorovan had completed his Contract. Vaelin had considered telling him, though what good would that do?

The actions that had led him to that single act of heroism were abhorrent. Dorovan still had much to learn. One action did not excuse many even if it had satisfied the contractual terms.

Vaelin trudged on, not sparing the panicked passersby a glance. The world around her tunneled as her vision darkened at the edges. She was tired—exhausted. She needed rest, but she refused to find it until she knew Cressena was safe.

The wood door felt solid under her palm—more solid than Vaelin felt herself. She looked up at the large doors of the Academy, then pushed them open.

XXV.

Sealed

It had been impossible to distinguish where they ended and the salt brine of the sea began once it had blanketed them wholly. The pressure of the water mounted, but they felt secure under its crushing weight. Time had slowed to a near standstill. They pondered three questions.

Who are we? How did we get here? Are we dying?

All three questions occurred simultaneously, though the third brought a spasm of alarm through their body. They opened the eyes they now shared and saw the faint light of the sun beyond the quivering surface of the water, like a milky cataract locking the surface world behind. They turned their head and saw one half of their former self. The color of its soft flesh was no longer as vibrant as it had been, now drained to the gray pallor of death. The soft waves gave its tentacles the thin illusion of life. They opened their lungs to take in the water, but they were quickly reminded why they must not. Lungs were not made for water.

Are we dying?

That question returned to their mind, and they suddenly realized they did not want to die. A dark shape obfuscated the dim sunlight above even further. It loomed into view like the body of a large aquatic creature. Fear returned to them like a forgotten memory. But also resolve—they resolved to reach the distant shadow. Either they would die from lack of air in the water or within the clutches of this mysterious beast.

They flailed their limbs, purposelessly at first, but quickly they remembered what to do. One in front of the other with the front pair. The back pair kicked, one by one.

They were rising upwards, away from the dead body they had left behind, and towards the surface of the water in the unity they now shared. The climb felt endless, and their lungs felt squeezed to nothing. The sea that had been their home for so many centuries was now rejecting them. The dark carapace of the beast above grew larger and more intimidating as they neared it. They almost wished it would see them and eat them so they could be spared their agony.

When their head escaped the water and entered the openness beyond, air poured into their lungs in a mad frenzy between wet coughs expelling sea water. They breathed, in and out, and each time they were reminded of how it was done. The sun above was much too bright for their eyes—it was as if they had opened them for the first time. They had expected the great beast to attack them. Now they turned to face it and were surprised by the sudden recognition. They were beside a large ship.

A humanfolk looked down at them from the railing. Concern creased his features as he yelled, incomprehensibly. As the sounds were repeated, they took on shape and meaning. "Drowner! We got a drowner overboard!" The cry was followed by the shuffling of feet on the ship's deck, and then a rope ladder being lowered into the water.

They stared at the rope ladder blankly. They knew what it was, but needed a moment to remember how to use it. "Climb it!" the sailors above cried out. *Climb*—like what they had just done to reach the surface of the water. They paddled to the ladder, then pulled themselves up. It took much more effort than swimming, and they weren't sure their limbs could hold on much longer. Thankfully, the sailors helped them on board once they reached the railing.

A woman handed them a jug of water. Why would they want more water? They had just escaped it. Nevertheless, they held the jug to their lips and drank deeply. The reminder that water could be both death and life was deeply unsettling.

"What's your name?" the woman asked. By the way the other sailors circled around her, it was clear she was the authority on board—the captain. They could not think up a response, so they shook their head. The captain's face took on a dark cast. "You're one of those Blue Scarabs, aren't you?"

The eyes of the crew were on them. What did those eyes see?

They looked down and noticed their blue cloak, a large scarab beetle embroidered at the front. Suddenly, they knew the answer to the captain's question had been yes, though they were no longer certain what a Blue Scarab was. They shook their head again.

"She sure looks like one, captain," a man behind them barked. Others joined him with their angry voices.

The captain held out a hand, and the deck quieted. "Send a boat to shore. Avoid the port. We will not harm this wretch, but I do not want it on my ship."

The disappointment among the sailors was palpable, though they abided by their captain's command. Soon, they were seated on a small boat being rowed to shore, towards a large city they knew they should remember.

"You're lucky captain is merciful," the man rowing the boat said, with a cruel sneer. "If it was up to me, I'd use your kind as chum for the fishes. Letting us sit in the bay for weeks without being able to dock. Who do you think you are?" The man didn't seem to expect an answer to his question, so they stayed silent and watched as the city approached.

The port was in absolute disarray. Many of the docks were destroyed and the waves were cloaked with shattered wood and viscous black sludge. *Did we do that?* The boat turned towards a beach outside the city, and the port grew distant behind them.

Who am I? A singular voice asked within their mind.

Who am I? Another singular voice echoed.

Who are we?

A flood of memories threatened to split them in half. They clung to each half dearly, knowing that, if they allowed them to separate, each would be lost forever. It was an agonizing task, at first. Slowly, it became simpler, like remembering how to breathe.

The beach neared, and suddenly they were sure of what they were. Memories were only a burden to them. They had been given a chance to start anew.

We are joined. We are together. We are never alone.

XXVI.

T<small>HE</small> G<small>OLD</small> M<small>ARK</small>

T he golden yolks of the two eggs steaming on his plate stared up at him like a pair of startled eyes. Dorovan broke their centers with his fork, spilling orange into the porridge beneath. He took a bite and swallowed it down without chewing or tasting. The world around him had suddenly lost all flavor.

This dining room was not nearly as opulent or grand as the one he'd seen at the Salviati estate, but it was well furnished and impeccably clean. The decor was too eccentric for Dorovan's tastes, as were the lord of the house's clothes and mannerisms. He understood clearly now why the man had hired his sister as his personal colorist. Every surface was saturated in a frenzy of contrasting hues. The lordling also seemed to have an affection for arches as there were arches of every shape and sort built into every single one of his doorways. Some were colorfully painted, others golden or covered in carved blossoms. It was as if a peasant had been given charge of the decor with no idea of what a noble's house actually looked like—a parody of fine taste.

Ensa sat a few chairs down from him, neatly eating her own breakfast. Lord Lorenzo had not joined as he had been summoned to a mandatory meeting between the Noble

Council and the Guild Union. Whatever stalemate had been reached in Sol Forne in the days since the *mer's* attack was a temporary respite—nothing but a brief sigh of relief. Everyone could feel the tension building, knowing well it would soon come to something more enduring than the now-infamous confrontation at the port.

"You should eat," Ensa said, in that irritating motherly tone of hers. Dorovan didn't have it in him to retort, so he took one more joyless bite of the now congealed yolk. Ensa seemed pleased. "I will be going to the market soon to pick up some fabric. You're more than welcome to come with me." Dorovan poked the egg with his fork as if he could summon a chick from it. "Dorovan?" Ensa called.

"Er, yes. I mean, no," Dorovan said. "I don't really feel like going outside today." He hadn't felt like leaving the house since he had arrived. The closest he had gotten was a brief walk into the courtyard the previous morning. A servant had offered him a puff of his cigarette. Dorovan had given it a try, but hadn't liked it very much.

"You should get some fresh air," Ensa insisted. "You've been through a lot. Getting out would be good for you."

She was right. Going to the market would be a good way for Dorovan to distract himself from the aimlessness of his life, at least for a few moments. It might abate the choke-hold of the deep sorrow he felt in his chest. But that sadness would always return to him, so what point was there in ignoring it?

Dorovan sighed. "Not today. But I promise I will make an effort tomorrow."

Ensa smiled, then wiped the corner of her mouth with a cloth. "I will hold you to it," she said playfully. She stood and walked over to him. "You know I love you, right?"

Dorovan looked into his sister's bright eyes. The instant flood of affection he felt towards her threatened to topple over the tower of guilt he had constructed and send it crashing on top of him. How could he have treated her in such a way? He didn't deserve her love and kindness. He had been nothing but an anchor weighing her down with talk of house names and strategic marriages, when all she had wished to do was succeed on her own merit. Perhaps it was time he finally did the same. "I love you, too."

Ensa kissed his head. With those words, "I love you," Dorovan had suddenly realized that he had needed his sister more than she had ever needed him. She would never stop looking out for him if he chose to stay. He felt fear at his sudden resolve. After Ensa left for the market, Dorovan packed the few things he possessed in a small sack. He left a note atop Ensa's bed. It was brief, but he hoped it would explain his reasons for leaving.

Where would he go? What would he do now that he had given up on restoring his name? No, not given up—he rejected it, refused to be defined by its absence any longer. Like the missing fingers of his right hand, it was no longer a part of him. The only thing to remind him of who he had been was the gold mark that still sat in his pocket. He held his father's coin, considering it. With such a bounty he would be able to buy passage wherever he decided to go. But this coin didn't belong to him—he had only thought it had because of an accident of birth.

His time with Vaelin had shown him, above all, the value of choice. From now on, he would pursue being a hero, not because he desired a noble title, or even because it was the mantle left to him by his father, but because that was his chosen quest. He felt embarrassment now for how certain he had been only days ago that heroism was a destination and not a journey. He doubted he could ever see himself in such a role now that he understood the full weight of what he had put Vaelin through.

No, he would never be a hero in his own eyes—no matter what he did going forward. But he would persist anyway. He owed Vaelin that much.

A woman sat near the western gate, cradling a silent infant. She wore a soiled bandage covering an infected right eye. On the ground in front of her was an old basket containing a couple dented coppers. This was Sol Forne—a city whose citizens lived at opposite extremes. Elaborate wealth was extracted from the common folk and hoarded only steps away from those it was plundered from. And the people whose circumstances were like Dorovan's—comfortable enough to have something to lose, yet precarious enough to exhaust themselves pursuing more—could only pretend they saw none of this.

Dorovan approached the woman, who looked up at him passively. Though her face was hard from life on the street, Dorovan was shocked by the realization that she was of age with him. It took no effort whatsoever to drop the gold mark in her basket and walk through the western gate, and out of Sol Forne forever.

In the years that followed, Dorovan would often think back on the last time he saw his sister. Much later, he would find out that her life path had led her to become the head of the Sol Fornian Fashionists' Guild. He had no regrets about how he had left things with her—it had been the right thing to do. He only wished that he could have told her how proud he was of her, and to hear her say it back to him. But that was not fated to be.

XXVII.

A New Song

"—and that's not to say that the elvenfolk never went to war, because they did. And often! Elveshar, in fact, warred for over one hundred years with the Elkesti. It was all due to a supposed slight from the Elkestian queen towards the Elveshari king. Elven wars were hardly ever about resources or territory. They were often just personal spats that could not be resolved peacefully. They took slights against their leaders very seriously to the point of happily throwing their lives away to defend their honor."

Cressena wrote down each of Vaelin's words as fast as she was able, though she really didn't need to. The two scribes seated behind her were already busy transcribing Vaelin's words onto parchment. "But how does that relate to the golden fruit?" Cressena asked, pointing to the chipped vase painted with the image of the Elkesti queen and Elveshari king both reaching towards a golden fruit that glittered just beyond either's grasp.

"Your guess is as good as mine," Vaelin shrugged. Cressena's gaze probed her through narrowed eyes. Vaelin sighed. "Elven art was often very figurative. The fruit was most likely not a fruit at all. It could have been a promise, or an action, or—"

"—a child," one of the scribes interjected, as if coming to a realization. "That would align with some of the inscriptions found in the Vizenian undercrofts."

"Or that," Vaelin agreed reluctantly. Cressena didn't seem particularly content with the answer. Vaelin continued, "Just because I lived through that era, doesn't mean I'm privy to every single detail of every historical event. The war between Elveshar and Elkesti eventually ended, and the result was that the Elkestian nation ceded itself to the Elveshari king in apology."

Cressena's eyes broadened at that revelation. "They just gave their entire nation away?"

"As I said, the elvenfolk didn't conceive of a people's identity in relation to who ruled. They were still the Elkestian folk, though now they were also Elveshari. To thank them for their gesture, the king of Elveshar allowed their queen to retain her place on the throne."

"That doesn't make any sense," Cressena interrupted. "If the Elkestians were still Elkestians, and their queen was still their queen, in what way were they part of Elveshar?"

"I don't know how else to explain it," Vaelin conceded. "They just *were*. This eventually led the Elveshari to enact the Four Corners Edict, where they established four separate rulers, all equal in standing, to watch over the four corners of the kingdom."

"The Nameless Gods," Cressena muttered under her breath.

"Precisely," Vaelin replied.

The two scribes glanced at each other, uncertainly. "I think this is a good place to stop for today," Cressena said.

"Perhaps tomorrow you will tell us more about these four... rulers."

"I have only met two of them personally," Vaelin replied. "It's not the most interesting story, unless you're fond of pigeon whistles."

"What in dirges is a pigeon whistle?" one of the scribes asked.

Cressena smiled brightly. "Looks like we will find out tomorrow."

After the meeting, Vaelin strolled through the almost empty halls of the Academy. Cressena was busy binding today's report so that it could be presented to the Academy Board in the morning. She was still paying dearly for all Vaelin had wrought. Vaelin was determined to make it up to the woman in any way she could, even if that meant squeezing every bit of history she was able to from her long memory.

Once Cressena had finished, they headed to *The Loathsome Scholar*, where Vaelin was still lodging. Vaelin kept her hood over her head. In the past few days, the Blue Scarabs had receded into their lodge but the frenzied rumors of the *mer* sighting had left the people of Sol Forne hostile to anything as unusual looking as she was. There were rumors that more Scarabs were on their way from Vizen to secure the city. The situation would become grim unless the nobility and the Guild Union heeded the Scarabs' demands soon. Vaelin wasn't sure that such a deal was possible.

Inside the *Scholar*, Vaelin and Cressena sat at a back table and shared a bottle, or two, of wine before turning in for the night. Vaelin really enjoyed these moments spent with the woman. It was as close as Vaelin would ever get to speaking to Myssa again.

On the stage, a young woman gave a lecture condemning the nobility for the recent tension that had befallen the city. She preached that the only path to true freedom of self was the dissolution of the noble class and all associated privileges. The gathered crowd whooped in agreement. Vaelin had seen this before—it was the prelude to revolt. Watching it play out once more made her still-aching chest tense.

"Seems like you're not the only one with a passion for freedom lately," Cressena said. Vaelin frowned as she sipped the delicious red wine Cressena had recommended. "What will you do with your newfound freedom?" the scholar asked.

"Why, tell you more about history, of course," Vaelin said, elbowing Cressena in the shoulder lightly.

"What about when there are no more histories left to tell?" Cressena asked. There was an unexpected somberness behind her question.

Vaelin had been pondering that very thing relentlessly for the past few days. She had been certain that Renna's death would ignite a degradation of the Cycle similar to what she had experienced in the past, before the Great Return. There was no way Renna's human body could withstand being *Sealed* to the *mer* forever. And yet, Vaelin had to admit that there was much she couldn't predict about the nature of Renna and the *mer*'s bond because, unlike her and the lucerne, they were originally two separate beings.

Infrequent quakes still moved throughout the city, alt-hough they were milder now. Freeing herself from the Compulsion had lent some stability to the Cycle of Nature, but Renna and the *mer* threatened to overturn that. Finding them would prove a fool's errand. But there was a place Vaelin could go where she could reinforce the Cycle in a meaningful way. The cost of such an act, however, would be substantial.

Vaelin had no idea how much time she would have left to enjoy her freedom, so she had resolved to savor it. She would no longer be subjected to the Compulsion's Hunger and forced to Contract folk to enact their unpredictable wills. The only will that mattered now was her own, and she found herself itching to wield it. She reached for her chest, where the wound had begun to heal.

"Perhaps I'll make some more histories," Vaelin answered. "Or maybe none at all."

Cressena smiled and raised her glass. "May you enjoy whatever you choose to do."

Vaelin smiled and clinked her glass against the woman's. After saying farewell to Cressena later that night, after many more toasts were raised, Vaelin teetered upstairs into her room, and enclosed herself into its quiet. Dorovan's sheathed sword still laid on the bed he had occupied. It was enough to make a dark flower of regret bloom in her heart. She could not, however, place her feelings. She did not feel guilt at leaving the boy, just... Perhaps she simply wished things could have been different. She saw potential in Dorovan—she hoped the boy would be able to use that potential for good. For him to become a fully realized person. Whatever he did, he would have to go about it on his own.

She turned away from the sword and grabbed the mandolin that sat on her bed. Her fingers nested on the strings with the familiarity of coming home. She strummed a half-forgotten song from a time long gone that she remembered enjoying, though tonight it sounded thin and trite. She halted her playing and smiled. Maybe Cressena was right. Old songs would no longer do. It was time to move forward—time to write a new one.

❧ ❧ ❧ ❧

The forest that had once brimmed with *life energy* now sat in what Vaelin could only describe as a stasis. Birds and other animals were reluctant to break its uneasy silence. During the past year, someone had attempted to restore it through a powerful enchantment. A great cost must have been paid to release even a sliver of that power. But it had not been nearly enough to finish the task.

Vaelin placed her hand upon the scarred skeleton of a tree. The *life energy* that it contained felt distant and tangled. The fires had scarred the forest of Albadone beyond recognition, dealing the Cycle of Nature a near-mortal wound. The *life energy* contained within its lifeblood—the *black water*—had been almost entirely depleted.

It would take an even greater power to aid it—a power Vaelin now possessed. Since the destruction of the lucerne, the totality of Vaelin's *life energy* had been returned to her control.

Vaelin removed her ash-stained hand from the tree trunk. She concentrated on embodying *Life, Power, Binding, Sealing, Warding,* and *Guidance* simultaneously. Like a too-full wineskin, she felt herself at the edge of bursting. She focused on the dormant forest around her and, embodying *Transference*, diverted the flow of the six essences into it.

Though the *life energy* expended was immense, she knew that it wouldn't be enough. She needed more—she needed to give up a part of herself.

She embodied the eighth essence.

Unity.

Not many knew of the existence of the eighth essence or the eighth chant that accompanied it. And that was for a good reason. *Unity* converted any matter or cost into *life energy* and restored it to the Cycle.

Vaelin chanted the eighth chant and fed her immortality into the Cycle. The forest of Albadone quaked in response, like a sigh of relief, as it was inundated with *life energy*. It would be the last of such quakes, at least until the next time the Cycle was substantially disturbed. But Vaelin would allow herself this victory.

Vaelin released her awareness from the eight essences and collapsed into the dirt. She felt spent, like a runestone. She was no longer a being of pure *life energy*. She was mortal now. Ancient aches began to make themselves known, and her head pounded from her drinking the night before. How did the humanfolk do it, waking up every day one step closer to the precipice of death? It was all new to her, and that was strangely exhilarating.

As the initial apprehension receded, it made way for Vaelin's usual curiosity. The air around her shifted, like a waking yawn. The melodic tweeting of a bird on a nearby branch awakened the, moments ago, silent forest. Vaelin wiped tears she hadn't realized she had shed from her face and gazed up at the bird. Its tentative chirps morphed sweetly into a song. While Vaelin did not know the words or melody, she found herself joining in.

EPILOGUE

FIVE YEARS LATER...

Pink clouds floated across the sky as the morning sun climbed lazily out of its cradle beyond the horizon. The girl watched them swirling above enviously: they looked so light and carefree. And here she was, tired and hungry, surrounded by bogland, and entirely lost. She had been turned around by the brief storm that had swept through the area the previous day.

Rain clouds had bullied their way across the sky, dampening her view of the moon and stars. Thankfully, she had managed to find shelter within a canopy of dead branches dangling from tall bare trees, which had partially shielded her from the chilled droplets of rain. Even so, her gown was more mud and water than cloth at this point. Frustrated tears blurred her vision. This challenge was stupid!

Complaints are like dandelions, Mother always said, although the girl could not remember exactly why. Why were complaints like dandelions? Who could say?

The girl trudged along the edge of a moss-tinted pool. She couldn't see past its murky surface, and that made her fearful of what lurked within. She had once witnessed a liongator of her exact size slither out of the water and swallow a muskrat whole. The image of the muskrat's legs twitching in the liongator's maw had brought nightmares to her for many nights. There could be an even bigger creature hiding beneath this pool waiting for the right moment to drag her with its fangs to the depths of the bog.

Stop thinking of scary things.

Her stomach rumbled. She spotted some brownish-yellow mushrooms climbing the trunk of a nearby rotting tree. A small white fringe surrounded their caps, making them appear as if they were melting. The girl squinted at the mushrooms hoping that her concentration would help her recall whether they were a type she could eat, but nothing came to mind. Better to avoid a potentially deadly mushroom than eat a potentially delicious one.

She sighed and turned away from the tree. At least she would be able to find her way back home now that she saw where the sun was rising. It was harder to navigate the boglands at night. The runestone of Life that she had pocketed from Mother's nightstand had helped defend against the worst of the chill. She knew she wasn't allowed to take Mother's things, but this would surely be forgiven.

It did a poor job though of soothing her hunger. The few animals she had seen around were beavers and muskrats. Those were too large and swift for her to catch, and Mother hadn't taught her trapping yet. She knew better than to eat the slimy sickeningly green moss frothing at the edge of the water, though even that seemed appetizing to her now.

She picked up a small pebble and placed it in her mouth. She had read in one of Mother's books that it could help prevent hunger, though she had a hard time believing it. The pebble only remained in her mouth for a few moments before the girl spat it out—it had not helped at all. She carried on north-eastwardly, her eyes scanning the ground for the rocky black soil and reddish dirt that would indicate she was near home.

As dawn bled into midmorning, the clouds she had watched earlier congregated together and turned gray. The girl's lip trembled—it looked like it would rain again. She hastened her step and proceeded onwards through the sparse boglands. For what felt like an eternity, the landscape stubbornly refused to change.

I need to find higher ground. I need to know where I am.

The girl looked around at the thin unsteady trees in the vicinity. Would she risk climbing one of those rickety trunks just to scan the environment? She carried on for an hour more, but the earth never sloped upwards to grant her a vantage point, nor did the trees appear any sturdier.

I really hate these challenges.

The girl resigned herself to climbing a tree with several skeletal but evenly spaced branches that offered decent footholds. She didn't weigh much, so the branches held her without much protest. When she reached the top and looked out, the bog extended far in every direction. A few trees much like the one she was perched upon dotted the marshy area, interrupted by the occasional pool of stagnant water. North-east, however, she could see an area where the tree line grew denser. On the horizon she could barely make out the bushy tops of verdant evergreens. She wasn't close, but at least she knew which direction to follow.

In her haste to descend the tree, a branch cracked loudly and gave away beneath her. She caught herself on the limp branch overhead, but, as her fingers lost their strength, the wood began to bend. If she didn't act, it too would break. The ground below swirled and swam, forcing her to look away.

She released the branch with one hand and felt into her pocket to pull out the runestone of *Life*. She reached up and passed the purple stone over the bending branch. Immediately, it became sturdier, lifting her upwards with its newfound strength. Tiny green leaves began to sprout from where the runestone had touched. She returned the runestone to her pocket and, assured now that the branch wouldn't break, used the last of her strength to inch her way closer to the tress gnarled trunk where footholds would be sturdier.

She took her time reaching the ground, then paced northeast, towards the more verdant tree line. Half an hour later, the bog made way for thicker woodlands, although they were still marred by the occasional mossy pool. The earth beneath her feet adopted the red tint she was accustomed to. She wasn't quite sure where she was yet, but she knew she was getting closer to home.

Suddenly, she felt something against her arm. Before she had time to look, the thing had taken hold of her, and her feet were hovering above the ground. The liongator had her!

"Let me go!" she screamed, kicking her legs.

A gloved hand covered her mouth tightly. "Quiet, lest she hears you." It was a woman's voice.

Eyes wide, the girl finally took a good look at her abductor: a woman of middle years, her skin as dark and weathered as bog tree bark; her black hair was trimmed neatly around her ears. The woman ran quickly, even while carrying her. Unfortunately, she ran in the wrong direction, delivering the girl back towards the heart of the boglands.

The girl kicked her legs rapidly, until the woman came to a halt. The woman set her down and looked into her eyes sternly. "Little girl, I am trying to save you," she said, her voice strangely soothing. "You cannot be out here."

"I will be fine," the girl protested. "I am just headed home."

"Home? Here?" The woman was skeptical. "Where is home to you?"

The girl pointed in the general direction she had been walking. The woman nodded. "Then I will escort you there."

"I'll be fine on my own," the girl protested.

"I cannot leave a defenseless child to walk through the boglands alone. Especially not when..." The woman looked around, as if someone was watching them. Her furtive glances raised the hairs on the girl's neck. The woman moved in closer to the girl and whispered, "The bog witch has been sighted."

"The bog witch?" A chill moved down the girl's spine.

"She's known to kidnap children. She eats their bones and... worse."

The girl swallowed. She wasn't sure exactly what a witch was, but from the description she could tell it was some species of beast. Her mother had lectured her endlessly about the dangers of speaking to strangers, but this woman was offering help. Perhaps it would be all right to accept.

"I am Viktri," the woman introduced herself. "What is your name?"

The girl grimaced. It would be best if the woman did not know her real name, in case her intentions were not as good as she had made them sound. "My name is Falma," the girl lied. She borrowed the name from a bedtime story Mother used to tell her.

"Falma," the woman repeated. The way she said it made it sound like she had spotted the lie. "Lead the way, then."

As they walked onwards through the slowly thickening woods, the girl stole secret glances at the woman. She didn't resemble any bogfolk the girl had ever seen. She wore thick leather across her entire body beneath a dark green cloak that draped around her shoulders. At her side was a short sword in a worn leather scabbard.

"My father gave this to me," Viktri explained. The girl blushed at having been caught looking. "I was a bit older than you when I received it. It's not very typical for a girl to inherit a sword where I'm from, but I never had any brothers growing up. If I hadn't learned to use it, this sword would have collected dust in our attic." After a few moments of silence, the woman asked, "Do you have a father?"

The girl thought about how to answer such a question. She knew a father was sort of like a mother, though she wasn't quite sure what the difference was. "I never met my father," she answered.

"And what about your mother," the woman continued, "Does she have a trade?"

The questioning made the girl uneasy. Her mother would not appreciate her divulging such information. "We only recently moved to the bog. She's been doing odd jobs for people in the village nearby." A half-truth.

"Where did you move from?"

"From the—" The girl bit her tongue. Was the woman simply trying to make conversation or was there something more sinister behind her questions? The girl met Viktri's golden eyes, seeking confirmation. When she found nothing there but polite curiosity, she resolved to tell the truth this time. "I don't think my mother would like me to share that with a stranger."

Viktri smiled pleasantly. "You're probably right."

They remained silent for most of the trek. A few times the woman asked how close they were, to which the girl always responded, "Almost there." It took another hour for her to reach an area she recognized and, soon, the stone house she shared with her mother came into view.

"This is it," the girl announced. "Thank you for walking with me. Goodbye." Her walk forward was interrupted by a hand on her shoulder. The girl faced the woman warily.

"I would very much like to meet your mother," Viktri said coolly.

The girl swallowed. Mother would not like this at all—she had worked so hard to build a private life for them out here. This intrusion would be most unwelcome, though something about Viktri's strange calm rendered the girl unable to protest. She nodded and led the woman towards the small home. Light gray smoke puffed out of the chimney—Mother was at work. She would not appreciate this interruption at all. The girl found the wooden door locked, so she knocked twice.

Her heart beat strongly in anticipation of the scolding she was about to receive. The door swung open to reveal her mother standing inside wearing confusion on her brow. "I was worried," was all she said. "Come inside, quickly now." The girl did as she was told. Mother glanced at the stranger in irritation, then closed the door. Viktri blocked it with her boot.

"My name is Viktri, madam. I found your daughter wandering about the boglands unattended. Do you know what sort of dangers lurk out there?"

The girl leaned closer to her mother instinctively, her mind wondering against her will what kind of fangs a witch creature would have.

"I have some idea," Mother said. "But maybe my daughter does not. You should leave so I can teach her about them."

Viktri's smile grew wider. "Madam, I am travel-worn, and hungry. May I trouble you for something to eat and for some water to replenish my drinking skin?" Mother remained quiet for a moment. "I did deliver your daughter safely to your home," Viktri added in hopes of sweetening her request.

Mother sighed in resignation. "Very well," she said, opening the door. She turned to the girl, and commanded, "Go gather some firewood so I can prepare dinner."

The girl glanced beside the fireplace where split logs were stacked neatly against the wall. This had to be one of Mother's tests. "I am hungry and tired, Mother. I don't know if I can."

"I will not ask twice!" Mother exclaimed. It was best to do as she was told after one of Mother's outbursts.

"Yes, Mother," the girl said, heading out the door with her head low. Viktri grinned at the girl as she stepped into the home. Mother closed the door behind them both.

The girl had not been exaggerating—she truly was too tired to be doing this sort of labor. Even so, she pushed a small wooden wheelbarrow ahead of her towards the nearby woods. For the better part of a half hour, she picked up as many thick and thin sticks as she could manage, until the wheelbarrow was filled. By the time she reached home, her legs were buckling, and her stomach pains had brought tears to her eyes. Mother could be so heartless at times.

The girl was only able to dwell on it for a second though before she noticed that the door to the home sat wide open. The girl's heart sank at the sight of the dark crimson liquid that stained the doorway and dirt below. No one was inside, so the girl reluctantly followed the trail of blood that led into the thicket behind the home. "Mother?" she called out. She thought back to the sword at Viktri's hip—to her incessant questioning. Was she a robber who had come to take their belongings? Had Mother put up a fight and been punished for it?

She could feel tears welling up in her eyes, but the situation was too urgent for her to let them overtake her. The dark muddy drag markings led her deeper into the woods until the sound of heavy breathing became audible. The girl padded forward with heavy caution, ducking behind every tree along the way. Finally, a figure came into view.

Mother dragged Viktri's limp body across the forest floor, and towards a nearby pool. The woman's throat had been slit, bright blood drenching the front of her leather armor. Her eyes gazed sightlessly at the sky above.

"Mother?" the girl asked doubtfully.

Mother looked up at her, dropping the body in the same motion. The way Viktri's head bobbed when it hit the ground made the girl shiver. "What are you doing here?" Mother asked.

"I saw the blood. I got scared."

"Oh, poor girl." Mother approached her and wrapped her tightly into her arms. "I am so sorry you had to see this. But this woman was not who she seemed. She lied to you— to us. She had come to take us away from here."

"Take us? Where?" The girl was unable to look away from the body.

Mother released her and knelt to meet the girl's eyes. "There are people in this world that wish us harm. They want the knowledge I am imparting to you for themselves. They wish to use my power and yours for their cruel purposes. I cannot allow that. *We* cannot allow that. We must be ever vigilant. Do you understand?"

The girl nodded, though none of this made any sense to her. She had never heard Mother speak so frighteningly of other people. Sure, strangers were to be treated with caution, but the role of an enchantress was to serve the needs of others and that meant doing no harm unless threatened. The girl thought of Viktri's grinning face, her eyes desperately falling on anything besides the glistening chasm at the woman's throat. Eventually the girl's eyes rested on the hilt of the sword Viktri's father had left her, which still peeked out of its scabbard exactly as it had before.

Mother kissed her on the forehead. "Go back home and let me finish up here. There is soup in the cauldron. It will be ready once it starts to bubble. I will be there soon. Can you serve me a bowl as well?"

The girl nodded.

Mother smiled. "I love you, Sesha."

Sesha met her mother's limpid eyes. "I love you too, Mother."

ABOUT THE AUTHORS

Élan Marché and Christopher Warman met in high school in Oklahoma in 2009. After dating for a decade, they got married in 2020. They currently live in Los Angeles where they work and spend their time watching TV, reading, writing, cooking delicious meals, and generally enjoying each other's company.

For updates and more visit:

www.marche-warman.com

CPSIA information can be obtained
at www.ICGtesting.com
Printed in the USA
BVHW081048230123
656900BV00002B/139

9 798218 122560